Abigail's World

VICTORIA WEBSTER

Grosvenor House
Publishing Limited

This book is published by
Grosvenor House Publishing Ltd
Link House
140 The Broadway, Tolworth, Surrey, KT6 7HT.
www.grosvenorhousepublishing.co.uk

A CIP catalogue record for this book
is available from the British Library.

ISBN 978-1-83615-111-1
eBook ISBN 978-1-83615-112-8

victoria-webster.uk

WHITE MOONLIGHT PRESS

E-book ISBN: 978-1-7376930-2-4
Paperback ISBN: 978-1-7376930-3-1

CHAPTER ONE
MAR

Time heals all wounds. That's how the saying goes, right? Several of the therapists I used to see told me that. It kind of negated the point they were trying to make —if all I needed to heal my wounds was time, why was I in therapy in the first place?

Needless to say, I never had a very good experience with that sort of therapy. I thought they would fix me somehow overnight, and I wouldn't have to try at all. I thought all the tears and bottled-up emotions would pour out of me, like a switch flipped from within, allowing me to unleash everything I'd tried to shove down over the years. That didn't happen. Not even close.

Maybe it was my teenage cynicism or my unrealistic expectations of therapy in general. But I think the most likely reason no one could fix me is because I was never broken to begin with. Not then, not now—as hard as it might be for you to believe. I can't remember a time I've ever been...*unbroken*. Actually, a better word to describe me would be "defective."

That's what Neil thinks of me, too—my biological father, finally making his guest appearance in my life after all these seasons. It's no major plot twist that he's the antagonist of the Mar Rochester Show, but the whole "demon" thing certainly shifts the genre. It's not surprising that he gave me up because he thought I was a powerless child, but now that I might have some hidden power, suddenly he's back in my life. To be more accurate, he's kidnapped me.

I can't say I've been curious about Neil Abbott. I didn't even know his real name for most of my life. The social workers told me he was imprisoned for dealing drugs. I didn't pry further, cursing him for resigning me to a childhood of foster homes. Blaming him for the circumstances of my birth. You know, teenage angst. Without it, half the YA novels in the world wouldn't exist.

As it turns out, the truth about my biological father is *much* worse than I thought. Neil Abbott is rich, and all my life he's only lived a few hours away in Pentington County, Georgia. Which, according to the county sign we just passed, is home to the world's best apple orchards. They can put just about anything they want on those signs, can't they?

"It's just another thirty minutes," Neil announces to the limousine. It's the first time he's spoken to me since the whole "Luke, I am your father" moment. But trust me, I'd much rather have Darth Vader as a biological father than Neil. Looking at him now, I almost can't believe we're related.

He's like a marble statue, which is just as well since I'm pretty sure his heart is as cold and unmoving as stone. With pale skin and slicked-back blonde hair, the light of his cell

phone illuminates his sharp facial features and makes his emerald green eyes glow.

I must take after my biological mother, who Neil claims is dead. My eyes and hair are dark, and while my features are also sharp and angular, no part of my face resembles his at all. Had I grown up with Neil as a father, I would have been the black sheep in his blonde-haired, green-eyed family.

"No one outside of this car knows," Neil reminds me, "that you are my biological daughter. I intend to keep this little secret between us."

"That's fine by me," I reply. More than fine, actually. The last thing I need is for anyone else to know I share DNA with this bastard. Ironically, I'm technically *his* bastard...

Beside me, Nic snickers. I don't know what's so funny, but my guess is he's mocking me in his head. It's pretty out of character for him. In my experience, he hasn't kept his insults to himself. Is this what they call character growth?

I understand why he thinks this whole situation is funny. From the very first time we met, Nic Woolridge has known who I am. My relation to Neil, my foster care situation, my characters...he's known everything. All the while, he's pretended to be my ally. Not that I ever really trusted him, but I didn't expect him to be working for my biological father. I thought he was assigned the role of "cannon fodder" and would die before the sequel. Oh, how wrong I was.

"I prepared the guest house for you, Maria," Nic says politely, though I know he's just using the name to get under my skin. I'm sad to report, it works. I'd love nothing more than to throw him out of the moving car, but he's much

stronger than me. What's that saying? Revenge is a dish best served cold? In my case, revenge might be served below freezing by the time I'm strong enough to fight back against Nic. It's fine—I don't mind waiting for the right opportunity to screw him over. "It used to be the slave quarters. Despite the renovations, everyone refuses to stay there. They say it's haunted."

"Neil is a demon, which makes me half demon," I reason, keeping my voice as neutral as possible. "It would be silly for a demon to be scared of a ghost, wouldn't it?"

"You are shadowborn," Neil agrees, "but you lack the physical strength of your peers. If not for the special properties your blood seems to hold, you would be no different from a human."

"You're a walking blood bag," Nic adds.

And you're a walking sack of shit.

No. I take a deep breath and count to ten in my head. I can't let him get to me, not now. If I lose control of myself, who knows what Neil will do to my family? Well, I guess I *do* know what he'll do. He said he'll kill them, and I believe him. He already wiped their memories of me.

My adoptive mother, Isabelle, has known me for eight years, since she first became my social worker. And my adoptive father and brother, Luke and David, have known me for even less time. But my sister, Tasha? We've known each other since we were kids. We were both in the system together. Wiping all her memories of me couldn't have been easy. Neil had to go *far* back in her mind.

Neil is powerful and ruthless; he'll do anything it takes to get what he wants, and right now, what he wants is me. He's made it clear where his priorities lie, and what type of person he truly is. As much as I'd love to rise up, transform

into some sort of overpowered superhero, and blow him to smithereens, I can't. Not with my current abilities, or lack thereof.

But when I think about all the pain he's caused me, and the way he's taken the people I love hostage...I want him gone.

Staring out the window into the darkness, I try to determine my next steps. Being Mar is too dangerous for me right now, rife with emotion. I need to be someone else.

Fake it till you make it, right? Tasha always used to say that I took the expression too seriously. Maybe that's true. After a rough patch during my formative years, I developed these characters: Mari, Marilyn, and Mary Alice. They're alter egos, of sorts—masks I use to hide who I really am.

But I can't be Mary Alice again, at least not now. She's my good-girl persona—a girl next door who isn't well-equipped to handle such adversity. Marilyn could work; a good dose of false bravado would be beneficial for me right about now. But in this delicate situation, Marilyn is...let's just say, she isn't subtle about using sex to get what she wants. I don't think that would work, considering the person in need of manipulation is my biological father. Yuck.

That leaves us with Mari, who is a ticking time bomb of emotion. Which is exactly what I'm trying to get away from at the moment. Her anger management issues probably wouldn't go over well with Neil.

Damn. Do I make a new character? I'm not sure who else I can invent, especially on the spot. I feel like I've covered the basic archetypes: the virgin, the slut, and the hothead. I'm not smart enough to be a nerd. What else does that leave? Gloomy goth? Jokester?

After going straight on the highway for so long, we

finally turn at a wooden sign half hidden by bushes. We pull into a long, narrow driveway blocked by a black gate. Fixed to the middle rail is an ornate sign carved out of wood and painted mahogany red. *Foley-Hill Plantation.* Below the gold lettering is a painting of a grizzly bear being strangled by some sort of giant black snake. How aesthetic—no doubt the custom design was commissioned by Neil.

The limo driver punches in a code and the gate opens. Thickets of trees surround the driveway, though the woods thin out the further we drive. Street lamps quickly come into view, illuminating rounded bushes of white flowers lining a freshly paved circular drive. Topiaries in various shapes and sizes decorate the perfectly manicured lawn, each with its own spotlight and wreath of flowers. Interspersed between the topiaries are gold and bronze statues, all headless figures casting eerie shadows in the night. There's no rhyme or reason to the design, no color scheme. It seems Neil chose a show of wealth over aesthetics. Tacky much?

The house doesn't look like a plantation, not any plantation I've ever been to. It's modern, to start, white and black boxes staggered on top of each other with all too much glass. The interior is completely visible from the outside, with no curtains for privacy. Just from the car, I see an indoor pool, a dining room, a living room, and a grandiose bedroom with white tiger fur pinned up on the wall. It reminds me of a horror movie, the type where a killer stalks the inhabitants of a remote house in a deadly game of cat and mouse. Except, I guess in this case, Neil's a demon. I don't think a two-bit serial killer would intimidate him.

"It's late. You should get some rest," Neil says, getting out of the limo. "Nic will take you to the guest house."

"And you?"

"I will return to my home, kiss my wife, and make sure my daughter is asleep in her bedroom. And then I will go to sleep myself, knowing that all the pieces are finally falling into place. That you, Maria, are unable to do anything but obey me."

I shouldn't have asked.

Clenching my jaw, I get out of the car with my lone canvas bag. Nic walks ahead of me, not bothering to check to see if I'm following him. He shoves his hands in his pockets, which is a pretty impressive feat considering how tight his jeans are.

I don't know what I saw in him before. When we first met, I thought he was incredibly good-looking; that impression has faded with every interaction, to the point where I can barely stand to look at him now. He's tall and fit, with dark features stark against pale skin. In essence, he looks like a vampire you'd see in some teen television show. All he needs is some glitter body gel. That's coming back into fashion, right?

His back is broad in front of me, and I can see the curve of his shoulder blades beneath his white T-shirt. A gravel path leads to a two-story Tudor house, the style of which can't be more different than the main house. I prefer it; the glass walls of the main house felt too exposing. At least this guest house has the blinds and curtains drawn.

It doesn't quite fit with the rest of its surroundings, an open field with patches of grass as tall as my waist. You can barely see the main house from here, and the outside lights don't provide nearly enough visibility to see toward the edge of the property. In other words, it doesn't feel safe. Then, I'm not sure anything would in this place.

Nic opens the door without a key, though I suppose there isn't much need for one. The property is secured by a tall fence, and if an intruder were to get in, they would be pretty unlucky to attempt robbery at a demon's residence. I would be mincemeat, probably. But I suppose Neil needs me. Or rather, my blood.

I can't explain its powers, or my own. But I also can't deny that there's something inhuman about me. Even before I realized Neil was my biological father, I had been having quite realistic visions. So realistic, I couldn't even tell they were visions. Adding to that, when my blood spilled on the magic summoning circle, the demon Astaroth rose from his time prison. A prison that isn't supposed to be very easy to open, considering it's sealed in an unknown place in space and time.

Neil doesn't know about the visions, but it's only a matter of time. I'm not sure if he really thinks I can kill Astaroth, but he's pretty much foisted the responsibility onto me because my blood freed him. How exactly I'm supposed to go about doing that is a complete mystery to me. But at this point, I'm so tired, all I can do is wash up and get a good night's sleep. My family is safe for now, and aside from a cult on the loose and a giant demon unleashed upon the mortal realm, there's no immediate danger.

Oh, who am I kidding? I'm screwed six ways to Sunday.

"Your room is the master bedroom upstairs. I heard several slaves were killed in there," Nic says casually. He doesn't turn on the light, so I do instead, revealing a lavish living room with two couches and a shelf filled with books. No television, though. I guess Neil expects me to spend all my time training to defeat Astaroth. You'd think he would

be able to come up with a better plan, rather than relying on an eighteen-year-old girl to slay his enemies.

"There's a kitchen over there," Nic says, pointing down the hall. "No food, though. Write a list of stuff you want, and I'll get one of the assistants to pick it up for you tomorrow. Tough luck until then. There's a laundry room somewhere, a few empty rooms upstairs, and...that's about it. No landline, so if someone tries to rob us and comes here first, you won't be able to call for help."

"I understand." *I understand that you're an asshole.* But I can't say that. I have enough self-control to refrain from angering Nic. It's late, I'm tired, and I'd rather him get out of my face as fast as possible.

But Nic doesn't take the hint and continues to antagonize me. "Neil is going to tell people that this was Allegra's idea, by the way. She's been asking him to help you out. You're like her little charity case, since you saved her life and all. Even though *I* did most of the heavy lifting. Isn't it ironic? She wants to help you find your shadowborn heritage, unaware that the truth is the last thing she would ever want. A bastard sister who could usurp her place as the heir of the family. You know that she's not officially named Neil's heir, right?"

"She's older than me," I point out, eyeing the door. "And I'm illegitimate. I don't pose any threat to her."

"Your very existence is a threat. She might be half demon, but she has some very *nasty* human habits," Nic says fondly. "She would be devastated to know that her father cheated on her mother, and what's more, had a bastard he abandoned. That would mean her perfect little family isn't so perfect after all, because of you. Because you were born. She would resent you, probably as much as you resent her."

"I don't resent her." I resent the *situation*. Or so I tell myself. Allegra isn't a bad person. Trust me, it would be much easier if she were.

"Come on, now. You don't have to lie to me," Nic coaxes. "We're cousins, after all—didn't Allegra tell you?"

"Wait. You're cousins?" I forgot about that little detail. "On whose side? Neil's?"

"Yeah. I'm your cousin, too, technically."

I feel bile rising in my throat. "If you knew that, then why the hell have you been flirting with me ever since we met?!"

"We're distant cousins," he says with a shrug. "I would have kissed you, too, if Archer hadn't beaten me to the punch. Or, should I say, to the *lips?*"

Distant or not, he was aware we were related the whole time. There's a lot to unpack there. "Oh my God. That's gross, not to mention illegal!"

"Maybe in the States. But in other parts of the world, and among the shadowborn, it's not unnatural for cousins to marry." There's a defensive edge in Nic's voice, reminding me of all the rumors I'd heard about him when we first met. That he was in a love triangle, fighting for Allegra's affection…and she didn't choose him.

"How distant *are* you?"

"Neil's my uncle. He and my mom are half siblings by blood."

"Wow, your explanation did *not* make things better," I say, moving toward the stairs. "I'm tired now. I'd like to rest."

"You're in for a long day ahead of you tomorrow," Nic agrees. "Get some rest. I won't be going easy on you, Maria."

The name halts me in my tracks, but I don't turn to face him. I can't. It takes a moment for me to level my voice, enough so the anger doesn't seep through. I've known guys like Nic all my life, and if you show that something bothers you, they'll keep doing it.

But as normal as I try to sound, even *I* hear the venom as I spit out, "Don't call me that."

"Why not? That's your name, isn't it, Maria?" He draws out the syllables, taunting me.

My entire body tenses, and I close my eyes, willing myself to calm down. It doesn't work. "No one calls me Maria."

"Then I suppose I'll be the only one," Nic says. "Unless...there's some *reason* you don't like being called Maria."

The statement hangs in the air for an awkward beat, but I don't take the bait to explain myself.

"Let me guess," Nic says, taking a step toward me. "You don't like being called Maria because you've been abused. Going from foster home to foster home, being beaten and unloved by practically everyone... You wanted to be someone else so badly, you made up fake personas. You began calling yourself different names, all to distance yourself from who you really are. These personas are your only chance to feel normal and wanted. But underneath it all, you're Maria. You only deny it because you're afraid of being hurt. How's that? On the mark? Am I missing some details?"

It takes me a few seconds to gather myself, to figure out what I'm going to say next. My instinct is to deny his claims, to tell him he's wrong and that he doesn't know me at all. He never will. But his guess hits too close to home.

You don't owe him, or anyone else, an explanation, I tell myself. All I owe Nic is a punch in the face, and maybe a kick in the crotch again for good measure.

With that in mind, I march upstairs with my bag. Though I'm not looking at him, I can practically feel him grinning behind my back. Go ahead. Once I gain enough power to protect those I care about, I'll be coming for Nic.

Right after I kill Neil.

CHAPTER TWO

Did you know that sleep deprivation is a form of torture? I know that *technically* I managed to sleep four hours last night, but when Nic wakes me up with an air horn, I don't feel like I've slept a wink. I do, however, feel a murderous urge rising in my throat.

"Rise and shine, sleepyhead," he calls in a disgustingly sugary tone. As if I didn't already want to beat him half to death.

I roll over and press the pillow to my head, trying to ignore him until he rips the sheets off and opens the blinds, blasting the air horn above my head until I sit up.

"It's time to train, Maria! I brought you an apple from the main house for breakfast. You can thank me later." He tosses a Granny Smith into my lap. "Let's go, lazy bones!"

Seriously, can I kill him?

I'd love to take the apple and toss it out the window, to make a point about how much (or in this case, how little) I appreciate his shallow gesture. But I'm hungry and there's no food in the fridge downstairs, so I take a bite and crawl

15

out of bed. I half expected worms to be crawling out of the fruit, or something else equally disgusting, but it's a regular apple.

"Yikes," Nic exclaims after getting a good look at my bare face. "Were you always this ugly?"

Were you always this charming?

I'm not ugly. Plain, maybe, but not *ugly*. If anything, *he's* the ugly one, on the inside.

"I need to wash up," I tell him, motioning toward the door. "I would like some privacy."

"Alright, princess. But only for today," he says, wagging his finger in my face. Should I bite it off? "Tomorrow, I expect your ass to be out of bed and ready to train by dawn. Or will that be too difficult for you?"

"Does it matter?" He's still going to make me do it. I'm not going to give this prick the satisfaction of resisting. Something tells me he's a sicko who gets off on stuff like that.

I set the apple down and go to the bathroom, washing my face and brushing my teeth. At least the house is stocked with toiletries. Pulling my hair back, I have no clothes to change into so I head downstairs where Nic is waiting. Sun pours through the windows, making the glass light fixtures above our heads scatter rainbows across the room. It doesn't improve my mood in the least.

"There are training grounds this way. Neil set up a makeshift shack out here, where no one will bother us."

Translation: No one will be able to see *me*. That's what Neil wants, right? I already know he is ashamed of me, but I guess this is just another confirmation. It's ironic—why is *he* ashamed of *me?* He's the one who cheated on his wife. I'm

the one who should be ashamed of sharing DNA with this asshole.

The sun is brutal today, without a cloud in the sky. Nic leads me past a field of tall grass, along a dirt path to a fenced-off portion of land next to the stable.

The red paint peels and chips off the walls, the entire structure held by decaying wood. Racks of weapons line the walls, sitting out in the open. With the windows wide, the sun heats the metal blades. I'm apprehensive to touch anything, afraid of burning myself. Thankfully Nic hands me a wooden sword to use. I use the term "thankfully" lightly—it's hard to be thankful toward Nic, especially when I'm fairly certain he's going to beat me up.

Granted, I don't know him that well. We haven't had many one-on-one conversations to get to know each other, and even through our short interactions on the cruise ship, we were both lying to each other. But I don't need to have a heart-to-heart with him to understand his type. He's an arrogant know-it-all, and he acts flirtatious to disarm people. I've dealt with guys like him before. Girls, too. High school, at least the first three years, were hell. I know this sounds judgmental, but I don't need to know much else about Nic to understand that he's a tool.

"I want to assess your skills," Nic explains, leading me outside. The training grounds are fenced in, with scarecrow-like targets in the distance. I assume they're used for archery practice, given the arrows sticking out of their stomachs.

"I don't have shadowborn abilities," I remind him, weighing the sword in my hand. It's blunt and looks like a child's toy, the "blade" not even the length of my arm. "I won't be able to come close to beating you, sword or not."

This exercise is pointless. To top it off, I'm not even strong compared to *regular* humans. Shouldn't strength training and basics be the priority? I guess they would be if the goal was to make me strong enough to defeat Astaroth. Nic seems more interested in humiliating me.

"Maybe your powers will show up out of sheer desperation," he says, sneering. "Either way, I'm looking forward to seeing what kind of painful expression you'll show me. It's exciting, if you know what I mean."

"We're cousins," I reiterate. "By blood."

"Debatable."

"We're first cousins."

"But we're both bastards," he points out, "so we're only distantly related. If you *wanted* to, we could fool around. But only if you begged me."

I'd rather stab myself through the eye with a live wire and pull it out my nostril.

"Let's set up some ground rules," Nic continues, putting a hand on my wooden sword. "You try to hit me with the sword. If you land a blow to my neck or the center of my chest, you win."

Sounds simple. But I'm not delusional enough to think I could beat him — not like this. For one thing, this is the first time I've ever held a sword. Nic is also much taller than me, faster, stronger, and has better reflexes thanks to his shadowborn heritage. Me? I have no such skills. The best I can hope to do is minimize the damage to my face and vital —

Nic plows into me, not bothering to tell me we've started. See? What did I tell you? He's a total tool. And he doesn't play fair.

A kick in the stomach sends me tumbling to the dirt, the sword flying out of my hand before I even get a chance to

swing it. Why did he give me a sword if he was just going to disarm me? And why feed me if he was planning on kicking me in the stomach? Embarrassingly enough, the blow makes me throw up. Thankfully not on myself, but it's still not a pleasant feeling.

Nic barely stops to let me catch a breath before he hits me again, this time right in the face. Pain explodes from my head, and I swear my nose is broken. Even if it isn't, I heard a crunch. That can't be a good sign.

Nic's blows are too fast for me to dodge, and he's not even out of breath. At this point, I can't get up from the ground. Every time I try to, he kicks me down and shoves my face in the dirt.

"Come on, Maria. Are you even trying?" he taunts.

The frustrating part is, I *am* trying. And he's not. But the angrier I get, the more each blow seems to hurt. My face, particularly, has quickly begun to swell to the point where my vision is severely impaired.

My teeth are still intact, though. And my ribs might be cracked, but they don't feel broken. So all in all, *not* the worst beating I've received.

I lose track of how much time passes. I'm on the ground, on my back, staring up at the sky and letting the sun scorch my skin. Nic might just kill me. There are plenty of weapons in the stable; he could easily do it and shove my corpse somewhere on these massive grounds. I assume he won't actually finish me off, because Neil needs me, but at this point who knows? Nic doesn't seem like the smartest cookie in the package. He's what I imagine demons would be: hedonists who put their own self-interests first.

"Nic." A sharp voice cuts through the haze of pain, and while I can't see, I can tell it belongs to Rhys. His voice is

unforgettable. English is his second language, but another romance language must be his first. It's not an accent I recognize, nor does it impair my understanding, but it's another mystery I've learned to accept about him. "You are going to kill her."

"Her? No way," Nic scoffs. "Stop being such a buzzkill. I'm just playing around."

"She has been invited to dinner in the main house. If Allegra or Mrs. Abbott question her appearance, I will not hesitate to tell them this was your handiwork."

"Aunt Faith won't care. Maria's just a stranger to her—a nobody."

"Incorrect. She is Allegra's savior, and Mr. Abbott's charge," Rhys says calmly. "Will you continue arguing with me like a petulant child? Or are you going to help her up?"

Nic scoffs. "She's bloody and sweaty and gross. *You* get her up."

I save them both the trouble. I manage to roll over and sit up on my own, though the world is spinning. I probably won't be able to stand, much less walk back to my room. But between crawling and being carried, I'd rather crawl.

Rhys appears beside me, helping me up. His skin is cool to the touch, while my own feels like it's burning. We walk back to the house slowly and I'm able to stand on my own two feet, but Rhys is practically carrying me anyway.

"Do not throw up on me," Rhys says, his voice cold as ever. I hope I do, just out of spite, but I haven't eaten enough. The best I'd be able to do is spit bile at him, and I'm not *that* petty.

Maybe Rhys is a bad omen for me. He only seems to show up when I'm in trouble. Not for *me*, mind you. The first time I met him, back in the cruise ship's sickbay, I had

just been attacked by a horde of cultists. He was assigned to protect me, probably because he didn't have a choice. The next time we met, he was helping Allegra in a hidden cultist ritual room. And now this.

Rhys opens the front door and helps me to the couch. I'm covered in dirt, blood, and a little bit of vomit that landed on my shirt. Unfortunately for Neil, I can't bring myself to care and lay down directly on the cushions.

Rhys drags a chair beside me, a first aid kit in his lap. He must have gotten it from the closet; I'm surprised this house is even equipped with one. Unless Neil knew Nic was going to beat the shit out of me. Entirely possible.

"Do not move. This is going to sting." He sprays disinfectant on my arms and legs, all scraped up and swollen from Nic's physical assault. My gut reaction *is* to jerk back, but my muscles don't seem to cooperate and I end up staying still while Rhys sprays liquid fire on my open wounds. "Does it hurt?"

"Take a guess," I manage.

"I suppose you are fine if you have enough energy to be sarcastic."

"It's the opposite. Sarcasm is my coping mechanism." One of many. Maybe I should get that printed on a T-shirt. "Is my nose broken? It feels broken."

"No. You will fully recover in a few days." He lifts my arm, wiping it with a towel and applying the salve. His hands are gentler than I expect. Or maybe I'm dying and the pain is so intense I'm going numb. One can only hope.

"How long have you known who I am?" I ask.

Rhys' hands pause, but I can't see his expression clearly. Even if I could, I doubt I'd be able to tell what he's thinking. "A long time."

21

Probably since before I came on the ship, then. Just like Nic.

"How did you hide it?" he asks. "The Blood Chalice did not expose you as shadowborn. Why?"

"I tampered with it," I reply honestly. There's no need to lie; he'd figure it out sooner or later. "I enlisted Ethan Kinsey's help, and he replaced the Blood Chalice with a fake one."

"Why would Ethan Kinsey help *you*?"

I'm not sure if he means to insult me, but I don't take offense. Ethan is the son of the chancellor of Northeastern College, a magic school in upstate New York. In other words, he's kind of a big deal. But I managed to convince him to help me, which may or may not have involved a meaningless little kiss. If I'm being honest, I would have done anything to get him to help me out. But I guess he has *some* morals, because he didn't ask to sleep with me. I would have if he'd asked. When you're—

Well, let's just say at some point sex became meaningless to me. And I wanted to get off the ship and as far away from the magical world as possible. Does that make me a horrible person? Probably. But if it makes you feel any better, I didn't get what I wanted. The universe, it seems, has other plans. *Neil* has other plans, most of them involving ruining my goddamn life and taking my family hostage by wiping their memories of me.

Of course, that's a lot to explain to Rhys. So instead, I simply say, "I'm a *great* kisser."

Rhys chokes on air. "Pardon me?"

"My lips are thin, but soft," I add, unsure of why I'm going into such detail. I barely know Rhys, and I haven't

even caught a good glimpse of him. "What? Are you curious?"

As soon as the words leave my mouth, I regret them. For one, I don't even know how *old* Rhys is. And I decidedly do *not* want to kiss him. Plus, I can't imagine I look very enticing. I'm swollen, bruised, and my face was Nic's punching bag a few minutes ago.

Thankfully, I can't see Rhys' expression of disgust. I'm guessing that's the kind of face he's making.

"It was a joke," I explain quickly. "A bad one. Sorry."

He sighs. "Mr. Abbott has requested you come to dinner this evening. You should rest before then. I'll have someone bring you a change of clothes, along with other things you might need. Do you need help getting to your room?"

"I'll be fine," I lie, mostly because I want him to leave.

Rhys hesitates, setting the first aid kit down on the coffee table. "I will return at 5:30 PM to get you. Be ready by then."

I won't be—but I guess, like everything else in my life right now, I don't have a choice.

MY FACE IS FUCKED. PARDON THE CRUDE LANGUAGE; I know you might not be used to it, because Mary Alice doesn't curse. But I'm not Mary Alice. Not yet, anyway. Though that seems to be the direction things are heading in.

I don't *want* to be. My other characters at least have some truth to them, while Mary Alice is the complete opposite of who I am. But Allegra doesn't know me as anyone else, and I don't have it in me to explain my characters to her. It could go one of three ways:

1. She'll think I have Dissociative Identity Disorder, which I do not. My characters are conscious efforts (read: lies) on my part, while DID is a serious and often misunderstood psychological condition.
2. She'll think I'm a total freak and want nothing to do with me, which would mean forfeiting what little protection from Neil I have. The only reason why I'm supposed to be "presentable" tonight, the only reason Rhys helped me, is because of Allegra. Neil wants to keep up appearances in front of the daughter he likes.
3. She'll feel bad and pity me, which is the worst option here for my pride. Not that I have a leg to stand on in that respect; what pride?

Even before I found out that Allegra and I are half sisters, I was admittedly a little envious of her. She's a better version of Mary Alice, sweet and kind, except Allegra is genuine. She's also beautiful and graceful, and even if she's been sickly since her youth, she's still stronger than me. Overall, she's *better* than me in every way.

The fact that we're related only exacerbates my jealousy. It's not *her* fault—I know that logically. But looking at her makes me wonder how different I would have been, had I been raised with love from a young age. Instead of hugs and kisses, I got kicked and—

Oh God. I just quoted *Annie*. It's a hard knock life.

Okay, you have *full* permission to kick me in the face as hard as you can! Seriously!

Now I *know* I'm too far into self-pity mode. Which only makes me hate myself more. It's a vicious cycle.

Snap out of it! I tell myself, staring into the bathroom mirror. My face is double its normal size, and I have two black eyes obscuring my vision, but I'm still alive and kicking. And unfortunately, this isn't even the worst beating I've gotten. It's up there, sure, but at least Nic didn't throw a hot plate at me. Now *that* hurts.

And really, all he did was hit and kick me a few times. Right out in broad daylight. I saw him coming. There was no element of surprise, no psychological factor he added or humiliation that made it worse. Would I have liked to *not* be beaten up? Yeah. But I've survived worse.

Look at me now! I'm a fully functional eighteen-year-old young adult. Do I have mental hang-ups? Sure, but who doesn't? Am I well adjusted? No, but I can fake it! And that's what I'm going to do at this dinner tonight. Pretend to be happy and normal, ignore my problems, and try not to let anyone get to me.

When you get strong enough, you're going to kill Neil anyway! I think, practicing a smile in the mirror. It hurts too much, so I settle on a more neutral expression. *You're going to save Tasha, Isabelle, Luke, and David. And then everything will be alright. As long as they're safe, as long as we're a family again… nothing else matters.*

With that, I walk downstairs and leave the house. Rhys hasn't come by yet, but I don't want to wait for him. If he intends to pick me up, I'm sure I'll pass him on my way. The path to the main house is narrow and not well lit, but the sun is still out thanks to the long summer days.

The dining room is fully visible from the backyard, with a wall made entirely out of glass. The Abbott family is already sitting down at the table, waited on by a staff of ten. The food on the table is enough to feed a

small village; there almost isn't enough room for it all. Half of it remains untouched, including the big turkey in the center. Allegra sits beside her father, laughing while he hands her a roll of bread. Her mother is beside them sipping on a glass of wine with a smile. It's picturesque.

The table is large, with at least twelve seats arranged around it. But sitting so close together, the Abbotts look cozy and happy. There might be a lot of empty seats, but there's no room for me to sit with them. Neil's made sure of it.

Nic approaches from the back porch, stepping in front of me to block my view. "Maria. I thought someone had already told you."

"Told me what?" I ask, a bad feeling worming its way through my stomach.

He smiles. "You don't look good enough to be seen by Aunt Faith and Allegra. Neil thinks you should stay at the house until your face recovers and you're a little bit more presentable."

"What about dinner?" I haven't eaten all day.

"Go back to the house." He puts two hands on my shoulders and spins me around, giving me a little shove for good measure. "You don't belong here."

I *know* I shouldn't say anything. I should be smart and leave without a second glance back. That's what Mary Alice would do. But I'm not Mary Alice.

"You're outside, too," I say simply, because I think that's what will hurt him the most. Not based on anything I know about him, but based on my own feelings. Maybe we're more similar than I thought, because it works.

Nic's expression changes. His hand whips out, grabbing

my arm and tearing me away from the window and into the bushes in the yard, out of sight.

"I could do anything I wanted to you right now," he murmurs. His hand crawls up my body, toward my throat. It's the one place left unbruised, but he remedies that quickly, tightening his grip. His full weight is on top of me, pinning me in place. "I could kill you. No one would say anything. No one would care, Maria."

"Neil needs me," I gasp, struggling to breathe. "And Allegra—"

"Allegra is my family," Nic says evenly.

I want to say that Allegra is my friend—but that's not true. She's Mary Alice's friend, maybe. She's not mine; she doesn't even know my real name. She only decided to help me based on her own self-interest, which I don't fault her for. But her self-interest happens to be maintaining her place as the sole heiress of the Abbott family.

If she finds out who I really am…

Nic laughs as if he can read my mind. "If Allegra knew who you were, she'd kill you herself."

He finally releases me, leaving me on my knees gasping for breath. I hate the way he looks down on me, figuratively and literally. But what can I do? He's already beaten me up. Even if I *did* manage to land a blow, which seems impossible in my current state, I'd fear his retaliation. All I'm able to do is swallow my anger and crawl back to the guest house on my hands and knees, like the beaten dog I am.

I try to convince myself that this is for the best. Do I *really* want Allegra to see me like this? How could I possibly explain my injuries in a way that won't piss Neil and Nic off? It's better to let myself heal and relax for the night.

But the rejection stings no matter what lies I try to spin

for myself, leaving a sour taste in my mouth. It would have been better if I didn't *see* the Abbotts through the window, like some voyeur. I was *literally* an outsider looking in, and frankly, I hate what I saw.

Why does Neil get to eat dinner with his family when he took mine away from me? Wasn't it enough that he abandoned me?

He shouldn't get to be happy. None of them should be.

If Allegra knew what her father had done, would she still smile at him? Would she *ever* smile again, knowing she's been raised by an asshole? Would Mrs. Abbott smile at him, would she ever fuck him again, knowing he cheated on her and had a baby with another woman?

I could ruin their happiness. I could march back up to the house and tell them everything. Even if they didn't believe me, the seed of doubt would be planted. I'm not sure they would ever be able to look at each other the same way. And if they believed me, then I'd be ruining their family. I wouldn't even feel bad about it. Their misery would be my delight.

Fuck.

This is why I can't be Mar. This is why she's just an in-between, not a full-fledged character. She's too much like Maria. The lines blur, and I can't climb out of the grave I've dug for myself.

I take a few deep breaths. I make it back to the house. My neck throbs, tender to the touch. I probably deserve it, after the dark mental path I just strolled down.

Walking upstairs, I lock the door and twist the faucet to "hot." I breathe in the steam from the tub, rising around me and fogging the mirror. The rushing water calms me, and

when the tub is filled high enough, I turn off the faucet and get in with my clothes.

I'm spiraling into my own personal hell. Maybe I'm too tired, too injured, and...too honest. But I can't afford to slip up now, to do anything that would push Neil to hurt the people I care about. Even if I hate him and Nic, it doesn't matter. I will stuff down my anger, my tears, *myself*, because I need to.

Because *they* need me to.

CHAPTER THREE

S omeone is at the door.

And before you ask, *no*, I did not gain supernatural senses overnight. That would be too easy, wouldn't it? I still have average human eyesight and hearing. But the doorbell has been ringing for the past two minutes nonstop.

I thought that if I ignored him, he'd go away. I don't want to see Nic's face right now and I sure as hell don't want him to see *mine*. While my eyes aren't as swollen as before, my face is still a landscape of bruising. At least the pain from breathing has subsided, though my entire body aches when I move a single muscle. Dragging myself out of bed, I crawl downstairs on my hands and knees. Reaching up to the door handle, I fling it open.

"What?" I spit out, using what little strength I have to stand.

"Good morning," Rhys replies, unfazed. He doesn't wait for me to invite him in before entering, carrying a brown grocery bag to the kitchen. As if it's the most natural thing in the world, he begins stocking my fridge. No explanation

or anything. Then, he's not exactly blessed with the gift of gab.

I have to cling to the wall to walk, not crawl, toward him. The kitchen is just down the hall, and while it's not large or luxurious, I prefer the cozy ranch style. There aren't any personalizations or decorations, but the green and cream color scheme and matching table set look like something out of a magazine. And, more importantly, all the appliances seem to be new and in working order.

"What are you doing?" I ask Rhys.

He glances up, putting down a big bottle of orange juice to pull out a chair for me at the table. "Sit down. You are aggravating your injuries by pushing yourself."

My pain outweighs my spite. I sit. "You didn't answer my question. What are you doing?"

"What does it look like I am doing?"

"Giving an injured girl an attitude at" — I check the clock — "nine in the morning."

He doesn't reply, though I swear he rolls his eyes a little. Speaking of, this is the first time I'm *seeing* Rhys. In the past, we've only met in the dark. And yesterday, my eyes were so swollen I couldn't see. And let's not forget the first time we met in the sickbay, when he hid his face behind a book on purpose. Because, according to him, he's "ugly." You know, there's a limit to being humble!

No. This isn't *humble*. He outright lied to me! Yeah, yeah, I'm aware of how hypocritical I sound. But I thought we already established that I'm a hypocritical liar. Actually, those are my two defining characteristics. Do you seriously need a refresher on that?

I'm getting sidetracked. Surprise, surprise — Rhys is hand-

some. Frankly, with all the shadowborn students being so good-looking, this doesn't affect me anymore. He's so attractive, it almost seems like he doesn't belong here. Not just *here*, on a plantation renovated by a demon, but in the mortal realm itself.

His hair is such a pale blonde it's nearly silver, but surprisingly it doesn't make him look old. I think having dark eyebrows helps define his features, though I'm not sure if they're natural or if he's using brow products. His lashes are as light as the hair on his head, framing eyes that are somewhere between sky blue and lavender.

It's his ears that stick out. Literally. I wouldn't have noticed it normally, but when he turns to put something in the fridge, I get a full glimpse. The tops of his ears are pointed, extended about an inch longer than mine.

Rhys must notice me staring, because he turns to face me with a frown. "What?"

"What, what?" I play dumb. As opposed to my usual self, which is dumb, but not playing.

"You were staring at me."

"You're just really handsome," I say.

His frown deepens. "You are lying."

"I was staring at your ears."

"Oh." He doesn't elaborate, and at this point, I'm not sure I should probe. He doesn't seem to want to talk about it...or *anything*, for that matter. Would it be rude to ask? I'm not sure how supernatural society would take a question like that, so I guess I'll refrain for now. He *has* brought me food, after all. What's that saying? The way to a girl's heart is through her stomach? Anyway, compared to Nic, Rhys has been saintly.

Rhys finishes stocking the fridge and pantry before

getting a pan out of the cabinet. He places it on the gas stove and turns up the flames.

"What are you doing?" I ask again, dumbly.

"What does it—"

"It looks like you're cooking—I get it, I can see," I cut him off. "I mean, why?"

"Because Neil wants you to kill Astaroth," he explains, breaking eggs in a bowl. They sizzle when he pours them into the hot pan, sprinkling them with salt and pepper for flavor. "To kill Astaroth, you will need to get stronger. To get stronger, you will need to train. A lot. And one should not train on an empty stomach."

"More training? With Nic?"

"Nic does not know how to train others. One doubts if he even knows how to interact with human beings. Neil has requested that I take over your studies." He frowns. "Given your current state, we will put a hold on physical training. Now, drink. I imagine you are severely dehydrated."

Rhys slides a glass of water my way, and I barely catch it before it falls off the edge of the table.

So, he's here under Neil's orders. I should have figured; he doesn't seem all that thrilled about it. I wouldn't be either if I were him. He's normally in charge of taking care of Allegra, so maybe in his mind, taking care of a bastard like myself is a step down.

I take a swig of water, realizing I haven't had anything to eat or drink since yesterday's apple. The rest of my body has been wracked with pain, so I hadn't noticed. As soon as I finish the glass of water, Rhys fills it again.

He finishes making breakfast quickly, putting a platter and utensils in front of me. Initially it looks like too much food, but I stuff it all in my face like an animal while he

rinses the dishes he used to cook and puts them in the dish-washer. It doesn't even occur to me until *after* I'm finished that he never asked me how I like my eggs cooked. Or what kind of toast I like, or which fruits I'll eat... I didn't even have to ask him for hot sauce—he had put the perfect amount on the eggs.

Either he's a good guesser, or Neil's been monitoring me for longer than I initially thought. Or I'm overthinking things, and my breakfast preferences are basic. Probably the latter.

"Thanks for the meal," I tell him, meaning it.

Rhys' expression doesn't change. "I have been asked to keep you alive."

"That sounds like something the accomplice of a serial killer would say."

He picks up my plate and rinses it off, filling my glass again and tidying the kitchen. "We will go into the office upstairs and begin our lessons."

"Lessons?" I echo.

"Your physical combat training will resume at a later date, but there are still things you must learn if you are to succeed at Southeastern University in the fall. You have less than a month to catch up to the other students."

"Back up a second." I know Neil said he wanted me to attend Southeastern, but his main goal is to have me kill Astaroth. Won't I just need strength training, and maybe some magic combat training? "What are you talking about?"

Rhys lets out an exasperated sigh, like I'm trying *his* patience. The feeling is mutual, buddy. "To defeat Astaroth, you must know more about him. In addition to combat training, you will attend academic classes. Neil has taken you in under the guise of a sponsor, so he cannot simply pay

your way through school as he—excuse me. I mean to say, he cannot bribe anyone. It would rouse suspicion. You must take classes and pass on your own merit."

"What *kind* of classes?" I press.

"Magical theory, history, supernatural biology— freshman remedial classes," Rhys says dryly. "At your current level, you will fail. You have no foundational knowledge. Neil has asked me to prepare you. Should you get poor scores, it will reflect badly on him."

Of *course*. I should have guessed. Neil abandoned me as a child and *lied* to me my entire life because he thought I didn't develop powers. This sort of shit is to be expected.

If I have to rely on myself to get good grades, then maybe being Mary Alice for a little bit longer would be the smart thing to do. On one hand, I'm already tired of her. On the other, she's the least offensive character and can get good grades. She's not the best suited for these types of supernatural situations, but maybe I just have to adjust her a little bit. Sure, she's kind of a...pushover, but until I have the power to protect myself, I can't afford to antagonize anyone. It's not just *my* life on the line.

"When are we going to start?" I ask Rhys.

"I need to bring textbooks from the main house. You can do what you'd like until then, though I recommend a shower. And a change of clothes. You look filthy," he says bluntly.

Ouch. I already know that, but he doesn't have to say it out loud.

"I don't have a change of clothes, and I couldn't find any detergent." I had to wash my clothes with body soap in the tub last night and throw them in the dryer so I wouldn't have to sleep naked.

Rhys stares at me for a moment, his expression impassive. "Fine."

And then he leaves. No explanation, no *emotion* at all. Like it's my fault I was kidnapped?

Whatever. I'm not going to chase after him. But he's right about one thing—I could use a shower. I took a bath last night, but I don't know how to turn the A/C on. As a result, I sweat like a pig last night. I can't exactly smell myself, but now that I think about it, I'm definitely not fresh as a daisy. Although I don't have a clean change of clothes, something is better than nothing.

It doesn't take me long to shower, but by the time I get out and dry off, Rhys is back. He's cleaning the living room, the sleeves of his white button-down rolled up to his elbows.

"Thanks," I offer. It probably wouldn't be a bad thing to get on Rhys' good side. We're going to be spending a lot of time together, and even if he *is* Neil's stooge, I'll be relying on him for the rest of the summer.

But apparently, Rhys doesn't care for the olive branch I've extended. If you can call a simple "thanks" an olive branch.

"This house is dirty," he retorts, straightening the cushions on the couch. "I thought you were a maid on the SS *Athena*. You cannot keep your own space clean?"

"I wasn't in the mood to clean, as you can see." I point to my face. "Nic bashed my face in."

"You will make a full recovery." There isn't a shred of sympathy in his voice. "Let us go upstairs."

He brings a bag of textbooks to the office next to the master bedroom, a small space lined with empty bookshelves. There's a big bay window overlooking the yard and

the forest surrounding the house. Rhys flicks the fan on, pulling over two chairs by the desk.

Setting the textbooks down, I get a glimpse of the spines. *Shadow World History for Idiots. Spellcasting Basics. Trueblood and Shadowborn Anatomy and Physiology 101. Northern Elvish for Beginners. The Old Man and the Sea.* One of these titles is not like the other.

"*The Old Man and the Sea?*" I question.

"Neil suggested I include some culture in our studies," Rhys explains dryly. "He is concerned others will question why he chose to sponsor you, as you seem to be an ignorant and unrefined person."

Wow, he doesn't pull punches. But I can't argue without getting too emotional, and I will *not* have a repeat of last night, so I drop it.

"And he wants me to take Elvish, too?" I ask.

"It will be an extracurricular of sorts," Rhys says carefully.

So I guess this more or less confirms Rhys is an elf, right? Thankfully he's more like Legolas than Dobby. No offense to the latter, but Legolas was played by Orlando Bloom in those movies. What can I say? I'm a fan.

"We shall start with history."

Ugh. My least favorite subject. Along with math, science, and English. It requires *way* too much brain power. At least I'm not getting graded on this, right? All that's on the line is my life and the lives of my family. But no pressure.

RHYS IS A TOUGH TEACHER, WHICH FIGURES. AND I WAS wrong about not being graded. Again, no surprise there. Not only is he giving me grades, but he's giving me *pop quizzes*. That's criminal. The only reason I haven't killed him this week, aside from him being way stronger than me, and my physical state being horrendous, is because he's cooked breakfast for me every morning.

His reasoning?

"You are incompetent when it comes to keeping your house clean. Why would I expect you to be any better in the kitchen?" He looks directly into my eyes when he says this.

My jaw is on the floor. When I manage to pick it back up, I tell him, "I can take care of myself."

"You are lying." He says this quite frequently. Most of the time, he's spot on.

"I've taken care of myself for most of my life. And I'm still kicking." Unpopular, maybe, with some strange coping mechanisms to deal with my feelings, but I'm still alive. That's gotta count for something, right?

Rhys doesn't have anything to say to that, but he puts a plate of eggs in front of me, and it pretty much makes up for all the attitude he's given me in the last twenty-four hours. As per usual, I gobble it down without holding back. My face is healing quite nicely, so it doesn't hurt to chew anymore. Having three full meals a day is definitely helping, and I'm taking multivitamins regularly for the first time in my life. So that's something.

For the last five days, Rhys has been keeping me busy with my studies. He leaves right before lunch, and while I have the rest of the day to myself, I don't have much else to do but rest and study more. Without television or the inter-

net, it's been a pretty miserable existence. And the heat wave isn't helping. At least I figured out the A/C.

"Eat slowly or you will choke," Rhys reminds me.

"You're surprisingly good at cooking," I reply, gulping down the rest of my water.

He refills it from a glass pitcher. "Surprisingly?"

"It's nothing. So what's on the agenda for today?"

"You are *surprisingly* chipper this morning," he says dryly.

"My face is mostly healed, and the detergent pods you gave me make this tracksuit a lot more bearable to wear." I shrug. "It's the small victories I try to focus on. Otherwise, the soul-crushing weight of this situation I'm in would, well, crush me."

"It seems we need to add more literature into the curriculum to strengthen your vocabulary."

Hey.

"Neil has requested your presence tonight," Rhys says, changing the subject. I nearly choke on a piece of bacon. "Are you alright?"

"I'm fine," I rasp, reaching for my water. "What does Neil want with me?"

"Allegra has been asking for you. She wishes to see you. I told him that your face is healed." He pauses. "They make a point to have dinner together on the weekends. Neil, his wife, and Allegra. It is usually quite the spread of food. But you will have to act the part. They will expect an update on your studies."

In other words, if I mess up, it will reflect poorly on Rhys. Got it.

Look, I don't *hate* the guy. Yeah, he's Neil's henchman and he's pretty rude and blunt, but he's not a sadistic jackass

like Nic. He's also the only one feeding me and giving me supplies, so I might have Stockholm syndrome. But I'm not sure what Neil will do to Rhys, and more importantly, to *me*, if I screw up this dinner.

"What should I expect?" I ask finally.

Rhys folds his arms over his chest. "I suggest you convince them that you need Neil's help, but also, that you can blossom under his tutelage."

Great. Not cryptic and general *at all*.

I guess I'm back to my usual strategy, then. Become Mary Alice and lie, lie, lie.

CHAPTER FOUR

"**F**uck!"

"Wow. What a way to greet your favorite cousin," Nic says sarcastically, looking up from the couch. I didn't even hear him come in, much less make himself comfortable in the living room. "You've got quite the potty mouth, don't you, Maria?"

"You surprised me," I reply. I can't be bothered to even *acknowledge* the "favorite cousin" shit he's spewing. "What are you doing here?"

"You don't have any clothes. Not any good ones." He looks at my tracksuit as if he has the right to judge me. He's wearing black skinny jeans. It's August in Georgia! I just *know* he has a heat rash under all that denim. "Tell me—if you're washing your panties every night, are you going to bed commando?"

"We're related." I feel the need to point that out yet again, even though I shouldn't have to.

"Sort of."

"Why are you here?" I ask repeat.

43

"You can't look homeless when you have dinner with Neil's family. What will they think of you?" He shoves a white plastic trash bag at me. "Here. I'm sure you'll find something suitable. Try not to make a fool of yourself. And don't be late. Dinner is at six. Neil will be *pissed* if you aren't on time. His policy is, everyone has to be seated before we can eat."

"Thanks." The clothes are useful—but there's not a chance I'm going to the main house at six. I'll be there earlier, just in case Nic is trying to trick me. It seems like something he would do.

I bring the bag upstairs, not bothering to show Nic out. Dumping the clothes on the bedroom floor, I sort through them to find something appropriate for tonight. Honestly, I assumed Nic brought me clothes he randomly found and shoved in a trash bag. But it's much worse—the clothes he brought are *nice*. Some still have tags, with prices in the thousands. It doesn't take a genius to figure out that these must be Allegra's hand-me-downs. All the tops have high necklines, and the skirts hang to my ankles. This is her style, and within Neil's price range. Is this a message from Nic? Yet another humiliation tactic?

Whatever. It doesn't make me feel *great* about myself, but I expect nothing less from Nic Woolridge. Besides, nothing he's implying with these clothes is untrue. I get it; Allegra is a high-class shadowborn, better than me in every way that counts. The reminder is unnecessary.

Shrugging on a blush-toned skirt, I choose a turtleneck to match and cut the sleeves and neckline with a pair of scissors in the office. Sewing isn't one of my talents, but the jersey material curls as soon as I cut it, hiding the raw edge.

I think this is what they call "street smarts." I'd like to flatter myself in thinking so, anyway.

It doesn't look bad, especially when I check myself out in the full-length bedroom mirror. But it's not *me*. Ironic, since I'm never really "me" to begin with. I usually consider that a good thing, but for some reason, in Allegra's clothes, I feel like a fraud.

I never felt this way as Mari and Marilyn—sure, they're just characters, but they aren't complete lies. They're founded in truth, and…well, very exaggerated aspects of my personality. Mary Alice has always made me feel the worst, because everything about her is a lie.

Now, staring at myself wearing clothes I don't belong in, in a house that certainly isn't my home, I can't deny how fucked up everything's become. What am I even *doing*? Parading around, playing houseguest when I should be spending every waking moment thinking of a way to kill Astaroth?

I guess Nic wins this round after all. If it weren't for him, I wouldn't be thinking about how ill-suited I am to even *visit* Neil's house. Putting my identity as his daughter aside for a moment, I feel like a little kid who just smeared Mommy's red lipstick all over her face in a poor attempt to copy her. It's pathetic. *I'm* pathetic.

I should have already known that, but apparently, staring at myself in the mirror is a strong reminder. I tremble like a little bitch in front of my reflection, trying so desperately to keep it together and hold in my bitterness and anger. For what? So I can pander to my half sister, whose whims will determine how difficult the next few years will be for me? She has no idea of the power she holds over me, and that is just another thing I resent her for.

MARY ALICE

I walk outside, down the path to the main house. I practiced my Mary Alice expressions in the mirror earlier, so it's a bit easier to slip into character now. Thank God for muscle memory. I have to make sure no other emotions can slip through my mask, and after a few tries, I get it down pat. A soft smile spreads across my face the moment I step onto the back porch.

"Maria." Neil is waiting for me, reading the newspaper by the pool. "There you are. You were almost late."

"I'm not late, though." No thanks to goddamn Nic Woolridge. "And Allegra knows me as Mary Alice. It would be strange if you or Nic were to call me anything else."

"Maria is your legal name. The name on your birth certificate," Neil says.

"I don't deny that," I reply calmly, glancing at my reflection in the window to ensure my smile hasn't slipped. "But we are strangers. It would be best for us both if you simply refer to me as Mary Alice."

Neil closes his newspaper. "Very well, *Mary Alice*. If you insist, I will indulge your little quirk."

It's a coping mechanism, not a quirk. Get your facts straight.

"Thank you," I manage. In an ideal world, I wouldn't thank Neil if I were on fire and he dumped a bucket of water over my head. But since I'm playing nice for now, I won't drop my manners. I'll probably get an ulcer from the snark build-up, though.

I'm not sure if Neil is trying to look like he stepped off

the set of *Fantasy Island*, but he reminds me of Mr. Roarke in his white penguin suit and shoes. Doesn't he know that it's over a hundred degrees? Even with the outdoor fans, I'm starting to melt!

But when we walk inside, it's like I've been transported to Antarctica. It won't be long until my teeth begin to chatter and my lips turn blue.

"You'll sit next to my daughter," Neil says pointedly. The room might be freezing, but he's become uncharacteristically warm in a matter of seconds. Maybe this is where I get it from—the phony, lying, insufferable part of my personality, that is.

The dining room table can seat twelve comfortably, but only five settings are arranged. And, lucky me, I'm seated under one of the modern metal light fixtures on the ceiling. Maybe it will fall and crush me. That way, at least I'll die eating.

That's me, ever the optimist.

What's with the décor, anyway? Marble floors, marble table, metal chairs—everything looks modern, in varying shades of cool beige. There's no warmth, both figuratively and literally. It suits Neil, but I can't imagine what type of person Mrs. Abbott is to agree to this. I've only met her once and she seems friendly, but she's married to *Neil*.

I'm grateful for Allegra's hand-me-downs now. At least they offer some warmth, and the skirt's multiple layers provide a bit of cushion from the metal seat.

Speaking of, Allegra sweeps into the room moments later. She looks the same as always: flawless. She and Neil share the same blonde hair and startling green eyes, but she gets most of her beauty from her mother. They look like a pair of Disney princesses when they

walk in together, wearing identical smiles when they see me.

Nic trails behind them, winking at me and taking his seat across from me. "Mary Alice. It's been a while."

"Hello, Nic," I greet with a wide smile.

"Now that we're all here, let's eat," Neil announces, clapping his hands together.

"Mary Alice, how lovely to see you again," Mrs. Abbott gushes. Her eyes sparkle like emeralds, and every gesture exudes elegance. "How are you liking the estate? I haven't seen you around very often."

"It's a big plantation, my dear," Neil replies for me. "And Mary Alice has been spending time in her guest room, recuperating."

Yeah, recuperating from Nic's uncalled-for beating.

"Are you settling in alright?" Allegra asks. "Dad mentioned you weren't feeling well."

"I'm better now," I drawl. "How are you feeling? The last time I saw you was in the hospital."

"My condition is stable now," she replies. "Mary Alice, about next semester—"

"Allegra, darling, I've told you that Mary Alice is being tutored by Rhys," Neil interjects.

Allegra frowns. "I don't mind helping out. And it wouldn't be very taxing for me physically. We'll stay indoors."

"Leave it to Rhys, dear. You won't need his help that much anyway," Mrs. Abbott cajoles.

"That's not it." Allegra looks down at her plate, struggling to find the words. That makes two of us. "I just thought it would be better if I taught Mary Alice. We're familiar with each other, and Rhys can be..."

"Mary Alice could use a little tough love, right?" Nic teases. "Something tells me she doesn't mind when things get rough."

"Let's eat," Mrs. Abbott says, no longer wishing to continue the conversation. Thank God.

The food is brought out on silver platters, by house staff dressed in sky blue polos and khakis. When a woman leans beside me to unveil a tray of broccoli, I notice the polo has the Abbott family crest embroidered on it. Neil doesn't spare any expense, does he? I bet he could have hired nannies to raise me in this mansion out of his sight. There are so many rooms, we might never have run into each other.

But then, I wouldn't have met Tasha. Or Isabelle, or Luke, or David.

"Thank you," I say, leaning back in my seat. The rest of the meal includes chicken, mashed potatoes, green beans, mac and cheese, fresh bread, and soup. Everything is put on my plate *for* me, and since I don't have the heart to say that I don't like green beans, I guess I'll choke them down.

"Have you chosen what classes you'll be taking in the fall?" Allegra asks me.

Before I can answer, Nic says, "She's going to be enrolled in remedial classes, Allegra. You probably won't see her. She needs to catch up on all the years she's missed out on. Right?"

"Right," I agree, keeping my voice calm. "I don't think I would be able to keep up with regular classes yet. There's still a lot I need to learn about."

"I'm sure you'll excel with Rhys' tutoring," Mrs. Abbott says kindly. "Neil tells me you've done very well in school."

Neil's a liar.

"If you need anything, Mary Alice, you won't hesitate to call, will you?" Allegra turns to her father. "Oh, Mary Alice's cell phone was confiscated. Can we get it back for her?"

"I'll have to discuss it with the provost, but I don't see why not," Neil agrees, putting a hand over his daughter's. "It's not as if she's going to put her family in danger by telling them about the shadowborn, right? She certainly wouldn't be that silly."

"Of course not," I assure him.

Allegra smiles. "You must have a good relationship with them. Did they take it well, when you told them you were coming here to study?"

"Yes. We have a good relationship. But it *is* hard keeping such a big secret from them," I say with a feigned sigh. "That's another reason why I'm so grateful you've invited me here. I don't think I could have waited around for the semester to start at home, without wanting to tell my parents. Or my siblings. My sister loves fantasy novels; she would be thrilled to know that magic exists."

"I didn't know you had a sister."

I take a sip of water and turn away, unable to look her in the eye.

"I guess it's a good thing you aren't home, then," Nic says casually. "Rhys says you're a bad liar."

I'm immediately taken aback. I didn't think Rhys and Nic were very buddy-buddy. It didn't even occur to me that they spoke, especially not about *me*. And bad liar? Excuse him! When did I lie? I've been Mar in front of him for the past few days.

"It's just a sign that Mary Alice is an honest young lady," Neil says graciously, barely able to contain his laughter.

"Well," I say, "I guess it runs in the family."

Mar

Rhys doesn't have breakfast ready for me when I get up. When I walk downstairs, instead of greeting me with a plate of food, he hands me a cup of pulverized vegetables. How appetizing.

"What is this?" I ask, not bothering to mask my disgust. I already don't like vegetables, unless they're dipped in batter and fried.

"A green smoothie. Since you've recovered, for the most part, we will begin physical training." He pauses. "I do not wish for you to vomit again, so you may eat a full meal *after* the workout."

"I might throw up just by drinking this," I mutter. But when I take a sip, despite its grass green color, I don't taste a single vegetable. Instead, I'm overwhelmed by pineapple and banana, with a hint of coconut. "This isn't some sort of potion, right? What magic did you use to make this?"

"A $500 blender."

"It's good," I admit. "Like, *really* good. Instead of being a brat babysitter, no offense to myself or Allegra, you should open a restaurant."

As usual, Rhys isn't flustered by the comment in the least. It makes me want to tease him and push his buttons, just to see how he'd react.

"Finish the smoothie and change into workout clothes," he says. "I left some in a bag, washed, by the front door."

I check the thermometer by the window, nearly choking

when I see the temperature. "It's over a hundred degrees out."

"I will bring ice water for you."

"You might want to bring an EKG machine, too."

"EKG? What is that?" he asks flatly.

"Something to revive me when I inevitably go into cardiac arrest."

He snorts. "You are very dramatic."

"I am," I admit, "but it's *way* too hot to do anything outdoors. Can't I just do squats inside?"

"You will only be doing warm-ups outside," Rhys corrects. "We will begin with a four-mile jog and a two-mile walk."

"*Begin* with a four-mile jog?" Four miles? I can barely run *one* mile! What happened with starting me off easy? "Are you insane?"

"Not any more than you."

"Okay, now you're just insulting *both* of us! I think." I can't do the mental Olympics right now. But what he's asking me to do is not only impossible, it's probably lethal. He hasn't coddled me during tutoring sessions, so I expected him to take my physical training seriously, but I didn't expect him to kill me with exercise right out of the gate!

"A shadowborn should be able to do this much," Rhys adds. Not helping *at all*. "So, shall we begin?"

CHAPTER FIVE

I've been here for two weeks now, and my mile time has only improved by thirty seconds. For a normal person, that would have been a miracle. For shadowborn, apparently, it's abysmal.

Those are Rhys' exact words, by the way. "Abysmal."

"Don't you think you overuse that word?" I press, bending over with my hands on my knees.

Rhys hands me a water bottle, his skin somehow still cool after jogging alongside me in the sun. I don't even think he's *sweating*, which is another sign he's not human. Aside from his ears, I mean.

His hair must grow insanely fast, because it completely covers his ears now. But I've gotten used to them, and more importantly, to him. I don't think I've been *that* affected by the attractive guys at Southeastern, anyway. Aside from Archer, I guess. Though, with everything going on lately, I haven't spared a thought toward him until now. And Nic disgusts me—not because he's my cousin. Okay, not *just*

because he's my cousin. He has a horrible personality, which must run in the family.

Rhys doesn't exactly have a shining personality, either. The "abysmal" thing is just one example of many, I assure you.

Case in point: "If I use 'abysmal' to describe your progress, to the point of redundancy, then perhaps you should reevaluate your efforts."

See what I mean?

"You're horrible at motivating others," I tell him.

"I am not here to motivate you. I am here to train you, and at a minimum, keep you alive."

Yeah, yeah. Rhys reminds me of that at least once a day. As if I need verbal confirmation that he's not on my side, that *no one* here is on my side. Rhys works for Neil, and Neil is my enemy. Which makes Rhys my enemy by association. Even if that weren't the case, I don't think I could ever get along with someone who takes the "brutal" part of brutal honesty so seriously. He doesn't pull punches, and while I don't need him to hold my hand through these trying times, *come on*. Neil is ruining my life, he's taken my family hostage, and he's going to pit me against an eldritch horror with an army of cultists. I'm not asking for a pity party, but throw a bitch a bone!

Rhys ignores my mental plea completely. I imagine he'd ignore me if I voiced my complaints aloud, too. "You still have another lap to run. If you do not complete it in under ten minutes, I will have to add another set of push-ups to your workout sheet."

Great. I already have a farmer's tan from all this outdoor exercise. Thankfully I haven't been sunburned. Rhys makes

me reapply thick sunscreen every two hours, going off the instructions on the bottle. Who does that?

"Does this matter? Can't I just, I don't know, nuke Astaroth?" I complain. "Getting launch codes might be easier than...whatever Neil plans on having me do."

Rhys doesn't even entertain the joke. "You will be devoured at Southeastern University if you continue at this pace."

"I think you mean 'eaten alive.'"

"Are they not the same?"

"The expression is 'eaten alive.' When you say 'devoured,' it implies that I'm going to be cannibalized." Which I'm *not*, with any luck. But if this summer has taught me anything, it's that I'm not lucky at all.

Rhys scoffs. "Your correction of my expression implies that you are trying to divert the subject because you realize I am telling the truth. You will be 'eaten alive' by the other students."

"That's a shame for them, then," I reply. Anything to get me out of exercising. "I don't think I'd taste good. I'm far too bitter for most palettes."

"I would say 'sour.'"

"At least I'm not over-salted."

"You would do well spending less time daydreaming about cannibals—" Rhys begins.

"I'm not *daydreaming*. It's not like I *want* to be cannibalized!"

"You should spend more time studying. Your last test score was—"

"Abysmal. I got it," I say dryly. "Are you done arguing with me?"

"Arguing?" he mocks. "Can you not tell that I am flirting with you?"

I laugh, in spite of myself. "Throwing that back in my face, huh? And here I thought you forgot about that."

Rhys looks like he wants to say something else, but drops it quickly when another voice calls out from behind us.

"Mary Alice!" Allegra shouts, jogging over to us.

MARY ALICE

"Hi, Allegra," I greet in my Mary Alice voice. Rhys doesn't say anything, thank God. He doesn't even turn his head to look at me.

"I haven't seen you in a while," she says, her cheeks red from running. "I've been meaning to find you."

"Allegra—" Rhys begins.

"My birthday party is coming up this weekend. I've been asking Dad to call the tailor, but he says you've been busy training." Her eyes flick to my sweat-drenched clothes. "I guess he wasn't lying. Are you alright?"

Not in the least. "Of course! It's refreshing to work out on a regular basis!"

Now Rhys looks at me, with an expression that says, *I can't believe how full of it you are.* Well, believe it, bub.

"That's a relief. I've been concerned about you," Allegra says, tucking a strand of hair behind her ear. "Well, the tailor is going to be here soon to fit me for my dress. I want them to fit you, too."

"She has training to do," Rhys says, shaking his head.

Allegra frowns. "This won't take too long, Rhys. Besides, what on earth will she wear to the party otherwise?

Mom and Dad want her there, and *I* want her there, too. What's the problem?"

Rhys' expression softens, possibly for the first time in his entire life. "Fine."

"I can't just wear my regular clothes?" I ask, as if I have a lot of options.

"The dress code is black tie. At my dad's insistence. He likes to make a big show of things."

I'm aware. "Black tie...so a dress?"

"A gown." She grins, though I'm not sure why. Floor-length gowns are pretty, but a hassle to move in. And, maybe this is the cult-induced paranoia talking, but I don't love the idea of not being able to run away if chased by some supernatural monster. "This will be *very* fun. And much better than the Fourth of July."

Well, on the Fourth of July I was attacked by a demonic cult and chased through the cruise ship. It's not a very high bar, but I see her point.

"I need to shower before I try anything on," I warn.

She nods. "Meet me in the foyer in thirty minutes."

IT TAKES ME LESS TIME TO SHOWER THAN I THOUGHT, AND I arrive at the main house early. I'm not going to wait around in the heat, so I let myself inside through the front door. Unfortunately, Nic is there, standing in front of a large painting of Neil hanging in the entryway. How full of yourself do you have to be to put a picture of yourself, *by yourself*, right by the front door? It's the first thing guests see, and it's not even a family photo. Not to mention, the frame is taller than me.

"Uncle is quite glorious, don't you think?" Nic asks, which is the complete opposite of what I'm thinking. Isn't this the very definition of a "red flag?"

In the nicest way possible, I say, "You and I have very different definitions of 'glorious.'"

"You haven't seen his true form yet. It's horrific." Nic's face splits in a grin. "Like Astaroth's."

No comment. The last (and only) time I saw Astaroth, he was taller than a building with big, leathery wings and bloody red eyes. Not to mention, he was *naked*. As hard as I've tried to erase that from my memories, it's burned into my mind.

"I thought Allegra was going to have a dress tailored," I chirp, trying not to break character. Not for this jerk. But Nic seems to bring out the worst in me, and maybe I bring out the worst in him, too. "Are you also having a suit fitted?"

Nic shakes his head. "I'm here purely for entertainment purposes, dear cousin."

So he considers watching his cousins try on dresses entertainment? Or is it the undressing part he wants to see? Ugh. Freaking gross.

But as if he can read my mind, Nic says, "I don't care about seeing your unimpressive body, Maria. What interests me is Allegra. More specifically, your interactions with her. Your long lost—"

"Mr. Abbott has agreed to keep up appearances," I interrupt. "He calls me Mary Alice. You should follow his lead."

"It's more fun this way. If you get found out, you're the only one who suffers." He smiles. "How will you convince me to keep your secrets?"

Kill you in your sleep? It's a serious consideration.

I don't have a chance to answer before Allegra arrives from the grand staircase, thank God. I have no idea how to convince Nic to do my bidding. Aside from resorting to violence, and I think we all know how that would turn out: not well for me.

"Mary Alice," Allegra exclaims. "Oh, Nic. Did you need your suit fitted?"

He extends a hand, helping her down the last few steps. "I was just chatting with our future classmate here. Wondering how her training with Rhys is going."

"I'm afraid I'm not very athletic," I admit.

"You don't have to worry, Mary Alice. You're human; it's only natural," Allegra says gently. "I'm not sure why my father insists on training you in combat. We can protect you. Nic most certainly will. No harm will come to you under our care."

Nic bursts out laughing. I almost do, too. Nic? Protect me? I need protection *from* him. Preferably a taser, but I'd accept pepper spray, too.

Allegra beckons me up the stairs. "Come up. The tailor, Miss Lewis, is all set up. Mom is here, too; she's going to get her dress altered after us."

"Do you do this every year?" I ask.

"Yes, my father insists. He's very...particular about social events. He'd prefer not to have me wear something another guest could have bought, so we go with custom designs."

Neil's an even bigger control freak than I thought. Why does that not surprise me?

The upstairs portion of the house is just as modern and tacky as the downstairs, with boxy metal statues around each corner that lend visitors the perfect opportunity to

impale themselves. It's certainly not baby-proofed. Heck, it's not even *adult* proof. If I'm running from someone and turn the corner too sharp, I'm a goner.

The room Allegra leads us to is exclusively for fittings. Mrs. Abbot lounges on a plastic blob I assume is the second most uncomfortable seat in the world. The first would, of course, be the electric chair. An older woman emerges from a curtained wall on the far right side, measuring tape in hand. She must be Miss Lewis.

"Oh, Allegra! I found it!" She totters over, carrying a large scrapbook of fabric samples. She points to one piece with a long nail, nearly snagging the cornflower blue silk square. "Look, this is the color!"

"Pastel suits Allegra more. I still think pink is the way to go," Mrs. Abbott interjects, helping herself to a pastry from the table. "Blue does not suit her skin tone."

"I don't need another sun dress," Allegra says kindly. "I just want to try on the dress for my party."

"Don't you want another outfit for school?"

"No, Mom. I don't have the space, anyway," Allegra insists. "Mary Alice, why don't you sit? I'll just be a few minutes. Mom will keep you company. Right?"

"Of course," Mrs. Abbott replies with a smile.

Allegra leaves to go behind the curtain with Miss Lewis, allowing an awkward silence to settle over myself and Mrs. Abbott. I don't exactly *pity* her, but it's strange to be in the same room as my biological father's wife. Allegra and I are only a year apart, maybe less. Did he cheat while Mrs. Abbott was pregnant with their only child? How could he possibly go home and face her?

Or maybe my biological mother hid the pregnancy at first. Maybe she ambushed him with it, and he killed her in

retaliation—no, that didn't happen. I wouldn't be alive, unless he waited until she gave birth to kill her. Then, that doesn't make sense, either. Neil clearly didn't want me. He still doesn't. If not for Astaroth and my growing powers, Neil would have never bothered with me.

Looking at Mrs. Abbott now, bathed in the warm glow of the afternoon sun, I wonder why Neil cheated on her in the first place. She's stunning, for one—Allegra certainly gets her delicate beauty from Mrs. Abbott. She's also been nothing but nice to me in the few instances I've met her. Though I guess that could be an act, considering *I'm* pretending to be nice, too.

"Why don't you sit down and make yourself comfortable, dear?" Mrs. Abbott says, gesturing to the seat beside her. She doesn't have a Southern accent, so unless she's purposely hiding it, I don't think she's from Georgia originally. Neil doesn't have an accent either, though I guess he's from the Veil, so he wouldn't have one.

"Thank you," I reply stiffly, sitting next to her. "I appreciate your hospitality, Mrs. Abbott. Your home is lovely."

Not that I've seen much of it, living in a separate house in the yard.

"You're a doll. I can see why Neil picked you up," Mrs. Abbott gushes. "You can call me Faith, dear. We're just so excited to have you stay with us. Allegra sings your praises. Nic, too."

Nic chooses then to stroll in, plopping down on the chair across from us. Where has he been? I thought he was right behind us on the stairs. "Aunt Faith, don't flatter her too much."

"Nic, dear, help yourself to some tea and cookies." Faith pushes the tiered cookie plate over to him. "They're fresh."

"Oh, I'm fine, Aunt Faith," Nic says. "By the way, when is *Mary Alice* going to try on dresses?"

"I don't need a new dress—"

"Nonsense. My husband told me you don't have a gown," Faith interrupts. "I want to make sure you enjoy yourself at the party. You should wear a fabulous dress."

My enjoyment of Allegra's birthday and wearing a fancy dress are two distinctly different things. But I guess I don't want to stick out like a sore thumb. And Faith *is* trying to be nice, in her own way. Unless she's secretly plotting to kill me with pins or poisoned fabric.

On that note, maybe taking a break from television is a good thing for me.

"While Allegra and Miss Lewis are still occupied, why don't we look at the dresses you can choose from? Unfortunately, we don't have time to make you a new dress from scratch, but I picked some out of Allegra's closet that you might like. You two seem to have similar styles," she comments. "Here, come along, Mary Alice."

My stomach twists. "I don't think Allegra's clothes will fit me."

"Nonsense," she says. "We'll *make* something fit."

CHAPTER SIX

They shouldn't have called it a birthday party. First off, there's not a single balloon in this entire house. Which is just as well, I guess, since the various modern art statues would have popped them. There are no streamers or party decorations, either. This could be *any* type of event; there's no indication it's a birthday party, specifically.

I knew it was going to be fancy—the dress code *is* black tie. But there's a difference between "fancy" and "throwing money down the drain." Neil seems to have mastered the latter. The plantation looks like the set of a Hollywood movie, swarming with uniformed waiters and waitresses in white eye masks and suits. Every suit in the joint is the same —black jacket and pants, black shiny shoes, crisp white shirt, and black tie. You'd think they'd at least add a little bit of color to the ties.

The dresses are, more or less, the same, too. The colors are different, but most of the partygoers in gowns have huge princess skirts fanning out and dragging on the floor. It

makes moving around difficult, especially when my own skirt is so wide.

I have to use both hands to lift the heavy layers of purple tulle, making sure I don't crush the silk flowers sewn to the fabric. The dress is easily the most expensive piece of clothing I've ever worn, and the most inconvenient. Just walking from the guest house to the main house's front entrance was a workout on its own.

"My, don't you look lovely? I guess what they say is true —any pig can look good in the right clothes."

I don't have to turn around to recognize Nic's voice — and his biting commentary. He comes around to me, holding two glasses of red wine. How much trouble would I be in if I knocked that wine out of his hand?

"Hello, Nic. You look very handsome," I respond, not even bothering to lie. Nic cleans up well, but the clothes can't hide his awful personality. I'm sure the same can be said about me.

"Allegra's dress doesn't suit you. You look like a child playing make-believe in her mother's heels," he says. "It's pathetic."

"I'm wearing flip-flops." I lift my skirt and stick my foot out to show him. "They have ducks on them."

"I can see that. So can the other guests." Nic clears his throat. "I came here to ask you for a dance. Aunt Faith insists I escort you."

I'd rather dance on shards of broken glass.

"Or, can you not dance? Don't worry; I can teach you," Nic says smugly. "You are, after all, my cousin. My family."

"Not so loud," I warn, looking around. Thankfully, everyone seems all too preoccupied with their own conversations to pay us any attention.

"I forgot, you're hiding it," he says, not bothering to lower his voice. "I wonder what else you're hiding, Maria."

"You'll have to excuse me." Before I kill you with that wine glass.

The safest thing right now is to put as much distance between us as possible. For both our sakes. I turn away from him and weave through the crowd, dodging trays of hors d'oeuvres until I reach the main ballroom down the hall. Musicians are playing classical renditions of pop songs onstage, which makes me think Allegra had more to do with this party than I initially gave her credit for. Still, no sign of her anywhere.

Maybe she's waiting to make a grand entrance. I don't blame her, but at the same time, I wish she'd just come out and get it over with. I was hoping to make a quick appearance and leave early. Not that I have anything better to do, except wallow in self-pity.

I learned a lot of hard life lessons growing up. Do I really have to continue going down that route? My life should be a goddamn romance novel right now, with all the shit I've put up with over the years. I'd even be happy as the heroine of an erotica novella! Oh, who am I kidding? I'd be *thrilled* with erotica as my genre. But instead, I'm in some paranormal fiction novel without even a hint of smut. You'd think, being surrounded by hot guys, I'd at *least* get a reverse harem. Instead, the only people chasing me down were cultists. Not in an enemies-to-lovers kind of way, either. They wanted to sacrifice me because they thought I was a virgin.

Life is hard! Maybe if I were *actually* a virgin, I'd be more qualified for erotica!

But no. I'm a sad whore who isn't even in a position to

sleep around right now, hanging onto my readership by a spider's thread.

I crane my neck, looking around the room for one of the waitstaff. I need some ice, for all that "breaking the fourth wall" I just did.

Instead of a waiter with ice (or alcohol), I lock eyes with someone else across the room. And, unfortunately, my heart skips a beat.

It's just because he's handsome. That's what I tell myself. Why else would my heart beat faster at the sight of Archer Kinsey? Of course, it's because he's good-looking! And he's wearing a suit, which only magnifies the effect of his handsomeness. I'm sure most would agree. His eyes—I still can't determine if they're grey or blue—meet mine for a long second. And then he begins to walk over.

Should I bolt? I feel like I should bolt. Because the last time I saw Archer, he was in the hospital for a knife wound. A knife that I pulled out of his back to stab a cultist in the neck. And then I didn't check up on him at all; I ran away.

We also kissed twice and haven't really discussed that. I'm not sure we ever will, considering it was a major lapse of judgment on my part. If you recall, I had just seen Neil's picture in Allegra's dorm and realized our familial relationship. How that led to me and Archer kissing, I'm not entirely sure. I think I just hate myself or something, because when I'm upset I make a lot of rash decisions that often come back and bite me in the butt. Kissing people I shouldn't is generally a given when I'm in that type of mental state.

Calm down! I chide myself. *It wasn't with tongue, so does it even count?*

It's more like I bumped into his mouth. With my own.

Distracted by all my internal monologuing, I don't make it out of the ballroom in time. Archer catches up to me, putting a warm hand on my elbow.

Leaning close to my ear for a brief moment, he whispers, "Meet me in the garden."

Garden? What garden? This is a huge plantation; there are five different gardens! He disappears into the crowd before I can ask for clarification.

Shoot.

Are we going to kiss again? That can't be why he asked me to meet him somewhere alone, right? The music *is* pretty loud, and with all the chatter from the other party guests, it's not easy to have a conversation in the house. Which leads me to wonder if we're going to be talking or making out. I'd much prefer the latter, despite it being completely out of the blue and inappropriate given our current relationship.

Which barely even counts as a relationship, by the way. Hence why my readership is probably dwindling.

Still, I'm Mary Alice now. Excuse the previous cursing. I'm Mary Alice, and I'm going to meet Archer and apologize for leaving him high and dry at the hospital. He'll forgive me, and we'll be on our merry way.

Yes. That is what I've decided will transpire, and since I've put it out into the universe with my mind…it definitely won't be that easy.

I wasn't kidding about this place having five gardens. I exit through the back patio door and follow the stone walkway through a maze of hedges, passing an empty rose garden and a greenhouse bigger than the guest house. It takes at least ten minutes in the sweltering heat to find Archer, sitting on a bench in a small alcove filled with creepy white sculptures. Way to set the mood.

"Mary Alice," he says, like he's surprised to see me. He asked me here, didn't he? I didn't just imagine that, right?

"Archer," I reply awkwardly. "I—"

"You left without warning. No one knew where you were," he says, his voice rough. "I thought someone had kidnapped you!"

Okay, well to be fair I *was* kind of kidnapped by Neil. But I get the point. "I'm sorry. A lot of stuff was going on, and I didn't get a chance to say goodbye."

"You could have left a note at least!" he yells. "Do you have any idea how worried I was about you?"

"Why?"

Archer pauses, the question hanging between us. I can't see his face well in the dim light, so it's difficult to get a good read on him. Finally, he says, "Do I have to explain myself?"

Frick. I swear I didn't plan this. I know I said that my life lacks romance and it's impacting my readership and whatnot, but that didn't mean I wanted to whore myself out for page reads. This is just a coincidence.

One second we're staring at each other, and the next we're kissing. Again.

It's not like the first two times we kissed. The first time was awkward, considering the lack of romantic tension leading up to it. And the second time *I* initiated the kiss, again without much leading up to it.

Not that there was a ton leading up to this, either, but at least I wasn't surprised. I could tell when he looked at me, and by the way he asked me that question, that he was going to kiss me. I just didn't expect it to be so…gentle.

He must use lip balm religiously because his lips are soft as silk. His hands cup my face, most likely smearing my foundation, as he draws me closer. I hope his super

hearing isn't sensitive enough to detect how fast my heart is racing.

I pull away first, my cheeks warm. "I'm sorry I made you worry."

"You're strange," he murmurs, still holding my face in his hands. "When I'm with you, I'm not myself."

"I can't tell if that's a good thing or a bad thing."

"I can't either," he confesses. "I didn't plan on...doing that. It's not why I called you here—to corner you."

"Do you regret it?" As soon as I ask, *I* regret it. Cardinal rule of questions—don't ask if you don't want to know the answer. And, from the way he's hesitating, I *don't* want to know.

But to my surprise, Archer answers, "I don't regret it. Do you?"

"No." It's not like we had sex. It was just a kiss, and not even French. So why is my heart still pounding? "We're probably going to be seeing a lot more of each other. I'm going to Southeastern this fall."

"I suspected. Allegra told me you were staying here, with her family."

She did? Since when did they talk? They dated in the past, and they were friendly with each other on the ship. They must be friends.

My cheeks immediately burn with a new horrible consideration—I'm wearing Allegra's hand-me-down dress. Is it something she wore before? Is it something she wore before *in front of Archer*? Maybe I'm overthinking things. Or underthinking them. Oh God, I need to sit.

Why did Archer kiss me? It doesn't *seem* like he planned this, but then, I can't tell with him. I'm not a rebound, right? It's not because this dress reminds him of Allegra, right?

Normally, I wouldn't mind if a guy was using me. After a while, I'd bein using them, too, and that would make me feel a little better about everything. I'm not sure how much I'd care if I found out Archer was just using *me* this whole time. Wanting me just for physical intimacy is something I can accept, but for some reason, being used as a replacement for my half sister is unbearable.

Is it Archer that makes me feel these things? Am *I* special to him, or is Allegra?

"It's not going to be easy," Archer says, breaking me out of my thoughts. We sit beside each other on the bench, and he migrates his hand down to hold mine. "You're human. The shadowborn won't be happy you are allowed to attend Southeastern."

"There's not much I can do about that," I say, my eyes drawn to our interlocking fingers.

"I know. And it's not like you can hide it—rumors are already swirling. Just stick close to Allegra," he suggests. "No one will hurt you as long as they think Neil is your backer. That's your best chance. I'm not sure I'll be able to protect you."

It would be a lie to say I don't need his protection, or that I don't want it. I do. What kind of heroine that makes me, I'm not sure. I guess that adds to the growing list of reasons why I'm not cut out for this.

"What is this?" I ask, holding up our hands. "What are...we?"

He stares into my eyes for a long time before responding. "I don't know. What do you want us to be?"

"I don't know," I repeat. "I...I want to know. I want to be able to respond to that question with a proper answer.

And I think I want you to do the same. But I have no idea how to achieve that."

"Hmm." Archer doesn't let go, tilting his head to look up at the smattering of stars across the night sky. "Maybe we get to know each other better. For example, I don't know anything about your family. How you grew up, what kind of house you lived in? I don't even know your favorite color."

It used to be green, because...well, money is green. And I like money. But now when I think of the color green, I'm reminded of Neil's eyes. And his daughter's.

"Gold," I answer. "I like gold."

"Mine is red. When I was little, my favorite meal to eat was tomato soup and half a grilled cheese sandwich," he shares, a rare smile forming on his face. "It didn't matter what the temperature was outside. I would have asked for that every day if I could have. My father hated it—he always said it was too ordinary, too common. But my mom cooked it for me anyway."

"Is there anything wrong with liking ordinary things?" For most of my life, all I wanted was *ordinary*. It turns out, that's a lot to ask for. And Santa doesn't give gifts to bad little girls like me, especially not when they ask for abstract ideas like "an ordinary family." He doesn't give cold, hard cash either, if you were curious.

"No. There's nothing wrong with it at all," Archer says. "I think people take the ordinary for granted."

I hadn't realized that, while we were talking, our faces had been gradually growing closer. Now, we're mere centimeters apart. My breath hitches, and just as I think we're going to kiss again—

"Dear guests." Rhys' sharp voice cuts through the stillness of the garden, startling me. Archer and I pull away

from each other quickly, but it's obvious Rhys saw everything.

"Rhys. What are you doing here?" Archer demands, his voice low.

"I have been tasked with gathering party guests to the ballroom for a special announcement. Including those who take advantage of the distant grounds' privacy." Rhys stares coolly at Archer. "Neil has an announcement to make, one you may not want to miss."

"We were in the middle of a conversation," Archer bites back. "We'll return after we've finished."

"It is rude to go against the party host's wishes."

"It's even ruder to interrupt a private conversation."

"Conversation? Is that what you call feeling up a young woman under Neil's care?" Rhys asks sarcastically. "This wouldn't be the first time."

"Excuse me?"

Ah, we're back to square one. Two hot guys are fighting, but it's *not* over me. If I had to make an educated guess, this is about Allegra. Everything comes back to her, doesn't it? Well, it *is* her birthday.

"I'll head back first," I interrupt. I have no interest in watching them make fools of themselves over someone who isn't me. Before either of them can say anything, I make a beeline for the exit. Powerwalking in this heat, in this *dress*, is no easy feat. But I manage to do it, driven by my hatred of awkwardness. Unfortunately, that particular hatred does not make my sense of direction any better. I get lost in the hedges, somehow managing to circle back around to the same garden. I try to turn and leave, but Rhys' voice catches my attention.

"You would do well to remember where you stand," he

remarks, which is a weird thing to say to Archer. If I'm understanding the situation correctly, Archer is from a wealthy and prominent family. While Rhys is a trueblood, he works for Neil as a caretaker and servant. "You are not acting appropriately, and it will be your ruin."

Archer isn't having it. "I should be saying the same to you."

"She is Neil's charge. Did you think, because she is human, it would not matter?"

"I don't forget that she's human."

"Then what?" Rhys challenges. And I thought he was cold to *me*. Turns out, he's extra icy with Archer. Though, if that story about them fighting over Allegra in the past is true, then I guess I understand.

"Do you really think you're in any place to question me?" Archer snaps. "I've always wanted to know why you care so much. You can't be with Allegra, and you can't be with Mary Alice."

"Neil has trusted me to look after them. That is all."

"That's not it. You had a personal stake with Allegra," Archer accuses, his voice filled with bitter resentment. "You made it your mission to sabotage us at every turn."

"You are mistaken," Rhys says firmly.

"So what, then?"

"What is it you want from me?"

"You act so full of it sometimes, Rhys. You can't admit that you are selfish, and that you stole Allegra away from me because you were in love with her, too."

There's a long silence. Rhys says, "You do not understand anything."

But I do. I understand that I need to get away from these men, from this house, as soon as I possibly can.

Kissing Archer won't derail my true mission: killing Astaroth and Neil. It was just a momentary lapse in judgment, is all. A lapse. That's what I tell myself.

So why do I feel like my heart is being squeezed whenever he says Allegra's name?

CHAPTER SEVEN

I know this must be a little bit difficult for you to believe, given I've kept my cool for one-point-two books by now, but I'm kind of a jealous person. Yes, you must be shocked. Let it soak in for a moment.

Sarcasm aside, there are those who come out of adverse situations better than before. Look at Cinderella—her life was horrible until she met that fairy godmother. Cinderella was constantly beaten down by her family and belittled, but she still kept a kind and pure heart. I'm nothing like that. The more hardships I face, the worse my personality gets. And jealousy always seems to rear its ugly head, more so than usual with Neil around.

Logically, I have no reason to be jealous. I don't want to *be* Allegra, and I recognize that she has her own struggles. She helped me over the summer *because* she's been struggling with succession. I get it.

But this negativity I feel toward her is on a deeper level, a raw part of myself that needs to be shut away forever. Allegra might be my only ally, at least for now. Not to

mention, she's been kind to me in the past. And all I'm doing now is repaying that kindness with a disingenuous smile.

It's not even that the situation is unfair. Neither of us chose the circumstances of our birth, or Neil as our father. I'm not so delusional as to think all this—the party, the expensive clothes, the status—should have been mine. But as I see the differences in our lives, of how Neil's decisions have made such an impact on who we are, I can't help the bitterness rising like bile in my throat.

I make my way back to the ballroom, dodging Archer and Rhys to the best of my ability. After circling the gardens twice, I finally reach the main house and follow the crowd inside.

The ballroom, at least, has a more traditional design. Chandeliers hang from the ceiling, dripping crystals and light onto the hardwood flooring. The walls are mostly glass, but at least the windows are outfitted with floor-to-ceiling red curtains for optional privacy. A stage on the far side of the room is big enough to hold a fifteen-person band of classical musicians *and* an area for Neil to stand and wave to his peers.

Allegra is with him. This is the first time tonight that I've seen her. She's radiant in her custom-made dress, a pink ballgown fit for a princess such as herself. She's not wearing a turtleneck today, but a sheer cropped coverup hangs over her shoulders.

Neil steps up to the microphone, smiling wide as he addresses the crowd. "Thank you all for coming here tonight to celebrate my daughter's nineteenth birthday. As you are all aware, Allegra is my only child of this generation, which makes milestones like these all the more special."

That wasn't aimed at me, right?

"I want to take this time, on her special day, to make an announcement," he continues.

I'm not *trying* to eavesdrop, but the couple in front of me is quite vocal. The woman says, "This must be the succession announcement."

"What else could it be?" the other woman responds.

Succession announcement?

Allegra wanted to be recognized as her father's sole heir. She felt she had to prove herself to the larger community, as Neil had yet to officially name her. She worried that, if he didn't choose her to be his heir and inherit his seat on the council of demons (aptly named the Ruby Council), Neil would try to have another kid. Most likely with another woman.

So, long story short, I guess this is a big deal for her.

"I will be funding a children's hospital in South Carolina dedicated to treating minors with cancer," Neil announces. "I will be calling it the Faith Abbott Children's Hospital, after my lovely wife of twenty years."

Mrs. Abbott smiles onstage, but it's forced. Allegra, on the other hand, doesn't hide her shock. The smile drops from her face while the crowd begins to clap.

Okay, I may not be part of their shadowborn community, but I can understand why Allegra and the couple in front of me expected the succession announcement. Neil went through the trouble of gathering everyone into the ballroom and making a big spectacle over *this*? It's Allegra's birthday party, and she's not even involved in this charity work. He's naming it after his wife.

Neil can't be keeping his daughter hanging on a promise he never plans on fulfilling, right? Oh, wait—that sounds

exactly like something he would do, something he *is* doing, to me.

"Now, I would like to lead my beautiful daughter onto the floor for a dance," Neil finishes. "Any other father/daughter pairs are welcome to join in."

Okay, I *know* that must have been directed, at least in part, at me.

Whatever. Even if Luke were here, he wouldn't be much use on the dance floor anyway. I've seen his and Isabelle's wedding video. The only person I'd trust as my partner would be Tasha, since we both took dance lessons as part of debutante training. She was always much more coordinated when it came to ballroom dance, probably because she actually *enjoyed* it.

I wonder how she's doing now. Probably great, even without me. Of the both of us, I've always needed her more than she needed me. Right now, if she were here, she'd probably tell me not to watch Neil and Allegra dance, knowing I'd do it anyway.

But that's one of the many reasons I love Tash. Even though I'm a self-sabotaging idiot, she never gives up on trying to help me. When I don't follow her advice, and things go horribly wrong, she doesn't say "I told you so." She asks me how she can help.

Neil smiles down at Allegra, but there's no warmth to it. That should make me happy, if I'm truly jealous of Allegra. But I'm not—happy, that is. Allegra doesn't exactly look at him with love and tenderness, either. Given his announcement, I wouldn't be surprised if she got upset.

But I don't know them well enough to analyze their situation and truly understand that relationship dynamic. It's not important anyway, not now, at least.

I turn away, searching the crowd until I catch sight of Archer. Our eyes meet, but he looks away quickly and disappears into the mass of partygoers. I guess it's better this way—if he'd asked me to dance, it would have brought attention to us. And while Neil never explicitly forbade romantic relationships, I doubt he'd be happy if I were to date anyone. Let alone his favorite daughter's ex.

"Care to dance?" Nic asks, appearing when I need him least. He extends a hand, but when I don't take it, he grabs me and pulls me onto the dance floor with his superior strength. "What, don't know how to dance?"

"I know how to dance," I say evenly. "I was a debutante, I'll have you know."

"Oh. I thought that was another lie." He sneers. "You do it so often, I'm not sure what's true and what isn't. Do you?"

On the contrary, my lies are a constant reminder of the truths I run from. I thought, given his own personality, Nic would understand that.

"Staying silent, my dear Maria?" he asks, lowering his voice. "Cute. But not entertaining enough for me. I'm growing tired of your Mary Alice act."

You and me both.

"When will you show me your true colors?"

"I don't think anyone wants that," I say carefully.

"Why not? It will certainly be interesting."

"Not for me. And not for you, either."

"I'm not so sure about that." He heaves a sigh and dips me, his hand on the small of my back. "If you won't entertain me, Maria, then shall I make my own fun? I told you, didn't I? I can do whatever I want to you, and no one will do anything."

"What are you—"

He doesn't let me finish before flinging me away from him. None of my training with Rhys prepared me for being catapulted into a waitress. One good thing about this dress: it cushioned the blow, and now I don't have shards of wineglass stuck in my ass. Wine drenches the front of my dress, leaving an ugly dark stain over the bodice. Glass digs into my palms, but the wounds are shallow.

Everyone's eyes turn toward me. I've become something of a spectacle, thanks to Nic. I guess this is the part where I'm supposed to feel humiliated. But I'm not embarrassed— I'm pissed.

Nic leans down, whispering, "Look at the mess you've made, Maria. You've ruined the dress Allegra lent you."

"Nic…"

"Didn't anyone tell you?" he asks smugly. "She wore that dress to her birthday last year."

I slowly rise to my feet, keeping my expression neutral as I walk out. Pushing past the crowd of people in the hall, I wipe my bloody palms on my skirt and walk back to the guest house. No one stops me, not that I expect them to. It's a good thing, actually—I'm seconds away from losing control.

MAR

My cheeks burn on the way back to the guest house. What a pathetic display—losing my cool over something that doesn't even fucking matter. I shouldn't be this upset, not because of a stupid spilled drink. Ophelia poured Coke over my head on the cruise ship. And that bitch from high school, Casey Lee, once spilled lemonade in my lap to make it look like I wet myself. This isn't anything new for me.

I know that this was Allegra's dress, too. I wasn't aware of how recently she *wore* it, but that doesn't make a difference. Right? So why am I so angry?

I stomp into the house and slam the door shut, peeling off the wet dress and leaving it on the floor. My makeup has mostly melted off, but I can't give a damn about my appearance now. I run the kitchen sink full blast, washing cold water over the cuts on my palms. The injuries are mostly small, surface-level scrapes. The deepest one is on the heel of my left hand, and I press my thumb to it hard with a wince.

"Wake up," I tell myself, squeezing my eyes shut. But when I open them again, I'm still here, standing in the kitchen alone.

Shutting the water off, I find the first aid kit in the hall closet and begin wrapping my hands. If this had happened to Allegra, I'm sure she'd be flocked by people helping her. Maybe they would have ulterior motives, but they would still help. Then, Nic wouldn't have done this to her. Probably. He seems to get off on making *me* miserable, just like—

Well, regardless of what happened in the past, Nic is a threat to me now. Things will only escalate unless I teach him a lesson or two. How I go about doing that is a mystery.

He's not some high school mean girl (or guy, for that matter). I can't just sleep with his significant other, slash his tires, punch him in the face, or splash hot coffee on him. Without fear of getting killed, that is. But I don't want to just sit by and do nothing.

When my hands are wrapped, I put away the first aid kit and walk upstairs to my bedroom. Shutting the door, I change into sweatpants and curl up under the covers. A TV would be great right about now—I could use a healthy dose

of sitcoms to get my mind off everything. But without that distraction turning my brain to mush, I'm trapped in my head, replaying my greatest hits. Or, should I say, greatest misses?

There was that guy in my eighth-grade history class who asked me out, only to blow me off when Mila Appleby told everyone my "real" mom was a crack whore. I handled it pretty poorly, crying and telling him it wasn't true. Or, when Casey Lee put the dead science lab frogs in my locker. I cried then, too, though I still don't understand why. I think things were going poorly for me outside of school, and I felt particularly sensitive at the time. Maybe that's what's going on now — I've reached some sort of breaking point, and even though I shouldn't, I want to cry.

I won't, though. It would be useless. Not only am I alone, therefore there's no one to manipulate with my tears, but crying doesn't make me feel any better. It just makes me feel worse about myself.

A light shines outside my window, which is odd since I'm on the second floor. Is someone waving a flashlight in here?

I tense, on high alert. It could be nothing, of course. But the light doesn't go away after a minute; someone is looking for something. For *me*.

Sliding out of bed, I keep low to the ground and drag myself across the room. I should have left the door open. Reaching up to the handle, I slowly try to pull it open, but something crashes through the window behind me and nearly crushes my hand.

I recoil, barely able to see from my vantage point. No — I can't wait for another projectile to be thrown at me. I yank the door open and bolt out of the room.

Not watching where I'm stepping, I rush to the stairs and immediately howl in pain. The window near the staircase was shattered, too, leaving broken glass everywhere. Now, a piece is lodged in my heel. I pluck it out, leaning against the railing and dripping blood as I limp down the stairs.

What if there's someone in the house? The door doesn't have locks, so it's a possibility. I head for the kitchen and grab the knife block, keeping one in my hand for protection. Or maybe it just makes me feel better. If a shadowborn is attacking me, I'm done for, knives or not.

This could be a stupid prank. It could be *Nic*. But I've seen enough home invasion thrillers to know that these situations should be treated seriously, and *not* as jokes. What if a cultist found me and snuck into the party?

Running outside would be a mistake; if the culprit is shadowborn, they will be able to outrun me. Even without my bleeding foot. I don't have magic or super senses to fight back. All I have is the element of surprise.

Making a snap decision, I hole myself in the first-floor bathroom and close the door. There are no windows, which means there is only one point of entry. But there's no lock on this door, either. I crouch in the bathtub with the lights on and my knife ready. As soon as I see someone enter the room, I can stab them. Or *try* to, anyway.

The minutes seem to turn into hours, but without any way to tell the time, I have no idea how long I've been waiting in the tub with my knife ready.

When the door finally creaks open, my legs are numb. My heart thuds in my chest, but I still manage to dive for the assailant's legs and knock them to the tile floor. Kicking

the door shut, just in case there's a group of people trying to kill me, I pin the person to the floor.

But the person underneath me doesn't move. She doesn't even make a sound. She just stares at me, eyes wide, mouth agape.

Who the hell is she? She's not wearing a cultist robe; she's in a ballgown. Could she have been a party guest? Either way, I've never seen her in my life. She couldn't have just stumbled in here, right? What if she's disguised as a guest to throw me off?

"Who are you?" I demand, holding the knife to her throat.

She only wheezes in response, blood pooling quickly from her body. Did she hit her head? It's possible. But there's a *lot* of blood on the floor, and when I finally lift myself off her, I realize that her stomach and chest are gushing blood.

That's the scene the police see when the bathroom door swings open—a party guest bleeding out on the bathroom floor, and me standing over her, covered in her blood, holding a knife.

CHAPTER EIGHT

The cop is a demon. Literally—it says so on the badge looped around her neck. SNPD is written in big gold letters, and Demon Class is written below it. I know Veil-based demons are different from Christian demons, but I'm still apprehensive, to say the least. Especially when she begins talking to me like we're friends.

This isn't the first time I've been questioned by the police. I know my rights. But this time, I'm not guilty.

"You must be shaken," she says, sliding a glass of water toward me. We sit at the kitchen table, while her coworkers take photos of the crime scene. "Your name is Maria Rochester, correct?"

"Yes. Most people call me Mary Alice," I reply.

She smiles, her red lipstick peeling from her chapped lips. Her hair is tied in a dark bun at the base of her neck, loose strands slipping out to curl around her chin and frame her heart-shaped face. It must be a long day for her, so I'm shocked she's being so patient with me. "Why don't you walk me through what happened tonight, Mary Alice?"

"Yes, of course. I left the birthday party early because wine got spilled on my dress when some glasses fell. I injured my hands on the broken wine glasses." I hold up my hands. "After cleaning them off and going to bed, someone shined a flashlight outside my window. I got up to go downstairs, but the window shattered. It must have been multiple windows at once, because the one near the stairs was broken, too. I didn't notice and stepped on a piece of glass."

"And the windows in the living room?" She's not as good at faking concern as she thinks she is. There's an underlying coldness in her voice that gives her away.

I'm not an idiot; I know what she's doing. She's trying to poke holes in my story, one I've already told two other cops who arrived on the scene before her. I've never understood it, but a single lie in a cop's eyes means definitive guilt.

Lies come more naturally to me than the truth, but with the added fact that these cops have magic powers, I'm not in the mood to get booked for something I didn't do based on a compulsive fib. "The windows were shattered upstairs, but I'm not sure who did it. I didn't want to look outside and see; I was just scared. I went to the kitchen to get a knife for protection and then I hid in the bathroom. I didn't notice a knife missing from the block. When that woman stumbled in, she had already been stabbed."

The cop nods. "If we tested your clothes right now for the victim's blood, would we find any?"

Of course. We fell on the floor together; her blood is all over my shirt. "I didn't hurt her. I don't even know who she is."

"That's funny," the cop says, in a way that clearly means it's *not* funny. "This guest house is quite far from the main house. She can't have just wandered over here."

"No," I agree. "She probably didn't. I'm not sure why she was here. Is she the one who broke the windows?"

"Look, Mary Alice. I'm going to be honest with you. This doesn't look good for you." The cop folds her hands in her lap. "You were caught in a very compromising position. And witnesses say you left the party visibly upset. Just tell me what happened. I can't help you unless you tell me the truth."

The truth isn't as shut-and-closed as she wants it to be. As *anyone* wants it to be. But she's not going to even come close to it without a little investigating on her part.

"The truth is," I begin, "that I no longer wish to speak with you."

That makes her crack a smile. "We are not humans, Mary Alice. We don't follow the same rules."

"No. We don't." Neil steps in through the back door, my knight in shining armor. *Not.* Where the hell has *he* been? "Maria's story holds true—all the windows upstairs are broken, and she is injured on her feet and hands. It would be difficult for her to fight a demon of Jessica Hardwicke's caliber, much less win, without a struggle. Aside from the glass wounds, Maria doesn't bear any marks typical of a brawl. And it certainly would be a brawl—Jessica is a member of the Hardwicke demon line and a Ruby Council member. Stabbing her from the front, even with the element of surprise, would have been difficult."

"Well, we'll just see what fingerprinting and toxicology reports come back with," the cop replies curtly, her dark eyes sliding to me. "We'll have to take her prints."

"Of course." Neil puts a hand on my shoulder. I think he means to look reassuring. If his hands weren't so skeletal and cold as a corpse, it might have worked. On the cops, not

on me. Never on me. Neil will never fool me. And no, that is *not* foreshadowing or building up to some twist in the story! I hope not, at least. Maybe this sounds arrogant—scratch that, I know it does—but no one will ever fool me with the whole "loving parent" routine again.

No, I'm not going to launch into a sad backstory or whatever. As I've said before, my childhood wasn't *all* bad. Things rarely are. But sometimes, the bad things eclipse all the good things. Happiness is comfortable but fleeting; misery is painful and intense. It can leave you filled with scars, scars that stay with you even when you're happy.

The cop takes a smartphone out of her pocket and opens an app, allowing me to electronically scan my fingerprints. I don't *love* having my fingerprints uploaded into some demon database, but I'm not sure how to refuse. Running away would mean breaking my agreement with Neil, which in turn would mean the death of my family.

Well, as long as she tests the knife for fingerprints, she'll hopefully see that mine aren't there. Rhys', maybe, since he's been cooking for me. But not mine.

"Thank you for your cooperation," the cop says sarcastically, and I have a feeling that's aimed more at Neil than me.

"Yes, of course. Anytime, Detective Baker." Neil is all smiles as he sees the cop and her team out, apparently finished with their crime scene analysis. He shuts the door before turning to me, his expression stiff. "It seems you've gotten yourself into trouble, Maria. You know that going to prison is a violation of our little deal."

"I'm hoping I *don't* end up in jail. But you know as well as I do that this is clearly a set-up," I reply.

"You wouldn't be strong enough to fight a shadowborn like Jessica," Neil agrees. "But Jessica Hardwicke is on

the Ruby Council—or, *was*. Her family consists of egotistical vultures, none of whom will take kindly to her death."

I don't think they'd take kindly to being called egotistical vultures, either.

"It isn't innocent until proven guilty here," Neil continues. "She died in your house. They will assume you did it, regardless of what the evidence says. Even if you are declared not guilty, they might think I bribed someone for you. Especially if they knew of our familial relationship."

"That doesn't even make sense. Any moron with two brain cells to rub together would be able to deduce my lack of involvement. I'm not strong enough, as you said earlier. And who called the cops, anyway? Isn't this whole thing too convenient? What would my motive even be?"

"I'm not sure. But 'logic' isn't something we demons pride ourselves on. We are creatures of instinct and hedonism." He smiles. "Well, perhaps that extends beyond demons."

I know it does. "Fine. And if the real culprit is discovered? *Then* will I dodge the hate train coming my way?"

Neil nods. "They will certainly still dislike you, but any actions taken against you will be seen as 'unjustified' by the larger community. They won't be quick to act. Keep in mind, Maria, that my sponsorship can only go so far. There are already many students who dislike your acceptance to Southeastern University. They think a human would dirty the name of the school."

"You could have said I was shadowborn," I point out.

"Yes. But they tested you with the Blood Chalice and determined you are not shadowborn," Neil replies. "You shot yourself in the foot there, with that one."

"I can't just say it made a mistake? Or fess up to it?" I mutter.

Neil says, "You can, but you would likely be punished by the school for your lies. It could result in expulsion, which would lead to—"

"Killing my family. I know." The threat is getting old—but he means it beyond a shadow of a doubt. Killing them means nothing to him, but for me, it would shatter my world. He knows it, too.

"I'm glad we're clear on that, Maria. Now, clean this mess up." He points to the bathroom. "Blood will stain the grout."

I HATE THE SMELL OF VINEGAR. IT DAMPENS THE KNEES of my sweatpants as I scrub the bathroom floor. I can barely keep my eyes open, but if the blood *does* stain the grout, there's no telling how Neil will react. The cleaning fumes are keeping me awake, thankfully. Barely enough to do a good job.

I haven't even *begun* to worry about the murder investigation. If demon society is as Neil described it, then I'm not sure how I can get out of this. It's clearly a set-up—luring me downstairs, sending a dying demon into the house, and calling the cops. The timing was a little too perfect, like... I'm being monitored or something.

Which I could expect from Neil, but he and his family gain nothing from this. Faith and Allegra were at the party, anyway, being watched by their guests. Neil needs me to kill Astaroth, so I don't think he'd set me up. Nic, perhaps...

But it's just a shot in the dark. I have no actual proof, no

leads, and no power to do anything about it. I'm *lucky* to have been set up like this, instead of killed outright. Which begs the question, why wasn't I killed tonight? Why frame me as a murderer instead?

My reputation is apparently already bad in shadowborn society. Yes, it's taken a nosedive with the murder of a prominent demon, but this plan to ruin my image seems sloppy and convoluted. The culprit is either insane or there's more going on beneath the surface. The worst part is, I'm at the mercy of the demon police.

The vinegar has soaked into the bandages on my hands, but the floor is clean now. I unwrap the thick gauze and throw it in the garbage. I should change the wrapping before I go to bed, at least. I move toward the door, hoping there are enough bandages left in the first aid kit.

Unfortunately, my foot injury renders me useless. I nearly slip on the wet floor, kicking over the bloody cleaning bucket as I open the door. A puddle of water, vinegar, and blood spills into the hall. *Great*—just what I needed.

Except, the hall of the guest house looks completely different. In fact, it doesn't look like I'm in the guest house at all anymore. A long, narrow hallway stretches out before me. Doors line either side, none labeled. Where the hell is this? Maybe I slipped, bonked my head on the sink, and died. Maybe this is hell.

That would be just about right: a shitty end to a shitty day.

I don't doubt I'm going to hell if it exists. But I didn't think it would be *this* soon. Isn't it a bit...anticlimactic? I mean, you haven't stuck around for this long to see me get offed in a common household accident, right? Not like this, with the main story left hanging.

The dirty spilled water puddles at my feet, and with my open wounds it's probably best not to step in someone else's blood. I keep the bathroom door open, walking further down the hall to get away from the spill. As I walk, another door opens on its own. And in walks Todd Glass.

Todd—the human kid on the cruise ship who tried to kill me over the summer. The one who went insane and attacked me multiple times, breaking into my room and making me think I was going crazy. *That* Todd.

My entire body tenses when I see him, but somehow, he looks different. The last I remember, he was haggard and pale. At least now, he's got some color to his cheeks.

He's still the tall, awkward boy I first met, with dark hair and eyes and a spray of freckles across his face. He says, "You aren't supposed to be here."

That's rich, coming from him. I'd laugh, but frankly, I'm too scared. I have no weapon, and even if he doesn't *look* crazy, that doesn't mean anything.

"Well," I reply, "you're supposed to be dead. Am...am I dead?"

"No—we're both alive. And judging by your hair and lack of a fake Southern drawl, you must be Mar," Todd says. It's a nice way to start our reacquaintance—by insulting me.

I contemplate running, but I don't think I'd make it back to the bathroom. Even if I reached the door, it doesn't have a lock. I don't even know if a mere lock would keep Todd out. There's something inhuman about him, there must be, because he's *alive*. Which shouldn't be possible. I saw him die; he was autopsied. Yeah, zombies can be raised through dark magic, but they wouldn't be as fresh as Todd looks. And smells. Besides, I can see him breathing.

"For your information, my Southern accent isn't fake," I

manage to reply. "You still haven't explained how you're here right now, instead of buried six feet under."

Todd shakes his head. "Look, I can explain everything. But you need to tell me where in the timeline you're at."

"You're not making any sense."

"What month are you in? What big events have happened so far? Did you enter Southeastern yet? Have you seen Jenna?"

"Jenna? No—I haven't seen her since she betrayed her friends on the ship. And I haven't gone to Southeastern yet, either."

Todd breathes a sigh of relief. "So this must be the night of Allegra's birthday. You've been framed, haven't you?"

"How could you possibly know that?"

"If you give me a minute, I can explain...a few things." I hate how calm he is, while I'm on the verge of freaking out.

"Why should I? You tried to kill me multiple times," I accuse. "Why shouldn't I just run away?"

"Because I know about Max."

I wince when I hear the name, a reflex I've never been able to conceal.

"So? That's not a secret," I say. "Everyone in Douglas County knows about what happened between Max and me. A version of it, anyway."

"No. I know what happened between you at the house that day. The real story," he adds, "not the one you fed to the police."

Well, fuck.

CHAPTER NINE

That's not a name I expected to come out of Todd's mouth, or anyone's mouth, really. Unless I was at the park and someone was calling for their pet dog. Which is what Max is—a goddamn dog. No, wait. That's an insult to dogs.

I don't even want to *think* about him, or any of it, but Todd's opened up a can of worms and my face twists into an ugly grimace.

"You told me that it would piss you off if I mentioned him," Todd continues, noting my expression. "But you also said it's the only way I could get you to trust me. Because you hate talking about him. It always makes you psychoanalyze yourself."

He's right—about everything. Especially the part about Max pissing me off.

"You don't like to think about him. I know," Todd says before I can come up with a response. "But you told me everything that happened between you two. Even the inci-

dent six months later—the one you've always lied to Tasha about."

"You need to start from the beginning, then," I concede, my heart finally calming down. "If I told you about…all this stuff, then I guess I must trust you to some extent. But when would I have told you that? Why? And how are you here?"

"I can't tell you everything right now. The timing isn't right. Things are going to get a lot worse before they get better." He gestures to the hallway, and the doors. "All I can tell you now is this: the key to your powers lies within you. Not in Neil, Allegra, or anyone else. It can only be you."

"And the award for most cryptic warning goes to—"

"This is all I can do for you right now," Todd says with a sad smile. "I'm sorry. For everything. But I can't change my future or your past. Now, you have to return before someone discovers your absence. All you have to do is go back to the bathroom and open the door."

"I can't just go back without even knowing how I got here," I argue. "I don't accept it."

"It doesn't matter whether or not you accept it."

"If you were in my shoes, what would you do?"

Todd holds his hand out, palm facing up. "Here."

He gently guides my hand toward him, placing it flat against his chest. His heart beats in sync with my own, his hands warming my skin. I pull away, the gesture enough to confirm to me that he's truly alive.

"We'll see each other soon," Todd says. "But you can't stay here. You have to go back, before you're missed."

"I could report you," I warn, but the threat is weak. Todd knows it.

"You could. But even if they believed you," he replies, "no one would know when to look."

MARY ALICE

When I was a kid, I made up all kinds of dumb lies to help me sleep at night. I told myself that my biological mom was a princess of a foreign country, and she couldn't pick me up because she was imprisoned by an enemy king. Or maybe she would be an international spy working undercover in a foreign country. Crap like that.

Isn't the "orphan with hidden abilities" trope common these days? It's popular for a reason. I know it gave *me* hope. Then, I expected to have an easier entry into the supernatural. Maybe falling in love with a vampire or a werewolf, only to find out that I'm magical, too. And then, with our love we'd overcome all obstacles thrown at us and get married at dusk. On a boat. Because obviously he'd be rich. Possibly British.

Man, things are *not* going according to that plan at all. Especially the "love conquers all" part. I'm pretty sure the moral of this story is going to be some shit about "being true to who you are" and "believing in yourself." Yuck.

I believe in myself, more so than anyone else around me right now, but I sure as hell don't advocate for "being true to who you are." Obviously. If I thought that, then I wouldn't be Mary Alice right now, would I?

But, in front of Allegra, I have to be. I already established the character and it would be disadvantageous for me to switch. I need to be on her good side, especially with Todd back in the picture. I don't even know what to make of him yet, and try as I might, I can't understand how he's still alive. I considered the

fact that he could have been lying, but he mentioned Max.

"We're almost there," Allegra tells me, pointing to the shoreline. "You can't see campus because of the trees, but it's close to the port."

"And we have to take a ferry to get there?" I ask, shielding my eyes from the sun.

"Yes. A boat is the only way to get to Kingsmarch Island. There's no airport, and the school has rules against helicopters."

Well, that figures. If I need to run away from the school for some reason, I won't have much luck, unless I want to swim a few miles. But Neil assured me that Southeastern University would be safe. Then again, he said that in front of Mrs. Abbott; it was probably lip service.

I wonder if Todd will be able to find me here. He seems to know more than he should about current events in my life; I assume he's all caught up on the whole shadowborn situation. Next time we meet, hopefully he'll be able to tell me more. Like how he survived, and why suddenly he doesn't feel like trying to kill me.

And, most importantly, why I don't remember telling him about Max. It's not like I can ask anyone else about this, either. I haven't told a soul about meeting Todd that night, and whether or not that's going to come back and bite me in the ass remains to be seen. But Rhys is Neil's lackey and Nic's totally out of the question. Quite frankly, I'd rather die choking on an embarrassingly large phallic vegetable than be helped by Nic. Allegra is Neil's daughter. Neil is…Neil. What would I even say? "I think I have the ability to open portals into a white hallway." What does that even *mean*?

With no one to ask and no internet access, I've been forced to look inward. In other words, I've been in a mental hell of my own creation with very little sleep and zero conclusions drawn.

"A penny for your thoughts?" Nic asks, leaning over the boat rail. I wish he'd fall in and get ground to mincemeat by the motor, but fate isn't that kind. "That's all they're worth, anyway."

"Nic," Allegra chides. "It's too bad we can't share a room, Mary Alice."

Agreed. Allegra is getting a place on her own, sort of. Rhys will be staying close by, as her caretaker. Which makes me all the more suspicious they have something going on between them. Aside from the conversation I overheard at her party between Archer and Rhys, he treats her a hell of a lot better than he treats me.

Case in point: he's holding a parasol above her head to shield her from the sun. She didn't even *ask*, he just did it. He also won't give me the time of day when she's around. I don't expect him to bend over backwards, but he treats me like air.

"We'll still see each other, I hope," I say, though it's probably a lie. I'm in remedial classes because despite the cram sessions over the summer, I'm far behind the other students. The only class we have together is a combat course, which doesn't have a remedial counterpart. I'm really looking forward to getting beaten up on a daily basis.

That's not to say Rhys' training didn't make a difference. I *am* stronger than I was at the beginning of the summer, as evidenced by the ease with which I lift my suitcase and carry it down the ramp to the dock. Granted, most of my stuff is being shipped directly to the dorm. But I have to

revel in the small victories so I'm not crushed by my large, repeated failures. Who says I'm not an optimist?

Nic watches me for a moment before turning to Allegra. "Can I help you with your bag, Allegra?"

"I'm fine," she replies, clearly lying. She uses both hands to hoist her luggage down the ramp, nearly stumbling and falling flat on her face. Rhys finally takes the bag from her and walks it down to the port himself. "Oh, thank you, Rhys."

Nic rolls his eyes and shoves past me. How much trouble would I be in if I threw my suitcase at his head?

"We can meet for dinner later, once you get settled," Allegra murmurs. "Are you nervous?"

Nervous? About meeting my roommate, about failing out of school and inciting Neil to kill my family, or about dying of stress-induced stomach ulcers from holding back my true feelings?

"A little," I admit with a sheepish smile. "But I'm excited, too, in a way."

Excited to be done with all this crap and get back home. I can't help but wonder if Tasha, at least, misses me. She might not *remember* me, but we've been such big parts of each other's lives. If I forgot her, I'm positive I'd still feel her absence.

Allegra stays by my side as we walk along the stone path. "You know I'm here if you need me."

I do—and that's what sucks. It would be easier if Allegra was a horrible person or if she hated me. But she's not, and here I am, keeping this huge secret from her. I do what I have to in order to keep my promises to Neil, but lying to her like this doesn't feel great. Especially when she returns my lies with kindness.

"I'm here, too," Nic interrupts. "You can always count on me. You know that, don't you, Mary Alice? I'll be watching over you."

"I'm sure."

At the end of the path, the trees thin and a wooden sign comes into view with "Southeastern University" painted on it in big blue letters. Otherwise, I wouldn't have been able to tell this is a college campus.

I won't lie—after seeing Northeastern, I thought Southeastern was going to be like Hogwarts. It isn't, not by a long shot. Houses line a newly paved road, each building a different pastel. They're all old Victorians with wrap-around porches and lawns that span half a football field. Each house is roughly the same size, so I'm not sure which is supposed to be the main building. They have wooden signs outside to mark them, but the signs are so far from the road I can't read what they say.

"The Sunrise dormitory is that way," Allegra says, pointing to my left. "It's on the corner of College Ave and 9th. You can't miss it."

You wanna bet?

"My dorm is in the opposite direction, but here." Allegra pulls a little black box out of her bag and gives it to me. "My mom told me to give it to you. Dad forgot— it's a phone. I put my number on it, so you can call me whenever you want. I'm sorry we couldn't find your old phone. Dad looked, but he couldn't recover it from the ship."

I open the box and look inside. It's the newest model smartphone, already charged and unlocked. "Thank you, Allegra. This will be helpful."

Allegra beams. "Message me with whatever you need. I

put Nic's number in there, too. If you can't reach me, you'll be able to reach him."

"Thank you," I say again. I have no idea if Neil has this phone bugged, and I wouldn't put it past him. But I don't care—having a phone will be useful regardless. I'll just have to be cautious. "Why don't we meet up for dinner after we've unpacked and everything? I'll need help finding the cafeteria, anyway."

"Sure! But there's a map you can access from the school's app, on the home screen," she tells me. "Just text me when you're finished, and we can meet at the rec center. That's the only building that doesn't look like a house here. It has a bunch of facilities, including the cafeteria."

"Thanks. I'll catch up with you later." Rolling my suitcase down the street, I make my way up College Ave. Despite the absence of sidewalks, there don't seem to be any cars on the road, so everyone is walking in the middle of the street. I do the same, mostly because it's easier to roll my suitcase on the pavement than in the grass.

The Sunrise dorm is easy to spot, even from far away. It's not like the other buildings, which look like huge doll houses. No, the Sunrise dorm must be the setting of a Southern gothic horror movie. Ivy covers the front of the weather-worn white building, surrounded by patches of bare dirt. As I get closer, I realize that even the sign has fallen. Dead trees and bushes populate the garden, dry branches and vines crawling over the porch rail. I have to dodge cobwebs to get to the entrance. All that's missing is a blinking red sign above the door that says "run."

I loiter around for a few minutes before gathering the courage to go inside. The door opens with a loud creak of the hinges, and a musty smell immediately overwhelms me.

"Oh?" A girl passing through the hall sees me and breaks into a big smile. "Are you a new student? Are you lost?"

"Hi, it's so nice to meet you!" I drawl, laying it on thick. "I'm Mary Alice Rochester. I've been assigned to this dorm."

"Oh, Mary Alice! I heard *all* about you. You're staying with the Abbotts, right? I'm Lilly. Why don't you come on in and meet the rest of the girls?" She takes me by the arm and pulls me into the living room, where three other girls are seated. All of them are blondes, making me the only brunette in the dorm. But Lilly is distinctly *strawberry* blonde, wearing her hair in short pigtail braids. "Girls, this is Mary Alice!"

"Mary Alice! Pleasure to meet you! I'm Kelsey, and these two are Natalie and Ellie-Jane."

"Ellie-Jane and I are cousins, so we share a room," Natalie adds. "And Kelsey and Lilly have their own rooms."

"They overbooked the dorms. This year's freshman class is big," Lilly explains. "But don't worry! There's enough space for all of us. I made sure to ask student services for an extra furniture set, Mary Alice. You'll have plenty of room."

"Thank you so much. That's so kind of you," I exclaim.

"Well, aren't you a sweet thing!" Natalie says.

"Bless your heart," Ellie-Jane chimes in. "We'd love to learn more about you, but I'm sure you're antsy to get unpacked. Your things came in the mail earlier, so we put them in your room."

"Yes, let's show her to her room. Here, let me help you with that bag." Lilly takes my suitcase from me and begins wheeling it down the hall. "Now, I know it's not much, but we tried to make it nice for you. Since you're, well, human and all."

"It must be a big adjustment," Natalie says. "You just let us know if you need anything."

Lilly opens a door near the kitchen, but I can't see much. It's far too dark.

Uh oh.

Before I can turn around, Ellie-Jane shoves me hard into the room. I tumble down a flight of stairs, my suitcase trailing close behind. Twisting away at the last moment, I'm able to dodge it and fall to a heap at the bottom of the steps. My head doesn't hit the ground, thankfully, but I land on my arm. It's too dark to tell if anything's broken, but I know for sure I'm going to be a mess of bruises later.

Lilly stands at the top of the stairs, peering down at me. "Let me reintroduce myself. My name is Lilly Hardwicke. And word around town is, you killed my sister."

Oh crap.

"Why don't you get unpacked and make yourself at home, in the basement where you belong?" Lilly drawls. "Welcome to Southeastern, bitch."

CHAPTER TEN

The basement isn't all that bad. I mean, aside from being cold and dark and damp, and that constant dripping from the bathroom sink. A bathroom in which I'm 60% certain someone's been killed.

At least I *have* a bathroom. My own, private murder bathroom. And hey, the soundproofing in this place isn't bad. If a ghost drags me into the bathroom mirror, no one will hear me scream.

I have to pull a string to turn on the light, and when I do, I wish I hadn't. The basement is unfinished and this one lightbulb is the only light source in the room. There's a bed shoved near a small boarded-up window, with a five-inch thick mattress and thin sheets piled up. Things are looking better and better for me.

Cheer up, Mary Alice! Your fall down a flight of stairs only left a few bruises, and now you don't have to share a bathroom with anyone when you need to poop. I call this a win-win.

Oh, even *I'm* not buying that crap! This place is something out of my nightmares, and probably against fire safety

codes. Just how I want to die: burning to death in a haunted basement.

All "joking" aside, my stuff *is* down here, thrown in the middle of the room. The cardboard boxes are filled with supplies I ordered on Neil's dime, including a luxury bedding set. You'd think, seeing as I hate Neil, I wouldn't want anything from him. Well, as I've said, I have very little pride. And hedonistic tendencies. I sprang for Egyptian cotton and a high thread count, so there are no regrets to be had. Only sheets to be washed.

The new clothes will also be a welcome addition to my wardrobe of Allegra hand-me-downs. I throw everything I can in the washing machine, turning it on.

Using the railing for support, I slowly inch up the creaking wooden staircase and try the doorknob to the first floor. Locked, as expected. But now that I have a phone, I can just call Allegra for help…if I had reception down here!

Fate is a cruel mistress indeed.

Well, here's one thing I bet those bitches didn't count on: my lockpicking skills. Allegra is much better at it than I am, don't get me wrong—but after all the investigating we did on the cruise ship, I learned a thing or two about breaking and entering. I also ordered a lockpicking kit online, so that should be with my stuff. You can order just about anything online, can't you? I rifle through the rest of the boxes and find the kit, pulling it out of the plastic. I also bought a safety lock, so I can lock the door from the inside. Isn't the internet amazing?

I'm not *that* eager to get out, mainly because I'd rather have a chance to change and make my bed with fresh, clean sheets. I could also use a hot shower.

I'm a bit apprehensive, given the amount of horror

movie jump scares that involve women showering, but it turns out I have nothing to worry about. It's *not* a hot shower, leaving me nearly frozen. This bathroom might not be haunted now, but it will be if I die from hypothermia.

After drying off, I switch the laundry and hang out in my towel. I should probably be doing something more productive, like studying those Elvish flash cards Rhys made me, but it's been weeks since I've watched television. And now I have a cell phone and Wi-Fi. It's slow, but it works.

I've always liked sitcoms. I can watch them on repeat, and often did, when I was a kid. It was something universal that every house had, even if the shows themselves were different. The format was the same, and that in and of itself comforted me. They made time pass quickly, something I wished for a lot when I was younger. *If only I was older*, I'd think.

Ha. If I knew then what I know now, maybe I wouldn't have been so quick to wish time away. There were a lot of painful memories, but there were some good times, too. Times I should have savored more.

Too late now.

When everything is dry, my clothes are put away, and my bed is made, I pick the lock on the door. I press my ear to it, just in case one of my new roommates is there. When I don't hear anything, I slowly open the door and manage to slip out the back of the house unseen.

My phone buzzes with the texts and calls I missed while in the basement from Allegra. She wants to meet for dinner, and I see no reason to refuse. We haven't gotten to spend much time together anyway, which is a good thing and a bad thing. A good thing, because her very presence makes me

feel…not so great. And then guilty, because all she's done is help me. With so much on my plate already to think about, the complex feelings I have about my biological half sister should *not* be added to the list.

That being said, she might be my only ally here. It would be stupid of me to push her away because of feelings I can barely make sense of.

I tell Allegra I'm on my way to the cafeteria and open the Southeastern app already downloaded on my phone. There's a map of campus handy, but it takes me fifteen minutes longer than it should to get to the rec center building.

Allegra stands outside, waving. Rhys is by her side, though he's wearing his usual cold stare. He doesn't greet me, doesn't even acknowledge my existence.

"Hi, Allegra. Hi, Rhys," I say warmly. "Have you both unpacked?"

"Yes. Rhys did most of the heavy lifting," Allegra replies with a smile. "I'm sorry service isn't so good in your dorm. Is the room alright? How are your roommates?"

"Great. Everything is much better than I could have imagined. The campus is gorgeous!"

Rhys scoffs at the lie but doesn't call me out in Allegra's presence.

The cafeteria is deceivingly large inside, with multiple food stations. We have to scan a QR code from the Southeastern app to enter, but once inside we can eat whatever we want. And we can stay for as *long* as we want. It seems too good to be true, but Allegra explains that the cost is included in the room and board charge.

"$30,000?" I sputter.

"It's the base price. For room upgrades, it costs more," she adds, grabbing us trays from the stack.

That's highway robbery and triple the annual tuition cost at the Douglas County Community College. God, I hope Neil isn't planning on making me repay him somehow...

Well, since he already paid for it, I suppose I'll have to help myself. I don't hold back, putting a pre-packaged steak on my plate. They even have Cajun waffle fries. Maybe when Lilly pushed me down the stairs, I died and went to heaven.

Just kidding. If heaven and hell exist, I'm not going upstairs, if you know what I mean. But thanks to the whole reveal of the shadowborn and the Veil, I've been questioning my faith. I've never been the most devout Christian, but I always believed. Now, with the existence of angels and demons from another realm, I'm not so sure.

Allegra selects a modest fruit parfait for dinner. Even with only one dish on her tray, Rhys holds it for her without taking anything for himself. We choose an unoccupied table in the middle of the room and sit down.

The steak cuts like butter, and I have no qualms about digging in. Allegra is much more reserved than I am, mixing the parfait without really eating it.

"If you weren't here, Mary Alice, I probably would have just taken this to go," she admits.

"Is that enough for you for dinner? Wouldn't you want to go back and get more?" I ask, stuffing a fry in my mouth. I would have offered her some but, well... When it comes to junk food, I don't share.

"I'm afraid I wouldn't be able to hold it down. The last thing I want to do is create a spectacle," she whispers,

glancing around. "Kind of like I'm doing right now, just by eating.

I don't even notice until she says it aloud, but looking around the room, there *are* some students blatantly staring and whispering. Normally I would brush it off, but with at least a dozen students acting the same way, I know it's not a coincidence.

"Why are they staring like that?" Don't they know their food's going to get cold if they continue to gawk?

"I'm a sideshow to them."

"What's to see? You're just eating." I lower my voice. "Maybe they're just looking at you because you're pretty."

"As much as I'd like to think so, that isn't the case," she denies. "It's worse now than during my freshman year. I suppose we're *both* attracting attention, since you're the only human student here."

"And she's been accused of murder," Rhys unhelpfully points out.

"Hey. I didn't kill anyone." Not this time, anyway.

Allegra gives a halfhearted smile. "I know you didn't, but the shadowborn world is less forgiving. I'm sorry, Mary Alice. At least…we have each other, right?"

I nod, my chest tightening. We have each other, huh? The staring must make her uncomfortable, so I understand why she would want to eat in her dorm. She has Rhys as her caretaker, so she's not alone, right?

After she finishes her parfait, Rhys wordlessly gets up and clears away her tray. It reminds me of how he would clean up after making me breakfast, tending to my needs without me having to ask. He doesn't do that now for me, mind you — even though I've finished my food, too. It makes

me wonder again what the relationship between Allegra and Rhys really is.

On the night of Allegra's birthday party, Archer accused Rhys of being in love with Allegra. He takes care of her, it's true, but he hasn't spoken much to either of us at all. He's taking care of her, but that's part of his job. Unless he's ignoring me because he doesn't want her to get the wrong idea.

"Allegra," I whisper, lowering my voice. While Rhys is gone, I might as well ask. It's not like his big ears give him better hearing, right? "I heard that you and Rhys are dating."

She bursts into laughter on the spot, attracting more attention from the other students around us. "I suppose that *is* the rumor going around. Where did you hear that? Archer? Mary Alice, in truth, it's—"

"Preposterous," Rhys finishes, standing at the end of the table. I have to crane my neck to look up at him, and he's *not* pleased. More than his usual blank stare, or even the slight furrow of his brow when he gets annoyed at me, his face is a mask of anger. "You would do well not to believe everything you hear."

This is the first time he's spoken to me today, let alone looked into my eyes.

"She was just asking." Allegra giggles, relaxing thanks to my apparently hilarious question. "Isn't it better to clear up that misunderstanding, Rhys?"

"It is not a misunderstanding, but an outright lie that Archer Kinsey and Nic Woolridge have been spreading. The latter seems entertained by it, and the former genuinely believes it."

"To answer your question, Mary Alice, Rhys and I are

not an item," Allegra clarifies. "It's true that Archer and I broke up before college, and that my father never approved of him. He instructed Rhys to be our chaperone, so I understand why Archer would think that something was going on. Even if I claimed there wasn't. Nic didn't make things any better, always joking that he and I would get married. I think Archer took him seriously. And that's how this whole love triangle rumor was born."

"Isn't Nic your cousin?" I ask.

Allegra nods. "We're first cousins by blood, though in the shadowborn world, a marriage like that isn't uncommon. My father considered it, but I declined. I can't see him as anything more than family, and I'm positive he's only joking around. Sometimes, he takes his jokes too far."

I don't think Nic is joking, but maybe now isn't the best time to point that out. I'm grateful she cleared up that whole debacle, at least.

Still… "So you and Archer are just friends?"

"We aren't as close as we used to be, but one day I hope we can be friends again." She sighs. "I don't think we would ever become involved again. We're too different."

"As are we," Rhys says, looking at her.

She smiles, but it doesn't reach her eyes. "Yes. You and I are also too different, Rhys. It…could never work."

Although she says that, one thing is crystal clear to me: there might not be anything between Allegra and Rhys now, but she wants there to be. And, for some reason or another, he doesn't.

CHAPTER ELEVEN

P rovost Mathers is a difficult man to read. On one
hand, he seems genuinely concerned about me. On the
other…why would he be? He has no reason to care about
me, and it's not like we've known each other for very long. I
would think he'd despise me because of what happened on
the cruise ship. But when I run into his classroom, two
minutes late, his first question is, "Are you alright?"

His thick drawl, cowboy hat, and boots make him seem
like a walking, talking stereotype. All he needs is a bolo tie
and a horse. His bright red hair, which I can't determine if
it's natural or not, is tied in a ponytail that runs down his
back. It's well kept, too, probably more so than my greasy
rat's nest.

To be fair, I slept through my alarm. You would have,
too, if you woke up in a dark basement! There's no sunlight
in there, no windows, which seems dangerous. I had to
sprint across campus to make it to class on time, tripping
over my own two feet as I tried to find this place with the

map on my phone. Even then, I went to the wrong building twice and my phone died. It's a complete miracle I found this class.

"I'm fine," I wheeze, though it's a complete lie. After being pushed down the stairs yesterday and tripping this morning, my legs are a mess. There's even a bruise on my butt, as long as a tube of lip gloss. Not that I measured.

I didn't expect Mathers to be my professor; I figured he would be busy as the provost, running the school and all. This is Independent Study I, and he isn't listed as my instructor. Given the name of the course, I thought I would be...studying independently.

"Please, have a seat," he urges, gesturing to the empty classroom. My instinct is to sit in the back, but since it's just the two of us, that would be awkward, to say the least. I take a seat up front, and I'm thankful when he sits across from me at his desk. At least we're at eye level. "How are you, Miss Rochester?"

Do I even need to answer that?

"I'm good," I lie.

He doesn't buy it. Not because I'm a bad liar—or so I tell myself. But if he's heard anything about me from the gossip vine, I'm sure he knows about the dead girl I've been accused of murdering.

"I heard that Neil Abbott is sponsorin' you," he begins. His accent is thicker than mine, though I can't place exactly which state he's from. Some of his words are slurred together with a heavy twang. "Since you grew up without any knowledge of the shadowborn, he suggested we place you in remedial classes. I requested you be placed in an independent study course, as well. I hope you think of this

class time as a free forum to ask questions. We can dive deeper into any topic you'd like. This *is* a class for credit, so we do need one assignment. You'll have a paper due at the end of the semester; any topic is fine."

"Am I the only student who...wasn't brought up with shadowborn knowledge?" I ask.

"At this school, yes. Very few children in the shadowborn community, at least in the Southeast region, grow up without any knowledge of their heritage," Mathers explains. "Even in those cases, more often than not those students do not end up at our school. There are five major magic colleges across the continental United States, and of the five, Northeastern has a much better program for beginner students. Washington State College of the Bizarre also has a robust instructional program and tuition assistance. Southeastern is quite exclusive."

Ah, so I've heard.

But what he's describing sounds like a terrible system. Taking kids out of their comfort zone, telling them that magic exists, and shipping them off to another part of the country? How exactly does that work? I can't imagine everyone goes willingly.

"You are somewhat of an exception. Neil Abbott was quite insistent on your admission, despite bein' human. I wonder why that is." But something about his tone makes me think he's not wondering at all. That he knows, somehow. Which is ridiculous, because how could he have guessed that Neil is holding my family hostage? Unless Neil has that sort of reputation in the shadowborn world? His face is kind of sleazy. Or maybe I'm just biased because I hate him with my entire heart and soul.

Neil doesn't want anyone to know that I'm his daughter, and I imagine if I let it slip, he'll do something awful to my family. I assume if I make him unhappy in any way, he'll hurt them. It's not a stretch, considering he wiped their memories.

"He's grateful to me. He thinks I saved Allegra," I explain.

"Curious." But he lets the subject drop, thank God. "I know we had our disagreements over the summer, Miss Rochester, but I hope we can put that behind us and work together this semester. It might be difficult for you to trust others, but know that I am your ally."

I *don't* know that. Realistically, is anyone here my *ally*? If they knew the truth…would they help me? I don't think so. I think they would blame me for freeing Astaroth, though I can't explain how I did that. Not to mention, I'm physically weaker than most shadowborn. They would probably treat me how they treat Allegra, with cold stares and constant, silent criticism.

The sentiment is nice, of course, but I don't trust Mathers as far as I can throw him. Which is not very far. On the ship, we found a corpse of a man made up to look like Mathers. It turned out to be a bit of a red herring, but I still don't know how that fits into the picture. At this point, I can't even concern myself with that little mystery. But it's enough for me not to put any faith in Mathers. Even if he does turn out to be on my side, the risk is far greater than the reward.

For politeness' sake, I smile. "Of course, Provost Mathers. And please, call me Mary Alice."

"Mary Alice," he repeats. "Are you certain?"

My smile falters. Mathers has seen my school file, and he knows my birth name. "Yes. It's a childhood nickname."

"Alright, Mary Alice. Do you have any particular topics you'd like to cover first? We can go over basics on the Veil, history, types of truebloods…"

"I want to learn more about demons. Particularly Astaroth." You know what they say—know thy enemy. So you can kill them. Knowing more about Astaroth's powers will be useful to avoid getting eaten by him. "Why was he so giant? Mr. Abbott is a trueblood demon, but he looks human."

"Astaroth was like Neil Abbott, once. Most trueblood demons look indistinguishable from humans," Provost Mathers explains. "As a blood magic practitioner, Astaroth's power grew exponentially. His size is probably due to that. Even after bein' caged in the time prison, he managed to use a surge of conserved magic to rampage upon his release."

"Why was he caged?" I probe.

"The Veil is separated into different territories, much like the mortal realm has country borders," he says. "If someone commits a crime in the United States, and they are a U.S. citizen, generally they would be processed and tried by a U.S. court. However, if that criminal committed crimes in multiple countries, what would happen? In the Veil, there is a sort of 'international police.' Once one commits an offense against multiple different trueblood species, they are handed over to an international council. But if they commit a world-endin' crime, they would end up in a time prison without trial."

"World-ending? Astaroth tried to start the apocalypse?"

"Not necessarily. But he did somethin' that could have caused mass devastation in the Veil. The thing is, blood

magic users can be executed on the spot. But he was imprisoned instead. Quite the curious case. I hadn't heard about it until this summer."

"Maybe they *can't* kill him because of the blood magic," I guess. "Can that make you immortal?"

"All information about blood magic is restricted to the general public. The knowledge itself is dangerous, and therefore off-limits. Even to me."

I hesitate to probe more about blood magic, for appearances' sake. But maybe that's the key to defeating Astaroth: blood magic against blood magic. From what little I *do* know, the limits of normal magic simply don't compare when it comes to blood magic. Jenna, for instance, was able to use necromancy to attack us.

"Why is blood magic so horrible?" I ask finally.

Provost Mathers looks at me like I have two heads. "I would think you of all people would understand the dangers, given the cult attempted to sacrifice you for their spell. Any magic which requires human body parts is considered blood magic, even if blood isn't used—though that is the main medium. For example, if I were to use a human eyeball in a spell, it would still be considered blood magic. This type of magic is dangerous because the user benefits from mutilation and murder. Not to mention, it can drive one insane. Astaroth is the prime example."

If I were to ask "how insane" or "when exactly does the insanity hit," I assume he would get suspicious. But I *am* curious. If I find the right blood magic spell and use it to go against Astaroth, how much harm would that do? I could use my own blood for the greater good.

Provost Mathers clears his throat. "Mary Alice, I sincerely hope these inquiries are coming from a place of

intellectual curiosity and *not* a desire to practice forbidden arts or take matters into your own hands. At Southeastern, as a student, you must follow the rules and leave these adult matters to our staff. There is no need to worry about Astaroth while you are here. Just focus on your education."

"Don't worry, Provost Mathers," I say. "I don't plan on doing anything dangerous."

RHYS DIDN'T TEACH ME HOW TO FIGHT. WE WORKED ON strength training and speed, but not weapons or hand-to-hand combat. Now that I have a combat class every afternoon, I imagine I'll either get good at it or get my butt kicked. Maybe a little bit of both.

Allegra is in the same class, at least. We sit together on the bleachers. It's like we're radioactive; no one dares sit near us.

It doesn't bother me as much as it bothers her. I get the feeling Neil spoiled her a little bit, and she's certainly treated well at home. Faith dotes on her, from what I can tell. Going from such a warm environment to this frozen hell of a social landscape must be jarring for her.

"I hope we get paired up together. I think we're going to be sparring today," Allegra tells me, tying her hair up. This is the first time I've ever seen her in anything but a turtleneck and skirt, or a long-sleeve high-neck dress that reaches the floor. For combat, she's wearing leggings. Everything is covered up, including her neck, but the new clothes are refreshing.

I tell her as much. "I like your outfit. It suits you."

"Thank you! To be completely honest, I was a little bit

nervous. I've never had combat class before." She's probably been too sick to participate. "I've been feeling better lately, though, so I got permission from my doctor."

"Don't push yourself," I say.

She smiles. "I won't. I can't. Rhys is off doing something else, so I'll have to be careful. If we're paired together, you'll go easy on me, won't you?"

"I think *you'll* have to go easy on *me*."

The combat professor enters two minutes after class is supposed to begin, dressed in a navy tracksuit. He's younger than I expected, probably in his early thirties, with short blond hair and a full beard.

"Alright, students! Today, I will be assessing your skills. I hope none of you were slacking over the summer," he announces. "For those of you who do not know me, I am Professor Hall. I do not believe in holding one's self back, so in this class, your grade depends on how hard you try. Now, you will all be paired off randomly and expected to fight in the ring. Rules are simple—no magic, only practice weapons for now. Get pinned to the mat for five seconds and you're finished. He who pins it, wins it. There are thirty of you and one of me, so only one pair will be fighting at a time. The rest of you may watch."

Oh, so we're fighting in front of the whole class? Great! I can already tell how this one's going to end: in a major butt-kicking. I only hope my partner doesn't hit my face too hard.

"Up first—Rochester and Hardwicke! Get in the ring!"

Of course. Why *wouldn't* I be paired up with someone who hates me?

It's not even like Lilly knows me as a person. If she did,

she'd probably still hate me, but at least then it would be justified.

Lilly rises to her feet and makes her way to the mat, snatching a wooden practice sword from a wooden weapons rack near Professor Hall. There's a white ring of tape on the ground, but it's not very large. Lilly and I stand on either side, but if I were to extend my arm, I'd be touching her. There's not enough room for us to fight, let alone for me to avoid her blows. This can't be a coincidence, right? Or, if it is, maybe I just have the worst luck in the world.

I glance back at Professor Hall as he blows his whistle, but in the crowd, I catch sight of Archer. He's sitting in the front row with Ophelia, on the opposite side of where Allegra is. I guess I didn't see him come in. I raise a hand to wave, but he doesn't move. Ophelia stares at me, though, and whispers something in his ear. What, I have no clue. Not even a guess.

I know he sees me. Will he ignore me because he's with Ophelia now? Or maybe he just doesn't know what to do?

Whatever. I can't think about this. I smile at Lilly, trying to make nice. Even if it's forced, and we haven't spoken since she pushed me down into the basement, I'm not sure how else to treat her. She *is* about to beat me up right now; showing a little kindness can't hurt, right?

"Let's have a good fight." I extend a hand toward Lilly to shake, but she knocks it away with the wooden sword. She doesn't even let me pick up a weapon from the rack before coming at me.

I immediately curl into a ball while she pummels me with the sword, using my spine as a drum. She could easily pin me to the ground right now, but she's not. I guess she's having her own kind of fun. That makes one of us.

She must be growing bored of hitting me with the sword, because she throws it aside and grabs my hair instead, lifting my face (and probably some of my scalp).

"You should have never come to this school," she whispers. "This should be more than enough proof that you don't belong here."

CHAPTER TWELVE

I t's about time I start fighting back.

That's probably what you're thinking, right? I can practically hear the heckling through the page. Well, I hate to break it to you, but I *did* try fighting back. Yeah, what you just read in the previous chapter was me...trying. And failing. It wasn't my greatest moment, okay? To be fair, nothing in this series is going to be my "greatest" moment. I may not be able to predict the future, but I have a feeling things aren't going to go my way anytime soon.

They say diamonds are formed under immense pressure. But I'm fine with being...whatever diamonds are before they're diamonds. Carbon deposits, maybe? I'm not sure— we learned geology in tenth grade, and I was too busy slutting around as Marilyn to pay attention in class. Those were the days.

Allegra, at least, is kind enough to invite me over to tend to my wounds. It's better than scrounging up bandages by myself in the basement.

But as soon as we enter her dorm, I regret accepting her

help. The Victorian smells like the ocean, which is appropriate considering everything is nautical-themed. I can't imagine why, after the experience we had on the cruise ship. She must not have chosen the furnishings. Even the wallpaper has seashells on it, bordering the top of the living room. Sand dollars are glued to the lamps on the table and the bookshelves leaning against the walls.

She sits me down on the blue couch, with fish printed on the fabric, and leaves to get a first aid kit. But not before sharing that she has this entire house to herself.

Not to sound *too* jealous (though I fear it's already too late for that), but this is a three-bedroom house. She's living here with Rhys. One, two...couldn't I have been the third person? I don't care if I'm the third wheel! Why am I living with Lilly and those harpies instead of with Allegra? The room and board would have been cheaper if Neil let me stay here.

It's not like he's afraid of me revealing my secret, with my family's lives at stake. This sounds like a persecution complex, but I swear that's not it: Why is Neil, and everyone else in the world, making my life so much more difficult than it needs to be?

Oh my gosh. Did that sound as whiny as it did in my head?

"Lilly didn't hold back," Allegra mutters, coming back to the living room with the first aid kit. She gently wipes my face and applies a salve around my eye, which will no doubt turn black later. It's not as bad as the one Nic gave me. Even Tasha's given me worse—my sister throws a *nasty* punch, something we're both proud as hell about. Even if I was the recipient at one point. I probably deserved it.

My back took most of the damage, already a mess of

bruises and cuts. Well, it's not like I'll be taking off my shirt for a guy anytime soon.

I thought, after that brutal smackdown, Archer would at least say something to me after class. But he left before I could catch him. If this were a more romantic novel, *he'd* be the one cleaning my wounds. I'd take off my shirt shyly, and he'd make a stupid comment. I'd get mad, but only playfully. It would start raining—

I wince as Allegra lifts my shirt, spraying disinfectant on my back. It might as well be lemon juice, the way it stings.

"She went too far. I'm going to report her and Professor Hall to the chancellor," Allegra announces. It's the first time she sounds *angry*, and I hate to say I'm a little touched.

We shouldn't be getting closer. She's my lifeline, and I want her to consider me a friend for my own benefit. I won't lie and say I feel guilty about it, because I can't feel guilty about doing what's necessary to keep myself alive. Even if it means being manipulative.

But the more I'm around Allegra, the more I grow to like her. It's going to be much harder if the truth ever comes out.

"I'm not strong enough to fight back," I reply honestly. Not physically, anyway. I guess I could steal Lilly's toothbrush tonight and clean the toilet with it. Or dunk it down the sink drain. Yeah, it's petty and childish and accomplishes absolutely nothing. The risk of being caught far outweighs the reward. Even so, I'm tempted to do it.

"I would fight her *for* you if I could," Allegra says eagerly. "She's a horrible person. This isn't even about revenge over her sister; it's pride and pure sadism!"

Agreed.

"I appreciate the sentiment, but I would never ask you

to fight anyone on my behalf," I tell her. If anything, I'd want to do it myself. But, as much as we can talk, or fantasize, about gaining super strength and beating Lilly Hardwicke into the dirt where she belongs, I know the reality of the situation. We live together. I have to walk home with my tail between my legs and wait until I'm strong enough to fight back. Until then, I'll just have to manage my anger. That shouldn't be too hard, right?

Rhys walks in from the kitchen. My shirt is still pulled up, the straps of my bra visible, but he doesn't show any indication it affects him. He simply sets the tray of tea down on the table—just one cup, I notice. "Allegra, it is time to take your medicine."

"I'll get going," I say, fixing my shirt and standing up. I can take a hint, though between you and me, Rhys is being awfully transparent about wanting me to leave. I should go back and take some painkillers, anyway. "Thank you, Allegra. I'll see you tomorrow, okay?"

"Are you sure you're going to be alright?" Allegra looks at Rhys. "Walk her home. Make sure she gets to her bedroom safely without anyone bothering her."

"I am not permitted in her dorm," Rhys replies curtly.

"Oh, campus security doesn't even patrol until after dark. Just walk with her, please."

He looks at me stiffly. Even though his eyes scream "no," he can't seem to refuse a request from Allegra. "Fine. Let us go."

Well, with that enthusiastic attitude, how can a girl refuse?

Rhys goes from refusing to spare me a glance in front of Allegra to, outside, staring at my face. I didn't think the black eye was *that* bad, but I stand corrected.

"Take a picture, it will last longer," I say dryly.

He doesn't take the bait. "Our tutoring will continue throughout the semester."

"Oh? Neil's making you tutor me? Aren't you supposed to be watching Allegra?" I figured she would take priority.

"This matter is of the utmost importance. Elvish lessons will continue and I will monitor you to ensure your assignments are completed. Previous records indicate you lack discipline."

That's an understatement.

"Previous records? You looked at my report cards?" How did Neil even get access to those? "It's not like I didn't try to get good grades. Have you ever considered that maybe I'm just stupid?"

"Yes. Constantly. Your lack of observation skills have been noted." Rhys might be insulting me, but I swear he's smiling. I mean, technically he's not—his mouth is a straight line. But if he didn't have a bad case of emotional constipation, I'm sure he'd smile. "I will pick you up from your combat class on weekdays, and we will study in the student lounge on the second floor of the recreational hall. I have reserved a room."

I'm not sure whether I should thank him. He's just doing his job. But the words slip out anyway, like a reflex. "Thank you."

"In Elvish."

I spoke too soon. "Thank you," I repeat in Elvish.

"Your accent is still off. Practice more." He stops in front of my dorm, which seems empty at the moment. No lights are on, and I have to unlock the back door to get inside.

"I'll see you tomorrow, I guess," I say, turning the porch lights on.

"One more thing. A piece of advice for you."

"Unsolicited? Well, I have to hear this."

Rhys gives me a droll look. "Shadowborn and humans have different values. You might be used to acting a certain way to achieve a desirable outcome, but applying the same technique you use on humans will not work here. Shadowborn value strength and power above all else. You would do well to remember that."

"I'm not strong, though." I point to my swollen eye. "Exhibit A."

"You will figure it out soon."

"Seriously? Can't you be a little bit clearer?" I sigh, putting a hand on my hip. "First Archer, now you. Is it just a policy for all hot guys to be cryptic? I'm not including Nic in this, because I'd rather gag myself with a broken bicycle chain than call him 'hot,' but he's just as bad! Let's rewind and explain this to me again. How do I get people to stop beating me up and hating me? Is there a simple answer here? Who does a girl have to pretend to be to make some friends around here?"

My rant, none of which is a joke, earns the smallest mouth twitch from Rhys. It's so slight, I almost don't catch the way the corners of his mouth pull up. Just for a second. Am I imagining things, or did he almost smile?

"Good night," he says.

"Yeah, yeah," I mutter. "Good night."

I'm not going to press him for an answer. Accidentally acknowledging his attractiveness was embarrassing enough, thank you kindly. Time to go shower and sink into bed. Hopefully I can fall asleep quickly, but I have a feeling I'll be up for most of the night reliving my most embarrassing moments.

I go inside, closing the back door and getting a cup of water from the kitchen. My eye continues to throb, a feeling I'm sadly growing accustomed to. That doesn't make the pain any less severe.

My vision is impaired, but as I stand by the sink and look out at the yard, I swear I see a figure standing directly below the street lamp. The sun is just starting to go down, so the light isn't on, and the figure is robed in black. They're not the easiest to see. Moving silently toward the back door, I quickly lock it. When I look back up, the figure is gone, vanished into thin air in a matter of seconds.

CHAPTER THIRTEEN

"A job," Provost Mathers repeats. "This is only the first week of school. Why do you think you need a job?"

"I would like to earn a little money." Since I have none right now. "So, does the school have any work-study programs?"

I figured Mathers would know, seeing as he's the provost and all. He sighs, leaning against his desk and crossing his arms. Today, he's wearing a bolo tie with the Southeastern University logo on it and blue boots to match. I have to hand it to him—he's very consistent in his cowboy style.

"I'll look into it for you," he says finally. "In the meantime, it might be best to wait until you feel better."

To be fair, I *do* feel better. A few days have passed since Lilly beat me up, but my bruises have already begun to fade. My eye is still bruised, but the swelling and pain have disappeared.

After all the beatings I received growing up, most of which happened at school, I can say with certainty I've

never healed this quickly. I think it started on the cruise ship, but what would the catalyst for this change have been? My eighteenth birthday? That happened shortly before I boarded the SS *Athena* for the first time.

Come to think of it, before I got on the cruise ship, Tash and I were in a car accident. But any minor injuries I sustained disappeared so quickly, I never thought about it again until now.

Why would I have a healing ability but no other shadowborn traits?

"Today, I brought you some light readin'," Provost Mathers says, putting a brick of a book on my desk. *Demonology: A Complete History.* At a glance I can tell it's more than 500 pages. "This is a book I found in the mortal realm, but it has quite a bit about Christian demonology, including a section on Astaroth."

"How will this help me?" I ask, trying not to sound rude. I fear I do anyway.

"Astaroth didn't choose his name randomly. By studyin' his origins, I believe we can learn more about him and his goals."

"There are no resources on the actual trueblood Astaroth?"

"Unfortunately not. Everythin' is being handled by the Ruby Council, which I am not privy to since I am not a demon. I am a siren shadowborn."

I wasn't expecting that. I thought Mathers would be a magician or an angel shadowborn. When I think of sirens, I think of mermaids.

Mathers must know what I'm thinking because he launches into a mini-lecture. "Sirens were named after the creatures from Greek mythology, but trueblood sirens are

humanoid without any bird-like or mermaid-like features. They look just as human as demons and angels. The only difference lies in their power — an allurin' song."

"Do you have a power like that, too?"

"No. Shadowborn powers, as you know, are diluted," he explains. "For example, a werewolf shadowborn cannot shift into a wolf. A vampire shadowborn doesn't drink blood. Well, I suppose they can, but most find it unappetizin'. The main ability of the shadowborn, aside from enhanced senses, is openin' rifts. Because we have the blood of a mortal and a trueblood in our veins, we can open rifts from either the Veil or the mortal realm."

"And truebloods can only open rifts from the Veil."

"Precisely."

Well, I'm glad I remembered *something* from class yesterday. "Okay, so are you saying that a werewolf shadowborn and a siren shadowborn don't have any differences in the type of powers they have?"

Mathers nods, clearly impressed. "Mary Alice, you have been studyin' well. You are correct — there is not much difference in terms of the type of power shadowborn hold. There are cases where siren shadowborn are more resistant to a trueblood siren's song, or werewolf shadowborn grow stronger under the full moon. But those differences are minute. The true dividin' factor between the shadowborn is social. Because of the biological differences in our trueblood ancestors, shadowborn can hold some discriminatory beliefs toward those of different heritages. They justify this because they believe their discrimination is backed by science."

"Do they hate humans because they see us as inferior?" This sounds awfully familiar to discrimination in human

society. "We don't have powers, so somehow, we're not as good?"

Mathers hesitates. "Well, I wouldn't put it that way."

I would.

"Has anyone ever spoken to you about beastbloods?" he asks, changing the subject.

"A little." Rhys briefly covered them when he was tutoring me this summer. While truebloods are humanoid monsters from the Veil, beastbloods are non-humanoid creatures from the Veil. They're closer to animals than humans. Like dragons or yeti.

"Discrimination against beastbloods is even worse than that among truebloods. But it is interestin' how Astaroth's giant form resembles a beastblood. At least, that is what I was told."

Right. Mathers wasn't there to see Astaroth rise from prison. "Why would he want to grow so tall? He won't be able to run his cult from the mortal realm, not without attracting attention."

"I imagine he can change form. He might be too weak right now to do that," Mathers guesses. "He is in hidin'. No one knows his whereabouts, which is difficult to believe. He might be hidin' in the Veil until he can get his form under control."

"He didn't *look* weak to me." He looked like he could crush me.

"Disregardin' his appearance, he's been in the time prison for over a century. There is nothin' in the time prison; no food or drink, nothin' to do, no one to see... It truly is a painful existence. It's probably driven him mad."

"If he's crazy, wouldn't that make him easier to kill? I mean, if he can't make rational decisions," I clarify.

Provost Mathers shakes his head. "Miss Rochester, I do not recommend seekin' him out. Astaroth might be weakened by his time in prison, but he is still a trueblood. He would kill you in a second."

"How would one go about killing a trueblood? Hypothetically speaking." This might come in useful for killing Neil one day.

Mathers shakes his head. "I will pretend you did not just ask me that. Now, I believe we've sidetracked enough for today. Why don't we read about Christian demonology together? You can start from the first page."

IT'S HOT TODAY, WHICH ISN'T UNUSUAL FOR THE FIRST week of September in Georgia. Climbing into the high 90s, Professor Hall has decided to end the week by having a swim lesson. Luckily for me, I don't have a swimsuit!

Allegra can't swim, so both of us get to sit out in the sun and watch the other students splash around for two hours. There's no shade, either, so we're both baking. At least I'm not in a turtleneck like she is.

"Are you sure you're okay?" I ask her.

Sweat pours down her face, but she dabs her forehead with a towel. "Class is going to be over soon. You don't need to worry about me, Mary Alice."

Someone has to, with how pasty she looks. "I can't believe Professor Hall won't let us go inside. Heat stroke is a real threat; doesn't he know that?"

"For humans, maybe," Allegra says, though I doubt all shadowborn are immune. "We should try to tough it out."

Everyone is watching. I know that's what she wants to say.

She doesn't need to remind me — I already know from eating dinner with her every day this week. And sometimes lunch, if we have time to meet. I thought the staring and not-so-subtle gossiping would ease up, but it's only gotten worse since school started. Partially because of me. I'm sure the entire school has heard how much Lilly Hardwicke hates me, to the point of beating me up in public. At least the bruises have faded.

"You shouldn't push yourself."

"Now you're starting to sound like Rhys." She laughs. "He's always worrying about me. Archer, too, when we were dating. But now, even though he's looking over here, I don't think he's focused on me."

What?

My head swivels to the other side of the pool, where Ophelia, Archer, and a few other students are sitting near the diving board. Archer isn't staring blatantly like the gawkers in the cafeteria do at Allegra, but after a few seconds I notice him stealing a glance at us. As soon as our eyes meet, he looks away quickly and slides into the water.

We haven't talked since the night of Allegra's party, and it's not like I have his phone number to call him. I'm not sure I want him to look at me, especially with Allegra bringing it up. Does this go against girl code? To date your friend's ex?

If it is, Tasha and I have violated the code several times. Then again, dating each other's exes was usually a revenge thing and nothing serious. Not that Archer and I are serious. I don't know *what* we are. But I didn't kiss him just to lower his guard and then shove him into a shaving cream birthday cake in front of his friends. I've only done that twice, and both times were deserved.

Are Allegra and I even friends in the first place? You have to be *friends* to break girl code, right?

Allegra grins and says, "I think he likes you. He's just shy."

Shy or emotionally constipated, like Rhys?

"We're finished, anyway. Don't hold back on my account."

She says that, but I'm not sure if I can take it at face value. What if she regrets it and gets angry later?

"Why *did* you break up? If you don't mind me asking," I add quickly. Did that sound rude? I'm curious, but maybe I shouldn't have asked.

"It's fine. We broke up because..." Her face scrunches as she's trying to articulate herself. "Well, I guess we're just two different people. But it was nothing dramatic, like cheating or anything. Even if Archer has a different opinion on the matter. Are you interested in him?"

Yes, if I'm being completely honest with myself. But it's not exactly a priority for me right now, and it probably won't work out. After I kill Astaroth, I don't plan on sticking around.

"We're practically strangers," I reply honestly. "We haven't exactly gotten a chance to know each other. And he hasn't approached me in class."

"I told you, he's shy. Why don't you talk to him?"

"About what?"

"I don't know. The weather? The field trip next month to the Veil?" Allegra suggests. "He likes dogs."

That's very helpful information. I'll just strike up a conversation about beagles, then. Yeah, right.

"Seriously, you should go before class ends and you miss your opportunity."

"I'm good. I think I'll catch him after class," I lie. "Anyway, some kids are already leaving to change. Why don't we make our exit now?"

I have to meet Rhys for tutoring. If I'm late, he'll ask, "I suppose you believe you no longer need to study?" At first, I thought he was joking. He wasn't.

"Good plan." Allegra grabs her bag and we walk out, passing Archer on the way. Maybe Allegra was right—he hasn't spoken to me, but I haven't exactly made an effort to approach him, either. Should I say hi?

Or maybe I should punch myself in the face first?

What the heck is wrong with me? "Does he like me? Why hasn't he approached me?" What am I *thinking*? Have I completely lost my mind? I have other things to worry about! That talk with Allegra was just girl talk. I shouldn't act upon it, right?

"Hi." The word just slips out. I blame Allegra for getting in my head.

Archer turns, but then, so does the rest of the group he's sitting with. Ophelia glares at me, which is to be expected. She never liked me, but if looks could kill I'd be dead ten times over. I'm sure she blames me for Jenna's betrayal, which isn't even my fault.

However, it's not Ophelia who decides to stir up trouble today. I thought she would be the top dog at this school, but maybe not.

I don't have great luck with roommates, and it shows. Lilly Hardwicke seems to be the center of everyone's attention this time. If she knew I stabbed my last roommate in the neck, would she be so rude to me now?

Not that I'm thinking of stabbing Lilly in the neck. Unless she tries to kill me.

"Hi?" she mocks, mimicking my high-pitched Mary Alice drawl. "What are you looking at?"

Don't answer that, I tell myself. Nothing good can possibly come out of my mouth right now.

"Hi, Lilly," Allegra greets, stepping in for me. "We were just going. Class is almost over, and Professor Hall already left. Come on, Mary Alice."

"Not so fast. I wasn't talking to you, Allegra. I was talking to the human."

This gives me déjà vu.

"I know we started on the wrong foot," I begin, "but I hope we can get along, Lilly. We're roommates, after all."

And your bedroom door doesn't lock. Watch out for a bowl of warm water tonight, bitch.

Unsurprisingly, she doesn't accept my lackluster lies.

"Get along? With a murderer?"

"I think there's been a misunderstanding," I begin. I didn't kill Jessica Hardwicke, but I killed my previous roommate. In my defense, she was trying to sacrifice me to a demon. In *her* defense, I probably wasn't the best roommate. But that's neither here nor there.

As my *current* roommate, maybe Lilly should watch her neck around me. Just kidding. Hey, don't throw tomatoes over a little dark humor!

Okay, okay. It was a bad joke. Let's just move on.

She's glaring, I'm tongue-tied and regretting coming over here, and Allegra is trying to help me. I think.

"Well, we should get going," Allegra says, tugging my arm. "Bye, Lilly. And Ophelia, Archer, and Marshall."

Oh. I recognize that redhead—Marshall. Wasn't he on the cruise ship?

"You're looking a little hot, Allegra," he says, a cruel

smile playing on his face. It doesn't suit him at all, not when he looks like Raggedy Ann's twin brother. Then, maybe it *does* suit him since Raggedy Ann is haunted. "Why don't you cool off?"

Shadowborn speed is no joke. One minute, Allegra is right next to me. The next, she's in the pool. And she can't swim.

My body moves on its own, immediately throwing my bag on the concrete and diving in after her. I was a lifeguard one summer, but none of that training comes back to me at all. Even though she's struggling, somehow I manage to get my arm around her and drag her to the edge of the pool without getting hit by her flailing arms.

The other students are laughing of course, or at the very least smiling. Archer isn't, but he's not *helping* either. I know he and Allegra are in a weird place friendship-wise, but why is he just standing there watching? At least Ophelia looks somewhat perturbed, even if she's not doing anything, either.

"Are you okay?" I ask Allegra, helping her climb out of the water. She's shaking like a leaf, her green eyes wide. Of course she's not okay, but at least she doesn't need CPR. I skipped our first aid class in high school, so I don't know the Heimlich, CPR, or how to properly take a pulse... Luckily, Allegra doesn't need me to do any of those things.

I pull myself out of the pool, ringing out my hair. I probably look like a drowned rat. Whatever, I guess.

"Come on," I murmur to her, picking up my bag. "Let's go back to your room."

Allegra barely acknowledges me, her shoes squelching as she walks ahead. I can't think of anything to say; all I can

do is walk beside her. When we get to her dorm, she finally speaks.

"You can shower downstairs," she tells me, her voice shaking. "I'm…sorry, Mary Alice."

"You don't have anything to apologize for. They're the ones who should be sorry," I say, maybe a little too honestly. I soften my tone when I speak next, trying to sound gentle and to smother my anger. "Do you need help getting upstairs?"

"No," she refuses quickly. "I'm fine."

Somehow, I don't believe that. She trudges up the stairs, rubbing her arms. Her turtleneck is lighter today, and now that it's wet, I swear I can see something on her arm. Beneath the fabric. A scar? A tattoo?

"What happened?" Rhys' voice startles me from behind. I nearly trip over the couch.

"Don't sneak up on me," I chide, but my heart's not in it. "You scared the cr-crud out of me."

"Where is Allegra?"

"Upstairs. We took a swim in the pool today," I say dryly. "I think she's shaken."

Part of me expects him to run to her immediately, but he doesn't. Rhys' attention is turned entirely to me. At first, I think he's going to blame me for what happened. Instead, he asks, "And your condition?"

"Excuse me?"

"Are you also shaken?"

It takes a moment for me to think before answering. "If it were just me, I wouldn't be. But since Allegra can't swim, yes, I was surprised."

"I see."

I don't.

"Shower. We can delay our tutoring session by thirty minutes."

"What? Can we just cancel for today?" I sputter.

"No," he replies curtly, walking up the stairs. The discussion is over. How typical of him.

It only takes me ten minutes to finish up in the shower, but when I come out there's a fresh set of clothes waiting for me on the doorknob. The dress is new with tags, and not Allegra's style unless she were to wear it over a turtleneck or something.

It fits me perfectly, which makes me think Allegra is the one who put it here. She was there when Miss Lewis measured me; maybe she bought a spare dress and decided to give it to me. I'm not sure. All I know is, it's a lot better than getting back into wet clothes.

Rhys is sitting in the living room when I come out, books spread across the coffee table. A cup of tea steams on the end table, waiting for me.

"Allegra is resting upstairs, so we may use this space for our session," he tells me in Elvish. "Do you understand?"

I nod. "My understanding is at a higher level than my... out speak?"

"Your listening skills are superior to your speaking skills," Rhys replies. "Conversation practice. Tell me what happened."

In Elvish? "What is the word for pool? And red hair? And bitch?"

Rhys translates seamlessly. Even the last part.

"I said hello to Archer. He was standing with the bitch Lilly Hardwicke and their friends. The bitch got angry. Marshall, the kid with the Crayola red hair, pushed Alle-

gra," I say slowly, trying to translate the sentences in my head. "Sorry."

"You feel sorry toward Allegra?" Rhys guesses.

I nod. If it weren't for my stupidity, she wouldn't have been pushed in. Even though I'm still working out my feelings about our relationship, I don't want anything bad to happen to her. I want to kill our dad, and that will probably hurt her...

But in a perfect world, I want to be her friend. Not because it benefits me or I want to manipulate her, but because I genuinely do like her.

"What will you do now?" Rhys asks.

I switch to English, unable to explain myself very well in Elvish. "I'm torn. I don't want Lilly to get away with this. But what can I do? I have to wait until I can fight back. If Marshall had shoved *me* into the pool, there's no way I could have dodged him, much less resisted. If I do anything, they will retaliate ten times worse. But at the same time, as hard as I'm trying to train and get stronger, I feel like I've made zero progress."

"You are quite honest with me."

"Yeah, because when I lie, you tell me. 'You are lying,'" I mimic, deepening my voice. "And I think I'm a *great* liar. So that's your superpower, isn't it? Figuring out whether or not people are lying?"

"It is hardly a superpower. All elves can distinguish the truth from lies. Likewise, fae are incapable of lying. You would think that would make us allies," he says. "Instead, we have a history of bitter wars. That is where the Elvish equivalent for 'bitch' comes from. It roughly translates to 'filthy fairy scum.' Of course, in our language, the term is much stronger."

"War? In the Veil?"

He nods. "Land disputes, mostly, but those spiraled into deeper issues. We can discuss it later. Right now, it seems you have a visitor."

Just as he says that, the doorbell rings. "Are you sure you're not psychic, too?"

"You may get the door."

"Yeah, sure." I get up, draining my cup of tea and opening the front door. I'm not sure who I expect, but Archer Kinsey doesn't even make the list. And yet here he is, standing in front of me.

"I figured you'd be here," he says. "Can we talk?"

Chapter Fourteen

I'm 90% sure Rhys can hear us from the kitchen, and 120% sure he's judging the hell out of me.

"I just wanted to make sure you were okay," Archer begins, sitting next to me on the couch.

Oh really? Because he did *nothing* at the pool. I don't expect him to become a knight in shining armor or anything, but I can't imagine he's unaware Allegra can't swim. Even if he couldn't get to her in time, he could have at least stuck up for her in front of his friends. Which makes me wonder if this sort of thing happened while they were dating.

"I'm fine. Allegra's the one in bed," I say.

"When she fell in, I just...froze, I guess," he mutters, clasping his hands together.

"She didn't fall in," I correct, trying my best not to sound as pissed off as I am. "She was pushed."

"I'm sorry" is all he can think to say.

"You should apologize to *her* when she's feeling better."

"I will," he promises. "Are you sure you're alright?"

"Yes." I guess he *did* apologize, even if it was a little late.

And he sounds sorry. And it's not like *I* haven't frozen up in times of duress. Can I blame him for it?

If it were just this pool incident, maybe I could overlook it. But he also hasn't spoken to me since we kissed at Allegra's birthday party. I'm sure he's heard all the rumors flying around about me. He doesn't owe me anything, and we're not dating. We're not even friends. But being ignored stings, even if it shouldn't. We've been in class together; he's had chances to approach me.

Am I being too sensitive because of what happened in high school? Is that pathetic of me?

This situation is different. Back then, everyone knew me as the daughter of a drug dealer. Sure, plenty of guys wanted to screw around, but none of them wanted to be seen with me. I was their dirty secret. Here, it feels like Archer is treating me the same way. This time, because I'm human.

But maybe he's been busy, and I'm reading too much into things. I haven't approached him either. And I thought we wanted to get to know each other. It takes two to tango.

Mary Alice would be more understanding, I remind myself. She's supposed to be my nice, goody-goody character. But being nice doesn't mean she can't confront people, right? Just…gently.

How the heck am I supposed to gently confront him?

I try to make my voice as soft and passive as possible when I say, "I haven't seen you around lately."

There, that's not too bad, right? Gentle, nice…I'm not breaking character right now.

Archer nods. "I know. Since we're in different classes aside from combat… No, that's just an excuse. I wasn't sure how to approach you after the party. And then I heard

about the death of Jessica Hardwicke and things got worse. Not only the demon shadowborn are angry with you—other groups are calling you a murderer."

Great. "So where do we go from here?"

"Where do you *want* to go from here?"

Ah, returning my question with a question. Helpful.

Before I can answer, Rhys comes in with a refilled tray of tea and biscuits. And only one teacup. Is that his go-to way of getting rid of an unwanted guest?

"We only have the one," Rhys explains coolly, which is a blatant lie. I saw several cups in the kitchen earlier! I know Rhys and Archer don't exactly get along, but this is just petty. And extremely entertaining. "If you are done with your conversation, we have studying to do."

"You're tutoring her?" Archer guesses, his brow furrowed. "If you need help, Mary Alice, *I* can help you. In combat—"

"Mr. Abbott has personally requested that I take care of her tutoring," Rhys cuts him off, handing me the teacup and saucer. "There is no need for you to offer help as an excuse to feel her up."

I choke on my tea. Archer has to pat me on the back several times before glaring at Rhys. "I want to help because the other students might try to hurt her."

"And you will not step in to help in front of your peers?"

"That's not it at all," Archer insists. "Mary Alice—are you okay?"

Am I okay? I'm *better* than okay. Two handsome men are fighting over me. Well, this argument circles back to another girl and doesn't seem to be about me at all. But I'm still going to bask in the excitement, just for a little bit.

Okay, basking over.

"I need to study," I tell Archer, taking out my phone. "I got a new phone, though. Can we talk later?"

His eyes dart to Rhys, but finally, he relents. "Sure. I'll text you later."

For a second, I forget about all the stuff I'm dealing with right now. A guy I'm pretty sure I'm interested in says he'll text me later. It's nothing overtly sweet, but still, my heart flutters. This is the first time in weeks, maybe even months, I feel *normal.*

That feeling quickly fades when Rhys opens his mouth, speaking to me in Elvish. "Let us continue with the lesson."

MAR

The last thing I want to do Friday night is work. It's been a long first week of school, and all I have the energy to do is scuttle back to my basement and watch YouTube videos. For training purposes, I've been getting up early and going to the gym, so my entire body screams "no" as I walk across campus.

Alas, the world is cruel. I brought this on myself by asking Mathers for a job. It's not like I can skip out now, even if the only job available is another cleaning gig.

It's a night shift, at least. There's no one here at 9 PM, probably because most students have taken the ferry back to the mainland for the weekend. There's a nice little board-walk right on the coast, and I'm sure it looks great lit up at night.

Meanwhile, I'm stuck sweeping up stale croutons and what I hope are blue cheese crumbs. Dumping the tray of crap into the garbage, I roll it to the back door and wipe

down the counters. Most of the food stations are cleaned by the individuals who work there during the day, so there isn't too much to pick up. A forgotten jar here, a paper plate there. At least this doesn't require much brain power on my part and I can listen to my headphones. Another "gift" from Neil.

Who needs friends or a social life? I've got Guns N' Roses.

The band, of course. I'd fit much better into the kickass heroine category if I had a gun. But I have no money and no gun license. The supernatural police already have me on their list; I don't need human cops to be knocking at my (basement) door, too.

Just as I'm putting away the mop, the cafeteria lights go out. Are they on a timer?

"Hello?" I call out, like every dumb bitch in every horror movie ever. Of course, there's no answer.

Call me paranoid, but after everything that happened on the ship, can you blame me? I try to turn on the light, but the switch isn't working. I'm out of here.

Except the doors are locked from the outside. Great.

I grab an air freshener and slink away to the kitchen, keeping my back to the wall. Something on the far side of the room falls—something made of metal. In the kitchen, at one of the workstations, I fumble around for a knife block. It's a horrible weapon, I know, but it's all I've got. My only other option is spraying them with air freshener, so I think the knife is an upgrade.

The back door might be locked, but it's worth a shot. It's harder to find from the outside of the building, and you can only get to it from inside the kitchen.

Heavy footsteps approach me from behind. I slip

between a fridge and a cabinet, hoping they can't see me. I'm right. The person passes by, but I can make out the faint outline of a hooded robe.

Not this shit again. Haven't I already dealt with enough cultists for one series?

They pause a few steps away, their back turned. The perfect opportunity. I brandish my knife and move forward as quickly as I can, stabbing them quickly in the back. They grunt, shifting away before I can attack again.

Night vision goggles gleam in the sparse light, giving them an advantage. I dart away, through the kitchen doors to the other side of the room. An ear-shattering boom sounds off behind me, and I don't need to be a genius to recognize that my purser has a gun. Even if their movements are slower, the night vision goggles and long-range weapon put them at an advantage. I just need to find a way to escape or have them run out of bullets. Then...

Then what?

Think, Mar!

A fire alarm. There should be one by the wall if I can find it. Another shot rings out, and I circle around to throw off the cultist. Jumping over the counter, I make a mad dash toward the fire alarm. But I'm not fast enough.

Pain tears through my arm as a bullet grazes me. It's enough to make me trip, falling flat on my face. Fuck! Trying to ignore the pain, I roll to my feet. But I'm too late.

The assailant stands in front of me, the barrel of the gun aimed at my forehead. In a world of magic and monsters, I didn't think gun violence would be what finished me. I guess I stand corrected.

Clutching my arm, my eyes dart around the dark room,

but I can't think of another play here. I'm not faster than a shadowborn, and I'm sure as hell not faster than a bullet.

But before they can pull the trigger, the door behind me opens.

The assailant's head jerks up, as surprised as I am. Using the opportunity, I knock the gun away and sprint inside the open door. The light is blinding, but I slam the door behind me and run. It takes a moment for my eyes to adjust, but when they do, I stop.

I'm back in the white hallway.

"Mar," Todd Glass greets. At least, I think it's him. He looks different than when I saw him last, his hair so long it brushes his shoulders.

"Todd," I say, still trying to catch my breath. If he tries to kill me right now, I'm done for. But instead of strangling me or shooting me, or something of that nature, Todd sits down on the floor with his back against the wall. I do the same, clutching my injured arm. It's bleeding, but I'll live. Probably.

"It's September, right? And you've just finished your first week at Southeastern. Which means you've only met me once," Todd says, thinking aloud. "It's been, what, three months since you first boarded the SS *Athena* cruise ship?"

"Yeah," I answer, too tired for any sort of mind games. "Are you going to tell me what's going on now?"

"It's been three months since you first boarded the SS *Athena*," he repeats. "It's been a year for me."

"I don't understand."

"Take a minute. You'll get there."

Okay. I know that Todd said some pretty cryptic things last time. And he's suddenly appearing to me in this hallway,

which could just be a hyper-realistic delusion. Except the cultist saw the light from the hallway, too.

It's been three months for me. It's been a year for him — even though I saw him die. And he was autopsied. But the last time we met, I felt his heartbeat. Maybe he was brought back to life somehow? But that still wouldn't make it a year since he boarded the ship. Unless...

"Time travel." It's the only explanation I can think of, but it's not plausible. Time travel isn't supposed to be possible. But Mathers explained that blood magic makes the rules of regular magic fly out the window, right? Could Todd be a blood magic practitioner, even as a human?

"I knew you'd figure it out." Todd beams. "I boarded the ship when I was eighteen. I died at twenty. That night, when you found me covered in blood...that's when everything changed."

I remember. How could I forget? That was when I truly began to believe something dangerous was going on and I wanted to leave. Also, after that incident, Todd tried to kill me. If he boarded the ship at eighteen and died at twenty, does that mean he was time traveling while he was on the ship?

"I can't tell you everything. If I give you too much knowledge, it will create a paradox," he explains. "But I can tell you a little since you already figured it out. Do you remember the night you found me covered in blood?"

"Yeah." Penny and I were taking the elevator when Todd stumbled in. We thought he had been injured, but there were no wounds on him — just blood. He started acting strangely after that. "You told me there was a demon on Deck 10."

"It was the night of the full moon and your roommate

Penny attempted to kill me as a virgin sacrifice." He laughs. "I managed to escape and found myself here, in this hallway."

"Aren't you human?"

"Yes. I'm a human fated to die—and that makes me the perfect candidate for this."

I sigh. "You're going to have to slow down and explain this timeline to me. How are you alive right now?"

"I boarded the ship at age eighteen, right out of high school," he explains. "That night, when Penny tried to kill me, I freed myself and ended up here. In the Infinity Hallway. I've been here ever since, fixing the timeline and all the paradoxes you've created. They call us Time Agents. Haven't you noticed all those instances I rewound time to save your life? Ironically, I've saved you more times than I've tried to kill you. I even saved you from myself. You remember that night when I broke into your dorm and slit your throat? I'm the one who turned back time to give you a fighting chance. Or that time you were hit by a car, right before you flew to Florida? That was me, too. But I can't use that power very often, so if you could try not to die anymore, I'd appreciate it."

So I don't have the power of premonition? And *Todd* has been saving me? "Why would you do that?"

"You weren't fated to die. As cheesy as it sounds, destiny has other plans," he explains. "I'm fated to die, though. You saw it yourself. I'm human, so I was never meant to be in this hallway, let alone time travel. In a year, I'll eventually go insane and be placed back on the cruise ship. I think you know what happens from there."

I do. But hearing him speak about his own death in such a nonchalant way makes me almost sad for him. Even

if he tried to kill me. Well, *tries* to kill me. His future is my past.

As if he can read my mind, he says, "It's okay, Mar. If I'm fated to die, I can't do anything about it. At least now my life has meaning. Even if you're the only one who will ever know. It's been a full-time job, too. A lot of people want to kill you."

"I've noticed," I say dryly. "And I guess you can't come to my rescue every time."

"No. It doesn't work like that," he confirms. "Just because I'm helping you out doesn't mean you should rely on me to save you."

"So what now?"

Todd stands, helping me to my feet. "Your mission hasn't changed. Kill Astaroth. The closer you come to reaching that goal, the more you'll learn about yourself and your powers."

"I feel like you told me a lot, yet nothing at all. How is it that I have more questions for you now than when we started this conversation?"

"It will all become clearer with time. I promise. But for now, you have to go." He taps on one of the doors. "This will take you back to your dorm. It will be the following morning, so you're in for a verbal lashing."

"Wait, what?"

"You left the cafeteria a mess. And your roommates are pissed off because—well, you'll see."

Great. "I have to go back to *this* time? Can't I just skip to the part where I kill Astaroth?"

"No, you'll create a paradox."

"Okay, I got it." I reached for the handle, but before twisting the knob I pause. "Tell me something. Last time we

spoke, you brought up…Max. I don't understand why I'd tell you that. I don't even know if I can trust you. How do I know my future self told you that, instead of you going back in time and seeing for yourself?"

"I guess that's a valid question." Todd thinks about it for a few seconds. "There's nothing I can say now that would make you trust me. You're just going to have to take a risk. Not that I'm even asking you to do anything risky. And you know, if I wanted you dead I would have just done it."

"By that logic, Penny could have killed me at any point. We lived together." I cross my arms. "You're going to have to give me something more substantial."

"You killed Penny as Maria, and you think because of that, you feel no remorse," Todd says. "You only feel guilty because you don't feel bad at all. You think that, if you were emotionally well-adjusted, you should feel bad even if she was your enemy."

My mouth dries, because he's right. I don't feel bad, and I don't regret it. If I could go back in time, which is apparently possible, I'd do it again.

"It wasn't out of hatred. It was just to further your own survival," he continues. "But part of you is relieved she's dead, and that you were the one to kill her. It's one less person you have to look over your shoulder for. And you feel that way about others, too. Max. His parents. Some of your teachers and peers."

"Okay, I get it." I don't want to go down that route just yet. "I'll go back now. I should get this wound checked out, anyway."

"I'll see you soon, Mar. But try not to get killed in the meantime."

CHAPTER FIFTEEN

My head is throbbing by the time I get back to my dorm. I stumble through the doorway into the bathroom, exhaustion hitting me all at once. I need to clean my arm and take a nice, cold shower. Maybe that will wake me up from what is obviously a prolonged nightmare.

Time travel. Seriously? Was it that obvious to everyone else but me?

Now that I think back on what's happened so far, it makes sense. Well, it doesn't *make sense*, but it explains a lot. The premonitions I thought I was having were very realistic. I assumed they were merely visions because time travel is so out of left field.

But it's not as though *I* can time travel. Todd was the one turning back time for me. Which leads me back to square one: I'm helpless and at the mercy of creatures much stronger than me. If I don't have any sort of special power, then what the hell do I have going for me? I'm supposed to be the heroine of this story, but I have no good traits!

I can't fight; I can't even *run away* unscathed, as

evidenced by the injury on my arm from where the cultist's bullet grazed me. My intelligence is average at best, and my personality is the worst part about me. I'm not even pretty enough to be a damsel in distress.

Existential meltdown aside, Todd mentioned that I wasn't "supposed" to die, which is why he saved me in the past. Does that imply free will doesn't exist, that *fate* or determinism exists and I have no say in my own life? If that's true, then what's the point of this? Why am I struggling so hard if I can't control the outcome?

I can't deal with this right now. I need to wash up and figure out what time it is. Todd said the doorway would take me to the following morning, but he didn't tell me what time in the morning. Despite my splitting headache and lack of sleep, I need to meet with Rhys for tutoring. As much as I'd love to just give up, I can't risk my grades and the lives of my family based on a flimsy theory about fate.

I check my phone and jump in the shower, cleaning and dressing the wound on my arm. It's not bleeding anymore, thankfully.

My hair has gotten much longer since the start of the summer, so it takes me an extra five minutes to blow dry it. After I put on some concealer and eye makeup, I look presentable enough to go to the cafeteria for a cup of coffee. God knows I need it.

Slinging my bag over my shoulder, I take the basement stairs two at a time. The other girls should be in their rooms, sleeping in for the weekend. I don't have the patience to deal with Lilly or anyone else right now.

But when have I ever been so lucky?

. . .

Mary Alice

My roommates gather in the living room, huddled together on the couches. Three security officers stand around them, talking and taking notes. The moment Lilly sees me, she leaps over with a snarl. Is she a demon or a dog?

"Where have you been?" Lilly demands, nearly slamming the basement door shut on my hand. "You weren't in your room earlier. And we've been monitoring the house. How did you get back inside?"

"Miss Hardwicke, we'll be asking the questions," one of the security officers interrupts. "Miss Rochester, I presume? Please have a seat. We'd like to ask you a few questions."

"Yes, of course," I reply warily. Todd mentioned I would be in trouble, but couldn't he have given me more details? I can't refuse to speak to security, even though I want to. From the glares my three roommates are giving me, something bad must have happened. "What is this about?"

"Where were you last night?"

Uh oh. Never a fun question to be asked.

"I was cleaning the cafeteria as part-time work." I can't refute that, not with security footage of me going into the cafeteria and record of me signing up for that job. "Someone attacked me with a gun. I barely managed to get away, but everything after that is hazy. All I remember is waking up in my room this morning."

I peel back the bandage on my arm as proof. One security guard inspects it, jotting something down in her notebook. "Do you know who attacked you?"

"I didn't see their face. The lights went out and the assailant wore black robes."

"How did you defend yourself?"

Apparently my weapon of choice these days is a knife. But I probably shouldn't mention that, especially not in front of Lilly.

"I don't remember," I lie. "Everything happened so fast."

Silence fills the room for a beat, and the security officers communicate through meaningful glances. That doesn't bode well for me. Did I say something wrong? Are they suspecting me of...something?

"Your roommate, Natalie Grayson, was attacked last night with a knife while walking past the cafeteria. The knife was taken from one of the workstations," an officer says finally. "We have footage of you being the only one to enter the cafeteria. When we checked this morning, there were bullet holes and blood found at the scene. Perhaps you had an argument with someone?"

"Someone attacked me."

"We found a knife with your fingerprints on it. The same knife used to stab Natalie Grayson in the shoulder."

Maybe the cultist attacked Natalie after I escaped. But why would they do that? And how did they manage to get off the island? The ferry stops at 9 PM. Unless they're still here, watching me.

"Natalie was attacked outside the cafeteria. It was caught on camera." The security officer folds his hands in his lap. "Your fingerprints are on the knife, and you can be placed at the scene of the crime. You have a motive—the girls here report that you dislike Natalie."

"Natalie doesn't like *me*." And trust me, if I were to do anything to her, I wouldn't skip right to stabbing her in the shoulder. "I feel horrible about what happened, but I was attacked last night. I didn't shoot *myself*—I don't have a gun here. Even if I did, I would have had to shoot from

much closer, and the wound would be much worse than this."

The security officer shakes his head. "I think we're going to have to visit the security office for a few more questions, Miss Rochester."

"A FEW MORE QUESTIONS" MY ASS. I CAN'T BELIEVE I'VE been interrogated *again* for something that isn't my fault! Probably. I know with absolute certainty I'm not the one who stabbed Natalie, but I guess it could be my fault the cultist was here in the first place.

After two hours of the same questions, the security office lets me go when Provost Mathers shows up to bail me out. We wind up walking to his private office for a little chat, which can't mean anything good.

The office is like a miniature library, with books overflowing from the shelves surrounding the small room. I can barely see Mathers sitting at his desk, behind a wall of books stacked to the ceiling.

"You were attacked again," he says, settling in his big leather office chair. "Are you sure it was a cultist?"

"They were wearing the same black robes," I reply. "I think. It was very dark."

Provost Mathers nods. "How did you escape?"

Valid question. But I'm telling him the same lie I told the security officers. "I don't remember."

"Mary Alice, I—" He cuts himself off and takes a deep breath. I'm the one who's been up all night, but the dark bags under his eyes rival my own. "I know we've had a very rocky past, and it might be difficult for you to trust anyone.

But I hope you can trust me movin' forward. I'm on your side."

How many times have I heard that *before?*

"I don't remember," I insist. Even if I told him, what could he possibly do for me? Trust issues aside, telling anyone about Todd would open a can of worms I'm not ready to unleash. I can barely figure out what's going on myself.

"Mary Alice, please. I know your past might make it difficult—"

"I'll keep that in mind, Provost Mathers," I snap, perhaps a little bit too harshly for Mary Alice's character. "Thank you for helping me earlier. I really must be going now."

"If you think that is wise, Mary Alice. But there's only so much you can do on your own."

I spin around, trying to control my facial expression as I walk out of the office. Only so much I can do on my own? My past might make things difficult? What the fuck does he know?

Nothing.

Maybe it's just been a rough day, but I'm more pissed off than I should be. Storming back to my basement, I lock the door behind me and turn on the light. Moving to the bathroom, I splash cold water on my face and lean against the porcelain sink.

Mathers acts like he knows me. What—did he read a few things in my school file and suddenly think he could help me? Does he have a savior complex or something? My high school was filled with adults like him. They "just want to help" and are "always willing to listen." "Everything you say in here is confidential." Sure. And as soon as they cure

me of my personality defects, we're going to ride off on a unicorn farting rainbows into the sunset.

I just want to sink under my covers and sleep off my bad mood, but with everything that's happened, I need a game plan.

Someone attacked me last night. Again. How did they get on campus? They probably know where I live—that attack couldn't have been random.

I can't be as passive as I was on the ship. I need to make a plan on how to defend myself. But now that I'm out of a job and out of money, I will have to get creative.

*M*AR

I looked it up, and Elvish isn't a romance language. Which makes sense, considering the way Rhys reprimands me in his mother tongue is not even remotely romantic.

"How many times must we review this?" he asks, sounding as frustrated as I feel.

"At this point, can't we just move on? Or admit that you're not a very good teacher?" I suggest, which unsurprisingly grates on his nerves even more. I can't help myself. When I'm with Rhys, I naturally revert to Mar.

"I might not be the best teacher," he admits, "but you are an atrocious student."

"At least I'm not abysmal."

"You just proved my point."

"It's too early to learn, let alone speak a foreign language," I say, pointing to the starfish-shaped clock on the wall. We're in Allegra's living room as she sleeps upstairs, the lucky duck. To be fair, she hasn't been feeling well since

the pool incident. She hasn't been attending combat class either, but I don't blame her after what happened. "It's a weekend, too."

"I am speaking a foreign language. And it is 9:21 AM; this is not early."

"It's the weekend," I repeat. "The weekend, may I remind you, after a shitty week. I've been attacked, questioned, shoved in a pool, and now I'm on the security office's watch list based on a false accusation by a roommate with a grudge against me."

Not that the security office has called me back since yesterday. I haven't seen Natalie either, though maybe that's a good thing. She's recovering in a hospital on the mainland. I'd love to question her, or at least figure out why she's accusing me of stabbing her. Aside from finding my fingerprints on the knife, did the culprit *say* something to her? Was there any other indication that made her believe I was the one who attacked her?

"Do you understand their suspicions?" Rhys asks.

I shake my head. "Not in the least. In their eyes, I'm human—how could I compete with a shadowborn?"

"Perhaps that is why they are scared, and they lash out. They fear you are more powerful than humans are made to be. You must remember, most of these students live in communities where humans are rare," Rhys explains, leaning back in his chair. "They fear the unknown."

"That's so cliché."

"You should tell them so."

"I don't appreciate the sarcasm. Nor the fact that you don't change your tone of voice when being sarcastic."

"English is my second language," he says, but he knows very well what he's doing. "I thought you would be someone

who appreciates sarcasm, given you seem to be so well-versed in it."

"Me, sarcastic? Never," I joke. "How do you relay sarcasm in Elvish? Now that's a lesson I want to learn."

"Ah, but it is not one I am willing to teach. I fear you will use what you learn for nefarious purposes and end up getting yourself killed." He's not smiling, but there's something in his eyes that tells me he wants to. Or maybe I'm reading into it, again. "Enough of this sidetracking. If you wish to converse, we should switch languages."

"No way. You're just going to make fun of me again."

"I promise I will not. Not aloud, anyway."

"That makes it *so* much better."

"You are being sarcastic again," he says, this time in Elvish.

It's a beautiful language, and admittedly, Rhys sounds great speaking it. His accented English is nice to listen to, but speaking his native language, he's more comfortable.

The good thing about Elvish is the grammar structure is similar to English, minus all the exceptions. But pronunciation is difficult, with sounds that don't exist in English and a thirty-letter alphabet. Rhys says my pronunciation after a month is "passable" at best, but we haven't focused on anything else.

"Try writing your name," he tells me, tapping on my open notebook.

"Which one?" I ask.

He doesn't reply, staring at me expectantly. I just write "Mar" in Elvish script, mostly because it's the shortest moniker I have. And I haven't exactly explained the other characters yet to Rhys. He only knows me as Mar, Mary Alice, and presumably Maria.

Rhys writes over the name in red ink, straightening the lines and smoothing the awkward curves until the spacing looks more legible. "Try again."

He ends up making me fill half the notebook with words, copying them while saying them aloud. My only reprieve is when Allegra wakes up, and Rhys goes to attend to her. She rings a bell to summon him. I thought she'd at least text.

"I do not have a phone," Rhys explains, completely unprompted.

"Stop reading my mind," I retort. "It's freaky."

"Your thoughts are written all over your face."

I have another response locked and loaded, but the bell from upstairs rings again. "I guess that's my cue to leave. I'll see you later."

Rhys doesn't look back before heading upstairs to attend to Allegra, so I see myself out. Without a car, I'm stuck on campus. Without a television or laptop in my room, I'm stuck in hell. At least I have a phone, although Neil is likely monitoring it.

The phone buzzes on cue—a call from Archer. I wait two rings before picking it up.

MARY ALICE

"Hello?"

"Mary Alice. What are you doing tonight?" Archer asks.

"I don't have plans." Except maybe searching Natalie's room, but I'll need to wait until the other girls are out of the house for a while. "What's up?"

"There's a fair in town. The last one of the summer," he adds. "I was wondering if you'd like to go with me."

Like a date? Seriously? Honestly, I didn't think he'd

speak to me after where we left off earlier this week. My anger from the pool incident has somewhat faded with his apology, and I *could* use some fun in my life to balance all the crap.

"What kind of fair?" I ask.

"There will be booths with games, rides, food... A funhouse. It might be a nice break from everything that's happening."

He's right. It might be an opportunity to get to know each other, without all the cult and magic stuff getting in the way.

"We could take the ferry this evening," he offers. "It's walking distance from the port. Ten minutes, max."

"That sounds like fun." Then, before I can change my mind, I say, "It's a date."

CHAPTER SIXTEEN

Dating has never been my strong suit. Kissing, sure. Sex, no problem! Flirting is fine. But a date? I've never been on one.

Once, a guy asked me out as a joke. I showed up at the agreed-upon diner and he didn't. Photos were taken, cake was flung, and somehow I'm the only one who ended up with an in-school suspension. But the pranksters ended up with food poisoning, so I can't say it was a horrible memory. I didn't poison them, just to clarify—that was just Lady Karma doing me a solid.

Given my lack of experience, the only thing I have to reference are the cheesy romance movies Tasha and Isabelle like to watch. I always kicked up a fuss about it, especially around the holidays, but now I miss it. You don't know what you have until it's gone, right?

No. Not gone. Tasha and Isabelle... We'll definitely watch some bad rom-coms together next year. And next Thanksgiving, I'll be home for Luke's famous turkey and stuffing, and David's questionable mac and cheese. Though,

to be fair, the kid is only twelve. He'll be thirteen this December and I'll miss it. I'll miss Tasha's parents' death anniversary, too. It will be fourteen years this year. Not that she needs me around for that anymore. But I still wish I could be there for her. I'm just a stranger to her now.

The thought hurts, so I brush it aside and take a deep breath. Right now, I am Mary Alice. And I am going on my first date with Archer. Archer, who is hot and who I may or may not have feelings for. Hopefully this date will clear things up. We've never had a chance to talk about ourselves, what with all the cult shenanigans going on.

Fixing up my hair, I take a look in the mirror. Concealer hides my stress pimples and dark circles, while plumping gloss stings my thin lips. I choose a plain outfit and comfortable white sneakers to go along with the girl-next-door look. And, most importantly, I haven't eaten much today. My body is ready for fried, artery-clogging fair food.

I walk down to the docks and meet Archer by the ferry. He's already there waiting for me, wearing a blue polo that makes his eyes lean more toward blue than gray.

"Mary Alice." He smiles at me, which lights up his whole face. It's a stark contrast to his usual self, so serious and stone-faced. I'm not ashamed to say that my heart flutters, just a little bit. "How is your arm?"

"Oh, you heard?" I laugh awkwardly. "I'm fine."

"You must be shaken. I heard about what happened from Ophelia. Lilly is—" He cuts himself off. "Sorry. I didn't mean to bring up something negative."

"No, no. I'm just trying to keep my head afloat." And attached to my body. "So, you went to this summer festival last year, right? What kind of attractions do they have?"

Archer takes my hand, helping me up the steps to board

the boat. I hate to say it, but I'm kind of disappointed when he releases me.

"They have a lot of different things. We can spend time doing whatever you want," he adds. "Not a lot of students will be there, so you don't have to worry about running into anyone. I guess they think these kinds of things are above them."

"You don't think like that, though."

He shakes his head. "I never got to go to fun attractions like this as a kid."

I didn't, either. At least, not as a kid. Most foster homes I was placed in didn't exactly want to spend money or time on "unnecessary" expenses. But I can't say that; Mary Alice was never in a foster home.

"Your parents didn't take you?" I press, keeping the spotlight on him.

"No. My family isn't exactly...normal. A lot of shadow-born families aren't," he explains. "Truebloods have long lifespans and age slowly, so in the mortal realm, they tend to get married multiple times and have different sets of families. Some have multiple family units at the same time, while others will wait a century or so. My grandfather had two sons with two different women: my father, born to his legal wife, and a child with a mistress. You met my uncle last month."

Yes—Chancellor Kinsey, the head of Northeastern College in New York, another magic school for shadow-born. He was British and kind of hot, though apparently good looks run in the family. I kissed his son, Ethan, in exchange for help with altering the results of the Blood Chalice. The memory makes me feel slightly guilty, even though it shouldn't. Archer and I weren't together then, and

we're not now. But if *he* kissed another girl, I think I would feel jealous. Does that mean I like him? Or is it a sign that I'm a toxic person? Both?

"Is your grandfather still married to your grandmother?" I ask.

Archer shakes his head as the ferry stops, allowing us to deboard. "My grandmother died during childbirth. Shadow-born births are always high-risk for humans. That's generally why interspecies relationships are discouraged."

He clams up, and the obvious occurs to me: he still thinks I'm human. Does that mean he's not taking me seriously because of it? Or does he like me so much that it doesn't matter?

Don't be so full of yourself. Of course he doesn't like you, I think. *He likes Mary Alice.*

The thought kind of pisses me off. He likes Mary Alice? Of course he does! I've only ever been Mary Alice around him. Except for when I stabbed Penny in the neck, I guess. That was all Maria, and I'm sure it didn't leave the best impression. But the idea that he likes Mary Alice rubs me the wrong way. Because, as I've been telling myself this whole time, I'm not Mary Alice. Not really.

But if I'm not Mary Alice, he probably won't like me at all. That's not meant to sound self-deprecating or anything, but I realize it kind of does. What I mean is, if I told him everything, would he still have asked me on a date today?

It's no use worrying about it. What can I tell him — where would I even start? Eventually, we'd get around to the fact that I'm Neil's biological daughter. And then Neil would be pissed if he found out and probably do something unspeakable to my family. I don't even want to think about it.

The smart thing would probably be to break things off before they blossom into something complicated. I know that. But I agreed to go out with him anyway.

"Is that why people don't like my acceptance into Southeastern?" I ask. The ferry stops and we deboard onto the boardwalk, where Archer takes my hand again.

"Shadowborn care about bloodlines," he confirms. "Stronger bloodlines mean more power. Once the bloodline dilutes, nothing can be done. So...in a way, mating with humans is looked down upon. It's seen as dirtying the bloodline."

"Ouch."

"My father always told me to marry a shadowborn or a trueblood. Anyone 'less,' like a magician or a psychic, would result in weaker offspring. Arranged marriages are common because of this." He grimaces. "I didn't think too much about it. And then I met you."

The first time we met was at the pool on the cruise ship, when Ophelia was chewing me and Penny out for bumping into her. The second time, I saw him naked. This isn't the direction I thought he was going with this conversation. "I'm sure you didn't have the best first impression of me."

"I was mistaken," he admits. "What was your first impression of me?"

"I was a little intimidated." *By how hot you are.* But I could never admit that aloud.

"Is that so?" he muses. "I thought you were a peeping tom."

"I remember." It's not a pleasant memory. Actually, it pissed me off. When did my opinion of him change? When did his? That, I suppose, is a safe question to ask. "When did you change your mind about me?"

"I don't know," he says, but he's not a very good liar. Strike that as another difference between us. Though, these days, I wonder if my lying abilities are getting worse. It seems like the amount of times I act out of character is increasing lately. Even the way I talk to myself in my head...

Well, I'll let this lie go. I'd be a major hypocrite if I didn't. Maybe he's too embarrassed to tell me.

The entrance of the fair has a big balloon arch. Archer buys us passes at the ticket booth, and I let him because I don't have a choice. I'm not swimming with cash; I don't even have a wallet. What would I put in it? Lint? My driver's license was cut up over the summer and I never got it replaced.

"Let's take a lap," Archer suggests. He doesn't move to hold my hand again, I notice. "If you see anything interesting, we can stop."

"Alright."

Everything looks interesting. Not that I've never been to a fair like this. Two years ago, we went on a family trip because David begged us. He ended up vomiting on one of the rides, cutting the outing short. We spent the whole car ride trying to cheer him up; he was devastated. Tash and I took it upon ourselves to make him funnel cake at home, but things...let's just say it didn't turn out too well. I learned that you shouldn't throw water on an oil fire.

I want to tell Archer *that* story, too, but I can't for obvious reasons. Thankfully, he speaks first to fill the awkward silence settling upon us.

"I guess this screwed up your college plans," he begins. "Coming here and all."

It screwed up my *life* plans. "It didn't, but it certainly

hasn't been very easy," I say honestly. "I still have questions from the summer that were never explained. Jenna and the fake provost...and the cult as a whole. And now, the death of Jessica Hardwicke and Natalie's attack."

"Those were coincidences," Archer says, but it's not convincing at all. "You could just have horrible luck."

Yeah, I know I do. "I want everything to work out for the rest of the semester, but it doesn't feel like it will. I have this feeling of impending doom that just won't go away."

But maybe that's the pessimist in me.

Okay, here's a dose of optimism: Whatever life throws at me next, I'll try to prepare myself. Even if I fall, I'll do a tuck and roll to avoid breaking my neck. Is that optimistic enough?

"Oh! Look!" I exclaim, pointing ahead. "Salt and vinegar fries!"

Our tickets came with a food stall coupon, and I know exactly what I'm spending mine on. Archer saves us a table while I get an order fresh from the frier. What's that expression? "Potatoes are a girl's best friend?"

"This is the happiest I think I've ever seen you," Archer comments as I bring the plate to the table. "Do you like fries that much?"

More than he could ever know. "Do you want some?"

"I don't eat fried food."

I nearly drop the fry on the table. "What? Like you've never eaten it, or you just don't like it?"

"Never eaten it. I've always been on a strict diet for training." He shrugs. "It's not that healthy for you, anyway."

Yeah, obviously! That's not the point.

"Are you sure you don't want any food?" There are plenty of stalls with different options, not all of them fried.

Just…most of them. "Well, maybe it's for the best if we're going to go on rides."

"What kind of rides do you enjoy?"

"Roller coasters can be fun. And the Viking ship. Do you have a preference?"

He shakes his head. "I've never been on any sort of ride. You can choose—I trust you."

He does? That's news to me. Maybe he just means he trusts I'll choose a fun ride? But the way he looks at me leads me to believe he trusts me in general.

Alarms blare in my head and my instinct is to run away immediately. Why does he trust me? He barely knows me and I've been lying to him since we met. I want to tell him that, to show him what a big mistake it is putting any faith in me. I'm only going to disappoint him.

But I swallow those feelings, because I'm a terrible and selfish person. I want him to like me. Not Mary Alice, but *me*.

I wouldn't even know where to begin explaining myself. So instead of coming clean or expressing how I feel, I muster a smile and say, "Alright. We'll go on the roller-coaster first."

IT TURNS OUT SHADOWBORN TRAINING DOESN'T PREPARE them for amusement park rides. Especially not ones that go fast, high, and backward. I'm glad I didn't make Archer eat anything beforehand because he looks pretty green. We have to take a break, sitting on a bench with his head in my lap. It would be a lot more romantic if I wasn't afraid of him throwing up on me.

"Sorry," he mumbles again.

"It's fine. I should have warned you," I reply, brushing his hair out of his eyes. "Maybe we take a break from rides. Are you feeling a bit better?"

"My head stopped spinning."

"That's a good sign," I encourage. "Look, why don't we go on the Ferris wheel? You can sit, and I bet the view is amazing."

"That looks like a metal death trap."

No kidding—that's what makes it fun!

He sits up slowly, taking me by the hand. There's not a long line for the Ferris wheel, so we don't have to share the car with anyone else. Archer sits across from me, glancing out the window as we slowly begin to rise.

"It's getting late. You can see all the lights from here," he says. "But we should probably head back to campus soon, before the ferry stops for the night."

"Yeah. Time passed faster than I realized," I confess. "Um, can I ask you something?"

"You're not going to ask me to go on another roller coaster, right?"

"No, no," I say with a laugh. "I... Look, I know we talked about it already, but I want to circle back to the topic. You said that you are encouraged to be with a shadowborn or a trueblood. But if that's the case, then why are you here? With me?"

Archer has to think about his answer before responding. "You asked me before when my feelings for you changed. I said I don't know, but that was a lie. I started having feelings for you when you kissed me, on the ship."

That wasn't what I was expecting. "You like me because I'm a good kisser?"

"You took initiative. I thought of you as weak before. And yeah, a peeping tom. Helpless, needy, in way over your head…"

Yeah, get to the point.

"But when you kissed me, I thought it was brave. My attitude toward you began to shift. Even though it's confusing now—I don't even know that much about you—part of me wants to protect you. And I guess that's its own kind of magic."

I'm not sure what to make of that confession. Should I be flattered? Or…

"Sorry. I don't think I phrased that correctly," he says.

"Do you think the spell would be broken," I ask slowly, "if I kiss you again?"

A smile spreads across Archer's face, and he lets out a relieved laugh. "I don't know. Do you want to try and find out?"

"We're not at the top of the Ferris wheel," I note. "It's customary to kiss at the top. Unofficial rules."

"Well, I won't tell if you won't."

So, with that, I lean forward and kiss him again.

CHAPTER SEVENTEEN
MAR

R hys might not have known about my date with Archer, but he senses my happiness before our tutoring session on Monday. And, being Rhys, he feels the need to crush said happiness.

"Get up," he barks in Elvish. He's never been *this* strict with me. Usually he's a cold and unfeeling block of ice. Now, he's running hotter than ever. His attitude, not his appearance. I feel the need to clarify that.

Somehow he's not breaking a sweat, which is either a testament to his physical prowess or my lack thereof. He always manages to look perfect and neat in slacks and a white button-down. Even after our sparring sessions, he smells like fresh laundry. Not that I sniff him. I merely observe his scent, compared to my own sweaty, smelly body. Thankfully, no one else is here to witness that. The gymnasium is empty.

"You hit me in the throat," I manage, massaging my neck. I stay seated on the mat, because he'll only knock me down again if I try to rise.

To be fair, this beating is nothing compared to what Lilly or Nic did to me. Rhys understands what "sparring" means and can fight without seriously injuring me. Lilly and Nic could use a few pointers in that regard.

Rhys uses force, don't get me wrong—but he hasn't left a mark. I suppose he's being kind. That, or my Stockholm syndrome is getting worse. Because that's exactly the kind of mental crap I need to deal with, on top of everything else.

"Your opponents will do much worse," Rhys tells me, but he bends down on one knee to examine me anyway. Slapping my hands away, he brushes hair from my shoulders and tilts my chin up. "You are overdramatic."

"You karate chopped my neck," I reply in English, mostly because I don't know how to say "karate chop" in Elvish.

"You did not block my hand."

"You were coming at me at fifty miles per hour!" Okay, maybe I *am* overdramatic.

"Your reflexes are sharpening, but your skills do not surpass that of a normal human's." I can't tell if he's complimenting me or insulting me. If I had to guess, it's the latter. "At least your Elvish listening comprehension is improving."

Yeah, we speak in Elvish every weekday during these training sessions. Rhys also gives me more homework than my normal college classes, sending me audio recordings and videos to watch on my phone. It's not like I have anything better to do.

"Your speaking skills are still—"

"Abysmal? Yeah, I got it."

"I was going to say 'improving' but I suppose 'abysmal' works, too."

"Do you give all your students a hard time, or is it just me?"

Rhys' eyes meet mine. "It is just you."

I shouldn't have asked.

I know it sounds insane, but sometimes, I have a feeling that Rhys is looking at me…*differently*. Which is weird, because most of the time I feel like he only barely tolerates me. And sometimes I wonder if he hates me.

It wouldn't be a stretch. I'm sure he's not thrilled to be tutoring me. It's double the work, and probably much more involved than watching over Allegra.

Allegra and I eat together most days, and Rhys joins us. For her sake, not mine. He never eats *with* us. He refuses to speak to me or even look at me when Allegra is around. If I ask him something, he'll only give a curt reply and find some excuse to leave.

Despite this, when we're alone, it's kind of a relief. I don't bother with the characters, and he doesn't make any snide comments about it. Strange, because it's not like I feel *safe* with him or I trust him. I'm just naturally…Mar.

And I can't tell whether that's a bad thing or a good thing. We're not allies, but it doesn't feel like he's my enemy, either.

"We will go again," Rhys says. He doesn't offer me a hand. In fact, he makes a point *not* to touch me unless we're sparring. And by "touch" I mean "hit." At least he makes it educational by criticizing my form and yelling out orders.

"I need a break. We've been doing this for how long, now?" I ask.

He checks the clock. "Fifteen minutes."

"That's fourteen minutes too long."

To my surprise, Rhys doesn't say anything, which I take

as a silent agreement. I drag myself over to the bleachers and sit, grabbing a water bottle he brought for me.

"Neil will be coming in October to see how you are doing," Rhys mentions casually.

"Why? Don't you just give him reports?"

Thank God Rhys switches to English, because otherwise I wouldn't understand him. "Halloween is an important holiday. Most magical colleges make it their 'homecoming' week and have festivities for students and their families. Midterms are held the third week of October, so students enjoy the celebration after testing is complete. Neil and his wife will be attending. They will be staying in a hotel nearby, but I imagine he intends to speak with your teachers and ensure that everything is going well."

Fantastic. This is just what I need—more pressure from Neil. At least I'm doing well in my classes so far. Aside from combat, the coursework is easy and interesting.

The door swings open on the other side of the gymnasium, and Rhys immediately tenses when he sees who it is.

"My, aren't you two *close*," Nic teases, waltzing in like he owns the place. Like he owns me, too. "Allegra isn't enough for you?"

"Your 'jokes' are humorless and tasteless as usual," Rhys replies coolly. Credit where credit is due: Nic is annoying as hell, but he doesn't manage to break Rhys' stony expression. "I told you that our tutoring sessions are closed. You are not to interfere."

"Uncle Neil wants to know how she's doing. Particularly when it comes to Astaroth."

"I'm working on it," I say, which isn't technically a lie. Between tutoring with Rhys, going to the gym, studying for

classes, and having miniature mental meltdowns every morning, I don't have much time to focus on killing Astaroth. I'm still in phase one of my plan to learn more about him with Provost Mathers during our Independent Study class.

But because of the blood magic he practiced, so much information about Astaroth is restricted. I'm stuck reading up on demonology and learning trueblood history at the moment.

"Work harder. Uncle Neil didn't give you a time limit, but if you have any hope of stopping Astaroth, it would be now. Deal with the cult later—kill him while he's weak," Nic replies.

"That would be a suicide mission." I can barely fight a shadowborn, much less Astaroth at this point. "Look, I'm trying to train—"

"Does it look like I care how you get it done, Maria?" he mocks. "Do you need a little reminder of what could happen if you fail?"

He takes out his phone with a wicked smile. A moment later, my own phone buzzes. I reach for it with shaking hands, but before I can open the message, Rhys snatches it from me.

"He is clearly baiting you." Rhys deletes the message and blocks Nic's contact before handing the phone back to me. "I am giving reports to Neil. You should be less concerned with her progress and more concerned with your own tasks. Or do *you* need a reminder?"

Nic grins. "You've gotten soft. You know she's still Neil's daughter, even if she's a bastard."

"I am aware of who she is. I do not think you are. She is not a toy, and she is certainly not yours," Rhys says placidly.

"Neil has a bargain with her. Getting in the way of that will only make him angry. Family ties or not."

"You forget yourself, elf."

"Are you two going to fight?" I blurt.

"Oh?" Nic laughs. "You wanna see us fight? Unfortunately, that won't be happening anytime soon. Maybe someday. Today, I came to deliver a message. You've been removed as a suspect in both Jessica Hardwicke's murder and your roommate's attack. Congratulations."

Honestly, I kind of forgot about that. Whoops. This is what happens when shit constantly gets flung at you.

"Why?" I ask. "What new evidence came through?"

"There's no evidence tying you to the murder," Nic explains. "But there's also nothing tying you to the attack on Natalie other than circumstantial evidence. There's no video footage of you leaving the cafeteria, either. So how did you show up in your dorm the next day? The tape hasn't been tampered with, and teleportation magic isn't possible within the same realm."

"I don't remember," I lie.

Nic only shrugs. "Well, it's none of my business. Kill whoever you want, as long as you don't get caught. Neil doesn't care, but he won't cover for you. Be more careful next time, Maria."

"There won't be a next time." But even as I say it, I know it's probably not true.

And Nic smiles, because he knows it, too.

I FLEX MY FINGERS, HOPING THAT MAKES A DIFFERENCE IN making the spell work. Because that's clearly why it hasn't

worked the last thirty times I tried—my fingers weren't loose enough.

Library books litter the basement floor as I sit cross-legged on the thin woven carpet, trying my hand at a rudimentary potion. It's a stain removal potion, basic but fast-acting, and the perfect way to test my spellcasting skills. Or lack thereof.

I've been learning about magic in class, but since I'm "human" I haven't gotten a chance to practice with the other students. This morning, I decided to try it. Maybe this is the key to defeating Astaroth—a cleaning potion.

If anything, the stain has gotten worse. And I'm going to run out of mugwort soon.

I chose the spell because all the ingredients were freely available in the greenhouse on campus: rose petals, mugwort, and thyme. I'll never get the smell off my hands. And I've ruined this shirt.

But I couldn't think of any other way to test if I can use magic. I'm not as strong as other shadowborn, and I don't have any special powers, so I figured maybe I'm gifted in spellcraft. Nope. Potion-making and spellcasting are two more skills I can add to the ever-growing list of things I suck at.

I've learned more about spells in class, so I know *how* they work. They require three things: magic, intention, and an anchor. An anchor is a physical object the magic attaches itself to; it can be a mixture of liquids, herbs crushed into powder, or even an object like a pencil. In this case, it's a concoction of smelly plants.

I try to follow the rules in the spell book one last time, crushing the ingredients together in a bowl while imagining

a clean shirt. But I don't feel tingly like the book says I should.

Spreading the mixture over the stain, I try again to imbue my intention and magic into the potion and wiggle my fingers over it. The book doesn't say to do this, but I figure it can't hurt.

When I wash the shirt in the bathroom sink, the result is the same. Stain city.

Sighing, I throw the shirt in the washing machine and begin cleaning up. I'm supposed to meet Allegra for dinner in thirty minutes, anyway.

I just don't know what I'm doing wrong, and more importantly, why I'm not like other shadowborn. I'm Neil's daughter, so I should have the same strength as any other demon shadowborn. Lilly and Nic are in a completely different league.

Super healing is useful, sure, but I'd rather be strong enough to avoid the beatings altogether. Just because I can heal doesn't mean I don't feel pain.

I want to kill Astaroth, to get this whole thing over with, but I'm still frustratingly stuck in the same position I was at the start of the semester.

Washing my hands in the bathroom sink, I lock eyes with my reflection. My dark circles have somehow gotten worse over the past week, thanks to the nightmares. I've also been getting up early every morning, studying in the library or weight training in the gym. I'm starting to see more progress when it comes to strength, but compared to my peers it doesn't feel like enough.

I don't feel like enough. And that's really the theme of my life, isn't it? Not being enough for anyone, even myself.

CHAPTER EIGHTEEN
MARY ALICE

Nothing I've learned so far prepares me for the Veil. I've been so focused on magic studies and theories, I haven't gotten a chance to see what it looks like in photos.

Maybe if Allegra came with me, I'd be more gung-ho about the whole situation. But an overnight field trip is too much for her to handle. Mentally, it's a lot for me, too. Without Allegra, I'm the one getting stared at and whispered about. I'm used to it, but in the past I had Tasha. In my combat class, I'm alone. Archer doesn't approach me, too preoccupied with his other friends to pay me any attention. Or maybe he just doesn't see me in the front of the gym.

Professor Hall takes attendance before we depart, checking off our names on his phone. When he's finished, he blows his whistle and unsheathes a sword from his belt.

I thought traveling to the Veil would be like walking through a doorway. I've heard of rifts in my classes, but this is my first time seeing one. I have to say, it's disappointing. Instead of "rift," they should have named it "rip."

Hall slices the sword through the air. After returning it to his belt, he reaches out and pulls open a portal with his bare hands from seemingly nothing. It looks like tearing fabric, revealing a blurred mirror suspended above the ground. The surface ripples like water.

I'm first in line, shoving my fears aside and stepping through the rift. It's not wet, but the moment I pass through, the wind blows back my hair and a rotting smell fills my nostrils. Did a fish die in here or something?

When my eyes adjust to my new surroundings, I have a difficult time hiding my utter disappointment. The Veil isn't mystical at all—I can barely tell I'm in another world. The sky is overcast with dark rain clouds, and the entire portside town is drenched in monotone.

"Move it," Lilly mutters, shoving past me. In her defense, I'm standing right in front of the other side of the rift. I shuffle to the side and take everything in, smell included.

Even the ocean looks grey, though I can't tell if it's clouds or pollution. Empty bottles and trash litter the shore-line, and not a single person is on the beach.

"Alright, students. The hotel is the Sunsetter, right there!" Professor Hall points to a building, which looks like it could fall apart at a moment's notice. Great. You know, before this trip I was worried I would be eaten by a dragon. Now I have to worry about dying in a hotel collapse. "Get some rest and explore the town. We'll meet back here at eight tonight, after dinner, for the Nightmare tour."

Oh, a Nightmare tour. How very appropriate for the start of October.

My classmates disperse, but I'm not sure where to go. I have a feeling that exploration will lead to getting eaten. I

can't even say I feel safe from the cultists here, since some could very well be truebloods and shadowborn. I'd rather not be in an isolated space, but before I can make up my mind about where to go, the rest of the class—Professor Hall included—have wandered elsewhere.

You know, I thought this would be more like Middle Earth or something. I guess vampires and werewolves are more "urban fantasy," but Rhys is an elf, and I know that dragons and stuff exist, too. I figured the Veil would be more...high fantasy-esque. Instead, it looks like a ghost town. Maybe literally—I have no idea if ghosts are real. Probably something to ask Mathers. Then again, zombies exist, albeit through witchcraft and not some sci-fi experiment gone wrong...

Or maybe I'm overthinking things. Either way, this town is kind of balls. Full offense intended. The drugstore is boarded up and the shops are empty. The only place that's open—though it doesn't look like it from the outside—is a tavern with a hole in the roof and dirt-speckled windows.

"Hey," Archer says, tapping my shoulder. I nearly jump out of my skin. "Whoa. I didn't mean to startle you."

"Sorry. I guess I'm just a bit nervous." Or, more accurately, completely taken aback by what a shithole the Veil is. No wonder the truebloods came to the mortal realm. "I'm not sure where to go."

"The town is run down," Archer agrees, which makes me breathe a sigh of relief. So I'm *not* going crazy. "A lot of towns in the Veil are. But there are some nice spots, too. Should we take a walk?"

He's gesturing to the woods, and I'm not sure if it's the past trauma or my general distrust of others, but I don't think I should go with him alone.

It's stupid. We went to the summer fair together, and he didn't try to kill me. He's helped me countless times, and I don't think he's a cultist. But when he offers to take me somewhere secluded, for some reason I flash back to what Nic told me at the Abbotts' house. He can do whatever he wants to me, and no one would care.

It's not a new concept. I've lived most of my life knowing that—because humans are cruel and selfish, even to kids. Especially to kids. I thought, after turning eighteen, I would finally graduate from being a powerless child. But in many ways, things haven't changed. It doesn't matter that I'm an adult now; I'm still physically weaker than those around me. No one has my back, and as much as I'd love to spew crap like "there are other ways to be strong," I don't think being a good kisser will get me out of being sacrificed by a cult.

So yeah. I'm a little bit apprehensive.

"Archer—"

"It's just a little bit further," he insists, pulling my hand.

I let him guide me through the trees, despite my apprehension. A short walk leads us to a clearing with a shallow pond. The water is sparkling and clear, unlike the ocean water in this realm. We sit on two large rocks near the water's edge. While the trees around us are bare and grey, plants sprout between the gravel and under the water's surface.

"We came here last year for a school trip," Archer explains, picking up a stone to skip across the water. "It's quiet here, despite being so close to the forest's edge. That's why I like it. It's easy to get back and forth, but it's still private."

"You didn't want to go to the tavern or hang out with your friends?" I ask, keeping my eyes trained on the pond.

"Not particularly." He doesn't elaborate, and I'm not going to press him on his social circle. Even if I find the inclusion of Ophelia, Lilly, and Marshall questionable at best. "I'd rather be here, with you."

"I'm afraid I'm not very entertaining," I say with a laugh.

"That's not true. Why don't you tell me something about your childhood?" he asks. "I'm curious about what a normal mortal experience looks like."

A normal mortal experience? It's not like the movies, if that's what he thinks.

Telling him the truth, *my* truth, would crush him. But at the same time, I don't want to lie. He's been so open with me, and I want to return the favor. It's an unfamiliar emotion. Maybe this makes me a horrible person, but for all the lies I tell, it's rare for me to feel guilty about them. My selfishness and self-preservation usually outweigh the feelings of others.

Now that I want to tell him the truth, I can't because of Neil. It's better this way, I tell myself.

"I never believed in Santa," I admit, settling on a truth that is both honest and inconsequential. "Or the tooth fairy, or any of those other kinds of fibs adults tell kids."

"Really? I always thought that human families, at least American ones, told their kids about Santa," he muses. "My parents didn't raise me with that. It would have been too confusing, they argued, because I was raised knowing magic exists. And they didn't believe in giving gifts for the sake of it; it would spoil me, they thought."

"Not even on your birthday?"

"No."

I guess we have more in common than I thought. But

this isn't a therapy session, thank God, so I'm not going to sit here and ask him how he *felt* about it.

"I can't imagine *not* being shadowborn," he continues. "But I think it would be interesting to experience a normal life as a human. Just for a little while. Like you."

I can't imagine a time I ever felt *normal*, without the pretense of Mary Alice. Even then, I rarely ever lose myself in the act. The key to staying humble is never losing sight of how much of a fraud I am at all times.

"What even *is* normal?" I ask with a laugh. "A white picket fence? A two-parent family? A cat? A dog? Siblings?"

"A family that makes you feel safe, maybe. People you can rely on."

"That's..." That's what I want, too. What I want to get *back* to, anyway. "You're right. Having people around you that understand you is important. I'm sorry if things aren't like that for shadowborn."

"When strength is everything, there's not much room for love or acceptance."

Love? Acceptance? Nice concepts — the mortal world seems to put a lot of stock into those things. But the truth is, so few people get to experience them. Even then, it's fleeting.

My stomach sinks at the thought. When I go back, if Neil lets me go, what will I be returning to? How would I even explain my absence to them? Would I tell them about Neil, about my shadowborn status? Or would it put them in danger?

If you had to guess, who would you think I'd be paired off with in a group? Let me clarify—this is a class trip, and the main event is a night tour. I'll give you a hint: I've used up all my romance points with Archer for the chapter. So obviously, I'm not lucky enough to be partnered with him.

No, my partners are the three people who hate me the most of all my classmates.

Marshall and Lilly don't seem that pleased to be placed in a group with me, but Ophelia is outright *pissed*. She keeps glaring at me, even though it's not my fault the universe hates me. We picked random numbers from a *hat* and this is who I get?

I *knew* I should have cheated.

"Let's just get this over with. We only have to do one lap around the lake," Ophelia mutters. "Mary Alice, if you wander off, don't blame us if you get eaten by beastbloods."

"That would be an improvement. An upgrade from the sad little life she's living," Lilly scathes.

Yeah, bitch, try being *more* cliché. I was taken off the suspect list for her sister's murder; you'd think she'd be a little nicer. Or, you know, apologize. Nope.

If I die tonight, I know who I'm haunting!

I mean that seriously. I know we're college students, and everyone here (myself excluded) has magic powers, but this whole "night tour" idea seems like a lawsuit waiting to happen. We know the area is overrun with beastbloods, and we know that Nightmares also frequent this lake in particular. Are we just tempting fate, or do they *want* us to run into monsters? And if the latter is true, why not prepare us better instead of creating this whole tour façade? This isn't a tour, it's a hunt!

I don't know if mosquitoes exist here, but if they do, at least my legs are covered by my jeans. I follow the dim glow of the lantern as Marshall leads the way.

Ophelia sticks with me, but I don't feel any safer. While she hasn't antagonized me nearly as much as Lilly has, I haven't forgotten how she treated me over the summer. She's made it clear she dislikes me.

Dodging dead trees and broken branches, we meander around the lake. Funnily enough, we don't come across any other student groups until we're near the end of the trail.

Students crouch behind the trees, shining their phone flashlights into a small cave half hidden by bushes. The entrance declines sharply inside, so I'm not sure why they're standing so close to it. The rocks shine with moisture, though it's not close enough to the lake to be water from there.

"What are you doing?" Lilly asks, putting her hands on her hips.

"We think it's a Nightmare cave," a girl whispers.

I'm out of here.

I haven't covered Nightmares in depth in my classes yet, but judging by the name alone, I don't need to gawk. Nightmares feed off of nightmares, hence the name, and while they appear humanoid, they're said to have underdeveloped brains. They're more like animals, according to my textbook.

"Cool," Marshall says with a grin, not bothering to lower his voice. Does he have a death wish or something? "Let's kill it. If we bring its carcass back to the hotel, I bet Professor Hall will give us extra credit."

"We don't have any weapons," Lilly points out. I never thought she'd be the voice of reason.

If there *is* a Nightmare in there, all other details aside, then isn't it wrong to just kill it for sport? We'd be invading its home at night. Then again, I assume it's nocturnal for feeding purposes.

"We should go," I whisper to Ophelia, hoping she senses how bad of an idea this is.

Shockingly, she nods in agreement. "Come on."

"We don't need weapons," Marshall says, picking up a large rock. "Isn't that the challenge? Making use of what little we have?"

I don't remember Professor Hall issuing *any* sort of challenge. But it's not my problem. Turning on my phone flashlight, I'm prepared to go right now.

Ophelia stops as another group approaches, waving their flashlights in our eyes. Archer is among them, leading the other students toward us.

"What are you doing?" he asks, crossing his arms. "We're supposed to keep moving."

"There's a Nightmare in the cave. I'm going to take care of it," Marshall replies, as if it's going to be the easiest task in the world. Well, it's his funeral. "Are you in?"

"No. That's stupid." Archer's eyes brush over me, landing on Ophelia beside me. "Professor Hall wants us back within thirty minutes. We're just supposed to take some photos."

"If we bring a Nightmare head, I bet we'll get extra credit," Marshall says eagerly, and something tells me this has nothing to do with extra credit. "What, scared, Kinsey?"

"No, I'm just not stupid," he shoots back. "You're going to fight it with a rock? It's a trueblood. It will tear you apart."

"And then we'll have to drag *your* carcass back to the hotel," Ophelia adds, moving to stand next to Archer.

"I have a good plan," Marshall assures the group. "All we need is bait."

Before anyone can move, Marshall slams the rock directly into the side of my head. I stumble to the ground, my ears ringing. It's already dark, but my vision blurs further as I try to blink the duplicates away.

"What the hell is wrong with you!" Ophelia screams.

"Calm down," Lilly snaps, bending down. She stares me dead in the eyes and laughs, pressing a finger into the wound. I wince, jerking my head back. "She's not going to die. Probably."

Marshall grabs my arm and throws me to the ground at the edge of the cave, sneering down at me.

"Be a good piece of bait," Marshall tells me, launching me into the depths of the cave with a sharp kick to my stomach. I land on my side, my entire body crying out in pain. "We're all counting on you."

Chapter Nineteen
Maria

The marble staircase is just how I remember, with the edge of the steps so sharp they could crack someone's head open. I always thought so, anyway.

I can barely reach the handrail, though I'm sure that's part of the illusion. I was the shortest kid in my class until my seventh grade growth spurt, but I wasn't *this* short when I lived there. Everything seems bigger now, and brighter. So bright the white of the walls hurts my eyes.

None of this is real—it can't be. It's a vision, or a dream, or more aptly, a nightmare. But I can't seem to wake myself up, and worse, everything *feels* real. The smooth metal of the railing, the shoes on my feet that are a size too small, contrasting with the hand-me-downs that are obviously too big.

Making my way up the stairs, I remember just where my bedroom was. The walls are still painted pink, and everything is princess-themed. Maybe other eight-year-olds would have liked it, but it was never my cup of tea. Still, I didn't say anything. I didn't want to make them angry or

sound ungrateful—those things could easily get you booted from a home. And moving was always a hassle. You never knew if the next house would be worse.

Baxter, the family dog, bounds up the stairs with a bark. The big golden retriever wags his tail when he sees me, jumping into my arms. Baxter liked me, more than my other family members. But not *this* much. Still, I rub the dog's head. He didn't live for much longer after I left.

Showing me Baxter must mean something terrible is coming. I can only assume that, given I'm in the Baker house again. Yeah, Baker—they named their dog Baxter Baker. It should have been a red flag.

Baxter follows me back downstairs, past the closed studies and bathrooms all the way to the kitchen. I drag a stool from the counter to the drawers on the opposite wall, climbing up to see what's inside. Unfortunately, they are all empty. This is just a prop house, an illusion, after all.

Maybe if I keep reminding myself of that, everything will be okay.

"What are you doing, silly bear?" Mrs. Baker comes in, sweeping me off my feet. I shudder at the sound of her voice, trying to wiggle out of her arms and put as much distance between us as possible. But she ignores me and picks me up in her arms. "Let's have dinner, as a family. You know Max is back from school. I'm sure he'll play with you if he doesn't have any homework."

Mrs. Baker brings me into the dining room. The table spread is grand, like something out of a magazine with all the glasses and silverware matching. A large turkey sits in the center of the table.

Thanksgiving, I note. Things really began to escalate at this point.

All the food on the table comes from a catering service, but Mrs. Baker uses her own dishes to serve dinner. It's her personal touch, to make everything look homemade. The kitchen is rarely used by anyone, but Mrs. Baker brags about her family's recipes to every guest who steps through the door. She told me once that because I was part of the family, she'd teach me all her mother's best dishes. I believed her.

Dr. Baker sits at the head of the table, fixing my plate. "Ah, Princess Maria!"

"We were getting bored waiting for you." Max's voice is so loud, it feels like he's going to pop my eardrums.

He's just like I remember him, so very *large* compared to me. At eighteen, he was a high school basketball star who later went on to major in finance at college. He was handsome to boot, with bright blue eyes and dark, perfectly coiffed hair. Maybe that's why everyone loved him. Even I was charmed, when we first met.

I know better now.

"Max, be kind to your sister," Mrs. Baker warns, putting me down in the chair beside him. "You have all weekend to play together."

Play? What world did *she* live in?

"I'm sure we'll have a great time. Right, Maria?" I hate the way he says my name, the way he draws out the syllables like a taunt. *Mah-ree-uh.* It almost sounds like *my-ria*, which is even worse. "Mine." I'm sure that's how Max thought of me.

"Right." I grab the plate of food in front of me and smash it on the table, breaking it into shards. Grabbing the sharpest one I can find, I lunge at Max and aim for his neck.

I can *feel* all my therapy and character growth flying out

the window. I've tried so hard not to think about Max, but when his stupid face is in front of me — even as an illusion — all the old, unresolved anger I have toward him bubbles to the surface. I can barely even think, just like back then. I see his face, hear his voice, and my blood begins to boil. He needs to disappear, not just in this nightmare, but in real life, too.

Before I can stab him, the scene shifts. Suddenly, it's so dark I can barely see my hand raised in front of me. When I move to hit the light switch, every muscle in my body aches.

The light flickers on, and I'm in a bathroom face-to-face with my reflection. My eight-year-old self is as plain and drab as ever. My leg is a mess of bruises and my ankle is swollen to twice its size. It hurts to breathe, mostly likely because of the cracked rib. Worse, the gash on my forehead is bleeding through the bandage. Ten stitches, all done at home by Dr. Baker.

"It was just an accident," a muffled voice says through the door. Mrs. Baker — she was the one who tended to me after her husband finished sewing me up. "You know that, don't you, Maria?"

That's what she always said. And I bought it — the first few times. A broken finger there, a black eye here, twisted ankles, and fractured ribs. Yeah, sure. Accidents.

I should have known. Age doesn't matter. When I look back, something I try *not* to do, shame is the first emotion to grip my heart. All the "what ifs" and "why didn't I's" flood my brain. I want to go back in time and scream at myself.

Why did you let them do this to you?

I know *why*, though: desperation. I wanted attention so badly that I was willing to believe any bullshit Mrs. Baker fed me.

I yank the door handle, but it's locked from the outside.

"Say it, Maria. It was just an accident."

I said it back then. I'm not going to now. If you say it's an accident once, it will always be an accident.

"Maria! Say it was just an accident!" Mrs. Baker begins pounding on the door, even though *I'm* the one locked in. "Say it for Mommy. Say it was just an accident! Say it! Maria!"

"Why are you doing this?" I ask, turning toward the mirror. "Making me see these things. They don't scare me — they just piss me off."

My reflection smiles, reaching toward me. Her arms break through the glass, hurtling me backward into another memory. Maybe I shouldn't have taunted the Nightmare holding me hostage in its illusion.

I'm somewhere else now — my old elementary school. Red and green streamers hang from the stalls in the girls' room; the custodians forgot to take them down over break, so the entire school is still decked out despite Christmas having passed.

Tasha is here, too, her hair cropped in a flattering pixie cut. But her eyes are bloodshot and puffy from crying, because of me.

My chest tightens, and I don't need her to say anything. I already know this memory.

"Where were you?" she whispers.

We're the only two people in the bathroom, but right now, it feels like we're the only two people in the world. Her voice echoes around me, and I swallow thickly. My ribs hurt, still healing from being kicked. Dr. Baker's bandages and painkillers do little to ease the pain, but I pretend like it doesn't hurt.

"Tash—" I start.

"You promised me! You promised you'd be there!" she screams. "I needed you."

This time, I don't speak. But the words come out of my mouth anyway. "Shut up!"

It's the worst thing I could have possibly said. I should have lied—told her I couldn't find a ride, or that I tried to make it but couldn't. Hell, I should have just apologized. But I didn't.

Because the truth is, I'm a much worse person than any of you realize. The truth is, beneath my characters, I am a selfish person who hurts everyone around me. Even the people I love most.

"Why do you even have to celebrate them?" I continue, no matter how much I want to shut my goddamn mouth. "Your parents are *dead*, Tasha. It doesn't matter how many years have passed. They aren't coming back!"

I've never apologized for this, either. It's been ten years, but I'm sure Tasha hasn't forgotten. I haven't, even though I try to.

Tasha fully breaks down crying, but I continue. Because I'm hurt, and it makes me feel better that she is, too. "You're alone, Tasha. Just like me. It's time you realize that."

I walk out of the bathroom just like I did then, even though I wish I could go back. To tell her that I'm sorry and I didn't mean it. But I physically can't turn around.

Through the door is the Baker house again. It's crawling with police, and I'm sitting on the couch. Dr. Baker and Max have already been carted away, but Mrs. Baker is sitting with me and the police. My social worker is there, too —the one before Isabelle.

"My poor son," Mrs. Baker keeps repeating, glaring at

me through tear-filled eyes. She's pasty from crying, her nose bright red. "My poor, poor son."

"Mrs. Baker, please calm down," one of the officers says.

"She did this!" Mrs. Baker screams. "It's all her fault!"

I didn't say anything at the time, just like I can't speak up now. Despite everything, I still wanted Mrs. Baker to love me. To choose *me* over her son.

The police offer shakes his head. "He filmed it, Mrs. Baker. He posted the beatings to a public online form."

Mrs. Baker jumps to her feet, grabbing me by the collar and yelling in my face. "You ruined his life! You ruined my son's life! And for what? It's not like he raped you!"

My social worker has to pry her away, wrapping an arm around me as she escorts me from the house. Outside, it's still a bit chilly for March. The flowers in the garden are just starting to bloom, but I won't be sticking around here much longer to see them. My social worker loads me into her car and sighs, adjusting the mirror.

"You should have just let it go, Maria," she tells me, starting to drive. "Half the county knows what happened. This is going to follow you for life, you know. You're going to be branded as a liar."

"No matter what I did, I would have been called a liar," I mutter.

"Any chance of a family adopting you is gone now. No one wants kids with baggage. The Bakers were your one chance. Do you understand that? I already had difficulty placing you. Now, they're going to put you in Group."

"With all the troubled children," I say, staring out the window. "I'll fit in well."

She drives under a tunnel, and again, the scene shifts. The next room I walk into is the principal's office. It's

spring, not that I can see outside. I remember because this is the month I'd be turning nine.

No one in the room has a face, but I can tell there are some police officers there based on their uniforms. I sit across from the elementary school principal, staring into my lap.

"We're just trying to figure out what happened, Maria," the principal says, his voice distorted. "You were asked what happened, multiple times. You said you had a series of accidents. Why are you changing your story now?"

"We're on your side, Maria. You should have told us sooner. Why didn't you trust me?"

"Maria, please tell us what happened."

"Your secrets are safe with us. But we won't know there's a problem unless you speak up."

"It wouldn't have escalated this far if you hadn't lied," the principal says. "We don't solve problems with violence, Maria."

"No, *we* don't solve problems," I snap, my voice finally free. I jump to my feet, my face red as a tomato. It doesn't matter that none of this is real. I know the Nightmare is purposely trying to show me upsetting things to feed off me, and I don't care. It's working. The words in my heart, festering like an old wound, come out of my mouth and it doesn't make me feel even a little bit better. "You did nothing to help me—all you care about is yourselves!"

Humans, I've learned, are cruel and selfish. There is no such thing as an act of kindness—only acts of vanity.

I'm cruel, too. I'm selfish. And maybe that's why I can spew such vitriol without an ounce of remorse.

"I wish you would all just disappear," I scream, my voice raw. "We should all disappear."

Maybe it's the sheer power of my hatred, or just good timing, but the world around me fades to black. My heart is still racing, my palms slick with sweat.

I'm back in the cave, breathing hard. Tears pour down my cheeks, but my body feels so foreign to me now. I wipe at my face with muddy hands, trying to find my bearings.

"Miss Rochester," Professor Hall says, shaking my shoulder. "Pull yourself together."

I can barely speak. My head is throbbing so much that I think it might explode. My legs feel like jelly, and I have to lean on Professor Hall for support to stand. Ophelia, Lilly, Marshall, Archer, and the rest of my class are at the edge of the cave, watching me like I'm some spectacle.

My hands shake uncontrollably and I want to do *something* to them. Something horrible. I want them to be as miserable as I feel.

They did this to Mary Alice, I try to remind myself. *Not Maria. They don't know Maria. They can't hurt me. It was just Mary Alice—and she's not real. They can't hurt a fictional character. It wasn't Maria.*

They can't hurt me. No one can hurt me.

"Come on. Let's get back to the hotel," Professor Hall says gruffly, pulling me along.

Provost Mathers, who wasn't even supposed to be on this trip, appears at the edge of the forest. "Did you find her?"

He jogs toward us, concern written all over his face. Who the fuck is he pretending for? I don't need his fake consideration. And no one else here gives a shit about me, so he's not earning any brownie points by being nice.

"We found her in a cave with a Nightmare. She

wandered off on her own, according to the students," Professor Hall says.

"Is that true, Miss Rochester?" Provost Mathers searches my face.

I laugh, drawing the attention of everyone around me. It must look bizarre, laughing with tears still streaming down my face. "I'm sure Professor Hall wants it to be."

"What is that supposed to mean?" he snaps.

I shouldn't talk. I shouldn't say anything, if I know what's good for me. But you know what? I don't give a shit.

"It means—"

"Miss Rochester, please allow me to escort you to the nurse on campus in the mortal realm," Provost Mathers cuts me off. "You're probably feeling very weak from the Nightmare."

"I'm tired," I agree. "I'm just so fucking tired of you all."

NOTHING'S WRONG WITH ME, OR SO THE NURSE SAYS. I still spend the entire day in bed, avoiding my classes and everyone else around me. I even skip tutoring with Rhys, which is bound to piss him off. But he hasn't come knocking on the basement door, so that's something.

I stop crying, too. It was difficult, but after showering, I did it.

It's not like I'm *sad*. I don't know why I cried. I haven't shed tears over that stuff in years. I told myself I needed to get over it, to shove it down so deep it would never surface and ruin what happiness I've created for myself. But Neil has already ruined my happiness, hasn't he? My family. The only people who believed me, who had my back and tried to

help me. Even Tasha, who stuck with me despite my lashing out at her. Not just the time in the bathroom—there was a period when all we did was scream at each other. It was usually my fault, my hurt feelings and bitterness that snuck their way into every interaction until I managed to get ahold of myself. And my characters.

I wish I could apologize to her, to all of them for being so difficult to deal with. I always meant to—I assumed she knew how sorry I was. But I've missed my chance.

I try to become Mari, or Mary Alice, or even Marilyn. But I'm so stuck on Maria that I can't get into character. All the things I've tried to forget and hide from have been quickly exposed. It's all over now, isn't it?

I'm a person filled with hate. I hate my past, I hate everyone who was involved. I hate how I can't seem to get over this.

The bathroom door opens, light spilling into the room. Todd Glass looks around, tentatively stepping into my bedroom. I didn't know he could leave the hallway. I'm so emotionally raw, I can't find the energy to act surprised.

"You're alone, so I'm not breaking any rules," he says sheepishly, sitting down on the floor beside my bed. "I thought you could use some company."

"When are you?" I croak.

"This is the first time we're meeting since you saw me on the ship. The first time we're meeting as...Time Agent and shadowborn," he clarifies.

"So you know what happened?"

"Not what the Nightmare showed you. But you looked so sad," he says. "Like you needed someone to talk to. Without breaching Neil's verbal NDA."

Ha. "One of my therapists told me that talking about

things is good, and that telling people about what happened will take a lot of the weight off me. But that's never been the case," I say.

"It's different with me. Because I've seen it, and I believe you," Todd replies. "I know what happened. I know it wasn't your fault. You were just a kid. Even if you hadn't been, what Max did to you was wrong. What his *family* did—"

"What his family did was just as bad," I finish. "I felt so ashamed for trusting them after that. I called Mrs. Baker 'Mom.' The first and only woman I've ever called that."

"Not even Isabelle?"

"I've never called Isabelle 'Mom.' I probably should have, though. She's my mother in every sense of the word." I stare at the ceiling, unable to look at Todd. "The Bakers were so kind to me at first, you know? I thought they were perfect. They threw me my first-ever birthday party and invited all my classmates. And then Max came home from college, and everything went to shit. It's hard to talk about."

It always has been. My feelings about the situation are jumbled and knotted. Thinking about everything all at once is overwhelming, but at the same time, it's impossible to unravel one aspect of it without the rest.

Time hasn't made anything better. I never fully processed what happened, so now, years later, I don't even know where to begin. I'm...the same age Max was at the time. But despite the ten years that have passed, it still feels like yesterday.

"Do you think the Bakers turned Max into a monster?" Todd asks, resting his chin on his knees.

"I'm not sure," I reply honestly. "Maybe Max was born that way. I had a fascination with true crime in high school;

some killers are just…unexplainably twisted. Even if no one wants to admit it. But I'm positive my characters were born because of Max."

"How?"

"I didn't know how to go on with my life after every-thing that happened. Nothing I did made me feel any better. I was put in therapy after a final confrontation with Max."

Thankfully, the Nightmare hadn't shown me *that* memory. Just the aftermath, with the police.

I continue, "We didn't get anywhere. After weeks of sessions, I didn't want to talk to her about it anymore. I also knew I couldn't continue living like that, with so much anger and hatred and sadness consuming my every thought. The only solution was pretending like none of it happened. Eventually, my rationale for the characters evolved, but that was the first reason why."

And they've served me well.

Todd doesn't say anything. What can he say? But he's listening.

"I see now why I told you that if you ever needed to earn my trust on future missions, all you had to do was mention Max," I say. "I hate talking about him. Even to Tasha—I lied to her about what happened."

"Tasha is your best friend," he says.

I know. I trust her more than anyone. But for some reason, I'm afraid of telling her *everything* about Max. When-ever I try, a knot forms in my stomach and I feel like I'm going to throw up.

"What are you going to do, then?" Todd asks quietly.

"I'm going to lie in bed and feel sorry for myself. And then, tomorrow, I will be Mary Alice," I say. "Mary Alice hasn't met Max or the Bakers. She's just a girl from Geor-

gia, and she has nothing to do with Neil or Astaroth or anyone else. When I'm her, I can pretend that nothing bad has happened to me. And that's the only way I can come close to being normal."

"Will that work?"

No. But if I ever want to see my family again, it has to.

CHAPTER TWENTY

I 've never liked the ocean.

I know a lot of people like it for one reason or another. The sun, the sand, the clear blue water, the dolphins leaping into the sunset... It's all very picturesque, until you see what the creatures from the ocean floor look like. Those are some of the ugliest fish to disgrace the ocean.

Those images have been burned into my memory since the summer, when I had to take a marine life class. Now, when I look at the ocean, all I can think about are those fish. I can't even *see* them from the shore, but just knowing they exist ruins the beauty of the ocean for me. There's another metaphor for you if you look hard enough.

It's been three days since I left the Veil, but I still haven't been able to change into a character. I've tried everything — cold showers, funny television shows, sleeping for fourteen hours straight... I can't turn back. Which means I'm essentially useless, more so than usual.

The Nightmare brought old memories to the surface, and all the negativity surrounding those memories bubbled

up as well. I just want to forget again, but no matter what I do, I'm stuck as Maria. And nothing good happens when I'm Maria.

Nothing productive happens, either. I can barely take care of myself, let alone study for midterms this month. All I can think about is how resentful I am, how much I *hate* Max and his family, and everyone else who's screwed me over. How I hate Marshall and Lilly now, too, even though I shouldn't. They hurt Mary Alice, not *me*. That kind of logic used to work in the past, but now, things are different. I'm different.

I only drag myself to the cafeteria when my stomach begins to hurt. Waiting until nightfall, when no one else will be around, I take a few yogurt tubes and go to the beach to eat them. They're not the most nutritious or satisfying meal, but at least I don't feel lightheaded anymore.

I need the fresh air, anyway. Lying in the sand, spread like a starfish, I can finally breathe. Maybe if I'm lucky, a sea monster will whisk me away to the lost city of Atlantis and I can forget my troubles. But I fear even then, I wouldn't be able to forget.

This is yet another reason why I hate Maria. When I'm her, it's like time rewinds and all my old wounds are fresh again. As much as I want to move forward, to move *on*, I have no idea how. My temporary solution was the characters, but you see how well that's turned out. Worse, it feels like the only person stopping me from being happy is myself.

I decide to stay at the beach a little bit longer, the tide rising to lick my toes. I nearly fall asleep, until I hear footsteps approaching on the sand.

The moment I spot Rhys walking toward me, I know

I'm in trouble. I've been skipping our tutoring sessions, so I figured he would come find me eventually. But I'm in no state to be chewed out right now.

Rhys jogs over. I don't even know how he sees me lying by the water, ruining my clothes. He glares at me, out of breath. "You were not in your dormitory."

"I've been out here for a while," I confirm, my voice hollow. "How did you find me?"

I chose the most secluded piece of beach I could find, a mile from the docks. There's barely any light here and the night sky is overcast with dark storm clouds rolling in over the sea.

"You have been skipping class. Your grades will suffer if this continues."

"If I continue to skip classes and flunk out of school, Neil will kill my family. But if I go back now as Maria, I'll still fail and my family will die. I'm stuck between a rock and a hard place."

"You are so confident you cannot succeed as you are?"

"There's no chance I'll be able to focus on my goals as Maria. When I'm her, I'm always on the brink of self-destruction."

It wasn't always like that. But as Max's beatings intensified, my grades plummeted. As much as an elementary schooler's grades could, anyway. I couldn't focus on anything but what was happening at home, and soon, Max was all I could think about from the moment I woke up to the moment I fell asleep at night. I was a fly caught in a trap of my own mind.

Rhys doesn't say anything, which is odd for him. I expected him to yell at me and drag me to the library to study. His silence only makes me grow more anxious, even

though I shouldn't be. Is he quiet because he's judging me? Does he think I'm weak and pathetic, too? Well, join the club.

"I assume you heard about what happened. In the Veil," I clarify. "With Marshall and Lilly."

His jaw clenches. "Yes."

He *does* sound angry. At me? He has a right to be. He's been training me to fight, and yet I still succumbed to Marshall in the Veil.

"The Nightmare stirred up old memories I wish I could forget. But I can't. I remember everything, and now I can't function without those nasty memories seeping into every thought," I explain. "They say what doesn't kill you makes you stronger, but some experiences erode your soul like acid to the point where you might as well be dead."

Not to be too depressing or anything.

"Perhaps it is best you do not forget," Rhys replies finally.

"Please don't tell me to be myself or be true to who I am. I don't think I could ever take you seriously after that."

"You do not take me seriously now."

"Now that's not true," I say. "If I didn't take you seriously, why would I be telling you all this?"

"Perhaps you have a point. You are honest with me even as you lie to all others. Yet you do not trust me."

Okay, valid. But I can't explain it. Rhys isn't trustworthy and he has his own motives; helping me is part of his *job*. Even talking to him now, I don't exactly feel at ease. Why do I keep talking so openly when I can barely admit these things to myself?

"I don't trust you. I don't know why I'm so honest with you. You make me feel comfortable, even though you

shouldn't. You're not on my side. Half the time, I feel like you hate me."

That earns me a deep frown, which is a departure from his usual stony indifference. "You believe I hate you?"

"Yeah, sometimes. So why the hell am I even talking to you about this?"

"Maybe you are the one who dislikes me, to the point where you do not care what I think."

"That's not it," I say immediately, dismissing the notion.

I don't *dislike* Rhys. I should, probably. He's not exactly sugar and spice and everything nice. He's only interacting with me because he was ordered to. But something about him makes me feel like I could tell him anything. Being with him is easy, which is yet another thing I cannot explain.

But maybe we're not meant to *explain* our feelings. We're just supposed to feel them.

Maybe there's something more to it, I think. Which is ridiculous for reasons I don't have to explain. The thought of us romantically involved is so out of left field, based on how gorgeous he is *alone*, that I can't entertain the idea without immediately shutting it down.

"Why did you come to look for me tonight?" I ask. "Was it because I skipped our tutoring sessions?"

Instead of answering my question, Rhys says, "Marshall's dormitory is currently unoccupied."

"What?"

"Marshall. He is at a party in the middle of the week and will be staying the night. His roommates are also at the party. It is currently empty and the back door is unlocked."

"How do you know this?" I ask incredulously.

"I have my sources."

"Okay, Mr. Mysterious. Why are you telling me this?"

"You are angry at Marshall and Lilly. You need to vent that anger, or you will not be able to change characters," he says placidly. "If you cannot change characters, you do not believe you can complete your mission. Neil has tasked me with helping you succeed. If I do not, I will be punished. Astaroth will reign free and the world as we know it will suffer. Must I explain further?"

"No, no. You've made your point. But what are we going to do in Marshall's room?"

"Something petty but satisfying," he decides, offering me a hand.

I take it, allowing him to pull me up. I dust the sand off my back. "I didn't take you for a petty person, Rhys."

"I have my moments."

He matches my pace as he walks beside me, not bothering to rush. When we reach the docks, it begins to rain.

The storm is finally here, and it's taking no man prisoner. Rhys and I dash toward the closest house, finding shelter under a wrap-around porch.

"I guess this puts a damper on our plans," I say, trying to catch my breath.

The lights outside the house turn on, and Rhys finally comes into view. Water drips down his face and from his hair, making it a darker shade of ash blonde. Not to sound debauched, but his white shirt has turned transparent. The fabric clings to his chest—I can't tell if it's naturally hairless or if he waxes it. I've always thought he looked slim, almost delicate, but my strength has never come close to matching his in training. Now I understand why. His clothes hide his lean muscles and toned torso.

His brows shoot up when he notices my gaze. "I must also keep fit and groomed. I am a professional."

"Can you please stop reading my mind?" I demand.

"But you make it so easy."

"I don't think that's the case." I point a finger at him. "You must have ESP or something."

"ESP?"

"Psychic powers!"

"Perhaps. But only when it comes to you," he says.

I shake my head. "Stop saying weird things like that. You're confusing me. You make me think…"

"I would hope I make you *think*, considering I am tutoring you."

"No," I say, letting out a frustrated sigh. "Just forget it."

"Anyway, the rain makes our plan work much better. Marshall's dormitory is up the road. Are you prepared to run?"

"Is anyone ever prepared to exercise?"

We take off running into the night, the rain soaking our clothes further until we reach a green Victorian off the main street. The back screen door is unlocked, and Rhys holds it open for me to enter first.

"Aren't there security cameras?" I ask.

"They do not work well in the rain."

That seems like a major flaw, but it's helping my revenge plan. Though from the looks of it, I might not need to take revenge at all. The house is a pigsty. We enter the small kitchen, littered with open snack bags and garbage. Gnats swarm the sink, which is piled high with dirty dishes. The odor is so strong I have to cover my mouth and nose. How can someone live in this place? Maybe this is why Marshall is such a pill.

Rhys motions toward the hall and I follow him upstairs to the bedrooms. Marshall's door conveniently has a sign

with his name on it, along with "Keep Out!" in bold red letters. Rhys ignores it and walks inside. It's just as messy as the kitchen, with clothes strewn everywhere. Thankfully, it's not nearly as smelly.

Rhys turns on the light. "His laptop is on his desk. The passwords are written on a sticky note."

"Again, I have to ask how you know this. And why you're telling me, knowing I'm up to no good," I add.

Rhys merely crosses his arms. "I suggest you delete his term paper."

Well, I'd be remiss not to take him up on that fine suggestion!

This doesn't make up for being hit with a rock, thrown as bait to a Nightmare, and nearly getting killed. But for the moment, it makes me feel a little bit better. Not because I'm imagining Marshall's face when he realizes his term paper draft is gone—though after reading the first paragraph, I might have done him a huge favor—I just didn't expect Rhys of all people to help me. He's always been so strict and by-the-book. Now, he's opening the window and tossing Marshall's personal belongings outside.

Rhys doesn't smile, but I get the feeling he's enjoying this. Which would be crazy, because it would suggest that he wants revenge on Marshall, too. For...hurting me? Doesn't that imply that he likes me in some form?

Not a chance. Maybe he just likes chaos.

"For Lilly, I recommend soaking one of her socks in a mixture of egg and milk. Hide it in her closet. It should begin to smell after a few days," Rhys says, confirming my theory about him. He likes chaos, and certainly doesn't have feelings for *me*.

"That's so petty and evil. I love it!" I yank the cord on

Marshall's alarm clock and whip it out the window. It sinks into a puddle of rain and mud below. "Where did you learn all these tricks?"

"Television."

"I didn't take you for a big TV watcher. I figured you spent your spare time reading the newspaper or something."

"You do not know much about me."

"You're right. But you tend to avoid my questions," I say with a laugh. "Thanks, though. I do feel a little bit better."

"Just a little?" Rhys hands me a mug from the night-stand. "It seems you need to continue vandalizing. Marshall's toothbrush is the blue one in the bathroom down the hall."

Never have I heard sweeter words.

Chapter Twenty-One
Mar

I thought, given how Rhys helped me with Marshall and Lilly, our relationship would change. Into *what*, exactly, I'm not sure. But not only has he gone *completely* back to normal, he's actually harsher on me during our tutoring sessions now. I didn't think that was possible.

"Is that the best you can do?" he mocks in Elvish.

I rest my hands on my knees, panting. "Yes!"

"This is not good enough. Four more laps!"

"You're crazy!" I bite out. "I have a test tomorrow!"

Midterms, to be precise. While I'm confident I'll pass, I still wanted to go back to my dorm after class and cram. Rhys seems to have other plans. Not only am I *not* studying for my exams tomorrow, he's having me exercise. Over the past two weeks, he's doubled our tutoring sessions.

On the plus side, I'm learning a lot. My Elvish has also improved exponentially since that's the only language he'll speak to me in. But I'm exhausted, and Rhys isn't the most compassionate person in the world.

At least I'm back to Mary Alice. Or, in this instance,

Mar. Trashing Marshall and Lilly's rooms made me feel better, enough to help me slip back into character. And I haven't gotten in trouble for the petty revenge scheme, either. I guess that's what happens when so many people hate you. Without video evidence, Marshall couldn't figure out who threw his stuff out the window. And Lilly hasn't found the sock yet, but she's been complaining about the smell lately. That's a win, I guess.

What's *not* a win is running two miles while an elf barks orders at you with a stopwatch.

"If you are not good at fighting, you must become good at running away!" he yells.

"I don't think that's how things work," I pant back. Just to put things in context, I've already been training all afternoon.

Unfortunately, Rhys isn't having any of it. After running the two miles, he makes me lift weights while drilling me on vocabulary. When our session finally comes to an end, I can barely stand.

Lying down on the bleachers with a groan, I announce, "It's official. I can't move."

"I did not push you *that* hard," Rhys denies, handing me a water bottle.

"My lungs feel like they're going to explode."

"Your Elvish vocabulary is growing."

"Is that a compliment?"

Rhys doesn't reply.

I gulp down the entire water bottle and wipe my mouth on the back of my hand. "Why are you pushing so hard these days, anyway? Did Neil say something to you?"

"Neil is coming to visit and see your progress after the

midterms," he replies. "He will not tolerate any imperfection. Particularly when it comes to you."

I know *that*. "Will he punish you if I'm not up to his standards?"

"He will punish us both."

I know Rhys mentioned it before, but I don't want him to get punished. Not because I have feelings for him or anything ridiculous. I'd have to be a major masochist to like him, with how hard he's been pushing me during training lately.

I just don't like the idea of him being punished for something I did. I'd feel guilty. There's nothing more to it than that.

There can't be.

WHEN I FINALLY TRUDGE BACK TO MY DORM, ARCHER Kinsey is waiting for me on the front porch. At least, I think it's *me* he's waiting for and not Lilly.

"What are you doing here?" I call out to him. I don't want to see him right now, especially after the Nightmare incident. And the fact that it's been *weeks* since the incident and he's been radio silent. If he had come to me earlier to apologize, to *explain* himself, maybe I wouldn't be so angry.

But he's been ignoring me in class, like he wants nothing to do with me. So it's ironic now that he says, "I wanted to see you."

How can I possibly believe that? How can I believe *him*?

I use my Mary Alice drawl, but my heart isn't in it, and it probably shows. "Why do you want to see me? I thought you were finished with me."

And you didn't even make it to home base. Your loss.

Archer has the absolute *audacity* to look surprised. "What are you talking about? When did I ever say we were finished? We've barely even…started."

Yeah, I'm well aware. "You seemed pretty done with me in the Veil, when you let your friends shove me into a Nightmare den. You haven't talked to me in what, three weeks? You haven't sought me out or asked me how I'm doing? And when the students told Professor Hall that I went into the den of my own volition, you didn't say anything in my defense."

"Mary Alice—"

"You act like you don't want to be associated with me," I say. "Well, you got your wish."

"Wait!" He jogs down the stairs, blocking my path. "That's not true. Just hear me out for a second."

I shouldn't. But I'm too tired to continue arguing. "Why didn't you do anything to help me?"

"I didn't think Marshall would hit you. You have to know that I would never let anyone hurt you," he explains. "It just happened so fast. When he kicked you into that den, the only thing I could do was bring Professor Hall over. I'm sorry. Things escalated in the blink of an eye. Marshall has never done anything like that in front of me. But I should have handled it better, you're right. He won't be bothering you again. He hasn't approached you since, right?"

"Why should I believe you? You have my number. We go to the same combat class every week. You didn't say anything to me then," I tell him.

"I thought you needed space. You looked…I've never seen you look the way you did when you came out of that cave."

That I believe. But the rest of Archer's explanation…is the same old excuse, isn't it? He didn't act quickly enough. Everything happened too fast. He froze.

But then I think about my own shortcomings and wonder, do I have any right to judge him when I'm not perfect myself? For all his faults, he has always come to apologize. Even though this one is *very* late.

Relationships take hard work and communication. Maybe I'm not mature enough to put in the work right now. I have so many other things on my plate; this doesn't take precedence.

"I don't even know what to think," I finally admit. All the anger drains out of me, and right now, I'm just *tired*.

"Look, once midterms are over, there's going to be a Halloween Dance. It will be fun. We'll go together and have a good time," he insists. "Can you please give me another chance? I know I messed up. But I *do* like you, Mary Alice. You know that."

"Do I?" I frown. "I'll think about it, okay? It's been a long day. I need to cool down and clear my head. But either way, we should talk again when I'm in a better head space. For both of our sakes."

"Okay," he relents. "I'll wait until you're ready."

It's a nice sentiment, but at this rate, I don't know if I'll ever be ready for romance. And certainly not with him.

CHAPTER TWENTY-TWO

Midterms were a breeze, thanks to Rhys' intense tutoring. Granted, the remedial-level classwork isn't difficult, and all the questions were multiple-choice. I took the tests on a computer, so my results came back immediately. Even if I fail the rest of the semester, I'll still average a C. Not that I plan on failing. I'm just not used to doing so well in school.

That's one area, at least, Neil shouldn't be able to complain about. I've barely gotten a chance to breathe between the tests and Neil's arrival. After my final midterm this morning, I went back to my dorm immediately to prepare myself. Look good, feel good, right?

Goodbye, woolly mammoth leg hair! Goodbye, peach fuzz! Hello, sheet mask, deep conditioner, and curling wand!

It feels good to take care of myself again, as vain as it sounds. I've been slacking in this department since the summer, but tonight, all will be redeemed.

I look in the dingy bathroom mirror, fluffing my hair.

The conditioner makes it glossier, falling in soft waves over my shoulders. For the first time in weeks, I feel pretty. Yes, it took quite a bit of legwork to get here, but it was worth it. My face is less angular with carefully-placed contour and blush, and my eyes pop with mascara. I'm more pulled together now than I have been since I arrived at school, which makes tonight all the more perfect for seeing Neil. Rhys informed me that I am expected to go to dinner with the Abbotts to celebrate the end of the midterms, and I have to be on my best behavior.

He repeated that five times, so I get the impression Neil is going to test me while he's here. On what, I can only guess.

Slipping on a pair of ballet flats, I'm ready to head out when I hear a knock on the door.

"Yes?" I call, hoping it's not Lilly coming to exact revenge for her sister again.

The visitor knocks again. "Maria."

My blood runs cold. Neil? Wasn't I supposed to meet him at the docks? Why the hell is he here?

"Maria, I know you're in there."

Crap. I race up the stairs, yanking the door open. Neil hovers in the doorway, looking impeccable, as usual. Funny, moments ago I was confident about my appearance. Seeing him makes me shrink back on the stairs, feeling quite small. Not just because he's taller than me; his very presence is overwhelming.

Neil descends the stairs, a mixture of amusement and disgust playing on his face as he looks around. I barely even see Rhys behind him, silent and unable to meet my eyes.

He's wearing a slate gray suit, which is a departure from his usual clothes. The cerulean tie at his neck brings out the

blue of his eyes and the silver in his hair. It suits him, but at the same time, the business attire makes him appear stuffy and out of place. He's an elf—he should be…well, not dressed like he's going to a 9-to-5 in a cubicle.

On Neil, the business suit looks much more natural. His green tie matches his eyes, and his blonde hair is slicked back with gel. He steps inside my small room, examining my unkempt bed and the clothes I keep in cardboard boxes. There's no dresser, so I don't have much choice.

Finally, he says, "Your roommates told me you were out of the house and tried to refuse me at the door. Luckily, Rhys has been keeping tabs on you and knew how to get to your room. It appears you are at the bottom of the social ladder, Maria."

"My roommate is Lilly Hardwicke. She thinks I killed her sister," I explain, straightening my back.

"Your roommate thinks you are a human without much backing. She enjoys stepping on you because she knows you cannot fight back."

What else is new?

"I don't mind. I can study all I want down here, and I don't have to share a bathroom." I hate the defensive edge my voice takes when I talk to Neil. Even *I* know how pathetic I sound. "Why are you here?"

"Can a father not visit his daughter and ensure her lodging is up to par?"

"So you came to make fun of me?"

"Now, Maria. Don't put it so crudely."

I take that as a yes.

Rhys clears his throat. "Your dinner reservation is at six."

"I am aware, Rhys. I am the one who made the reserva-

tion," Neil says dismissively. "I am just surprised that Maria, after her extensive history of violent temper tantrums, allowed herself to be cowed into basement accommodations."

I cross my arms. "*You* told me not to get kicked out of this school or you'll kill my family. Besides, I can't win against Lilly or anyone else here in a physical fight. If I did anything, they would come at me with ten times more force."

And I've received enough head injuries for this book, thank you kindly.

"Is Rhys not training you?" Neil probes.

I freeze, looking at Rhys. His gaze is cool and calm, but he still won't look at me. "Rhys is training me just fine."

"And yet you cannot fight a low-level shadowborn. How do you expect to fight Astaroth?"

Time, training, magic. A miracle.

"You didn't give me a time limit," I argue. "It hasn't even been a year since I found out about this. I'm doing my best."

"Am I supposed to cut you some slack?"

Yeah, that would be nice. But judging from Neil's tone, he's being facetious. "I will kill Astaroth. But I am halfway through my first semester. If I try now, I will fail."

"Well. I wouldn't want that," Neil says, circling me like a shark. "You look different."

"I'm wearing makeup."

"It's not the gunk on your face that makes a difference to me."

Well, fuck you, too.

"We really must go," Rhys cuts in, looking at his watch.

Neil stares at Rhys for a long, hard minute, and none of

us move. Finally, he says, "Do you have a problem with me speaking to my daughter, Rhys?"

The question hangs in the air like a guillotine over Rhys' neck, waiting to swing down. My chest tightens.

"Astaroth will die by my hand, I can assure you of that," I interrupt. "But it won't happen today, and having you come here and question my progress won't make me work any faster. I know what's at stake here. So tonight, we're going to go to dinner and we'll play 'happy family,' which seems to be your favorite game. You're going to call me Mary Alice and I will act like you're a god on earth."

Neil's lips curl into a smile. "You really *are* my daughter. My Maria."

MARY ALICE

Despite Rhys' numerous warnings, we're late for our reservation. We end up at a different restaurant down the street, an upscale Italian place with private rooms for VIPs. And who is Neil if not a VIP? He's a demon with excess income. A Very Important Prick.

At the large table, I'm lucky enough to be sandwiched between Nic and Neil. My two least favorite people, edging out even Max. Faith and Allegra sit opposite us, and Rhys doesn't come into the restaurant at all. I'm a little bit relieved he won't be joining us.

I don't know *why*. I thought Neil was going to hurt Rhys for my weakness earlier, and while I can't explain it, I can't have that happen. I don't like anyone getting hurt for my sake. Unless they deserve it. Or unless it's two (or more) men fighting for my affections. What can I say? I love the

love triangle trope. But Rhys is different. I guess I've grown fond of him, even if he doesn't feel the same way about me. Probably.

Even though he claimed to help me get revenge on Marshall because of his job, I have a hard time buying that. He could have just forced me to study, or tried to. Instead, he seemed to know exactly what would make me feel better. Not to mention, he knew Marshall would be out at a party and how to get into his dorm. That had to be premeditated, right? And earlier, Rhys risked Neil's wrath by reminding him about the reservation twice. He couldn't have been trying to help me then, too, right? If he was, what does that mean?

"Are you alright, Mary Alice?" Faith asks, bringing me back to the present.

"Yes. Sorry. I'm still a little bit distracted from all the tests this week," I reply with a smile, going full Mary Alice mode on her.

Faith returns my smile, showing her dimples. She's wearing a dress made of emerald silk, matching Neil's tie, held together with a diamond broach.

Meanwhile, Allegra is haggard beside her mother. Her dark circles look like black eyes, and her skin is pale as paper. She's so skinny she's skeletal, her bony fingers working to pull apart a piece of bread. She didn't look like this when we had dinner yesterday. What happened?

"Allegra, are you feeling okay?" I ask.

"I'm fine, Mary Alice," she replies. What a horrible liar. That's one thing we don't have in common.

"She's just a little tired," Nic replies with a hearty laugh, slinging an arm around my shoulder. He brings his mouth close to my ear and whispers, "Not that it matters to you."

What's that supposed to mean?

"Are you finding your coursework challenging, Mary Alice?" Neil asks, passing the basket of bread down the table. "Make sure you're eating well, Allegra."

She mumbles a response, taking another piece of bread with shaking hands.

"My coursework is exciting. I'm so grateful for the opportunity you've given me to learn. It's like a dream," I gush, laying it on thick.

"I'm glad we were able to help Allegra's dear friend," Faith replies, patting her daughter on the back.

Allegra winces in pain, draining her glass of water in one sip. She's starting to look greener than her mother's dress, but she doesn't make any moves to get up from the table.

Against my better judgment, I say, "I need to use the restroom. Allegra, come with me?"

"Why does she have to go with you?" Neil challenges.

"Oh, it's a girl thing." I giggle. "We always like to go to the bathroom in pairs. Right, Mrs. Abbott? Come on, Allegra!"

I help her stand, wrapping an arm around her for support. We make our way to the bathroom, which is thankfully a single room, and I lock the door behind us. Acting quickly, I pull a hair tie from my purse and throw Allegra's long blonde hair into a bun.

"You look like you're going to puke," I murmur, shrugging off my sweater and bunching it up on the ground. She kneels on it, leaning over the toilet as she throws her guts up. I run the faucet to drown out the noise, turning away to give her what little privacy I can offer.

I thought she was supposed to be the family jewel. Why

didn't anyone at the table help her? She didn't even look that great on the ferry ride, thinking back.

Allegra hasn't eaten much, so not a whole lot comes out of her. As soon as the toilet flushes, I turn around and check on her.

"Rinse out your mouth with water," I instruct. "And maybe wash your face, too."

"I'm sorry," she croaks, hobbling to the sink.

"You're sick. You don't have to apologize for it. Let's get you back to the dorm —"

"No, I can't!" She looks up with pleading eyes, water dripping down her face. "I have to go back out there."

"I mean this in the nicest way possible, but you look like a corpse. If your illness is flaring up again, you shouldn't push yourself."

"If he sees me like this, he'll pull me out of school. And I can't go back home again." She dabs her face with a paper towel. "I've worked too hard for it to mean nothing."

"It won't mean that much if you're dead."

"This hasn't killed me yet."

"That's not a great argument," I say.

She hesitates. "I told you before, didn't I? I want my father to see me as his successor. I thought he would make the announcement at my birthday party, but he didn't. Because he knows I am lacking."

I try not to be brusque with her, but I don't succeed. "So by pushing yourself to the point of throwing up, you're showing him that you're strong?"

Allegra slides to the bathroom floor, defeated. "I was born with the body of a human."

"What?"

"I was born with the body of a human," Allegra repeats.

"But I have the powers of a shadowborn. Because of that, my body can't contain my magic. It constantly attacks itself, like an autoimmune disorder. It views my magic as something foreign, like a disease."

She lifts the hem of her skirt, revealing scars crisscrossing over her legs. Black tattoos like thorny vines wrap around the scars, making a mess of her skin. Her arms are the same.

"Who did this to you?" I ask, even though I already know the answer.

"My father keeps my magic bound with spells. It's the only thing keeping me alive," she explains. "As a result, I'm not much stronger than a human. I can't even open a rift. And even with all these tattoos and spells and medications, I relapse if I do too much. But my 'too much' is what *you* do daily when you train."

That explains a lot. I knew I saw something on her skin the day she was pushed into the pool. But I'm not sure why she's telling me all this, especially in a public toilet. Maybe she never had anyone to talk to about it, which makes me feel bad for her. And guilty, for all the times I made small talk with her over a meal instead of genuinely asking if she was okay.

Someone knocks on the door impatiently. "Hello? Is this bathroom occupied? You've been in there for quite some time."

"I have explosive diarrhea. Come back, or don't, in an hour!" I yell back.

Allegra snorts, leaning her head against the wall. "In truth, I'm a bit jealous of you."

That's not something I would have *ever* expected to come out of Allegra's mouth. Then again, she only knows me as

Mary Alice.

"I'm sorry about your illness," I reply, sitting next to her. "And I'm sorry your dad makes you think you have to prove yourself to gain his approval."

"It's not my dad's fault. It's mine. I want to be stronger, to be able to defend myself. But I can't even learn how to swim because it puts too much stress on my body. I can't eat the foods I crave without vomiting, and I can't wear what I want because of these tattoos. I'm not supposed to tell people about my illness because my father doesn't want it to be widely known. Having offspring like me would make him seem weak. That's another big reason why everyone hates me; I've always had to be vague about my disease, and they think I'm faking it for attention. That's why I'm a little bit jealous of you, Mary Alice. You're so normal."

"I'm not normal," I assure her. "Everyone has their own struggles."

I've been jealous of Allegra, too. She carries herself with such elegance and hides her weaknesses. She's the picture of a Southern Belle, a better version of Mary Alice. I can't imagine how she must have felt holding all this in. Aside from me, she doesn't have any friends. Archer is her ex, and Rhys works for her family. I'm sure it's been difficult not having anyone to talk to.

"And yours?" Allegra asks. "What do you struggle with?"

Given her courage to talk to me about her problems, I return her question with honesty. "My heart is really small. Because of that, I have a much larger capacity for hatred than I do for love. The love I am capable of giving is finite; the hatred is infinite and consuming, like a void swallowing me whole. And even though I know this about myself, *hate*

this about myself, there's nothing I can do about it. Every time I try to change, I fail."

Allegra is quiet for a long time before she finally says, "I think you're selling yourself short."

"Excuse me?"

"You might not *love* me. But you are kind to me when no one else is."

"I have ulterior motives," I reply honestly.

"You saw I was feeling sick and you helped me. Even when the people who 'love' me would rather turn away and ignore the reality of my situation. You listened to me, and now, you aren't looking at me like I'm a freak. Or like I've disappointed you. Even if you have ulterior motives, I'm grateful for you."

I stare at her for a moment, then reach into my purse. "I brought my makeup pouch. Do you think you can make it through the rest of the meal without passing out?"

"I feel better now that I've thrown up, but I don't think I can eat anything heavy," she admits.

"That's fine. I have an idea."

I wash my hands before starting. I don't have enough to give her a full makeover, but I can at least make her look healthier. Swiping concealer under her eyes, I begin trying to make her skin even. The rest of the look falls into place naturally, with highlighter and blush being the main stars of the show. By the time I'm finished, she looks passable. At least, she looks alive.

We exit the bathroom arm in arm, giggling as we walk back to the table.

"What took you so long?" Neil asks. "The food is getting cold."

So, he already ordered for us. Figures.

"Someone was holding up the bathroom line," I lie with a pout. "I'm sorry. I didn't realize you were waiting. Or that you ordered. Allegra and I are on a diet."

"A diet?" Faith echoes, turning to her daughter. "What kind of diet? You don't need to lose any weight."

"It's this healthy diet I read about in a magazine to boost our immune systems. We're going to need some lemon sorbet," I say, piling lies on top of lies. But I'm on a roll. "Scientists have discovered that consuming cold lemon products is the best way for your body to absorb vitamin C. Something about the cold makes it more effective. Right, Allegra?"

"Right. It's a groundbreaking discovery," she replies, playing along. "As soon as Mary Alice told me about it, I wanted to try it. We decided to do it together, to motivate each other."

"You can't skip the diet for today?" Neil asks.

"Absolutely not! We can't have a cheat day or it will ruin our progress," I exclaim. "All we need are the lemon sorbets and a pitcher of water. Hydration is *so* important."

Neil sighs, waving the waiter over.

Allegra beams at me, mouthing "thank you."

I can't help smiling back, knowing this small gesture will never be enough to make up for the sin of my birth.

CHAPTER TWENTY-THREE

A llegra admires my handiwork in the bathroom mirror, swiveling her head from side to side. "Wow. This looks great—like I was in a horrible accident!"

A bubbling blister frames her face, running across her forehead, down her nose, and on either side of her eyes. Blood drips from her hairline and eyes, like ruby tears. It's positively gruesome—and some of my best work yet.

"You sound a little *too* happy about that," I tease, swiping more gelatin on her face. "Don't smile until this sets."

"I can't help it. How did you learn special effects makeup, anyway?" she marvels.

"YouTube." Where I learn all my makeup techniques. "I'm much better at daily looks, but I can't do normal makeup on you. You're already too pretty. Enhancing your natural beauty wouldn't do anyone any favors."

"Oh, stop," she says. "You flatter me."

It's not flattery; it's the truth. Allegra is stunning, Halloween makeup or not.

Our relationship changed after the dinner with Neil a few nights ago. And, more importantly, she's feeling worlds better. I think her family stresses her out, more so than she'd like to admit. If Neil was my father—*IF*—I would be anxious, too!

Growing closer to Allegra should be a good thing, but instead of being happy, *I'm* the one who feels sick. She's opened up to me, but I can't return the favor even if I want to. The thing is, I'm not sure I want that in the first place. Does that make me a bad person? More than I already am?

I like Allegra, don't get me wrong. I feel for her, and I want to be there for her. But I don't want her doing the same for me. Keeping secrets from her makes me feel guilty, but how can I stomach telling her the truth? Even if it were possible without Neil's repercussions, I don't know that I would. And relationships are a two-way street, right?

"Are you sure you don't want to go to the dance?" I ask, putting the finishing touches on her makeup. "You'll be the ghoul of the ball."

"I'm not a huge fan of school dances. The other Halloween festivities should be more than enough to keep me occupied. I heard there's going to be a hay maze!" she exclaims giddily. "You can borrow a dress from my closet if you need one."

"I'll wear something I have." I don't plan on staying long, anyway.

I debated whether I wanted to go at all, but after what Archer said last week, I've decided I want to talk things through. I've been running from my problems for most of my life, but if I run from this like I do from everything else, I'll spend the rest of my life wondering "what if."

The way he handled everything sucked, but it's not like

I'm Miss Perfect. I *am* lying to him about who I am. I guess either way, I'll be more satisfied with the outcome if I know I tried to work things out. Even if whatever it is between us ends.

The thing is, I'm not sure *what* to feel anymore. I like Archer, otherwise I wouldn't be so hurt by him ignoring me. When we're alone, he makes me feel special, and I enjoy his attention. But even after deciding to get to know each other better, I don't know him at all. Although we've talked about ourselves, he's still a stranger. And I have to ask myself if being with him feels natural, or if I'm forcing something to happen.

As cheesy as it sounds, he makes my heart beat faster, and I enjoy kissing him. The attraction between us is real. But that's not enough to base a relationship on, is it?

"Allegra's makeup looks very realistic," Rhys comments, standing in the doorway. "You have quite a skill."

A rare compliment from Rhys. I'll cherish it forever. "Do you want me to do you next?"

He blinks, bewildered. "Do me?"

"Your makeup," I clarify with a laugh. "I can give you a burn, too. There's a ton of gelatin left."

"That is quite alright," he replies, his voice clipped. Jeez, first he compliments me, and now he sounds angry.

"Mary Alice needs to get ready. She's got a *date* with Archer," Allegra teases. "Don't stay out too late."

"It's not a date." It's probably a breakup appointment.

Rhys frowns. "Archer Kinsey?"

"He's taking me to the dance. But all I want to do is talk to him. After the situation in the Veil, I want an explanation."

Allegra's eyes widen and she covers her mouth with a hand. "Wait. Was Archer there when Marshall hit you?"

"Yeah, and he didn't do anything about it," I explain. "I don't expect him to ride in on a white horse, but when students told Professor Hall I walked into the Nightmare cave myself, he didn't say anything in my defense. And he ignored me afterward, only approaching me last week about it. Like he expected me to forget."

"He's always been like that. Even when we were dating," Allegra says. "That's one of the main reasons I broke up with him. He was the sweetest boyfriend in private, but in public, all he cared about were appearances. He never stood up for me."

My jaw drops. "Why didn't you tell me sooner?"

"It's been years. I didn't want to ruin your relationship based on my own experiences," she says. "Sorry. I also feared you'd think I was trying to sabotage your relationship."

"Well, we're going to hash things out tonight. I don't think it's going to be a fun conversation. So with that, I have to go prepare, mentally and physically."

"Okay. Good luck! I'll be around campus if you need me for backup," Allegra promises.

Rhys looks like he wants to say something, probably snide, but he lets it go and walks away without a word. Okay, bye.

I head outside, zipping up my jacket. Allegra's little revelation about Archer doesn't change things. I still want to hear what he has to say.

A large white box sits on the front steps of the dormitory when I get back. It's hard not to notice the orange bow — how festive. Judging by the lack of lights on inside the

house, I'm guessing none of the other girls are home. I pick up the package and bring it inside.

When I place it on the dining room table, I notice a tag sticking out from the bow with my name on it. It's for me? Is this some kind of prank? It *is* Halloween. You know —*trick* or treat.

Cautiously, I open the lid and peer inside. It's not a dead animal, at least. Underneath a layer of silver tissue paper lies a white ballgown with a note and a ticket to the dance attached to the bodice.

Mary Alice,

I'm sorry. I hope you come tonight.

Archer

I lift the dress out of the box, holding it up. The tulle skirt sweeps the floor, attached to a rigid bodice adorned with intricate beadwork. The dress is fit for a princess, which I am not.

But bringing it downstairs, I'm still eager to try it on. I shower quickly and pull up my hair, doing my makeup before touching the dress again. I don't want to get anything on it, and God forbid my fingers slip and I drop my mascara wand.

When I'm finished, I pull the dress on. It's a bit tight at the waist but I manage to get the zipper up without ripping it. The fit is awkward and not made for my body type. It would look much better on a more petite girl with a shorter

torso and bigger bust. Nonetheless, I can't expect Archer to know my exact size. The gesture itself is generous.

Throwing on a pair of shoes, I shove the ticket from Archer into my purse along with my phone and leave through the back door. Night has fallen, but the sky is lit up from the Halloween festivities around campus. Allegra was correct—there are plenty of activities tonight aside from the dance. I pass a booth with balloon darts, whack-a-witch, and numerous food stalls handing out candy. There's the hay maze Allegra mentioned, though it's not nearly as crowded as the funhouse. The doorway looks like you're walking into the mouth of a clown—yikes.

The dance is held in the gymnasium, right next to the caramel apple stand. Black and orange streamers hang from the open doorway, blowing in the crisp autumn breeze. All the guests lining up outside are thankfully in gowns and suits, not in costumes.

When I finally reach the doorway, an attendant checking tickets holds her hand out to see mine. After verifying that it's legit, she hands me a white plastic mask like the one from *The Phantom of the Opera.*

"No thank you," I say, shaking my head. The mask will ruin my makeup.

"You have to. This is a masquerade," the attendant explains patiently. "The masks are spelled to conceal your identity."

My heart plummets. "What?"

"This is a masquerade," she repeats. "You need a mask."

That's not written on the ticket. But now that I can see inside, all the partygoers are wearing masks.

Maybe it's a coincidence, I think, but even I'm not stupid

enough to fall for that. It's no coincidence. Even now, Archer is ashamed of me.

Why else would he invite me here? All I wanted to do was talk, but he made a show of inviting me here instead. Why?

I'm such an idiot. Why did I expect things to be different here? Just because no one knows about my characters, about my "drug dealer" father? The problem, I'm realizing now, is *me*. Who I am, not Mary Alice or Mari or Marilyn. Not even Mar. It's Maria. She ruins everything.

Spinning around, I get out of line and head back the way I came. Shame dyes my cheeks red, and all I want to do now is run from it. But how fast do you have to run to escape a feeling within yourself?

I race past the caramel apple stand, holding my skirts as I stop to catch my breath by the hay maze. I can't go back to my dorm alone, feeling like a loser. But I can't be out in the open, either. Most of all, Archer can never know how much he's hurt me. I've learned that, if you let a guy know he's gotten to you, he's won. I've already lost so often here—to Nic, to Neil, to Lilly, to Marshall… I don't want to lose to Archer, too.

I duck into the hay maze. It looks dark and abandoned, the perfect place to collect my thoughts. Or be murdered by a serial killer. But that would be leaning way too far into the horror genre, and we already established this as a paranormal fantasy novel. I should be fine, right?

I take a seat on a bale of hay inside, trying to collect my thoughts. It doesn't make sense why I'm so upset about this. I was prepared to break up with him tonight, and I'm already aware he's a coward. None of this is new informa-

tion, so why am I freaking out? Am I more hurt by him than I wanted to admit earlier?

It doesn't make sense. What he did was shitty, but he didn't ignore *me*. He doesn't even know me. He rejected Mary Alice, ignored *Mary Alice*. Which only goes to show how poor his taste is. Mary Alice is my best character. She's not me. When did the line between Maria and Mary Alice begin to blur?

I take a deep breath. Maybe I was too hasty. I should go back and sort things out with him like I'd originally planned. Making my way through the hay maze, I find the exit that leads to the back door of the gym. Perfect. I can just go in, find him, and leave for a more secluded place to talk —

"Well, well. If it isn't Maria." Nic stumbles into me, clearly having had one too many drinks. Where did he even get alcohol here? There are no stores on the island that sell it. "What are you doing, looking like that?"

"I'm not in the mood, Nic," I say, taking a step away from him.

"I just want to keep you company." He pulls me into an awkward embrace, and I can smell the alcohol on his breath. "You love my company."

*M*AR

"That's bullshit and you know it," I snap, trying to extract myself from his arms. "I'm not in the mood for games."

"Well, I am. And whether you like it or not, Maria, you're going to play."

"Just tell me what you want from me and get out of my face."

"I want you to stop pretending like you're someone you're not," he says, his words beginning to slur.

His touch repulses me, his clammy hands on my shoulders, but I can't shake him off. He's drunk but strong. "Why does it matter to you?"

"Because your very existence sickens me."

And there it is.

"I'm sure you can relate to that. I read your file, Maria. Your full file. Just got my hands on it last week. I have to say, you're a real piece of work. You play 'poor little orphan girl,' but in reality, you're just a psychopath, aren't you?"

I don't reply. Anything I say will fall on deaf ears since he's plastered. Even if that weren't the case, it's Nic we're talking about. I just need to get away from him, as soon as he lets me go.

"You go on pretending to be something else, pretending like you're better than me. But at least I didn't push someone down a flight of stairs as a kid. How old were you, eight? Nine? Why did Neil take *you* in?" He's beginning to sound angry, and not in a playful way. This isn't good. "We should have just drained you dry and used your blood ourselves. But he insists that you stay alive. For what purpose?"

"Why don't you ask him? I have no clue," I whisper. "I'd *prefer* it if you left me alone!"

"See, here's where I don't believe you. I think part of you is excited by all this. The adventure, the thrill of being *special*." He sneers, his voice rising.

"You know why I'm here." He knows all too well. "I don't have a choice."

"You're Neil's daughter."

"What?"

Time seems to freeze, and I slowly turn around.

Archer stands behind me, his expression a mix of shock and disgust. He's heard everything.

No. No, this isn't happening.

I have to lie, to convince him somehow that Nic is just messing around. But the words get stuck in my throat, and before I have a chance to fix the situation, Nic begins to laugh.

"You didn't know? Sorry to break this to you, but she's not who you think she is," Nic taunts. "She's shadowborn. A weakling shadowborn, just like her sister."

"Shut up!" I struggle against Nic, but he has me locked in his arms, nuzzling against me. "Archer, he's just drunk—"

"Neil Abbott is her father," Nic tells Archer. "She's shadowborn, just like you and me."

"Mary Alice, what is he talking about?" Archer asks.

"He doesn't know what he's saying. He's a liar," I say quickly. "He's a *drunk* liar."

"A liar? Talk about the pot calling the kettle black," Nic replies. "Your real name isn't even Mary Alice. It's Maria. Isn't it?"

I wince. If I react, if I deny it too strongly, Archer will suspect me. I have to be careful, but at the same time, Nic isn't giving me any opportunity to weasel my way out of this.

"Archer, he's drunk," I repeat, trying to keep my tone calm. But I think my expression is telling a different story, because Archer isn't buying it. He's barely even looking at me.

Nic continues his rant, holding a hand tightly over my

mouth. "She's lied to you about everything, Archer. Her name, her family, her status… And you bought it, like a fool. Why else do you think Neil took her in?"

I elbow Nic in the stomach, hard. He grunts, loosening his grip enough for me to wiggle away. "Don't listen to a thing he's saying —"

"Your accent is different," Archer interrupts. "You usually have a Southern drawl. Now, it doesn't sound like you have a drawl at all. Have you been faking it this whole time?"

"I —"

"What is going on here?" Rhys asks, walking in at the worst possible time. He comes around the back of the gym, examining the scene. "Nic. Archer. Do either of you care to explain?"

"I was just telling Archer here about Miss Maria Rochester," Nic says with a wide grin. "Or should I say, Miss Abbott? I don't know. Do bastards get to take the father's last name?"

What can I do? Continue denying it? Cry on cue? I need to sell this lie. Screw whatever feelings I had toward Archer; now, I need to do whatever I can to convince him Nic is delusional.

But I don't get a chance to say anything before a flash of white light illuminates the sky, so bright it looks like it's daytime for a few seconds. The sound of an explosion follows from inside the gym, and it isn't long before I hear a chorus of screams as students pour from the back door of the building.

Chapter Twenty-Four

I know what it feels like to think you are going to die. The anticipation, the dread, the retrospection…all mixed with something raw and primal that I can't quite put into words. Over the past few months, I've narrowly escaped death time and time again. But nothing compares to this.

Screams fill the air, along with smoke and the distinct scent of burning flesh. Inside the gym, flames shoot from the sprinkler system, raining fire and death onto the students still trapped within. A stampede of people pours from the doors, some still ablaze.

"We have to go," Rhys says, pulling my arm roughly. "Come on!"

He drags me away from the students, away from the blaring alarms and the corn maze toward the beach. But I can't run very fast in this dress. In the end, Rhys picks me up and throws me over his shoulder. It's more practical than a princess carry, I suppose.

He only sets me down on the sand once we make it to the water.

"What just happened?" I ask. My legs feel like jelly and I slide to the ground to sit, breathing hard despite Rhys doing most of the work to get me here.

"I do not know." He looks around, scanning our surroundings for something I can't quite comprehend. "Do you have your cell phone?"

"Here." I hand it to him, my hands shaking. "Call emergency services. I—I wouldn't even know what to say."

He takes it from me and dials, but none of his words register as he speaks to the person on the other line.

Do I go back and help the other students? I should; it's the right thing to do. But I can't move. What if, by trying to help, I make things worse? Actually, on that point, what could I possibly *do* to help? I'm useless.

Am I behaving like Archer, freezing up when people need me? Am I more of a hypocrite than I realized?

"Look at me." Rhys kneels in front of me, forcing me to stare into his eyes. "Everything is going to be fine. You are going to be fine. I promise."

"I don't understand why this is happening. *How* this is happening. Someone committed arson at a magic school. What use is magic if we can't prevent situations like this?"

What use am I?

"Everything is going to be fine," he repeats. "But you and I need to stay here."

"We should go help—"

"We cannot do anything to help. Emergency services are on their way. Just try to breathe."

I do—but it doesn't make me feel any better.

THEY CALL IT A MIRACLE IN THE SCHOOL PAPER. ONLY fifteen students died, eight of whom were hospitalized for serious burns. The other seven were killed in the stampede outside.

Rhys was right about not going back to the gym. We wouldn't have been able to do anything, and we could have gotten injured ourselves. He waited with me for hours in the dark, until he deemed it safe for me to return to my dorm. He didn't even go to find Allegra, though she's fine, he assured me.

I don't know why I'm so shaken by the whole incident. Maybe it's one of those "that could have been me" feelings. Either way, it won't disappear no matter what I do.

Two days later, I go to the cafeteria to calm my nerves over a bowl of soup. It feels like I haven't stopped shaking since the incident.

Could this be related to the cult? Is this...my fault? Were they looking for me?

Invasive thoughts flood my mind, and my only reprieve is going on my phone and scrolling through shopping websites. Not that I can buy anything anyway. I just need the distraction.

I forgot all about Neil, until he approaches me in the cafeteria.

"Maria. Let's go for a drive. I need to update you on a very serious situation," he says. "This is not a request, but an order."

A serious situation? Did something happen to my family? I shoot to my feet, following him out of the cafeteria. "What happened?"

"Come along. We don't have any time to waste. We need to board the ferry. My car will pick us up on the other side."

I try to keep up with him, but he walks too quickly. I have to jog to maintain a place beside him. We board the ferry just in time and get into a black SUV parked by the boardwalk.

Neil sits across from me while I fumble with my seatbelt. "Are you going to tell me what's going on?"

"In light of the arson incident a few days ago, I've been quite preoccupied. I've lent my aid to the school trying to find the culprit, but they seem to have evaded everyone's grasp."

"That's horrible," I say, "but what does that have to do with me? What's the urgent situation?"

"I've been told Archer Kinsey has been made aware of our familial relationship."

Silence falls between us, and I'm caught between lying about it or begging for mercy. But I don't think either will be very effective.

"Nic told him, didn't he? He always had a big mouth," Neil continues. "But I specifically told you to keep this a secret. Part of it was a test, to see how you would handle Nic. And you did nothing."

"Nic got drunk and started shouting it because he hates me. I'm not stronger than Nic; I couldn't physically do anything to him," I argue. "And we're related, so how was I supposed to persuade him?"

"You should be stronger than him. Nic is only shadow-born, and you are to defeat Astaroth, a powerful trueblood. Have you made any progress?"

"It's not my fault I wasn't born with shadowborn strength. I'm doing my best," I say. "Nic is the one spilling your secrets."

"I don't care for excuses, Maria. If I don't discipline you

now and make good on my promise, you won't believe me in the future. And I only want what's best for us. You know that."

"What are you —"

The car stops, and so does my heart. We're in front of Isabelle's house. The tinted windows in the back open, just a crack.

Luke is outside in the front yard, laughing with David. They're passing a football around, and doing a horrible job of it. Luke's not the biggest sports fan, but David enjoys it.

My heart sinks to my stomach as I turn back to Neil. He pulls a gun from his jacket pocket, pointing the barrel out the window.

I lunge for him, but the shot rings out before I can even get my hands on Neil or the gun. I think I scream, or David does. Someone screams. I look outside, and Luke is on the ground. David stands stock still, splattered in blood.

I try to open the car door, to run outside and cover David's eyes, but the door is locked. Isabelle's car isn't parked in the driveway, either. Is she not home? Or did Tasha take it? Does David even know he needs to call 911? They can save people who have been shot, right? It's all about timing.

"Let me out!" I yell, yanking the handle. "Oh my God. What have you done?"

"I think the real question here is, what did you just make me do?" Neil closes the windows and signals for the driver to speed away, forcing me back in my seat. "You should be thanking me, Maria. Now, you only have one father: me. It's as it should be."

CHAPTER TWENTY-FIVE

The first time I met Luke, I was twelve. Isabelle had to pick me up from school because I got into a fight with another girl. Luke drove. I was in rough shape when I slid into the backseat. And Luke said, "Yikes. I hope the other girl looks worse."

"She doesn't," I replied.

"Well, in that case," he said, "I think we need to stop for ice cream on the way home."

When I first moved into Isabelle's home, Luke was in charge of preparing our bedroom. I looked inside and the room was empty.

Isabelle turned to Luke, pissed. "I thought you said you'd take care of it!"

"This is going to be Tasha and Mar's room," Luke replied, completely calm. "Shouldn't they be the ones decorating it? I thought we could take a trip to Target and let them pick out their own stuff."

"Where are they going to *sleep* tonight? In the guest room?"

"Of course not. They're not guests." Luke laughed. Unlike mine, his was never forced. "This is their home now."

"Don't mind all that stuff your teacher said. You don't have to call me Dad," Luke told me. I was sixteen.

"It would feel weird," I agreed. Not because he wasn't my father. I'd never called *anyone* Dad. I didn't explain it well, but Luke smiled like he knew exactly what I was thinking.

"Take your time, Mar," he said, patting my back. "I can wait as long as it takes."

IT'S A LONG DRIVE BACK TO SCHOOL. TIME PASSES MORE slowly when your lungs feel like they're filled with broken glass.

Neil drops me off at the pier. I don't even remember boarding the ferry, much less getting back to my dorm. I run down to the basement, locking the door and turning on the light.

"Todd!" I scream, opening the bathroom door. But it's just a bathroom. I shut it and open it again. "Todd! Where are you! Todd!"

The third time I open the bathroom door, Todd is standing on the other side. The Infinity Hallway glows behind him, illuminating his silhouette.

"Todd," I breathe, my voice shaking more than my hands. "Thank God. I need you to turn back time."

"Mar, calm down. What happened?" he asks, helping me sit on my bed.

"I need to turn back time to earlier today. No, to Halloween." If I can go back a few days, I can change everything. "Do you need my blood? I'll give you whatever you want. Just rewind—"

"I can't rewind time to bring someone back to life. It doesn't work that way if someone is fated to die," Todd explains. He already knows what has happened.

"But Luke wasn't fated to die. Neil…he hurt him. But I can change that. I can fix things. How can someone have such a horrible fate? I need to fix it. It's my fault, so I need to fix it."

"Mar, you can't rewind time to bring someone back. You're a different story, but everyone else…"

"That's not possible. That's not *fair*," I say. "Why did you save me and not him? Why am I here and he's not?"

"I'm sorry, Mar," Todd says softly. "I'm so sorry."

"So am I."

Todd returns to the bathroom without a word, closing the door and disappearing back into the Infinity Hallway. There's nothing he can do, nothing he can say to make it better. The only thing I can do for myself right now is…change.

I dig through the boxes stacked in my room, searching frantically through the supplies I bought before coming to school. In the bottom of one box, I find several packages of hair bleach and dying kits. I lock myself in the bathroom and brush my hair out. It's gotten longer since I last dyed it, so four boxes should suffice. I've had enough at-home hair disasters to know: always buy more than you think you need.

The light above me flickers as I brush the bleach on, sectioning with hair clips and coating each strand meticulously. Focusing on getting this done quickly and precisely helps keep my mind from wandering down a long and dark winding mental hallway I shouldn't dare go. But it's hard to focus when everything is numb, right down to my fingertips.

It's been a while since I went blonde. Full-blown blonde, that is. I got highlights senior year, but they looked so horrible I had to re-dye my whole head the next day. My hair was a mess of split ends.

My hands tremble as I mix more bleach in the plastic bowl, the smell stinging my eyes. But pain is good. It reminds me that I'm still alive. And if I'm still alive, I can ensure Neil won't be by the end of all this.

The end.

Will this ever be truly over?

It's not "over" between Max and me. He's still alive, yet he's capable of haunting me like a ghost. Neil will do the same, even if by some miracle I *do* manage to kill him. But as long as I have that goal in my mind, I have something to move toward. Something to hope for in a sea of misery.

It takes the entire night, and several bottles of toner, to achieve an acceptable shade of blonde. I end up chopping off several inches, letting it fall just past my shoulders. Even after the conditioning mask, the ends were fried; I had no other choice but to cut off the dead weight.

With the transformation complete and dawn approaching, I admire myself in the mirror. The golden blonde color doesn't suit my palette, but after I get dressed and put my makeup on, I'll look better. More importantly, I'll *feel* better. Because I won't be myself.

After all that crap with the Nightmare, I'm shocked at

how easy it is to get into character as Marilyn. She comes to me naturally. It would be concerning for a therapist, I suppose, but I don't have one of those right now. I don't have anyone but myself.

Marilyn is perfect because she doesn't have parents. She doesn't have a demon for a biological father, and her adoptive father, her *real* father, didn't die. Her family isn't being held hostage. She has nothing but herself, nothing to lose. She's alone, and that's what makes her strong.

I need her strength. Even if it's a lie, if it's just pretend, I can't bear being myself right now.

MARILYN

I can't believe I haven't found any cute boys on campus. It's a dry November, to cap off a barren year. Why, I'm not sure what I'll do if my third quarter metrics continue to be so low.

Maybe I'll try to find a party to go to. Colleges are full of parties, right? And with these silicone inserts, I should be able to get into any party I want. Even if I'm an undesirable human, my breasts have never looked better.

I guess having a spare outfit for every character does come in handy. I don't think I could have felt like Marilyn without the push-up bra. Thank you, Neil. I'll be sure to exercise your wallet before I exorcize your soul!

My heels click on the pavement as I walk toward Mathers' office. The main building is still under repair on account of what happened at the Halloween dance. Funny, what happened just a week ago feels like a lifetime away.

I don't want to be late for Independent Study, especially

since I plan on being a little bit more direct with Provost Mathers. No more pussyfooting around, excuse my word choice. He's going to tell me how to kill Astaroth, no matter what the method.

I've been too sidetracked, lately. That's my problem — I should have gone straight for the jugular. And as a result...

Well, it doesn't matter now. I'm Marilyn, and if the other characters couldn't kill Astaroth that's too bad. I know I'll succeed because I'm not weighed down by morals. Those are just pathetic human constructs that only certain groups of people have to follow. For most of my life, I've been resigned to the fact that I have to follow the rules or face the consequences. But why can't I have my cake and eat it, too?

I grab a soda from the vending machine and head up to Mathers' private office, only a few minutes late. But Provost Mathers doesn't look too pleased to see me, which is a gosh darn shame, given my outfit is so on trend.

"Mary Alice, you are fifteen minutes late," Mathers chides, writing something in his notebook. When he looks up from his desk and sees me, the pen falls from his fingers. "Mary Alice? Is that you?"

"Not quite," I drawl, sauntering inside. "I'm Marilyn. Like, Marilyn Munster. I loved that show when I was a little girl. Did you see it, Professor?

"I'm afraid I'm not familiar," he stutters out, bewildered. "Mary Alice —"

"Marilyn," I correct. "It's a shame you haven't seen the show. A family of classic monsters like Dracula and Frankenstein live in California. The comedy of it makes use of dramatic irony. I learned that from Rhys when we were studyin' Grecian plays. It's when the audience knows some-

thin' that the characters don't. In *The Munsters*, the family of monsters don't realize they're monsters."

"Miss Rochester—"

"Marilyn. And it's a bit rude to interrupt someone, isn't it? As I was sayin', the family of monsters is completely unaware of how scared their human neighbors are of them. They have one non-monstrous member of the family, Marilyn Munster, who they consider plain and drab despite the actress herself bein' a real beauty. But you know what I think, Professor? Despite her appearance, she's just as strange as the rest of the Munsters."

"People *do* judge others based on appearance," Professor Mathers agrees weakly. "But I fail to see what this has to do with you."

"I wonder. But Professor, you don't need to be so tongue-tied. I don't bite, promise. I don't *usually* bite, anyway. Not unless they ask me to." I shrug. "Now, I'm ready to continue our lesson. More importantly, I want to know how to kill Astaroth."

I settle in the chair across from him, crossing my legs. In truth, I haven't worn heels in a while, and this particular pair pinches my toes. I need at least thirty minutes to recover enough to walk back to my dorm later.

"Miss Rochester, *Marilyn*, we discussed this." A stern look settles over his features. "You must leave Astaroth to the professionals."

"The professionals who let his cult run rampant on the ship? The professionals who allowed the use of blood magic and human sacrifice to free him from the time prison? The people who cannot find him now?" I press. "Forgive me if I don't trust these 'professionals.' Haven't you ever heard the phrase, 'If you want somethin' done, do it yourself?'"

"Do you think you, a human, can kill Astaroth?" he asks incredulously.

"It doesn't matter if I believe it or not. I have to." I smile, leaning over my desk with my chin propped up on my hand. "Did you ever wonder why I was admitted to Southeastern, despite bein' a human? Why would I come to this school when, at the hospital in Boston, I ran away despite your warnin'?"

I can't tell him my situation outright, but I hope the good old provost here can put two and two together.

"I thought you came here for protection," Provost Mathers says warily, which is the wrong answer. But I won't penalize him for it, because I'm generous like that.

"You're a smart man," I purr, "but I'm gonna need you to think about this harder. I risked everythin' to go home, to be with my family. Why am I here? Why am I with the Abbott family? What could I benefit from learnin' at a school for shadowborn, when I'm human? Do you think Neil Abbott is a generous man?"

It takes a minute longer than it should for realization to dawn on Mathers' face. I was hoping I didn't have to spell it out for him.

"I can't talk about it, and neither should you. For all I know, you're on his side, monitorin' me and such."

"Do you truly not trust me?" Provost Mathers asks, which is a silly question.

"I don't trust you. But I need you. I need you to tell me how to kill Astaroth once and for all. You can either help me or I can find someone who will, no matter what I have to do to convince 'em."

"I'll help you," he croaks. "Of course, I'll help you."

I clap my hands together. We've wasted enough time on

these mind games; now, the real work begins. "We should get started, then. Tell me what magic I can use to kill a demon."

"But you're human—"

"You let me worry about the execution."

Provost Mathers straightens, picking up a book on his desk. "I did find somethin'. It's just a theory, though. A legend with no real backin'. There is...a sword."

"Go on."

"It's called the Divinities Sword. Not much is known about it. I only happened upon it while readin' a passage in this book about medieval weaponry." He opens the book to a dog-eared page in the middle, placing it in front of me. The image is black and white, and blurry to boot, but it just looks like a regular sword from what I can tell. "The sword is enchanted, like the Blood Chalice from Northeastern."

"What makes it so special?"

"It's..." He hesitates, which I don't have time for.

"Spit it out, already."

Provost Mathers sighs, like this interaction is stressing him out. Well, Marilyn tends to have that effect on people. "It is said to use the opposite of blood magic, which in theory makes it strong enough to repel and destroy blood magic. I have no idea what that means, or what the 'opposite' of blood magic is. But it's considered a relic and owned by the Ruby Council. It's on display in the Veil, but I don't—"

"I want to see it. Do you think you could gauge if the 'theory' is true if we ran a few tests on it?" I ask.

"Tests? Miss Rochester, this is the Ruby Council we're talkin' about," he insists. "They won't just let you *take* the sword."

"Of course not." I'm not an idiot. "We're goin' to steal it."

Provost Mathers is speechless when I leave his class. With Independent Study over, I plan on skipping combat class and spending a little more time looking into the Divinities Sword at the library. Why even bother with combat when I can get someone else to help me out? Which is what I should have done from the start.

I'm nothing to Astaroth. Aside from my blood, I can't ever hope to defeat him in battle. Why should I? If I can get someone else to kill Astaroth by supplying them with whatever tools they need, the chances of success are much higher. And it's not like I can't find someone else to do my dirty work.

Look at Allegra. She helped me on the ship because she wanted to take credit for catching the cultists and prove herself. Who *wouldn't* want to take credit for killing Astaroth? All I need to do is find someone strong and desperate.

Nic's out, for obvious reasons. Rhys is out, too. I need a shadowborn. Archer would have been perfect—clearly, he cares about what other people think of him—but I don't think he wants anything to do with me after Halloween. Which is laughable. Between the two of us, at least I had a *reason* for lying. He's just a coward, like all the other guys I fucked. Except Archer didn't even get under my shirt, which is a gosh darn shame for him.

If it weren't for him…

Nope. Not going there.

I walk across campus, flashing smiles at any good-looking guy I see. Which seems to be just about everyone. Only a few smile back, probably because they don't know who I am.

By happy coincidence, I spot Nic Woolridge by the library's entrance and race to catch up with him.

"Nic!" I yell, waving my arms.

He spots me immediately, but recognition only dawns when I get closer. "Is that you, Maria? I like the new hair."

"It's not new, sweetheart, but I'm flattered all the same," I say. "You are just the man I've been lookin' for."

"To what do I owe the pleasure?"

I latch onto his arm with a big smile, my heels bringing me nearly to his height. "Neil found out about Archer. I just wanted to know who I have to thank for that. You were my first guess."

"Ah, so he found out. Well, unfortunately I wasn't the one who broke the news to him." He nods his head at Rhys and Allegra, who come up the walkway behind us.

Allegra has reverted back to her sickly, pale appearance. Why she's up and about is anyone's guess, but Rhys has to support her as she walks. They're speaking in hushed tones, real intimate. I should have known where his allegiance lies. Rhys works for Neil, and he has been giving him reports on me since the summer.

"Thank you, honey." I squeeze Nic's arm and walk away from him, toward Rhys and Allegra. Her eyes are bloodshot and red, like she's been crying. If I were a better person, I'd comfort her or at least ask her what happened. She's probably still shaken from Halloween, poor thing. But I'm Marilyn. I don't have to give a shit about anyone but myself.

Rhys is who matters right now. Rhys, who told Neil

about Archer and subsequently got Luke killed. Nic could be lying, but if it *was* him who squealed, he would be bragging about it. Instead, right now he's just watching the show. And I can't let my *favorite* cousin down, right?

"Rhys. I heard from Nic that you told Neil about my secret bein' exposed," I begin, crossing my arms. I try to read his face, but I can't tell if he's surprised because of my appearance or my words.

Either way, he doesn't deny it.

"Nic told you?" he asks, his voice low. His eyes dart to Allegra, sniffling beside him. "This is not the best time—"

"Then I'll be short." There's not much that needs to be said, anyway.

Rhys' words are all the confirmation I need. He told Neil that Archer knows my identity. He knew about my deal with Neil—about what would happen if I breached any of Neil's terms.

It's his job to keep tabs on me. Neil is his boss, and Rhys was just following orders. I can't fault him for that. It's not even like he betrayed me or pretended to be my friend. Maybe I was the one overreaching, making our interactions into something they weren't.

But whether it's his mistake or mine, whether he meant to or not, the result of his actions remain the same: Luke is dead.

"What happened to you, Mary Alice?" Allegra whispers. Does she have any right to be asking me that now, looking like a member of the living dead?

"Your father made good on a promise to me, is all," I drawl, staring into Rhys' eyes. "Thank you, Rhys. Really. You've helped me remember my mission here. Who my friends are, and who my enemies are."

"What are you talking about—" Rhys begins.

"Forgiveness is not my strong suit," I say. "I won't forgive you for this. I never want to see you again. I don't want to think about you or hear your voice. I don't care what Neil has ordered you to do. Don't ever show your face in front of me again unless you're prepared to die."

CHAPTER TWENTY-SIX

Word to the wise: The cure to a hangover is *not* more alcohol. It's not sex, either. Now I have a headache *and* lower back pain. Who knew whoring around school would be such a bad thing? Oh wait—I did. And I did it anyway. Because I hate myself.

Being Marilyn is freeing, in a way, but I don't have much impulse control or time to think about consequences. Even if I know something is going to bite me in the ass later, I still do it if it seems fun. This particular spiral, however, is not like the others. I've been hedonistic in the past; now, I'm trying to forget the pain. Nothing is working.

Nights are the hardest. I spend mine in bed with different guys, because the thought of going back to my basement alone is unbearable.

My latest conquest, if you want to call him that, kicks me out of his dorm in the morning. He doesn't want his girl-friend to see me, so he makes me crawl out the window and climb down the trellis, as if that won't draw *more* attention. He didn't mention he had a girlfriend, but now I can see

their silhouettes entwined in the window, kissing on the same bed we just had sex on. Classy. I know how to pick 'em, don't I?

I've always been like this. I can't even blame Marilyn; every single character seems to choose the wrong men to partner with. That's what happens when you have low self-esteem: You let people do anything to you because you think you deserve it. You constantly make excuses for them, but when it comes to yourself, you are crueler than you are to anyone else.

I thought I'd gotten over this, that my self-esteem had risen and rehabilitated thanks to Isabelle and Tasha. But nothing has changed, has it? I made excuses for Archer, too, and forgave him because I wanted to believe in him. In the end, I'm still alone.

It's Saturday, so I don't have class. Not that I would have attended, in my sorry state. I should stay near a toilet for the day.

I go back to my room and shower quickly, trying to wash away any traces of the guy from last night off my skin. I don't even remember his name, but he left some nasty marks on my hip. If need be, I have his dental imprints.

Just to be clear, I haven't been sleeping around because I'm a whore. Okay, not *just* because of that. After sex, they tend to be more loose-lipped. I thought pillow talk would help me discern who could be a hero candidate. Obviously I need a better tactic.

The perfect hero candidate to defeat Astaroth is someone strong and desperate for recognition—so desperate they will be easy to manipulate. This person doesn't have to be a *guy*. But what girls do I know? My roommates hate me and so does Ophelia. Allegra is too weak and too close to

Neil. Georgia Kyle is a prospect—she was the class representative on the cruise ship, and supposedly a talented swordswoman. But we're not friends, and aside from seeing her a few times in the cafeteria, I haven't talked to her all semester.

Am I...a friendless loser?

Nope, not going down that trap door!

The second part of my plan is the weapon. If the Divinities Sword doesn't work to defeat Astaroth, I'm fresh out of ideas. Astaroth is a blood magic user. How can I compete with that? How can *anyone*?

I spring up in bed, thinking back to what Todd told me once.

The key to your powers lies within you. Within me. *Within* me. At the time, I thought he was just being motivational. Trying to be, anyway. But what if he meant that literally? My power lies within me—within my blood?

It makes sense now that I think about it. Neil and Nic also confirmed my blood opened the time prison.

If not for the special properties your blood seems to hold, you would be no different from a human.

You're a walking blood bag.

The key to your powers lies within you.

I scramble to my feet, digging out my spell supplies and the stained blouse I practiced on earlier. Magic spells require intention, magic, and an anchor. I crush rose petals, what little mugwort I have left, and thyme in a mixing bowl. For the final step, I find a pin from my sewing kit and dip it in rubbing alcohol from the bathroom.

"Here goes nothin'," I mutter, pricking my finger. A single bead of blood drips into the bowl, and I crush it with the other ingredients. Moment of truth time.

I picture a clean version of the shirt as I smear the mixture on it. Rushing to the bathroom sink, I immediately rinse the shirt. Wiping away the chunks of herbs, I hold the shirt up to the light.

It's clean.

Wet but clean, without any signs of a stain.

My blood *is* key. I'm not sure why I didn't think of it sooner, but now that I know what I need to activate my powers, I want to see what else I'm capable of.

My body is buzzing with energy, and all the possibilities I've just opened up. I need to get another spell book and more materials for testing. The library should have grimoires. Even if I can't check the books out, I'll take pictures with my phone.

I grab a jacket and my bag. There's no time to waste. Racing across campus, I skid into the empty library and run up the stairs to the spell section. I need something more than a cleaning spell, something with easy ingredients that won't create a mess or kill me if it backfires.

After rifling through several grimoires on display, I choose twenty different spells to take pictures of. I'm not sure how heating cold soup—soup specifically, not tea or coffee—requires spellcraft instead of a microwave, but I'll try it anyway. Other inconsequential spells like that will be easy to try. The only useful spell I've taken a picture of is a flashbang, which is going to be hard to test out but possibly useful in a fight.

I'll have to come back later, but for now, I should head to the greenhouse and get some of the ingredients on my list. As I'm walking out, I bump into Archer Kinsey. Of all the people I don't want to see, he doesn't *top* the list...but he's still on it.

Archer pauses when he sees me. At first, I think he's going to turn around and leave without saying a word to me. That would be fine—it's not like I have anything to say to *him*, after what happened with Nic. But instead, Archer stops in front of me.

"I've been looking for you." It's not a good way to begin the conversation, but I guess this was coming sooner or later.

If I were Mary Alice, I'd be wondering how to play everything off. Now, I can lie, beg him to believe me, distract him with the promise of sex. But I can't bring myself to do it, even as Marilyn.

As confused as I was when we were together— "together"—it's even worse now. I can't determine whether or not I feel angry or guilty. Maybe both. Usually, my guilt would outweigh my anger and I would forgive him. Logically, I know what happened isn't his fault. And he didn't even hurt me—he hurt Mary Alice. A fictional character. As much as I try to tell myself that, my heart isn't listening. My ears are on my head, not my chest.

His rejection shouldn't sting, it shouldn't *feel* like a betrayal, but it does. I built him up to be someone he isn't, and that's on me. And he certainly has a right to be angry, given I lied to him. Maybe this *is* my fault, after all. I was deluded enough to think we could have a relationship, that I could get close to him, all the while knowing my mission to kill Astaroth was more important.

"You could've called, honey. I would've answered," I reply playfully, forcing a smile. "It's just us now. What did you want to talk about? I thought everythin' was settled on Halloween."

"Have you completely lost it? *Nothing* was settled. You

lied to me," he says incredulously. "Were you just playing with me? Did you only string me along because of my past relationship with Allegra?"

"You bring her up a lot. Are you sure that relationship is still in the past?" I brush by him, walking up the stairs toward the nonfiction section to ensure the librarian can't hear us.

"Don't make this about something it's not," Archer warns, following me. "How long were you going to keep this up? Pretending to be weak, pretending like you needed help when you didn't. Were you laughing at me behind my back with Nic?"

"Oh. So this is about how I hurt your pride, huh? You were the one ashamed to be seen with me."

"Don't deflect and pin the blame on me, when everything you've told me has been a complete lie! I don't even know who I'm looking at right now!" he bellows.

"What do you want from me, Archer? Do you want to yell at me, scream at me, hurt me?"

"I want the truth. I want to know why you lied."

"I'm a horrible person. I'm a bitch and a slut, a liar and a freak," I admit. "Does that make you feel better?"

"It doesn't," he denies. But I don't believe him.

"Knowin' that I am a villain, a monster who tricked you, I imagine you don't want anythin' to do with me. It's best if you just forget everythin' that happened and don't breathe a word of this to Allegra."

"Why shouldn't I? Why shouldn't I tell her *everything*, to warn her away from you?"

"Because..." Because I've dug myself into a hole and now I can't think of an answer. If it were anyone else, I

would have offered myself to him in exchange. But Archer would be disgusted by that.

The library door opens before I can respond, the little bell ringing. I look down and make eye contact with Nic Woolridge, the last person on earth I want to see.

He waltzes up the stairs, slinging an arm over my shoulder. "Ah, Maria. Archer. What are you talking about?"

"Nothin'," I mutter, shrugging him off. "I was just leavin'."

"Not so fast." Nic grabs my arm, shoving me back. "What's the big rush?"

"Three's a crowd, sweetheart."

"Oh? I'm your sweetheart now, am I?" Nic laughs. "I can't say I dislike this side of you, Maria."

I don't have time for his games. Not when I have the overwhelming urge to kill him. Even though Rhys was the one who told Neil, Nic is the reason it happened in the first place. I want to move past him, but Archer stops me.

"We aren't done here," he says roughly, grabbing my shoulder.

Stop grabbing me! I want to scream at them. I'm not a doll for them to just throw around. But instead, I say, "I'm very busy."

And I need to get out of here before Nic sets me off. I can already feel *her* at the surface, begging to be freed. Begging me to make Nic disappear, just like I tried to do with Max.

Nic mentioned Max on Halloween, didn't he? He knows what I did.

Nic smiles. "Hey Maria, how's your father doing?"

I freeze, squeezing my eyes shut. I can't freak out here, I can't lose it.

MARY ALICE

I'm in the library. Nic hasn't spoken to me yet. Everything is fine, and I am Mary Alice.

I'm Mary Alice. I have a family in Georgia. I am happy and nice and a good student.

I'm Mary Alice.

"I didn't think you'd be with Archer again," Nic says, barring me from passing by. "After what happened with your dad and all, I thought you would hate his guts. But I guess your file did mention what a slut you are."

I'm Mary Alice.

I'm not a slut. I do, however, feel the imminent need to throw up.

You're fine, I tell myself, swallowing it down along with any other unpleasant emotions rising from within. *You have to be fine.*

"What?" Archer looks between us frantically. "What is he talking about?"

"Nothing at all," I reply quickly. The last thing I want is for Archer to be dragged into this any deeper. For as

awkward as it is between us, I wouldn't want him to think that this is his fault. But Nic doesn't get the message.

"Didn't Maria fill you in? Part of her contract with Uncle Neil is to keep her origins a secret," Nic says. "But you found out. So he shot her fake father in the face."

MAR

No.

This isn't happening. I need to leave the library.

You are fine, I tell myself quietly, trying to control my breathing. Now, instead of throwing up, I feel like I'm dying instead. Like the world is ending around me and my heart is being crushed by the weight of Nic's words, the truth behind them.

No. You are fine. This isn't happening, I repeat to myself like a mantra.

"Why are you so upset? He wasn't your real father," Nic goads. I almost clamp my hands over my ears like a child to drown out his voice.

I'm hungry. I should go to the cafeteria.

I'm Mar. I like fries. I'm sarcastic. I'm strong-willed. I'll be okay.

I'm Mar. It's okay. I'm just Mar.

"I heard his blood splattered on your little brother."

Count to ten. Breathe. Go easy, now. You can't be Maria. You're Mar. Maria doesn't exist.

"I'm sure he'll never be the same, after seeing his dad get killed like that. Knowing that it's your fault. But really, Maria, Uncle Neil did you a favor."

Breathe. 1. 2. 3.

"You think they would have stayed with you, knowing the truth? That you're the bastard of a demon?"

4. 5. 6.

"If they knew what you cost them, your 'family' would never accept you."

7. 8. 9.

"You have a lot of weaknesses, Maria. Now you have one less."

10.

MARIA

Nic's voice sounds distorted. I can barely hear him over the blood rushing in my ears. It's too late to think about the consequences of my actions, too late for any regrets.

"Mary Alice — Maria," Archer corrects, shaking my arm. "What is he talking about?"

"It's nothing," I say.

"How magnanimous of you, Maria!" Nic gushes. "To forgive Archer for killing your fake father."

"Neil isn't my father, no matter what a genealogy report may say. Neil *murdered* my father. Not because of Archer, but because of you and Rhys." My voice is shaking. "Even then, Rhys was doing his job. But you were being malicious. You knew what would happen if anyone found out my secret and you told Archer anyway. Because you want to hurt me. You hate me, everyone seems to, for something out of my control. I didn't ask to be born. I don't *want* any of this. I just want to go home."

"I hate you," Nic confirms, "but not for the reason you

think. You are a snake in the grass, Maria. Or should I say *the hallway?*"

"It doesn't matter what your reasons are. In the end, Nic, you win." I turn, standing directly in front of him. "I'm Maria. You got your entertainment. I've lost my father. I can't even be *sad* about it because I can't tell anyone about Neil. I have to pretend like everything is hunky dory, that it *doesn't* feel like my goddamn heart is being ripped out every single second of every single day because of what you've done! But I guess that doesn't mean anything to you. You only care about yourself. You are just like Max. And you said it yourself: I'm a psychopath. I tried to kill him when I was eight. No matter how much I pretend, nothing has changed since then. No matter how hard I try, nothing ever will."

Nic's reflexes might be sharp, but I manage to catch him by surprise. All it takes is a little shove—a push of his shoulders and he loses balance, toppling over the railing and landing with a heavy thud on the first floor.

CHAPTER TWENTY-SEVEN

Nic's screams echo throughout the library, but Archer and I are slow to respond. I walk down the stairs leisurely, staring at him on the ground wiggling like an insect.

The librarian rushes over first, and seeing the blood, she screams, too. "What happened?"

"He fell," I reply calmly. "He thought he was cool, sitting up on that railing. But he lost his balance."

"You bitch!" he spits. "She *pushed* me!"

"I'm human. I wouldn't have had the strength," I retort, staring at the librarian.

"She's right," Archer says quickly, his voice shaking. "He fell on his own."

"I'll call the nurse," the librarian says with a nod, rushing to her desk across the room.

I bend down, looking at Nic's leg. "Max was surprised when I pushed him. I don't know why; he had been tormenting me for months."

But bullies never think their victims will stand up for

themselves. They are arrogant, and that is their fatal flaw. Maybe I was arrogant, too, because I thought pushing Max down a flight of stairs would kill him and end everything.

It didn't, not by a long shot.

"Max got a compound fracture, too," I say. "He made a full recovery, though. Not even a scar. Isn't that always the case? He walked away from everything without any consequences."

Nic doesn't quite register what I'm saying, and by the panicked expression on his face, neither does Archer. But I don't care. This is for *me*. Me, Maria.

"Even after they found Max videotaping himself beating me, they blamed *me*. Did you know that? Was that included in my file? I'm the one who took it too far. I'm the bitch, the slut, the liar. The foster freak. And Max was my victim." I look at the bone sticking out of Nic's leg and press on it hard, eliciting another scream from him. "Because before me, they swear he was normal. It was *my* fault he changed, my fault for not reporting him so they could get him help. I 'seduced' him into hurting me because I wanted attention. Were you normal before you met me, Nic? Were you seduced by me, too? Or is it all just fucking bullshit?"

I take a deep breath and stand. Archer looks at me as if I'm a stranger. I guess to him, I am. There's no turning back now, no crying over spilled milk. Or blood.

I was upset Max didn't die. I'm *not* upset Nic survived— because he deserves so much worse than this. So do I.

I don't wait for the campus medical staff to arrive. I leave first, walking out the back door as the two boys watch me go. I can't guess what they're thinking, nor do I care to.

Killing Nic would have been easier, but that requires more careful planning if I'm going to attempt to get away

with it. Neil might care, which would make things difficult and risk my remaining family members.

Well, I suppose what I've done here today already put them at risk. I should have thought things through better, but I was so angry I snapped. I'll just have to deal with the consequences as they come.

To think that I'm in control of my own fate is laughable. I lack so much, and it's put me at the mercy of those who despise me. But it's about time I return the favor in earnest.

I go back to my room and lock the door behind me, turning on the shower and stripping naked. The water is cold, but I let it rain on me anyway, soaking through my hair and down my body.

I can't function like this. To think that Nic pushed me this far. Maybe I'm still sensitive from Luke's death. Yet I can't seem to shed a fucking tear. What the hell is wrong with me? Don't normal people break down from this? I can't afford to right now, I know. But a small part of me wonders if I'd feel better that way, crying with abandon.

Luke deserves so much more. He deserves to be mourned properly by the people who care about him. What if heaven and hell *do* exist? What if he's looking down at me right now, thinking I don't love him?

I didn't say the words, but he knew...didn't he?

I slide down, my back against the tub and my legs leaning on the wall. Losing Luke is bad enough on its own, but Nic was right about one thing. If my family knew what happened, that he died because of *me*, what would they say? I'm sure they wouldn't blame me aloud, but they would in their hearts. How can I face them after this? How can I face David, knowing he had to watch it happen?

Max changed my life. And now I've changed David's.

He won't ever be the same again, because I stole his father from him.

I still remember the sound of the gunshot, the look on Neil's face. It should have been *him* instead. He's a monster and I wish he was gone forever. It's not about killing or enjoying it; I want him to just disappear, and with him, all my negative emotions. My fear, my hatred, and my disappointment.

By the time I get out of the shower, my fingertips are wrinkled and my teeth chatter uncontrollably. I towel off, blow dry my hair, and curl under my covers.

I'm Marilyn, I try to tell myself. But as much as I repeat it, I can't turn back. All I can think about is how much I hate Nic, how Neil has ruined my life. And how I can't do anything about it.

*M*AR

Returning to the Veil isn't my idea of a good weekend, but that's where the Ruby Council headquarters are. That's where the Divinities Sword is.

Provost Mathers is the one I have to thank for this little excursion. He booked everything and arranged a tour guide for us. The earliest day we can visit just so happens to be the Saturday before Thanksgiving.

"Are you ready, Miss Rochester?" Mathers asks.

I stand behind him on the beach, the wind whipping my dark hair into my face. My short-lived stint as Marilyn has come to a close, thanks to Nic. After what happened, I haven't been able to revert back to anyone but Mar. It's just as well. My grades have taken a nosedive, and I haven't

gone to tutoring with Rhys in weeks. All my spare time is spent studying and testing spells.

I'm avoiding Allegra, too, though that's easier nowadays. I don't see her much on campus, and assume her illness has flared up again. Nic has taken a leave of absence to recover, and thanks to Archer backing up my story, I didn't get into trouble for pushing him over the balcony. But Archer hasn't spoken to me since then, either.

At least I'm able to take care of myself, remembering to shower regularly and brush my teeth twice a day. On good days, I remember to eat. And my class attendance is the same. This is the most productive I've ever been as Mar.

"I'm ready," I confirm. "Ready as I'll ever be."

Mathers unsheathes his sword and swings it down, slicing through the open air. We pass through the rift together, and once we reach the Veil, Mathers closes the portal with both hands.

The rift brings us to a city center, though it's distinctly different from Atlanta or any other U.S. city I've seen photos of. There are a handful of tall brick buildings around us, but the rest of the shops and offices are two-story houses similar to the gothic Victorians on Southeastern's campus. The sidewalks aren't as crowded as Atlanta, either. Actually, there's no one around—not even any cars on the street.

"Why is the Veil like this?" I wonder aloud.

"War, industrialization, rampant magic—many things have caused a decline in some areas of the Veil," Mathers explains. "Others are still quite beautiful. The vampires have their own capital, and there are schools across the Veil, just like in the mortal realm. The elves and fae have preserved lands."

"And this?"

"Demon territory. Many demons live in the mortal realm," he replies. "As a result, the city is not as lively as it once was."

"It looks like no one lives here."

"There will be more people near headquarters." Mathers leads me down the street, looking both ways before crossing over to a skyscraper on the righthand side. It's a sleek glass building I'd expect to see in Manhattan, but there still aren't many people around.

Or inside, for that matter. Two guards check our IDs and make us sign in with a receptionist before we're allowed to enter.

The lobby looks like Versailles, with intricate gold embellishments on the walls and ceiling. It clashes with the modern art sculptures around the room, making me wonder if all demons lack interior design skills or if it's just the members of the Ruby Council.

"Ah, Mr. Mathers!" A tall man appears from behind a statue, tucking a feather duster into his back pocket. His fashion, shockingly enough, suits the room perfectly. The white powdered wig and intricately embroidered frock are very "French Nobility" while the pleather skirt and go-go boots are "Robo-chic." I respect it.

"Miss Rochester, this is Mr. Callan. He is one of the top Curiosities Curators in the Veil, and he's doin' a special collaboration with the Ruby Council."

"Hello." I extend a hand, but he fist-bumps my palm instead.

"Well, aren't you just darling?" I cannot for the life of me tell whether that's sarcasm. "You two are interested in the Divinities Sword, correct?"

"Yes. Anythin' you can tell us or show us would be beneficial for Miss Rochester's school paper," Mathers replies.

"Of course. Follow me." Mr. Callan talks as he walks, flaring his hands on occasion to emphasize his points. "The sword is a real mystery. It was first found by a fairy in the 1400s, who told all her friends that she saw a barbarian slay a blood-crazed wyvern with it in a single blow. At the time, no one believed the fairy. She couldn't explain how she *got* the sword in the first place, and soon after, she disappeared and took the sword with her. But prior to her disappearance, she showed it off around town. Some accounts say that no one could pick up the sword, regardless of their strength. The fairy claimed the sword only answered to its master."

"If the sword's abilities couldn't be verified, then why is it rumored to use the opposite of blood magic?" I ask.

"The sword disappeared and reappeared several times throughout history. There were 'sightings' of it, so to speak. The most famous sighting happened in 1886, when a woman was seen with the sword battling a famous tribe of blood-moon lycans. A huge ray of light erupted from the sword and slayed the dark beasts no one else had managed to kill," Mr. Callan explains. "There were quite a few witnesses. The sword hasn't been seen since."

We come to a stop in front of a display case with a sword inside. A red, knotted tassel hangs from the hilt, and a squiggly line is carved into the flat of the blade. Other than that, it looks like an average sword.

"This is a replica, one of the best by all accounts," Mr. Callan adds, as if I care. I don't want a *replica*, I need the actual sword!

"So, the real sword is lost in time?" I ask.

He nods. "Unfortunately it is. But I'm sure you could write your paper on the legends, little missy."

I turn to Mathers, who laughs uncomfortably. "Mr. Callan, thank you so much for all the information. Might you point us in the direction of the library so Miss Rochester can do more research on the topic?"

"Of course." Mr. Callan leads us down another hallway toward the records room, a gothic-style library with all-black furniture and candle lighting that goes with the theme but makes it very hard to see. He takes us to a section about magic relics on the bottom floor, running his hands across the spines. "You cannot check a book out, but feel free to read it here and take notes, darling. I'll be around if you need me."

I wait until he's out of earshot before speaking, whispering to Mathers, "Great. What do we do now?"

"Perhaps a new sword can be created," he suggests, but I highly doubt it. I can only tap into my powers if I incorporate my blood into a spell. How am I going to create a sword that is the opposite of blood magic when blood magic is all I can use?

We crack open a few of the books solely dedicated to discussing the Divinities Sword, but as we continue, it just seems more hopeless. No one knows where the sword came from. There are hundreds of accounts, but none of them line up. All they know for sure is, the sword killed a beastblood wyvern in a single swing. It had a spell written on it in a language unknown to the Veil residents, making them believe it could be an ancient language. But they can't even replicate it properly, hence the reason why only a squiggle was drawn on the replica.

"We should go," I say with a sigh. "This was a waste of time."

"We'll find another way," Mathers promises. "Miss Rochester —"

The sound of an explosion interrupts him, and the entire building shudders. Mathers reacts quickly, pulling me under a nearby table as the bookshelves around us begin to tip over and the leather-bound volumes rain to the ground.

I clutch my bag and the book, *A History of Divinity*, to my chest. What the hell is happening? First the Halloween explosion, and now this?

Another loud *boom* rocks the room, and a hand grabs me from under the table, pulling me backward.

"Miss Rochester!" Mathers tries to grasp my arms, but he's too slow. I fly out from under the table, kicking and screaming as a figure pulls me into another room.

The white light is so bright it's blinding, but at least my legs are freed. I scramble to my feet, looking around. Is this the Infinity Hallway?

It certainly looks like it, but I didn't think Todd would *drag* me here like this.

"Todd?" I call, spinning around.

A door down the hall creaks open, and a woman enters. She's probably in her forties, with short brown hair and dark eyes. She adjusts her jacket as she walks toward me, looking very professional in her charcoal grey pantsuit.

"Not Todd," she says, stopping in front of me. "Do you seriously not recognize me, Maria? I know it's been a while, but I don't look *that* different, do I?"

"Oh my fucking God," I mutter. "Jenna?"

CHAPTER TWENTY-EIGHT

"What the hell? I'm actually pretty offended," Jenna Cooper says, putting her hands on her hips. "I do a sheet mask once a week, exercise every day, and maintain a very healthy and well-balanced diet. The same can't be said about you, Mar."

"Don't call me that," I snap. "I don't have time for this. Explain to me what's going on right now, or—"

"Or what? You'll stick a knife in my neck? You know, you were a lot nicer as Mary Alice."

"You're stating the obvious."

Jenna leans against the wall, heaving a dramatic sigh. "I didn't think I'd have to spell it out for you. Come on. We're in the Infinity Hallway, and I just saved your life. Sound like someone you know?"

"Todd?" I guess.

She takes a small notebook out of her jacket pocket and flips through it, clicking her tongue. "Okay. So it looks like I can't provide a full explanation yet, but I can tell you this. Todd and I are Time Agents. We make sure

the timeline is kept nice and neat, hence saving your ass a bunch of times. But you know that. Where's my thank-you basket?"

"You both tried to kill me," I point out. "Though I guess Todd's case is justified, since this hallway will make him go insane. What's your excuse?"

"Todd was pulled out of his timeline and given a choice to become a Time Agent," Jenna explains patiently. "I was born one. It's my fate. So my 'excuse,' as you so succinctly put it, is teenage angst. I tried to fight fate, but instead, I played right into their hands. I guess I *do* owe you an apology, though. For attacking you and cutting up your license. And drugging you."

"Wait, you *drugged* me?"

"Only a little. But I'd think you would have more of a problem with my multiple attempts on your life, over slipping you some magic hallucinogens," Jenna says. "After our confrontation in the secret room on the ship, I tried to escape through a hidden passage and wound up here instead."

"And you changed your mind about trying to kill me? Just like that?"

"Look at me. It took years of— It took years to change my mind. Wasted time, ironically," she says with a laugh. "I'll be real with you, Mar. I don't care if you believe me or not. And I'm not in the mood to play nice like Todd. I just saved your life. So how about you listen up for a change and let me tell you something that might help?"

Harsh. But I'm listening.

"What is one thing all shadowborn have in common?" she asks.

"Is this a trick?"

"Just think about it," she says, losing patience. "What is a time prison? How did your blood free Astaroth?"

What is a time prison? A prison that no one can find, because it constantly travels through time.

How did your blood open it? No clue. But it did.

What's one thing all shadowborn have in common? Trueblood lineage?

Think, I tell myself. My blood opened a portal to a prison lost in time. My blood was a key—no. Magic needs an anchor, and I've proven that my blood can act as one. My blood anchored the spell that opened the portal to the time prison. Not anyone else's, despite the bloodshed. Archer bled in the circle but nothing happened. So did Penny. My blood is different.

And what am I? Despite my weaknesses, I'm shadowborn. Shadowborn can have a lot of different powers because of their lineage. But they do have one thing in common—the ability to open rifts from either realm. I've never tried before, but maybe...

Maybe it's a power I've also inherited.

"Rifts are portals through space," I begin slowly. "Are you trying to say that I can open portals through space *and* time?"

"Finally. Give the girl a prize."

"But that's what this hallway does, right? So what use is my power?" Even if it *is* kind of cool.

"Todd and I need this hallway to travel, and we can't pick and choose where we go. You have a lot more freedom. If you wanted to go back and, say, make out with Abraham Lincoln, you could. I would ask that you don't, because the more paradoxes you create the more work I have to do. But it's possible."

"I don't want to make out with Abraham Lincoln," I say. "What about the butterfly effect? Can I go back and erase my own existence from the timeline?"

"Do you listen, Mar? Time Agents take care of inconsistencies. All you have to worry about is getting the Divinities Sword. It's lost in time, right? Well, you just so happen to have the power to retrieve it. If you are about to overstep, a Time Agent will find you and stop you."

"That's reassuring, I guess. But why? Why are you helping me?" I question.

"You're special." But Jenna doesn't say it in a way that sounds like a compliment. "You're the chosen one. You're the specialist snowflake to ever flutter to the ground. You should change your name to Mary Sue instead of Mary Alice."

"I don't appreciate or need your sarcasm."

"It's time for you to get back to the fun. I did my job," Jenna says, turning the doorknob. "Try not to get killed in the meantime. And if you could pick up some R-rated comics for me, that would be great. I prefer BL, but I guess BG or GL work, too."

I don't know what those acronyms mean and I don't want to know.

"I'm not doing that. Can't you find that on the internet?" I hiss.

"All the good ones are locked behind a paywall," she whines. "Just make an account for me on DLsite and attach a credit card—"

"I'm not buying you porn! Especially not when you can read it for free!" I yank the door open and walk through, finding myself in a bathroom stall.

Another explosion shakes the building, and I use the

sink to steady myself. The ceiling tiles shake, but thankfully, they don't fall.

I have to get out of here. Once the tremors stop, I push through the door and dart out into the hallway. Truebloods stampede toward the front door, and I follow them, hoping to exit the building before another explosion hits.

I barely make it out the door before the entire building begins to collapse, raining fire and dust from the sky.

THERE IS NO HOSPITAL IN THE DEMON DISTRICT OF THE Veil, which seems like a major oversight in my opinion. Provost Mathers has to be pushed on a gurney through a rift and driven away by an ambulance on the other side.

Both his legs are broken, but apparently he's lucky that's all that happened. No one died (yet), but paramedics at the scene say at least fifty people were injured. That's truebloods for you.

I wish I could have taken Provost Mathers with me into the Infinity Hallway. I'm not sure if I trust him, but this whole thing is *kind of* my fault. Not the explosion, but Mathers being with me here in the first place. I don't get why he's helping me at all. Yes, I'm his student, but after seeing everything I've done to him, he shouldn't like me. So why would he go out of his way to help me? It's not like he gains anything from it.

Maybe it was a mistake to rely on him for help. If I'd just pretended like everything was fine and not insisted on finding the sword, he would be okay. Now he needs surgery, and I'm stranded in front of a hospital.

I'm still in Georgia, at least. I confirmed with the

hospital staff. They let me use their phone since mine died. I don't have money to call a car, so I call the school instead. And they call Neil, even after I expressly tell them not to.

But Neil is considered my "guardian." Funny, I don't feel like he's doing a thing to guard me. He *does* get his driver to pick me up, in the same black SUV he drove last time.

As soon as it pulls up to the curb, my mind flashes back to Luke. I don't want to go in; I don't even want to touch the car. My instincts tell me to run inside and hide from my problems.

Neil rolls down the window, holding a glass of red wine. "Maria, come inside. You are delaying the inevitable."

I hate the way he cracks the window, just like that day. I can almost see the barrel of his gun poking out, but when I blink, it disappears. Just a hallucination.

Maybe I did die in the building collapse after all, and this is hell.

"Maria, don't make me tell you again. I do not like repeating myself."

And yet he repeats the same threat to me over and over. It works every time.

I open the door and slip inside. As soon as I'm in, the driver hits the gas at a speed that can't possibly be legal. But Neil is unfazed, and not a drop of wine spills from his glass.

"I am having a Thanksgiving banquet in a few days. I expect you will join us," he says. "I've already made the arrangements for you and Allegra to miss class. You won't be missing much, anyway."

"A Thanksgiving banquet? I didn't know demons celebrated."

"Any excuse to have a party."

Sounds about right.

He doesn't ask me if I'm okay, or what happened to Mathers. Not that I expect him to care about the well-being of others. He probably already knows what happened, being on the Ruby Council.

I turn my head toward the window, unable to look at Neil in this car. He doesn't say anything, but out of the corner of my eye, I swear he smiles.

"I heard what happened to Nic."

My heart drops.

"No need to give me that frightened expression, Maria. I don't plan on intervening in a spat between my children. Family rivalry can be healthy, especially for him. He enjoys goading you."

"He didn't *goad* me," I grit out, hating how dismissive Neil is about the incident.

"Oh? What would you call it, then?"

Not "goading." It's more malicious than that, and Nic knows it. Neil knows it, too.

"You are goading me right now. What Nic does is torment me. He enjoys it," I add. "That's who he is."

"Oh? And who are you, then?" Neil mocks. "The type of girl who pushes men she doesn't like from great heights? A girl who has sex with any willing sap on campus? Or are you the type of girl who cannot let go of the past?"

I hate how he says "girl" with the implication that I am young, and somehow because of that, beneath him.

"You can learn a lot about someone by observing how they react during times of great hardship," I say. "I was just a kid when I learned who I really am. I'm the type of person who doesn't know how to forgive. The type of person who divides the world into allies and enemies. The type of person

who wishes death upon others, who acts impulsively, and who doesn't feel remorse. There is something unfathomably hateful and wicked within me. I guess I can't escape my blood, because underneath all the characters I play and lies I tell myself, I am an inherently malicious person. I am just like you."

CHAPTER TWENTY-NINE

Thanksgiving is Isabelle's favorite holiday. It's a time when people come together, not with gifts, but with food. And homemade food, in excessive amounts, is her love language.

It's never a family-exclusive event. She invites everyone and their mother to her house. She invited *me* when we first met, knowing my record and penchant for destruction. I was apprehensive at first, but I ended up having a great time. Every Thanksgiving after that was filled with joy and laughter. It was almost enough to overwrite the horrible holidays that came before.

This Thanksgiving will be my worst in years, and not just because of Luke's death. Foley-Hill Plantation is filled with classical music and party guests who hate me, the tension thick enough to choke on. The last person I want to be with on *Thanksgiving* is Neil, because the only thing I have to thank him for is ruining my life. Not to be too dramatic.

Neil has invited all his Ruby Council associates,

including Lilly Hardwicke and her family. They glare at me from the corner of the living room; if looks could kill, I'd be dead ten times over. I'd flip them off—I *am* feeling quite self-destructive today—but a waitress saves me before I can and offers me a glass of champagne.

Down the hatch.

I take two more after finishing the first flute. With any luck, I'll be throwing up in the bathroom by my sixth glass. That should get me out of dinner, right?

But by glass five, the room is spinning and I need to pee. I must have skipped the "happy drunk" stage and run right to the "easily agitated" stage. Fantastic. Wobbling up the stairs, I clutch the railing for support. Maybe I can say I'm sick and skip out on dinner. Or at least hide in my room until the food is served.

Neil put me in a guest room in the main house for a change, but not out of the goodness of his heart. He wants to keep tabs on me, and possibly torment me with Nic's presence. Thankfully I haven't run into him, but he's staying at the house, too.

After finishing up in the bathroom, I stumble toward my room, narrowly avoiding impalement by Neil's modern art monstrosities. My mind doesn't feel *too* clouded, but I'm starting to see double, which isn't a good sign. Fumbling with the doorknob, I can't get into my room until the door opens by itself. Rather, someone opens it for me.

I nearly fall to the ground, but a hand shoots out from behind and steadies me.

"Rhys?" Somehow I know it's him before I turn around. "What are you doing?"

"You have been drinking." A statement, not a question.

He helps me inside to lie on my bed, his hand so hot on my arm it feels like it could burn through my skin.

"Why are you here?" I mutter. Why does he have to see me in such a sorry state?

The last time we met, I told him I'd kill him if he showed himself in front of me again. Thinking back, that was...over-dramatic. Even by my standards.

I was angry, I still am, but it's not like I *hate* Rhys. I don't like him, either. Between him, Nic, and Neil, though, he's the least of my concerns.

"I thought you would be coming up here sooner or later," he replies quietly. "We need to talk."

"We don't *need* to do anything." And I'm not quite in the right state of mind. Maybe it's the alcohol, or maybe it's the fact that this will be the first Thanksgiving without Luke. It's probably *both*. But if he stays with me any longer, I'm probably going to say things I'll regret later.

"Please listen to me for a moment." Rhys has *never* said "please" to me. He's not impolite, but he doesn't strike me as the type to beg for anything. Something feels different, something in his voice. All the more reason we shouldn't have this conversation now.

"I can't listen to you."

"This is important. I left something in your room for you—"

"Looking at you reminds me of *him*," I say, the words coming out harsher than I intend. I squeeze my eyes shut, trying to regain my bearings. It doesn't work well. "And I can't think about that, especially not when I'm supposed to be playing nice with the man who killed him."

"Maria."

It's the first time he's ever called me by my name. I open

my eyes and sit up to look at him, but I wish I hadn't. Despite his usual stone-faced expression, he looks as hurt and raw as I feel. But I have no words of comfort for him; I don't have any for myself, either.

"Don't call me that." I roll to my feet, shoving past him and back into the bathroom in the hall. Looks like I didn't need the sixth drink to make myself sick after all. Closing the door, I make it to the toilet just in time.

I won't describe to you what happens next, out of consideration. All you need to know is, after I'm done puking my guts out, I still feel dizzy and gross.

I brush my teeth to get rid of the sour taste in my mouth. While I'm rinsing, someone knocks on the door. Rhys.

I don't want to see him now, especially not after what just happened in my room. "Go away, Rhys!"

The knocking persists. Maybe I should hear him out — he sounded serious. Probably. But it's better to wait until I can think clearly.

"I said, go away! I don't want to talk to you right now!"

"Mary Alice? It's me," Faith calls from the other side. "We're going to serve dinner soon. How are you holding up?"

"I'm sorry," I reply, my cheeks red. I unlock the door. "I thought you were Rhys."

Faith opens the door with a warm smile. "I heard you two were in a little spat. Do you want to talk about it?"

Not in the least. "It's nothing. I'm sorry, I'll come down in a minute."

"Oh, it's no rush, dear." Faith is dressed impeccably as usual in a green silk dress. Meanwhile, I probably look like I just rolled out of bed after a night out. She brushes a tear

from my cheek. "You look upset. Maybe it's best if you wash your face and collect yourself."

I'm...crying? Why?

"Come on, now." Faith ushers me inside the bathroom and turns on the faucet. "I have some face wash you can borrow."

She rubs my shoulders as I bend down, splashing warm water on my eyes. She shouldn't be so nice to me, especially now, when Neil is hosting a party with their friends and acquaintances. She should be enjoying herself downstairs. It's not my cup of tea, but it seems like something Faith would like. Instead, she's wasting time on me.

"This is the least I can do for my daughter's savior," she soothes.

"I'm not anyone's savior," I mumble. I couldn't do anything for Luke. I can't do anything now, either.

"My husband told me you saved Allegra in Massachusetts over the summer. He always likes to remind me that you stepped in to help our daughter, that you are her friend," Faith says. "He thinks I'm foolish. And so do you, right?"

"What are you —"

Faith laces a hand through my hair, grabbing the back of my head and slamming my face into the porcelain sink.

CHAPTER THIRTY

I t makes sense that Faith has lost her marbles. Anyone would, after being married to Neil.

"You don't look like my husband at all," Faith muses, "but did you both think I wouldn't know as soon as I laid eyes on you? No matter how he dresses you up, you look exactly like the Leighton bitch."

I have no idea what she's going on about, but I take it she knows that Neil is my biological father. Which begs the question, why isn't she attacking *him* right now? It's not my fault he can't keep it in his pants! Everyone blames the other woman, but in this case, I'm not even the other woman. Why do I have to get injured?

Blood pours down my face from a deep gash on my forehead. It almost looks fake in the mirror, like another one of my special effects makeup tricks. Unfortunately, it's real and it *hurts*. Not that Faith cares, using my hair to slam my head repeatedly against the floor. Luckily, the floor is tile, so there's nothing to cushion the blow. Things are going well for me, as you can see.

"He thinks he can *humiliate* me like this? I would have allowed you to live if you had just minded your own business. But coming into *my* house, befriending *my* daughter, even as you're trying to usurp her rightful place as heir? I didn't spend twenty hours in labor just to have my husband's bastard come in eighteen years later and steal what is Allegra's birthright. You're nothing compared to her!"

As much as I'd love to argue with her, it would be pointless. I need to put as much distance between us as possible, to go downstairs and get help. But who's going to help me? Lilly? Neil? Nic? Allegra? None of them are going to lend a hand, especially if it means going against the lady of the house.

I just have to get away from her. Using what little strength I have left, I sweep her feet with my legs, catching her by surprise. While she falls, I manage to slip out the door and down the hall. Wiping the blood from my eyes, I hurry into my room. Except, there's no lock! What the hell?

My head throbs and I imagine by this point I've had more concussions than an NFL player. But I can't pass out, I can't go downstairs, and I can't get help. I'm screwed. I'm going to die here.

Faith rips the door open, straight off its hinges, and flings it aside as if it's nothing. "Where do you think you're going? Do you think you can run from me? Who's going to help you?"

No one—that's the problem. One of many, at the moment.

She knocks me to the floor and sinks her nails into my ankles, drawing blood as she drags me down the hall. The cherry on top is the interior design providing absolutely no

help whatsoever. There's nothing in the hallway for me to grab hold of, and the floors are slippery marble. Once again, fuck you and your modern plantation house, Neil!

Faith doesn't care who's listening. She's too busy yelling at me, being angry at *me* for something I can't control. I don't want Neil to be my biological father, much less have him intervene in my life. I just wanted to go home!

But by killing Luke, I'm not sure what I would even be going back to now. How can I face my family knowing that I failed them so tremendously? How could they stand my presence if they knew Luke died because of me?

And that's what it comes down to. I didn't pull the trigger, but I failed Neil's test, and Luke died for it. For *my* failure.

"Neil doesn't care about me," I say. "Neither should you."

Faith pauses, looking down at me with a sneer. "I threw the Hardwicke girl *in your lap*. I put evidence in your dorm room after Halloween, *and* after the recent explosion at the Ruby Council headquarters. But nothing happened to you. I stabbed your goddamn roommate and you weren't arrested. Do you know why? My husband stuck his neck out for you. He got rid of the evidence and saved you."

Neil didn't save me. Jenna and Todd saved me, and not being in the gymnasium during the dance was just a coincidence. How did she even know I would be at those places?

"The phone," I realize. "You've been tracking my phone. You had Allegra give it to me."

"You accepted it so easily. I thought you would be more cautious."

I thought Neil was monitoring me—but it was Faith.

Meanwhile, Neil probably realized that his wife was trying to kill me. And he didn't say anything!

"Enough of this," Faith mutters, pulling a gun from the pocket of her dress. Seeing the pistol in her hand brings back painful memories. Luke's face flashes in my mind. The sound of Neil's gun going off, the look on David's face, and all that blood...

My throat tightens. Faith clicks off the safety, but before she can pull the trigger, someone barrels into her and knocks her down. The gun flies out of her hand, clattering on the floor.

Rhys.

He came out of nowhere, pinning her to the ground as she screams colorful expletives.

"You must run," Rhys yells, holding Faith beneath him. "Something is wrong. She is too strong to be human."

"Rhys—"

"Run!" he shouts as Faith breaks his hold.

Rhys is a trueblood. And Faith is supposed to be human. Now, all I can see is a monster. I dive for the gun, springing up and aiming it at Faith. But I can't pull the trigger; I've never fired a gun, and Rhys is too close to Faith. I could shoot him by accident.

As angry at him as I am, as *confused* as I am, I don't want to hurt him.

But Faith takes care of that for me. With an animalistic yowl, she unsheathes a hidden blade from her ankle and stabs Rhys three times in rapid succession. His eyes widen as she throws him aside, barreling toward me despite the gun in her face.

I pull the trigger.

The gun kicks back in my hand, harder than I expect.

The bullet hits Faith in the shoulder, but despite the blood, she acts like it doesn't affect her at all. Rhys is right—she's not human. Not anymore.

She tackles me to the ground, her eyes wild and blood-shot. "You should have never been born."

"What is going on here?" Neil's voice booms across the hall. Faith turns her head, and while she's distracted, I kick her off me. Neil's eyes are trained on me, but he doesn't say anything about how I kicked his wife in the stomach. He drags her farther away from me, throwing her against the wall.

The other partygoers rush to the stairs, watching the scene unfold with rapt interest.

Allegra pushes through the crowd, her eyes falling on me.

"You had your *bitch* give birth to a bastard behind my back!" Faith's voice is a mixture of sobs and screeching. "You thought I wouldn't notice if you brought your halfling into our house?"

"Faith. Enough."

"You *promised* me Allegra would be the last!"

"Faith killed Jessica Hardwicke," I interrupt, sitting up. "She's been trying to kill me since this summer. The cafeteria, the Halloween dance, the Ruby Council explosions...it was all her."

"I needed to get rid of your mistakes, as usual!" Faith glares at her husband. "I am always cleaning up your messes. And yet, you can't even name our daughter as your heir. Is she the reason?"

"No. I have big plans for Maria," Neil replies placidly. He looks at the gathering crowd, watching his every move. Hanging on his every word. "None of which involve Alle-

gra. But you have disappointed me, my wife. Now, I will have to clean up *your* mess."

Neil breaks her neck with a single twist, turning it so far it looks like it's on backward. No one moves, no one even *breathes*, as her body falls to the ground with a heavy thud.

Allegra is the first to react, wailing as she crawls to her mother's fallen form on her hands and knees. She looks up at her father, tears pouring down her face. "What have you done?"

"Criminals must pay for their crimes," Neil replies simply, looking to the crowd. "Now. The food downstairs is probably getting cold. Shall we eat?"

CHAPTER THIRTY-ONE

Neil isn't the kind of man to comfort his daughter, even as she cries over her mother's body. I thought he would say *something* to her. This is his fault, but he acts like Faith's corpse is nothing more than trash as he steps over it and toward me.

He walks past me, examining the blood on the floor from where Faith dragged me. "That might stain. I should call a housekeeper to get this wiped up immediately."

Just when I thought I couldn't hate him more.

I try to stand, but Faith got my ankles good. I'm reduced to crawling on my hands and knees, my head swimming. Rhys leans against the wall, clutching his side. Blood pools on the floor, soaking part of his shirt.

"That doesn't look good," I say stupidly. He was stabbed —of *course* it doesn't look good. "Why did you come back?"

"Did you see the envelope I left on your desk?" he asks, his voice barely above a whisper. The color has all but drained from his face.

"Now isn't the time for that."

"You must take it with you. I put everything else in your closet, but the envelope is most important." His voice grows softer as he struggles to get the words out.

Neil finally pulls away from the goddamn floors and his attention snaps to us. He picks up Faith's fallen knife from the ground, covered in Rhys' blood. "Iron. My wife prepared well, even in the end. I wonder if she knew she'd have to face you, Rhys."

"You have to call a doctor," I tell him. "He needs medical attention right away. I don't know what the trueblood protocol is—"

"Elves cannot heal wounds made by iron weapons," Allegra cuts in, her voice sharp like a whip. "It is their one weakness."

"If magic can't heal him, then call an ambulance," I insist. "A doctor can get him stitched up in no time! What are you standing around for?"

"This is all because of you!" Allegra rises to her feet, pointing a finger in my face. "This *never* would have happened if you hadn't shown up. This is all your fault. Nic warned me about you; he told me I shouldn't trust you. He said you were a snake. But I said he was being ridiculous, that you were a good person. And it turns out he was right!"

"Allegra, go downstairs and entertain our guests," Neil orders.

She ignores him, striding over to me. "You should never have been born."

Neil shoves her back before she can get closer, wrapping a hand around her throat and slamming her into the wall. "What did I just tell you to do?"

Allegra chokes, but doesn't struggle out of his grasp. Has this...happened to her before? I don't want to think it

has, but judging from her reaction, she isn't surprised. The moment he releases her, Allegra scurries away, sending one final backward glare at me. Like I'm the one who had her in a chokehold.

But she has a right to be angry. I would be, if I were in her shoes. In a twisted world, I would say that I lost a father, and she lost a mother, which makes us even. It doesn't, not by a long shot.

Once she disappears back downstairs, Neil steps over Faith's body and looks down at me with cold eyes. "I had to kill my wife for you."

"You didn't have to *kill* her."

"I did. A public trial would have ruined my reputation. But I suppose it's ruined anyway, now that everyone downstairs knows you are my daughter. I am not pleased, Maria. Not pleased at all. And I think you know what happens when you displease me. Tell me one reason why I should not kill your entire family because of this."

"You wouldn't have any leverage left," I grit out. "Faith tried to kill *me*. She's the one who exposed me — "

"Yes, and I had to kill her for it," Neil snaps. "Otherwise I would be under scrutiny, more so than I already am for this disaster of a party."

Does he care more about the party than his own family? Or does he care more about himself, about his reputation? Probably the latter. Truebloods outlive humans and shadowborn. We're probably nothing to him, just temporary annoyances he can use to achieve his goals.

"Well?" he asks impatiently.

My mind spins. All I can think to say is, "I found a way to kill Astaroth."

That piques Neil's interest. "Go on."

"There's a sword," I explain quickly, my eyes darting to Rhys. "It's called the Divinities Sword. It can kill Astaroth in one swing."

Theoretically. But at least this will buy me some time. I have nothing else, no leverage to preserve my own life or my family's. Or Rhys'.

"The Divinities Sword is lost in time, but I can find it. If I open a rift, I can go back in time, get the sword, and bring it back to kill Astaroth," I say quickly. "It's the only way."

There's a long pause, and for a whole minute, Neil just stares at me. And then he smiles. "Well done, Maria. Truly, you've exceeded my expectations!"

"I'll do it, but I won't if you harm my family. I can go tomorrow," I promise. "Just call an ambulance for Rhys. Do *something*. Even if iron wounds can't be healed with magic, they can still sew him up and give him a blood transfusion, right?"

"They can," Neil confirms. "But I fear it's too late."

"No, it's not!" I say, but when I turn to my side, Rhys' eyes are closed. With a shaking hand, I feel his neck for a pulse. He's still warm, but I don't see his chest moving. And I don't feel a heartbeat. "You need to call someone *right now*. Maybe they can save him—"

"He can't be saved, my dear Maria. He doesn't deserve to be," Neil says calmly. "Now, why don't you go downstairs like a good girl and help your sister entertain the guests? After you clean yourself up. You look disgusting."

I DON'T NEED STITCHES, ACCORDING TO NEIL. I DON'T trust him to know whether I need them or not, but I have no

choice. Neil controls everything in my life right now—even my access to a doctor.

By the time I return to my room, Rhys' and Faith's bodies have been moved into cold storage downstairs. The hallways have been mopped and waxed to the point where it's dangerous to walk. But I don't imagine I'll be getting up tonight and wandering around.

Weariness sets in my bones. Whether it's the alcohol, or the blood loss, or the general distress caused by today's events, my body doesn't want to move out of bed. I don't even have the energy to pull myself under the covers.

Tomorrow, I go to the Veil. There's no time to waste, according to Neil. It doesn't make sense—I can *time travel*—but Neil insists I go tomorrow. I'm getting a little sick of the "or I'll kill your family" threat he keeps throwing around. But how can I not take him seriously?

I wish Luke were here. He would know exactly what to say at times like this to make me smile. Or at least, to help me sleep. But every time I close my eyes, I see his face. His blood.

And Rhys.

The guilt bites me, flooding me with venom in the form of more questions. What was he trying to tell me earlier? Why didn't I just listen to him? What could I have done differently to save him?

He told Neil about Archer. But he also helped me today. He died because of me. I'm not one to relish in the death of my enemies, but at the same time, I've never felt remorse for it. I don't feel guilty about hurting Max. I haven't spared a thought toward Penny. Rhys' actions caused Luke's death; I shouldn't care what happened to him.

But I do. I didn't want him to *die*, especially not like that.

Before he died, Rhys mentioned an envelope he left for me on my desk. I haven't had the courage to open it, but now, in the dead of night, I feel like I have to. He used the last of his energy trying to tell me about it. It must be important.

Slowly, I rise from bed and inch toward the desk. My muscles scream, but I try to ignore the body aches and pounding in my head.

The envelope is sealed with wax. How very old-fashioned; I wouldn't expect anything less from Rhys. Cutting it with a letter opener, the contents spill into my hand.

A gold necklace shimmers between my fingers as I hold it to the light. The circular pendant is inscribed, but I can't discern what it says. If I had to guess, it looks like some sort of coin.

The letter that comes with the necklace is in Elvish. Rhys' handwriting is beautiful but it's in the Elvish equivalent of cursive, making it harder for me to decipher. But, line by line, I begin to read.

Dear Maria,

I realize you are unhappy with me at the moment, but please know that there are things beyond your knowledge. I would think, after our many tutoring sessions and your constant questions, you would have figured that out by now.

You asked me to stop reading your mind, but sadly that is an ability I do not possess. I wish you could read my mind and understand why I have come to work for Neil. It is not a choice I made lightly. I trust you will find out soon, and when we meet again, it will be on better terms.

This necklace was passed down in my family for six generations. It will protect you, as it has protected me for all these years. May it bring you luck.

Yours,
Rhys

P.S. I prepared a bag in your closet. You will need it on your trip for the Divinities Sword. How do I know, you may ask? I told you; I have my sources.

Chapter Thirty-Two

There's no time like the present. Or should I say the past?

Get it? Because I'm going back in time? Too cheesy? Well, *excuse* me for trying to mask my crippling guilt with a little humor.

I barely slept last night, especially after reading Rhys' letter. I had to break out my Elvish dictionary to ensure I understood everything properly. I would have just *asked* him, but now I can't. Which complicates my feelings even more. I can't even dwell on it, because I have a mission to complete for Neil.

It's a great day to time travel, and by that, I mean it's a horrible day because a huge storm is coming. The sky rumbles, filled with dark clouds ready to downpour at a moment's notice.

Neil stands behind me, checking his Rolex every thirty seconds. Good things come to those who wait, but I hate Neil and don't want anything good to happen to him. The only reason I'm trying to move so quickly, his threats aside,

is because I'll finally be able to escape him for a little while. He won't be able to watch over me in the Veil, right?

One can only hope.

"How long is this going to take, Maria?" he asks, questioning my process yet again.

By "my process," I mean I'm bullshitting everything along the way. I don't even know if I can do what I claim, but it's worth a shot. My life motto seems to be "fake it till you make it." I'm faking it, but I don't know how the hell I'm going to make it. Dumb luck? Main character plot armor?

"I'm ready," I lie, unsheathing my sword and ignoring his direct question. We're at his training grounds in a big open field. The wind whips my hair into a frenzy, but I try not to let it bother me. Taking a deep breath, I raise the sword above my head. Time for a little pageantry.

Spells require magic, intention, and an anchor. I have magic. I have intention. And now, I need an anchor.

I run a finger along the blade, tapping just lightly enough to draw blood and smear it across the flat of the sword. I tested kitchen spells before with my blood but opening a rift is something different. Maybe I should have practiced last night instead of lying in bed wondering where it all went wrong. The worst thing that can happen is the sword bounces back in my face and slices my head in two. Another doom scenario is surviving, but having nothing happen, which would result in punishment from Neil.

Shifting my weight between both feet, I close my eyes and focus on what I want. Intention. I envision a rift opening up and leading me directly to the Divinities Sword.

This better work, I think to myself. I'm going to feel really stupid if it doesn't. Also, there's the whole "family death"

thing hanging over my head. But we've beaten that threat to, well, death throughout this installment, haven't we?

I swing the sword down in one fluid motion, hitting the grass hard as the rain begins to pour. When I open my eyes, I don't see anything. Taking a step forward, I drop the sword and reach my arms out in front of me.

I didn't do it wrong, right? Waving my hands around, my fingers catch on something. Silk, it feels like. Layers and layers of silk, at least five inches thick.

I pull on the invisible silk, opening it like a curtain and revealing a rift unlike any I've seen before. The surface is iridescent, rippling like water. The fabric of time and space frames the portal, the layers sheer but colorful.

Picking up the backpack prepared by Rhys and shrugging it over my shoulders, I step through the rift.

On the other side, I'm immediately plunged into cold water. I was wet before from the rain, but now, I'm drenched from head to toe. I spin around and close the rift before doing anything else, pulling both sides of the portal shut before trying to kick up to the surface, toward the light. But as soon as I break through and take one big gulp of air, the backpack drags me back down. It's even heavier underwater, and with it on, I can't stay afloat.

My lungs burn as I struggle to get it off, freeing one arm but not the other. Finally, I manage to extract myself from the straps and swim up. Once my head is above water, most of my strength is drained. I float on my back, taking a moment to breathe.

I'm in a lake, which is a good thing. It's not the middle of the ocean. But I thought I pictured the Divinities Sword when I opened this rift. So where the hell is it?

A forest surrounds the lake, but I can't make out much

in this lighting. It's dusk, and freezing, which is just what I need: to die of hypothermia before getting the sword.

As heavy as my limbs feel, I need to get the backpack and drag it to shore. I assume Rhys packed essentials in there. I looked through it briefly this morning and saw several changes of clothes, which I initially thought was silly. I didn't plan on spending too much time in the past. I still don't, if I can help it.

Taking a deep breath, I dive down to the bottom of the lake and search for the backpack. The water is clear enough that I can see, but it doesn't change the fact that I'm running out of strength. The best I can do is drag it to shore, making multiple trips up to the surface and down to the lake floor to bring the bag closer to the water's edge.

By the time I make it to the shallow end, I'm exhausted and it's nightfall. Flopping on the sand panting, I look up at the stars.

There are so many here, more than in the mortal realm. I wonder if there are aliens here, too. What would those even look like in the Veil? Would they have magic?

I should be trying to warm up, finding fire and a place to set up camp. But just getting to shore has taken everything out of me. I don't even know how to start a fire. Do I rub two sticks together? Maybe I should have read more about survival before I came here.

Or maybe I can find a nearby town and stay. With no money. Damn.

I don't even know if there *is* a town nearby. If there's not, what am I going to do about food? I guess I could go back through another rift and—

Another rift. That would be useful. If I had brought the sword with me.

Seriously, can I just go back in time and beat myself up?

I'm fucked! Excuse my language, but that's the only appropriate word to describe my current situation.

To make matters worse, because trust me, they can *always* get worse, I hear footsteps approaching. Not one or two people, but a whole bunch of them coming from behind.

Shit.

I roll on my stomach and push up to my feet, grabbing the backpack. But the intruders are closer than I anticipated.

A man comes into view, holding a torch. He sticks it in the sand, joined by a group of at least twenty others. And get this: they're all naked.

I swear to God I'm not a peeping tom. I don't know why handsome naked men keep showing up in my life, but they do, and frankly I'm getting a *little* bit tired of this kind of meet-cute. At this point, it's just meet-creepy!

Meat-creepy. Heh.

Okay, that was a lame joke. Don't throw tomatoes! I'm not a weirdo, I swear!

I dive into the woods between the trees before they spot me. I need to get the hell out of here before I'm caught. I know Jenna mentioned she and the other Time Agents will fix any paradoxes my time traveling will inevitably create, but I don't think interacting with others is the best idea.

Darting through the trees, I try to put as much space between the group of men and myself as possible. But the deeper I go into the forest, the darker it gets. I reach out, trying to feel my way around the trees. As I move forward, my hand touches something warm and smooth. And moving.

I yelp, yanking my hand away and tripping over my own two feet as I try to back up.

A man lights a lantern and hangs it on a low tree branch, peering at me curiously. He's tall and, if I have to guess, around my age. I *really* wish he was wearing clothes, though. He must be with the other group.

He kneels in front of me, his braid of dark hair swinging like a rope and brushing my leg. Childishly, I clap both hands over my eyes to shield myself from his bare form, my cheeks on fire.

With my hands on my face, I feel blood oozing from my forehead. Great—the wound opened up again. For all I know, this guy is a vampire or something.

But he quickly proves me wrong when he asks, "Are you injured?"

His voice is deep but gentle, his words melodic. And Elvish.

Elvish. Peeking through my fingers, I notice his pointed ears poking out from his hair. So he's an elf. I can't tell if that's a good thing or a bad thing.

"Who's there?" someone else calls out to us.

The elf in front of me turns, answering, "I found someone. A boy."

"A boy? In these parts? Is he fae?"

"No," I respond quickly in Elvish. Telling the truth is the best move right now, considering elves and fae don't have the best history. "I'm not fae."

The elf studies my face. "You are not an elf."

Well, no. But I'm not a fairy, either, so please don't kill me and barbecue me. Not that I'm accusing elves of being cannibals. Would that even *count* as cannibalism?

Another man approaches us, wearing silver armor like

some sort of knight. A longsword swings at his waist, and when he spots me, he looks like he wants to draw his blade and press it against my throat.

"Theodas, what are you doing?" he asks. "It is your turn to bathe."

"But this boy," the elf replies. "He is bleeding."

"Suspicious. There are no travelers in this forest. It is too dangerous, especially for —"

I don't catch that last word, but I doubt it's a compliment.

"He is not fae."

"That hardly matters."

"The prince will know what to do with him." Both elves turn as a third man steps between the trees, his expression sullen.

"What is going on here?" he asks.

"Your Highness, we found this boy sneaking around near our base. He is not fae, but might be working for them," the gruff man says.

"I'm not!" I deny it forcefully.

"Fae cannot lie, but they use deceit to swim around the truth," the gruff man sneers.

The brown-haired elf closest to me, Theodas, stands. I cover my face again, because when he bows to the third man, I can see his bare bottom.

"Theodas," the man barks. He approaches me slowly, putting his gloved hands on my wrists and pulling my hands from my eyes.

My first thought is, thank *God* he's dressed. His fair complexion glows in the warm light of the lantern above us, illuminating his eyes.

He studies my face before saying anything, releasing my

wrists. For a moment, all we can do is stare at each other, suspended in time. His long, thick silver hair cascades over scaled armor, matching the color of his eyes caught somewhere between pale blue and lavender. He looks different now, younger somehow. And yet, despite his hair and his clothes, and the pitch of his voice, I recognize him immediately.

Rhys.

EPILOGUE

Todd Glass didn't have a good feeling about the new recruit. He wasn't supposed to question management; the first few times he did, he got an earful and was forced to watch the training video three times in a row. Somebody took a little too much inspiration from *A Clockwork Orange* if they asked him.

No one *did* ask Todd, though. No one ever asked him anything.

His opinion didn't matter in the grand scheme of things. His existence didn't; otherwise, why would he be here in this goddamn hallway?

Had he known what he'd signed up for, perhaps he would have chosen differently. Figuratively, of course. Todd only had the illusion of choice. Isn't that what free will was supposed to be? The greatest illusion?

He walked down the white corridor, having spent months getting to know his way around. There were no signs or directions, and he didn't have a cell phone with

GPS on it. They didn't even give him a map, at first. He made one himself, in his trusty little notebook.

Turning the corner, he walked past a set of glass doors until he reached the farthest door on the right. He could hear the tail end of the training video playing and slipped inside the room, trying not to make too much noise.

Jenna Cooper sat at the projector, her eyes glazed. She must have seen the video hundreds of times. Perhaps that was why she was so adamant about "the cause" and Maria Rochester. Even when, before, Jenna worked actively to *kill* Maria.

Just like Todd would, one day.

Just like all the human recruits would eventually want to do. Because they saw the future, and the past; they knew what Maria really was. And what she was created to do.

Jenna cut the video as the credits began to roll. "So, rookie. How did you like the video?"

"Inaccurate," the new recruit replied casually. "Offensive."

"I didn't make it," Jenna replied with a shrug. "Todd, turn on the lights."

He did as he was told. He had to.

The new recruit blinked, trying to adjust to the flood of lights above their heads. He was older than Todd expected, which meant his term of service would be little more than a year, if that. Todd was young, and he could only survive for two years in the Infinity Hallway before losing his mind.

Why would the big bosses agree to have such an old man become an agent?

Not that he was *old*. Todd guessed the rookie was in his mid-forties. But what could he have possibly been offered to accept a job here?

Well, it would be rude to ask.

"From now on, the three of us will be working together," Jenna announced. "I'm still handling the inconsistencies with Rhys, and Todd will continue to support the time-rewind function. You might be new, buddy, but we're giving you the Armageddon project."

"Armageddon project?" Todd questioned. He'd never heard of such a thing.

Jenna bristled. "Confidential, Todd."

"Right." Everything in this place seemed to be, for good reason.

Jenna's watch buzzed, and she looked down at her wrist. "Ah, I'm up. Todd, show him to his sleeping quarters."

"Yes. This way." Todd escorted the man out to the hallway. "There are bunks over here."

The man scanned the halls, frowning. "This place..."

"You get used to it," Todd said gently. "It might sound difficult now, but trust me, it gets better."

"How long does it take to get better?"

Todd wasn't sure how to answer, but finally, he decided to be honest. "For me, it took a couple of months."

"I only have six months."

Todd's mouth dried. Six months? "What kind of deal did they offer you for six months?"

He couldn't imagine doing all the work of a Time Agent for a measly six-month life extension.

Todd was young, so he agreed to it because he wanted to see the world before he died. He didn't mind the work; he found it *meaningful*.

But seeing the man's face, Todd regretted prying. "I'm sorry. I didn't mean to be rude."

"No, it's a fair question," the man replied patiently. "For me, the contract wasn't about the time extension. I wouldn't have accepted it if that were the case. With the way I'm slated to die...it's not very peaceful. But the big bosses told me that if I accepted, they would let me see my daughter again. To say goodbye, and to tell her that it wasn't her fault."

Oh.

Todd's heart dropped to his stomach as he stuttered out a weak apology. "I'm so sorry."

"It's fine. I'm coming around to accepting it," the man said, forcing a laugh. "Thank you for showing me to the sleeping quarters. I think I need to rest for a little bit and absorb everything I've learned so far."

"Of course," Todd said quickly. "If you need anything, let me know. I'm Todd, by the way. Todd Glass."

The rookie gave Todd's hand a firm shake. "My name is Luke."

Glossary

Astaroth: A powerful demon known for practicing blood magic. Astaroth was once imprisoned in a time prison, but due to certain events, was released. He has a cult following in the mortal realm.

Beastblood: Non-humanoid creatures originating in the Veil. They are often associated with animalistic traits and remain within the Veil, usually unable to get to the mortal realm on their own. Some examples of Beastbloods include lycans, chimera, and dragons.

Infinity Hallway: A corridor used by time agents to travel through time. It contains multiple doorways, each leading to a different point in history or the future. However, the hallway can be dangerous to humans and may cause madness or disorientation to those who stay for extended periods.

Magician: The offspring of two shadowborn. Generally, magic weakens as the generations are mixed with human genes. Magicians can perform spells, although their abilities are not as potent as those of shadowborn. They cannot open rifts like their shadowborn counterparts.

Mortal Realm: The realm where humans and non-magical creatures live. It is separate from the Veil and lacks the magical properties and creatures that exist in other realms.

Psychic: The child of two magicians. While they cannot perform spells, psychics possess limited abilities and are born with a connection to the Veil. They are unable to open rifts, however.

Rift: A magical portal between realms that can be opened by swinging a blade through open air and concentrating on the desired destination. This ability comes easily to most shadowborn, and allows them to travel between the Veil and the mortal realm.

Ruby Council: The governing body of trueblood demons in the Veil. They hold significant political power and are responsible for maintaining order and enforcing laws among demonkind. One of the most powerful and wealthy members of the Ruby Council is Neil Abbott. As a member of the council, he wields a great deal of influence and is respected by many in the demon community.

Shadowborn: A hybrid born from the union of a human and a trueblood, possessing traits from both species. They are

considered half-bloods and are often seen as shadows of their trueblood parents. Shadowborn have the ability to open rifts between the mortal realm and the Veil, and are stronger, faster, and more durable than humans. They can also perform magic, with some being born with rare and powerful abilities. Generally, the child of two shadowborn will either be a shadowborn or a magician.

Time Agent: A highly trained agent responsible for maintaining the timeline and ensuring that all events occur as they are supposed to. Time Agents use the Infinity Hallway, a special place that enables them to travel through time and space. They must be well-versed in historical events and possess advanced technology to prevent paradoxes and other disruptions to the timeline.

Time Prison: A highly-secure supernatural prison designed to hold dangerous beings. It's a place where inmates are isolated from the rest of the world and thrown in a different time period, making it nearly impossible for them to escape.

Trueblood: A magical humanoid being originating from the Veil. Truebloods identify themselves with human-categorized monsters such as angels, demons, vampires, shifters, and more. They are not affiliated with any religion. Truebloods can only open rifts from the Veil to the mortal realm but cannot close a rift if they are in the mortal realm. They migrated to the mortal realm during the 1800s. Truebloods possess magical abilities and often hold positions of power and influence in the Veil and mortal realm.

Veil: A mystical realm imbued with magic that is filled with unpredictable and often dangerous forces. It is the birthplace of all truebloods and beastbloods, and it is separated from the mortal realm by a thin barrier that can be traversed by opening a rift.

About the Author

Samantha Gao is a New Adult author with a passion for all things fantasy and paranormal romance. Her writing is fueled by her love for paranormal romance, and she enjoys creating compelling characters that readers can relate to and root for. After graduating from college with a degree in a completely different field, Sam decided to pursue her life-long dream of becoming a writer.

When she's not busy crafting stories that will transport readers to another world, Sam enjoys watching Asian dramas (with subtitles, of course!), listening to music, and indulging in her weakness for chocolate.

Sign up for her newsletter here: subscribepage.io/SamGao

facebook.com/whitemoonlightpress

instagram.com/whitemoonlightpress

amazon.com/author/samgao

bookbub.com/profile/sam-gao

goodreads.com/samgao

SAM GAO

HOUR OF NEED

THE TIMEKEEPER'S DAUGHTER
BOOK 2

Penny laughed delightedly. "You're a sweet kid, Nora Osborne, but you're a little on the naive side. Anyway, don't lose any sleep by blaming yourself, if Dave doesn't get his promotion. You're sure to pass inspection. Any girl as cute as you would. Sometimes I think that's all it takes—cuteness. My theory is that the wheels simply want to keep a stable of sweet young things for their own amusement."

"You don't really mean that, Penny?"

"Don't I? After all the passes I've had to cope with—passes made by Worden-Forbes' top brass?"

"You're joking."

"Me? A charter member of the Ninth Floor Club, joking?"

Nora looked at her in bewilderment. "What in the world is the Ninth Floor Club?"

"You haven't heard of the suite the company keeps on a permanent basis on the ninth floor of the Harrison Hotel?"

"No, I haven't."

"Well, how unenlightened can a person be?" Penny said. "You ask Dave about it." She took another, longer swallow of her drink. Then, with a trace of bitterness: "Anyway, my Bart didn't get to be Director of Engineering and Design through his own efforts alone. After all, there are plenty of other men as capable as Bart Austin—as the corporation wheels well know. And Penny did her share, believe me. She gave her little all to help her man."

Nora did not reply. She was sure that Penny could not mean what she semed to imply.

"Now I've shocked you," Penny said. 'Well, child, you'll learn. You've only been one of us for a few months. Give the gray-haired boys time." She stood up abruptly. "I've got to rush. I've been roped into helping with the new hospital fund drive and there's a meeting this afternoon. Oh, but it's fun being an executive's wife, Nora. Never a moment free from being a public-spirited, do- gooder."

She started away, then turned back.

After a moment of hesitation she said in a friendly, confiding tone, "About your Dave: He's all right. Smart, and a hard worker. But I have it from Bart that he isn't exactly aggressive enough. Tell him to be a little more pushy, darling. Tell him not to be scared of the brass. Do that, now—you hear?"

She hurried off, disappearing into the entrance of the bar.

Nora sat for a few minutes longer going over Penny's conversation and disturbed by her disclosures about the Ninth Floor Club. She told herself that she did not believe half of what the redhead had said. Penny had been pulling her leg. The top men at Worden-Forbes were not like that at all. She'd met most of them during the past few months, and without exception they seemed—well—quite proper. True, she had occasionally caught one or another of them appraising her in a speculative wolflike way. But all sorts of men gave her the eye, just as they did to any woman who was not downright repulsive. Men's minds were always on one thing—even Dave's. Many a time she had seen him look with warm admiration at another woman. At Penny, for one. Penny's lush figure always caught Dave's eye and he made no secret of it. But he did not mean a thing, really.

Still, what if Penny had not been kidding her? What if she, Nora Osborne, would have to cope with passes made by some man who could make or break Dave's career? Would she—could she—lend herself to such a thing even to help Dave?

She would not, she decided definitely. She simply could not. Such a thing as Penny had hinted at was unthinkable for Nora.

So Nora told herself but still she was troubled. She remembered bits of gossip she had heard, gossip about members of the crowd that now comprised Dave's and her friends. There was gossip of affairs and assignations. Perhaps there were deals made between the young wives of ambitious junior executives and the men who wielded the power at Worden-Forbes. Maybe there was more than one sort of payola.

Nora had come from a straightlaced, middle-class background and she could not shake off the sense of shocked dismay that such things actually went on among the people she now knew. Suddenly she did not want to think about it longer. She set down her unfinished Coke, rose and hurried to her Ford station wagon in the parking area alongside the clubhouse.

The station wagon was new and had replaced the ten- year-old second car she had formerly driven. Like the Buick that Dave had bought at the same time, the station wagon was a must. They had moved into a better neighborhood and so their cars, too, must have more prestige. Dave's income had jumped from seventy-five hundred a year to twelve thousand when he had been given the duties of a vice-president. On his own, he would not have moved from their old house in the inexpensive development until he had been given the title—and the permanency that went with it—as well as the duties of the office.

But he had been advised by his friend, John Fletcher, Worden-Forbes' comptroller, to make the change. John was backing Dave for the vice-presidency and he had urged the Osbornes to live on a scale consistent with that office. This, John had insisted, would permit them to socialize with the firm's top men and their families. Through socializing they would be accepted. And it was vitally important, John Fletcher had pointed out, that Nora as well as Dave be found acceptable.

All this meant, Nora reflected as she drove away from the Lanford Country Club, that she was constantly on exhibition. She must measure up to the concept, held by the corporation high brass and their wives, of a proper wife for a Worden-Forbes executive. She must prove to the company's elite that she was not only capable of giving Dave a happy home life but also that she was adept at functioning as his social partner. A rising young executive's wife must indeed be a helpmate.

But was a helpmate really expected to go as far as Penny Austin had intimated?

And was the answer yes, if the husband wasn't quite able to make it on his own?

Nora didn't know.

She wished she could stop thinking about it.

CHAPTER TWO

DRIVING HOME along the curving, tree-shaded streets of Wilshire Heights, past the handsome ranch-type and split-level homes, Nora lost her uneasiness. Everything was snug and safe here and she was able to rid herself of the ugly, weedy idea that Penny Austin had planted in her mind.

The neighborhood was as substantial-looking as it was attractive, and the people who occupied these fine houses were, Nora assured herself, much the same as Dave and she. Most of them were, certainly, couples in love and faithful to each other. They were solid, decent families, who took loving pride in raising their children in these homes. The parents were church-goers; they belonged to the PTA as well as the country club. There was togetherness here and certainly morality. If there were misfits in Wilshire Heights, misfits like Penny Austin, they were in a very small minority.

Yes, Nora felt better now.

She turned in at her own house, a gray-stone and clapboard split-level on a full acre of landscaped grounds. Their home was still new enough to her to evoke a little thrill each time she turned into the driveway. Although far from being among the more imposing homes in the Heights, the house and grounds were completely beautiful in her eyes.

She pressed a button on the dash, and one door of the two-car garage rose magically. She ran the station wagon inside, pressed the button again, and the door descended. She switched off the motor, got out of the car and entered the house proper by a connecting door.

Mrs. Jensen, the housekeeper whom Nora did not really need but accepted for status' sake, was busy in the gleaming, appliance-loaded kitchen with early preparations for dinner.

"Any guests this evening, Mrs. Osborne?"

"Not tonight, Martha," Nora said. "Were there any phone calls?"

There had been none, Mrs. Jensen told her and she went upstairs to the bedroom she and Dave shared. The chamber was done in ivory-white provincial and it was, of course, her favorite room. Why should it not be, she thought. Here she experienced the intimacies of love with the only man she had ever wanted. Here in Dave's arms she was lifted by soaring passion to ultimate ecstasy. She was, for all her considering herself a rather ordinary young woman, an extremely passionate one. The pleasures of the flesh were for her an important part of being alive. She lived through many a day waiting impatiently for bedtime with her husband. When she heard or read of frigidity in women, she could not understand or even imagine such a thing. *

She removed the plain blouse, skirt and heavy shoes that she had worn for her golf lesson and then examined herself critically in the dressing-table mirror. There was nothing of the narcissist in her makeup. She did not admire her physical self.

She was of average height but she would have preferred being tall. She was curvaceous when she would have preferred being slender. Her features were, it seemed to her, too ordinary. But her hair, a rich, lacquer-like black, pleased her and her eyes, of gold-flecked brown, were certainly another good feature. When she was angry her eyes seemed to spark. When she was happy, as when in Dave's arms, they glowed. Or so Dave had told her on numerous occasions.

Removing her bra, for she intended to shower, she revealed shapely, roseate-tipped breasts. Too big, she thought with her usual self-disparagement but certainly, thank heaven, not quite so bovine as Penny Austin's. She—

The phone began to ring.

She made haste to answer, going to the extension on the nightstand between the twin beds before Mrs. Jensen had to bother to take the call.

"Nora Osborne speaking."

"Nora, this is Julia Hoyt."

"Oh, Mrs. Hoyt. How nice," Nora said, her mind conjuring up a picture of the caller. Though fortyish, Julia was as lovely and trim as a high-fashion model—a true honey-blonde with a patrician beauty. She was the wife of Brandon Hoyt, a Worden-Forbes senior vice-president and board member. "How are you?" Nora said, asking that trite question because she was a bit flustered. Julia had never before called her. Too, Nora stood somewhat in awe of her.

"I'm quite well, thank you," Julia said. "I called to ask if you and your husband are free this evening. Brandon and I are having an informal little party—a cookout, actually, with just a few friends in, and we'd like so much to have you come."

"Why, we'd love to come," Nora said, trying to keep sudden excitement out of her voice, "unless Dave has already made an evening engagement today." She could not help feeling thrilled. This was the first invitation the Osbornes had received from the Hoyts. "Shall I call him, then call you back?"

"Oh, that won't be necessary," Julia told her. "Just come if you can. And I do hope you can. 'Bye now, Nora."

Nora said goodbye, thinking: Now we're really in. To be invited to the Hoyts meant that Dave and she were being accepted by them. It meant—

She had to tell Dave the good news right away.

She dialed Worden-Forbes' number, asked for Mr. Osborne in Public Relations. She was given Dave's secretary who asked who was calling. Nora told her and a moment later Dave came on.

"Hi, honey," he said. "What's up?"

"Guess who just called me, darling!"

"The White House."

"Goof! It was Julia Hoyt."

"Oh. Well, I'd never have guessed in a thousand years. What's with Julia Hoyt?"

"She wants us over this evening for a party," Nora said, then waited for her husband to express pleasure or even an excitement to match her own. When there was no response, she asked, "Well isn't that something?"

"Uh-huh. It's an invitation that was due."

"Couldn't it be a good omen, for heaven's sake? After all, Brandon Hoyt is a member of the board. And now that he and Julia are accepting us socially—"

"It must mean, you think, that I'm definitely on my way to that vice-presidency," Dave cut in. "Honey, for Pete's sake, don't pin your hopes for that on an invitation to a cookout."

"Well, I still think it's a promising sign," Nora said, refusing to be deflated. Then, after a pause: "Dave, honey ..."

"Yeah?"

"Could you come home, maybe?"

"At three-thirty in the afternoon?"

"I'm lonely."

"A nice cold shower is a cure for that sort of loneliness, baby."

"Beast!"

"See you about five-thirty, sweetheart," Dave said and broke the connection.

In his office at the Lanford plant of the Worden- Forbes Corporation, Dave Osborne lost his smile the instant he put down the phone. A scowl replaced it. The scowl had nothing to do with Nora, however. Dave seldom had reason to be displeased with his wife. Nora became unreasonable only infrequently and he was pretty well satisfied with her. Pretty well? He was damn well satisfied with her. Nora was a doll, fun to have around at any time and especially in bed. That she was fun in bed was important to Dave, for he was, he would have admitted with all modesty, a pretty warm guy. At thirty-six, he showed no signs of slowing down in the bed department.

For a moment he considered doing what Nora had suggested, knocking off for the rest of the afternoon and going home to her—to take care of her itch. The thought caused his scowl to ease a little.

But the temptation of playing hookey passed and the scowl, which had come at Nora's reminding him of Brandon Hoyt, deepened.

The invitation to spend the evening with the Hoyts was not the good omen Nora believed it to be. For just this afternoon Dave had heard, via the office grapevine, that Hoyt planned to sponsor a retired Air Force general for the vice-presidency that Dave had been working for. Evidently Hoyt felt that Worden-Forbes should follow the example of other corporations that now numbered high-ranking military men among their top personnel.

What under the sun a retired Air Force general would know about business management and industrial production, Dave could not imagine. Of course, Worden-Forbes did manufacture electronic devices and space vehicles on Air Force contracts.

The general might be able to help the firm in its dealing with the USAF top brass. Perhaps that was what Hoyt had in mind.

Dave leaned back in his chair and lit a cigarette, then, still scowling, gazed about his office, or rather, he sourly corrected himself, the office he was momentarily occupying. It was a large room, with brown wall-to-wall carpeting, relieved by several small but good Oriental throw rugs. The desk was a conservative mahogany, the chairs and sofa of mahogany and brown leather. In one corner stood a large terrestrial globe, in another a flag of the United States. Three walls were panelled in walnut to shoulder height and finished to the ceiling in opaque glass brick, and the fourth was a picture window of reflectionless glass. By turning in his chair, Dave had a panoramic view of the company's fine new research and development building, set amid the well-kept, velvet-green expanse of lawn. And the atmosphere in which he worked was, of course, air-conditioned.

A voice in his mind: Boy, you're going to miss all this.

He would, indeed, when, and if he was moved back to the cubicle he had formerly occupied. He had worked in this handsome office for nearly six months now, ever since its former occupant, J. P. Vinson, then vice-president for Public Relations, had resigned unexpectedly and taken three key men from the department with him.

It had been due to the loss of those four top executives in Public Relations that Dave had been moved into this office and given the duties of a vice-president. He had been the only man left with the experience and ability to head the department. And, if anyone asked him, he had done a good job. He had reorganized the working routine to function more efficiently and had hired some good, new people to work with him. He felt that he was doing a better job than J. P. Vinson had done to protect and enhance the company's good name, both in the eyes of the organizations with whom Worden-Forbes did business as well as with the general public. On the other hand, he had the empty, bitter feeling that his efforts were not appreciated or even noticed by the big boys upstairs. Yet he realized that his non-recognition must be blamed partly on himself. Why was it that he could sell Worden-Forbes to the public but was such a flop at selling himself to Worden-Forbes, the people who mattered most in his present world? He was painfully aware of the deep-rooted shyness that kept him from tooting his own horn, but he seemed unable to conquer, or even to combat, this lack of aggressiveness.

Yes, it would be hard, damn hard, to go back to his old job as a junior executive. And costly, too. He would have to take a big cut and suffer the necessary retrenchments his lower economic status would demand. How could Nora and he possibly be able to keep the house in Wilshire Heights? Why, running the place kept him broke even now, on his two hundred and fifty a week.

The intercom on his desk buzzed softly.

He flicked the switch, said, "Yes, Miss Marvin?"

"Mr. Harmon of the *Herald* is on the phone," his secretary said from her desk in the anteroom.

Dave said, "Okay," and reached for the phone. "How are you, Mike?" he asked. "Something I can do for you?"

He knew the newspaperman well. As financial and industrial editor on the *Lanford Herald*, Mike Harmon was a good contact for a public-relations man and especially for one in Dave's job.

"Just confirm a rumor for me, if you can," Harmon said.

"What rumor is that?"

"Rather a big one. I heard that General Lyle Wyman, USAF Retired, will become a Worden-Forbes vice-president. Anything to it?"

"That is a big one," Dave said. "This is the first I've heard about it. How about letting me call you back?"

"Okay. But don't hold out on me, boy."

"Do I ever?"

Harmon ignored that, saying, "General Wyman is still hot news, you know. The ex-glamor boy of the wild blue yonder. How soon can I expect your call? I've got a deadline on my neck."

"Half an hour. Okay?"

"Right," Harmon said and hung up.

Dave's scowl was back when he put down the phone. Obviously, the rumor had been purposely leaked. And almost certainly the leaking had been done by the fly-boy's sponsor, Brandon Hoyt. Oh, Nora, Dave thought, you and your high hopes just because of a little invitation. This would hit her hard. He pressed the switch on the intercom and told Miss Marvin to call John Fletcher's secretary and find out if Mr. Fletcher could see him immediately.

Mr. Fletcher could, Miss Marvin informed him a minute later, and he went upstairs to the comptroller's office.

As usual, John Fletcher's oversized desk was littered with papers to the point of chaos. This was not due to untidiness on the man's part but to the nature of his work. As comptroller, he was constantly checking and rechecking the company's financial affairs and consequently he spent his days working his way through a paper maze.

He was a thin, gray man of sixty-one or two and he looked every year of his age. He wore glasses, and still seemed not to see too well. He smoked a pipe, and never appeared to be ruffled. A soft-spoken, mild-mannered man, he was not at all typical of the Worden-Forbes breed of executives. Somehow, he had taken a liking to Dave Osborne. In turn, Dave Osborne was more relaxed with him than he was with any other of the company's executive officers.

Reaching for his pipe, Fletcher leaned back in his chair and said, "Sit down and tell me what's on your mind, Dave."

Seating himself, Dave said, "John, I just had a call from the *Herald*. Mike Harmon has heard a rumor that a retired Air Force general, Lyle Wyman, will join the company as vice-president. I heard the same rumor here at the plant this afternoon. Harmon wants the rumor confirmed or denied. I thought I'd ask your advice before calling him back."

Lighting his pipe, Fletcher said, "How did Harmon learn of it so quickly?"

"The so-called rumor was leaked, of course."

"I suppose so," Fletcher said. "Well, I heard of it only a few minutes ago, myself. Brandon Hoyt was in here trying to sell me on Wyman. The idea is his. He served under the general during World War Two, and it seems that Wyman, since his retirement, has been putting out feelers to industry. Wants to find himself a soft, big- payment job now that he's retired from the service, just like a lot of other former brass. I can't say that I blame him, but—well, I question the value of most military men to industry. Business just isn't their game. Still, Brandon is enthusiastic. He's going to do a lot of spadework and then bring the General's name up at the next board meeting."

"There's only one vice-presidency open, John."

"Unfortunately."

"I feel that between Wyman and myself—"

"I know," Fletcher said, "You're the better man for the office. I agree absolutely. And I'm going to bat for you. Like Brandon Hoyt, I also happen to be a member of the board."

"He'll give you a fight, and he's tough."

"Yes," Fletcher said. "That, I know."

"Well, I'll just have to sweat it out," Dave said. "There's nothing I can do personally. But what shall I tell Harmon for publication? I can issue a statement either confirming or denying that General Wyman is to join the company. Either way, the next board meeting could prove me wrong. The only way I'd not be going out on a limb would be to say that Worden-Forbes hasn't heard the rumor. If I go to Hoyt, he'll most likely want me to issue a statement to his and Wyman's advantage. If I go to H. M. Forbes, the chief, he'll tell me that I'm the public relations man and bounce me out of his office."

John Fletcher chuckled. "Well, so you are the public relations man, Dave. And if you're a good one, you won't go out on a limb on this thing—even though you are personally involved."

Dave smiled ruefully. "You're right, of course." He got to his feet. "I'll give Harmon a statement that says absolutely nothing."

"Such as?"

"Such as: David J. Osborne states that no agreement has been reached between Worden-Forbes and General Wyman and that no negotiations are underway at the moment."

"So," Fletcher said, smiling, "you've solved your problem."

Dave showed that rueful smile again. "I guess my real problem was that I wanted to hear that Hoyt wasn't planning to bring Wyman into the company, John."

"Yes. And I wish I could tell you exactly that."

"Well, thanks for your time."

"Any time at all, Dave," Fletcher said.

Brandon Hoyt was getting off the elevator when Dave came from John Fletcher's office. Seeing Dave, he waited for him to come along the corridor. In his early fifties, Hoyt could have posed for a man-of-distinction ad. Middle-age had put gray at his temples and stamped his handsome face with character. He was lean and fit. He was also sharp and shrewd. Only one man in Worden- Forbes' widespread organization wielded more power than Brandon Hoyt, and that was Mark Hammond, retired president and current chairman of the board, who one day would almost certainly be replaced by Hoyt.

Hoyt had charm as well as distinguished good looks, and he now turned it on for Dave. He smiled, placed a friendly hand on Dave's shoulder and asked him how he was feeling.

Then: "Mrs. Hoyt and I are having a few people over tonight, Dave, and we'd like you and Mrs. Osborne to drop around. Make it about six-thirty, if you have nothing better to do. My wife has probably called yours by now, but I thought I'd mention it to you."

Dave nodded. "I'm sure we'll be able to make it, Brandon."

"Good, good," Hoyt said. "It's high time we got together socially. By the way, I've been wanting to mention another matter. I've already discussed it with John Fletcher and a couple of others and I feel that you should be told, in your capacity as sort of an acting vice-president." He paused, letting the significance of those last half dozen words register. Then: "General Wyman, a good friend of mine who's just retired from the Air Force, is looking for a connection with a concern like Worden-Forbes and I personally feel that he would fit in here. I'd like your opinion on the subject, Dave."

Choosing his words carefully, trying to conceal his feelings, Dave said, "I've a lot of respect for your judgment, Brandon."

"Then you wouldn't be opposed to the General joining the team, eh, Dave?"

"Not knowing the General, I could hardly be opposed."

"Actually, I'm merely sampling opinion."

"Oh?"

"It's not definite yet. It will be for the board of directors to decide, of course."

"The *Herald* contacted me about it," Dave said. "I'll have to come up with a statement for Mike Harmon over there."

Hoyt frowned with spurious annoyance. "Those newspaper-men," he said. "It beats me how they get onto something you're trying to keep under wraps. What sort of statement are you giving him?"

Dave told him exactly what he'd told John Fletcher. Then he added, "If you'd like something more definite, I'll be glad to quote you."

"No, no," Hoyt said. "Your statement covers the matter as it now stands. Let it go like that for the time being, and everybody will be happy." He gripped Dave's arm. "See you this evening, Dave."

He moved briskly away, and Dave, staring after him, supposed that he should be grateful. Hoyt had given him fair warning. He was not slated for that vice-presidency if Brandon Hoyt could swing it his way.

Thanks, Dave thought bitterly. Thanks so much for nothing.

CHAPTER THREE

Arriving home at five-thirty, Dave was greeted by a silent house. No sound of activity came from the kitchen. Evidently Nora had let Mrs. Jensen go home early, since they were dining out. Nora failed to appear to welcome him, contrary to her usual custom. Nor did she answer when he called her name.

He went searching for her. She was not in the living room, nor anywhere upstairs. He went back to the first floor and found her in his study, sitting in his favorite leather chair and turning the pages of his latest copy of *Fortune*. She did not look up. Her expression as well as her silence told him she was in a mood.

He sighed resignedly. "All right," he said. "Just what did I do?"

The silence continued, except for the sound of magazine pages being flipped.

"I asked you—"

"It's not what you did, Dave Osborne," Nora said, looking up at last. She wore her angry face, eyes sparking and lips thinned down. It's what you didn't do."

"So what didn't I do?"

"You know very well what you didn't do," she said, getting to her feet and dropping the magazine into the chair. "You didn't come home when I needed you. For all you cared, I could have been deathly sick and—"

"Sick, hell—You just wanted to be laid."

"I *what?*"

"You heard me," Dave said, his temper slipping.

"I certainly did hear you," Nora said coldly. "And you needn't be so vulgar. You can find more proper ways to express yourself, you know."

"Excuse it, please," Dave told her. "But I'm an illiterate." He stared at her, having seen her lips quiver. "Damn it, you're kidding, aren't you?"

Nora began to laugh.

He grabbed at her. She tried to elude him but too late. He caught her by the arm, turned her about, slapped her across the backside, not gently.

"That'll teach you not to get kittenish," he said. "After all, a man expects his thirty-year-old wife to have a little more sense and dignity."

"Twenty-nine-and-a-half-year-old wife," Nora said, rubbing where he'd slapped her. "But you could have come home, darn it."

"I'm home now," he said, pulling her to him.

"There's no time now," Nora said. "We're to be at the Hoyts' at six-thirty. You just have time to shower and dress."

"Dress for a cookout?"

"Well, don't wear that business suit, for heaven's sake."

They left the study arm in arm, and went up to their bedroom. Nora was wearing a housecoat and merely had to change it for a dress. Dave began stripping down for his shower, going to the bathroom wearing only his T-shirt and shorts. He took along a fresh change of underwear. When he came back to the bedroom Nora was wearing her dress, a beige sheath, and was sitting at the dressing table doing her face. Getting a sports shirt from the dresser drawer, he wondered how he was to tell her about Brandon Hoyt's sponsoring General Wyman for the vice-presidency she so desperately wanted him to have.

Noticing that she was watching him in the mirror, he said, "I wanted to come home, honey, but I'm not exactly my own boss."

"Just so you wanted to come, darling," Nora told him. Then: "You were scowling a moment ago. Is something wrong?"

"No—No, not really," he said.

He got into slacks, put on socks and a pair of loafers. He kissed Nora on top of the head, then went downstairs to the kitchen and fixed a drink. He took a swallow and went back upstairs with the tumbler in his hand. He knew that he should tell Nora about General Wyman but he still did not know how to do it. It would be a blow, no matter how gently he broke the news.

Nora paused in putting on earrings, saying, "Don't tell me you needed a bracer just to visit the Hoyts."

"Well, I sometimes find Brandon Hoyt pretty hard to take," he said. "I'm not exactly in love with the guy."

"How about Mrs. Hoyt?"

"Too old for me."

"Just so I'm half as attractive when I'm forty."

"You will be," he said, meaning it. "Don't fret about that."

"Dave …"

"Yeah?"

"What is the Ninth Floor Club?"

He gazed at her blankly for a moment, then with curiosity. "Where'd you hear about that?"

"From Penny Austin," Nora said. "I saw her at the country club this afternoon after my golf lesson. We got to talking about how hard it was for a junior executive to make top executive and how a man's wife must stand inspection. Penny mentioned this mysterious Ninth Floor Club, without telling me what it is. She said I should ask you about it." Rising from the dressing-table stool, Nora faced him. "Come on, give, darling. After all, I'm a big girl now."

"There isn't any Ninth Floor Club. It's just a gag."

"Penny says she's a member."

"She did, eh?" Dave said. Then, after a pull at his drink. "Why did she say it?"

"She was telling me how she helped Bart get to be head of Engineering and Design," Nora said. "She said she'd given her little all' to help him. If she meant what I think she meant—well, you know."

"Don't let Penny Austin put ideas into your head, sweetheart," Dave said, grinning suddenly. "From what I hear, she's got the morals of an alley cat."

"You think she did help Bart in that—that way?"

"All I know is the gossip I hear. A long time ago somebody told me that she was Mark Hammond's part-time mistress."

"Mark Hammond? The chairman of the board?"

"No less."

"But he's—old."

"Sixty-one his last birthday."

Nora thought about Penny Austin and Mark Hammond. She looked as though she felt shocked. Then: "So what's the Ninth Floor Club? Explain the gag to me, Dave."

"Well, the company maintains a large suite on the ninth floor of the Harrison Hotel," Dave explained. It's for putting up visitors from the firm's other plants and its branch sales offices and for VIP's who come to Lanford to do business with the company. If these people request feminine company and are important enough to be given the full treatment, arrangements are made to send women up to the suite. Call-girls, of course. One of the guys in my department takes care of it."

"Don't tell me that Penny is a call girl."

"I won't. The girls I'm talking about are real pros."

"But what did Penny mean, saying she was a member of the Ninth Floor Club?"

Dave shrugged. "I can only guess. She probably had dates with Mark Hammond there. But don't ask me about Penny Austin. I'm not one of her boy-friends."

"Still, I've seen you ogling her more than once," Nora said, making a face at him. "Anyway, my curiosity is now satisfied—about the Ninth Floor Club, I mean. Now shall we call on the extremely wealthy and socially prominent Brandon Hoyts?"

"I guess we have no choice," Dave replied, grinning at her. Then: "You look wonderful, honey. I like the dress."

"You should by now," Nora told him. "I've worn it often enough. But I'm glad you think I look wonderful. You look cute, too."

They went downstairs together and Dave disposed of his empty glass in the kitchen.

As they went to the garage he said, "It's too blamed quiet around here. I miss the kid."

"I do too," Nora told him. "But we'll be driving up to Camp Wee-ni-toka on Sunday to see her. And after all, Louise has been gone only ten days."

"That's a long time for a seven-year-old to be away from home. And she'll be away almost three weeks longer."

They got into the Buick, Dave starting the motor and pressing the button that controlled the garage door.

As he backed the car out, Nora said, "We can't keep our child tied to our apron strings. It's not done any more."

"But camp," he said. "I don't know that I approve."

"It'll make Louise self-reliant."

"Like you?"

"Well, aren't I self-reliant?"

"You are. And you didn't spend your summers at camp as a kid."

"I had very few advantages in my childhood, darling."

"But you survived."

"Full of complexes and frustrations."

Dave snorted. He was silent until they had turned from their driveway onto Elm Drive. Then: "Sunday, I think I'll withdraw *my* daughter from Camp Wee-ni- toka."

"Over my dead body," Nora said.

He grinned at her. "You and your body. Always flaunting it."

"As you expect me to," Nora said. Then, in a more serious tone: "Dave, Penny was trying to be kind and helpful this afternoon. She told me you should be a little more pushy. She said you shouldn't be scared of the brass."

"Oh, she did, did she?" Dave said, his voice barbed.

"She said that Bart told her you aren't exactly aggressive," Nora went on. "And you're not really, you know."

"Thanks, Thanks a heap. Next thing, you and Penny Austin will decide that I don't handle my job properly."

"That's not so, darling," Nora said. "Everyone knows you're doing a swell job of handling your department. But you aren't pushy enough. You don't mix with the top men." She looked at him anxiously. "Am I making you sore?"

"Not at all," he said flatly. "You're making me feel just dandy."

"I just want to be of help. A wife has got to help."

"Yeah. Like Penny Austin helped her husband."

"Now you are sore," Nora said contritely. "I'm sorry, darling."

Dave merely grunted.

They were silent the remainder of the way to the Hoyt's estate in the Crestwood section. Brandon and Julia Hoyt lived in a huge ranchhouse that looked like something out of the pages of *House Beautiful.* It stood atop its own rolling hill in snobbish aloofness and was reached by a long, curving driveway. Around back were tennis courts, a putting range and a swimming pool. A dozen cars were already parked in front of the house when Dave and Nora arrived and one of them was the Austin's Lincoln convertible. Penny, alone, was just getting from the Lincoln. Seeing the Osbornes, she waved to them and then waited until they had parked and gotten from their Buick.

His feelings still ruffled, Dave eyed the redhead with sudden dislike. But his new distaste for her did not keep him from admiring her as a woman. She had the ripe, statuesque figure of a showgirl and, at times, the pixyish expression of a sex-kitten. There always seemed to be an excitement in her just below the surface and Dave, in male fashion, assumed that was due to the fact that passion, sudden and explosive, lay at a shallow depth within her.

Penny was an outgoing person; that was sure. In greeting Nora, she exclaimed, "Darling, you look wonderful," and then touched cheeks with her in that ludicrous pretense of two females kissing. The next instant she turned to Dave and gave him a warm, sensual smile. The instantaneous thought flashed through him that there was a promise—even, perhaps, an invitation—in her crinkled green eyes.

"And you have that handsome husband of yours along," she said. "How are you, Dave?"

"I'm fine," Dave said. "And you?"

"Just fine," Penny replied. "Except I'm in a mood because I have to come stag. My husband is off trying to settle some damn problem at the Dayton plant. Look—may I make my entrance with you two? I just loathe arriving alone."

"Of course you may," Nora said. "Come along."

And Dave said, "Sure. Three makes no crowd."

He walked behind them around the house to the terrace where the cookout was being held. His gaze was on Penny's shapely rear. She made sure that he notice her by walking with an exaggerated swaying of her hips.

Two dozen or more people were already gathered on the terrace between the house and the swimming pool. Dave spotted a half-dozen Worden-Forbes executives. He recognized other of the male guests as prominent business and professional men. The women were, for the most part, middle-aged like the men, but were as sleek and lovely as expensive clothes, cosmetics and hair stylists could make them.

Brandon Hoyt saw the newcomers and came striding across the velvety lawn toward them. He was delayed by one of a foursome; someone who evidently had a story to tell for Hoyt smiled and nodded and finally broke into laughter. His wife joined him, and host and hostess came on to meet Penny Austin and the Osbornes. They made a strikingly handsome couple, Brandon with his virile good looks and Julia with her fine-drawn and rather cool blonde beauty. After telling Dave and Nora how happy they were to see them, Julia turned to Penny: "My dear, it was so sweet of you to come, even though Bart is out of town."

"I long ago decided," Penny told her, "that if I waited for my man to take me places I'd be sitting home most of the time. The guy's as much married to his job as to me—and maybe more so. And I think"—this to Brandon Hoyt—"that I hate Worden-Forbes with all the venom of a jealous woman."

"With Bart pulling down thirty thousand a year?" Hoyt grinned. "I'll just bet you do. Well, come along, you people, and we'll have some drinks. This little affair is by way of celebration—yours truly's birthday. The day actually isn't until Sunday, but we're celebrating now because I have to be out of town for the weekend." He smiled that charming smile. "Now please don't ask which birthday the old man is celebrating. That's a touchy subject."

Penny said, "You didn't warn us, and so we haven't come bearing gifts. Still. . ." She moved close to Hoyt, kissed him on the cheek. "So there," she told him. "Many happy returns."

Everybody laughed.

Each of the Osbornes privately decided that the evening promised to be a pleasant one; a forecast that made Nora warmly happy but one that filled Dave with a feeling of bitterness. For one fact stood like a threatening black cloud before his eyes: Their host, charming and hospitable though he was, was doing his level best to keep Dave from the vice-presidency.

CHAPTER FOUR

Dave did not purposely set out to get stoned but he was in a low mood from thinking constantly of that vice-presidency slipping away from him. So by nine o'clock, having drunk far more than he had eaten, he discovered that he was a little looped but he felt no exhilaration from his drinks. Rather, he was filled with an oozy, alcoholic self-pity. He stood around morosely on the edge of the crowd, working on his drink and taking no part in the talk and laughter of the other guests.

After Nora rebuked him by saying, "Really, darling, you're not being exactly the life of the party," he fixed a rather vacuous smile on his lips so as not to appear downright antisocial.

Actually, he had plenty of company in his mildly looped condition if not in his low frame of mind. The Hoyt's bartender was a busy man, and more than a few of the guests—both men and women—were feeling their liquor as much as Dave. But they were high rather than glumly tight and consequently the party soon showed signs of turning into something of a brawl.

There was, for example, the matter of the floating key. A dozen or so guests had gathered by the pool and the noise they made caused the Osbornes and still others to join them.

A man's voice yelled, "Go on, Georgie! Don't chicken out!" And another voice, no soberer than the first, called, "Go to it, boy I You've got everything to gain and nothing but your life to lose!"

Georgie was George Mason, famed as a playboy and heir apparent to Lanford's largest trucking firm. He was standing alone at the end of the pool and apparently contemplating a dive into the water. He had removed his jacket, shirt and shoes. As more and more people called to him to take the plunge, he grinned and said, "All right, here goes nothing!"

Quickly removing his slacks, he dived into the water and with a great deal of splashing started swimming toward a small yellow disc which floated in the center of the pool. The yellow disc bobbed up and down on the now agitated water, and Dave saw that it was a paper picnic plate from the buffet table.

Turning to Herb Sundersen who stood beside him, Dave asked, "What gives?"

Sundersen nodded in the direction of a young woman who stood at the edge of the pool, watching the swimmer with a half-musing, half-mocking smile. She was Connie Barron, one of Worden-Forbes' largest stockholders and a granddaughter of one of the company's founders. She had been recently divorced from a major-league ball player who had turned out, so gossip said, not nearly so virile as she had hoped.

"Connie floated her apartment key out on that plate," Sundersen said, chuckling, with the implication that whoever retrieved it could make use of it tonight."

"And Mason was the only taker?" Dave said. "Connie must feel let down that there aren't more chumps playing the game."

"Too many wives present," Sundersen said.

Nora tugged at Dave's arm and whispered, "Does she really mean it, do you suppose?"

"My naïve little wife," Dave said, grinning at her.

Mason finally came within reach of the paper plate. But he was both a clumsy swimmer and too eager, and in grabbing the plate he tilted it and the key slipped off and sank to the bottom of the pool. A collective groan, mingled with hoots of derision, went up from the watchers. A moment later several people called to the swimmer to dive for the key, Mason did make several tries at finding it but then, winded and tired, he was forced to come out of the water.

A moment later a second paper plate was launched, this one by Jim Matthews, vice-president of production at Worden-Forbes, and this plate carried not a key but a hundred-dollar bill. A heavy-set man with a coarsely handsome face and iron-gray hair, Matthews was a grass widower. He grinned, announcing that this was a contest for the ladies.

The ladies were more competitive than the men had been, and four young women decided excitedly to try for the money. One of the four was disqualified because of her tipsiness and one was restrained by her husband. The other two, Connie Barron and Penny Austin, quickly stripped to panties and bra, to the noisy delight of most of the spectators. They took their places at the end of the pool, waiting for Matthews to give the signal. He was agitating the water with his hand in an attempt to float the plate out from the side of the pool.

Matthew finally called, "On your mark. Ready. Go."

The two young women dived into the water. The spectators chose sides, some shouting encouragement to Connie and others to Penny Austin.

Dave Osborne watched glumly, rooting for neither. But beside him, Nora yelled excitedly, "Come on, Penny—come on!" Dave glanced at her amusedly. This wasn't at all like Nora. But she had been caught up by the spirit of the crazy stunts, probably because she had had one or two daiquiris more than her quota during the evening. "Come on, Penny—come on!" Nora cried.

Penny Austin was the stronger swimmer and drew ahead of Connie Barron. However, when they got close to the plate with Penny slightly in the lead, the Barron girl grabbed Penny by the hair. Penny's reaction was swift and vicious. She whipped about and drove her elbow into Connie's neck and Connie, with a shriek of pain, let loose her hair. Penny laughed and swam on and the next instant reached the plate. She took hold of it gingerly with one hand and with the other plucked off the hundred-dollar bill. Her supporters cheered, Nora among them.

Laughing, Penny swam to the side of the pool and was helped from the water by Jim Matthews. Her wet panties and bra clung to her like a second skin and her magnificent body gleamed in the soft glow of the garden lights. Wet though she was, she flung her arms about Matthews and kissed him. He slapped her on the seat of her soaked panties.

It was quite a party, Nora Osborne decided, a good deal wilder than the parties that Dave and she had attended before. She was a little surprised by that, since the extremely proper Brandon Hoyts were the hosts.

After the horseplay at the pool Dave and Nora went to the bar for another round of drinks. She was drinking too much, she realized. She felt a little tipsy. This will be my last, she told herself. She also told herself that this one should be Dave's last, too. He was drinking far too much but surprisingly he did not seem to be enjoying himself and she couldn't understand that. He no longer seemed peeved with her for her having said that he was not aggressive enough in his dealing with the key men at the plant. But something was certainly bothering him. She would have to ask him what it was when they got home.

A ilittle later, feeling a fine warm glow from the last daiquiri, she went into the house to powder her nose. Coming from the bathroom, she saw Brandon Hoyt about to turn into a room farther along the hallway. Seeing her he stopped, then, after a moment of hesitation, he came to her.

"Enjoying yourself, Mrs. Osborne?"

"Immensely, Mr. Hoyt."

"I'm Brandon to my friends," he said, smiling at her.

"And I'm Nora to mine," she said. Then, noticing that there was still a smudge of lipstick on his cheek where Penny Austin had kissed him, she giggled. "There's nothing sillier," she told him when he looked at her uncertainly, "than a man wearing lipstick."

"I didn't know that I was," he said, grinning. He took out his handkerchief, wiped at the smudge.

"Tell me," Nora said, knowing it was the daiquiris prompting her. "Tell me. ... Doesn't Mrs. Hoyt object to other women kissing you?"

"Not when I'm celebrating a birthday," he said. Then, eyeing her in a speculative way: "As for myself, I'm not averse to accepting kisses as birthday presents."

"Be careful," Nora said, and again felt the impetus of the daiquiris. "I can take a hint."

"Can you?" Hoyt smiled. "Well, if you're in a gift-giving mood—"

She was tipsy indeed, for she would never have considered kissing him when sober. She slipped her arms about his neck to do it. It was a brief kiss but a kiss, nevertheless, and with it she was committed. She would show him that at least one of the Osbornes was not shy with Warden-Forbes' executives. She slipped her arms farther about his neck, and this brought her body in contact with his. She kissed him again, more lingeringly. He put his hands at her waist, held her tightly to him.

Afterward, drawing back, she said, "Now. Many happy returns."

"I couldn't have had a nicer present," he said, and now his way of looking at her was definitely calculating. "We'll have to get together sometime, you and I."

"On your next birthday."

"That's a long way off."

"A safe way off," Nora told him. "And right now I'd better get back to the party."

"Look," he said hastily. "I'll call you one day soon."

"Don't you dare," Nora said, and in spite of her tipsiness hurriedly left him.

Dave and she left at eleven o'clock, among the first to leave. It was time to go home, Nora knew. Dave was well on his way to becoming stoned, and she—well, she herself had had far too much to drink. Her behavior with Brandon Hoyt was proof of that. Whatever had possessed her, she did not know. One thing was certain—she had left herself wide open for a pass. He had said he would call her and, worriedly, she knew he would. She remembered the direct, intimate look he had given her when Dave and she said good night to him and Julia ... Yes, he would call her. She felt suddenly frightened, actually frightened.

To get her mind off him, she commented to Dave that it had been quite a party.

"A brawl," Dave said, his voice thick and his words slurred. "That's what it was, a brawl."

He sounded not only more than a little drunk but also in a foul humor. She did not try to talk with him again on the way home, and once they arrived there he went straight to bed and was instantly asleep.

Later, lying in her own bed and listening to his slow, heavy breathing, Nora felt an annoyance that was very close to anger. She wanted him tonight, right now, this minute. She needed urgently to be loved. She was wide awake and in a state of excitement. She lay there thinking of George Mason trying to get Connie Barron's key from that floating plate. She wondered if Connie had taken pity on George and let him come to her apartment, anyway.

She wondered if Jim Matthews had not expected more than a kiss from Penny Austin for that hundred-dollar bill. And if Penny, with Bart in Dayton, had not known that Jim expected more.

She thought of her ridiculous behavior with Brandon Hoyt, and his promise or threat to call her, and wondered if her morals, like Connie's and Penny's, were not becoming a little elastic. Was it a case of when in Rome doing as the Romans do?

At any rate, she wanted to be loved tonight.

Her loins ached for male caresses, and her mind was full of sexual fantasies.

And her husband lay deep in sleep in the other bed.

CHAPTER FIVE

Aᴼᴛᴇʀ ᴡʜᴀᴛ seemed hours, Nora finally slept and then over-slept. Dave's bed was empty when she awoke and the clock on the night stand indicated the time was nine-twenty. Dave had gone to the office without having awakened her. She wondered uneasily if he were still peeved with her and then, getting from bed and finding that she had a pounding headache, she also wondered how he managed to get up at his usual time. He must be suffering a much worse hangover than she was, having drunk so much more.

The door chimes sounded just as she came from washing her face and running a comb through her hair. They continued to sound with urgency, unanswered by Mrs. Jensen. Nora became aware tardily that this was Thursday, the housekeeper's day off, and so she put on slippers and robe and went to the front door.

Penny Austin stood there and she was her usual buoyant self. "Hi," Penny said. She was in skirt, blouse and low heels. She appeared as bright and fresh as the fine July morning. "Did I get you out bed, darling?"

"Two minutes earlier and you would have," Nora said, forcing a smile. "Come on in, Penny."

Penny came in, asking, "Hangover?"

"Sort of."

"Me too," the redhead said. "But I've just got to rise above it. She frowned thoughtfully. "I know it sounds corny, but have you tried a cup of. black coffee?"

"Not yet."

"Let me make a pot for you."

"All right," Nora said and went to the kitchen with her.

She sat at the table while her visitor put water and coffee into the coffee-maker, and wondered about this early-morning visit of Penny's. The redhead lived only three blocks away but they were not on such intimate terms that they ran back and forth to each other's home. Knowing about Penny's extra-marital activities, Nora wasn't sure that she wanted to be on such friendly terms with her. Still, she did like her. Suddenly she realized that she was glad Penny had stopped by.

Penny sat down and lit a cigarette while the coffee perked and said, "It was quite a party, wasn't it? And as usual, I had one drinkie too many and made a fool of myself."

"How did you find the nerve, Penny?"

"I was just feeling devilish, I guess," Penny said. And then, in a serious tone: 'i came over to buck you up, Nora. As soon as I saw that lousy thing in the paper, I decided that I ought to lend you my shoulder to cry on."

Nora looked at her blankly. "What lousy thing?" she said. "I'm sorry, Penny, but I'm pretty fuzzy-minded this morning. And I haven't seen the morning paper."

"And Dave didn't mention it?"

"Mention what?"

Penny frowned. "Now I've done it," she said contritely. "I would have to be the one to break the bad news to you. Still, maybe it's nothing to be taken seriously—since Dave didn't say anything. It's just an item in Mike Harmon's column in the financial section of the *Herald*— something about a rumor of some retired Air Force general becoming a Worden-Forbes vice-president."

Looking stunned, Nora cried, "Oh, no!"

"As I said, if Dave didn't mention it …"

"So that was why he was in such a foul mood last night," Nora said, more to herself than to Penny. "He was worried about this. He didn't mention it because he didn't want me upset."

"He should have known you'd hear of it," Penny said. "A thing like this is like a pregnancy—you just can't keep it a secret. I'm sorry, Nora. I truly am."

Nora nodded, believing that the redhead was sincere. Getting from her chair, she said, "I've got to see it for myself. Excuse me, Penny, while I look for the morning paper."

She found the Herald on Dave's desk in the study. She opened the paper to Mike Harmon's column. The item, at the very end of the column, read:

> Interesting, to say the least, is the rumor that General Lyle Wyman, USAF Retired, is to join Worden-Forbes Corporation as a vice-president. W-F executive David J. Osborne in a statement to this column would neither confirm nor deny the rumor. According to Mr. Osborne no agreement has been reached between his company and General Wyman and no negotiations are underway at the moment.

This had been a blow for Dave and she—heaven forgive her—had made him feel worse by saying those things about his not being aggressive enough. What good would aggressiveness be against such a deal as this? A retired Air Force general. Damn. Why couldn't the man be content with having had one career? Why did this General Wyman have to take a job away from a deserving young man like Dave?

Poor Dave, she thought, and she felt like crying for him.

She returned to the kitchen and said bitterly, "Oh, darn, Penny, why did this man have to bob up? After all, there's only one vice-presidency open. That's the one Dave should have."

"Somebody at Worden-Forbes bobbed him up," Penny replied. "And I've an idea who that somebody is."

"Who it is?"

"Brandon Hoyt. He was in the Army Air Force during World War Two. A major, I think. Anyway, I'd bet that he's the culprit." She rose, saying, "You'd better have that coffee now, for sure."

They sat at the table, sipping black coffee.

After a lengthy silence, Nora said, "Penny, could you help Dave?"

"I?" Penny said, looking at her with astonishment. "How in the world could I help him?"

"Well, you helped Bart. You told me yesterday that you did. And Dave said—" She broke off, suddenly embarrassed. "Sorry, I didn't mean to say that."

"Sorry for what? For discussing me with Dave?"

"Well, yes."

Penny laughed. "Don't be sorry about that. Everybody discusses me—because everybody knows about me. It's not something a girl can hide. Not an affair with a man like Mark Hammond."

"Couldn't you talk to Mr. Hammond on Dave's behalf?"

'I'm sorry, Nora, but my affair with him is pretty well over and done with," Penny said. "He isn't the man he was when I needed a favor of him. He's six years older now and that makes a big difference in a man his age. I seldom see him any more—and I mean seldom. Actually he comes to Lanford only for board meetings nowadays. He spends his time between Maine and Florida. I'm sorry, darling, but I don't see how I could help."

"I shouldn't have asked."

"Sure you should have. And I only wish I could have said yes. That damned Brandon Hoyt. One day he'll replace Mark as chairman of the board and that day I dread to see."

"He told me last night that he's going to call me."

"Brandon?"

Nora nodded.

"Well, in that case maybe you can do yourself some good." Penny gave her a knowing smile.

"Oh, I couldn't. I just couldn't."

"You've never had any man but Dave, have you?"

"No, never."

"Really? What a rare bird you are."

"Had you other men besides Bart—before Mark Hammond?"

"A dozen," Penny said matter-of-factly. "The first when I was fifteen. My father came home from the war with a lame leg and a nervous condition. He was in and out of the veterans' hospital all the time and my mother took a lover. Or rather she kept the lover she'd had while Dad was in the service. My father and I had never been close. He was preoccupied with sports every spare moment and forever going out with the boys. He hadn't much time for a daughter—or for a wife, for that matter. My mother and I weren't exactly buddy-buddy, but I understood her. Somehow I understood her need for a lover—young as I was.

"Anyway, this boy-friend of hers, Max, was a sweet guy and nice to me. He was always bringing me gifts, when he came to see Elaine—Mother. Bribes, I guess they were, to keep me from telling tales out of school. The older I got, the nicer he was to me. So one day in the summer when there was no school and Elaine was at work, he stopped by when I was alone. He said that he'd just happened to be in the neighborhood but of course he'd planned it. He came with a present. Not a bribe this time; it was an enticement."

"And he was the first man?" Nora asked as Penny paused.

Penny nodded. "He was on the fat and forty side but that didn't matter. I liked him. More important, I was wild to know what really went on between men and women. I didn't know from nothing but I met him halfway ... My mother married him after my father passed away but that was after I was grown and had left home. After Max, there was a boy. He wasn't any good at it; too young and clumsy. There were others before I married Bart."

Penny paused, seemed to think about it. Then: "With me, sex has never had anything to do with love. It seems a separate thing—an urge, an appetite, sometimes a hunger. Bart's my guy, and I'm fond of him. He's the only man I've ever known that I wanted to spend my life with. But where sex is concerned, well, a number of other men have been more fun."

Penny laughed suddenly. "Lord, but I'm being candid. What is it about you that makes me yak-yak about myself?"

Nora smiled faintly, feeling too low to be amused. "Maybe if I'd gotten off to the same sort of start as you," she said soberly, "I might be able to play the game like you do. But I can't imagine my giving myself to another man. Besides, I'd be terrified that Dave would find out. Aren't you afraid that Bart may find out you're playing around?"

"He knows about me," Penny said. "He knew from the start and he's always acted accordingly. He's never said a word but he keeps the score even. He probably would have done his own playing around even if I'd been as faithful as you. Like a lot of men, Bart's a chaser by nature. He—" The redhead suddenly burst into uncontrollable laughter. "Does Bart know about me and Mark Hammond? I'll say he does. Mark did a crazy thing a few months after Bart was promoted to his present job. One stormy Saturday night, I remember that Bart and I decided we'd stay home. We had a couple of drinks and played gin, then went to bed early.

"We were having a cozy time—nothing wildly exciting, just making love like two people used to each other. The phone rang. Bart answered because his mother was sick and he was worried about her. But it wasn't Dad Austin; Mark Hammond was on the phone.

"If you knew Mark well, you'd understand his pulling such a stunt. It didn't faze him at all that my husband answered. He simply said, "Bart, I'd like to borrow Penny tonight. My chauffeur is on his way to pick her up."

Penny paused to finish her coffee and light another cigarette, then continued, "Bart was sore, of course. But he couldn't object, or he felt that he couldn't. He was still feeling insecure in his job. He owed it to Mark, and knew Mark could break him as easily as he'd made him. So I rolled out of the hay, put on a dress and shoes, slipped into a raincoat and tied a scarf about my head. By the time I was ready, Mark's chauffeur was pulling up in front of the house. I ran out into the rain and got into the car and spent the rest of the night in the company's ninth-floor suite at the Harrison." Penny laughed again, this time a bit ruefully, as though at a joke on herself. "That was one time when Bart definitely knew about me."

"And still you have a good marriage," Nora said, marveling.

"A lot of good marriages in our crowd have a dash of infidelity mixed in with them," Penny pointed out. "It would be a sorry world if a little extramural sex broke up all the marriages touched by it."

"But my Dave isn't at all like Bart," Nora protested. "He'd never let me get away with cheating on him."

Amused, Penny said, "Are you trying to convince me or yourself darling?"

"You, of course," Nora said, smiling. "Why should I need to convince myself of it? I know."

"But aren't you, right this moment, half-seriously considering a little cheating—if it could help get Dave that vice-presidency?"

"He wouldn't want the job if I had to sleep around to get it for him."

"You could be right, of course," Penny said thoughtfully. "But he really wouldn't have to know."

"There's no sense in even talking about it, when there's no Mark Hammond offering me a trade."

"But there is a Brandon Hoyt. Remember? You said he's going to call you."

"Oh, that," Nora said, trying to dismiss the possibility as meaningless.

Penny, however, refused to drop the subject. "When a man says he's going to call you," she said, "he means he has only one thing in mind—to have you for a playmate. Believe me, I—" She broke off abruptly, having glanced at the wall clock. "Good Lord, it's quarter past ten already. I've got to run or I'll miss my date with the hairdresser." Snubbing out her cigarette she got up from her chair and smoothed her skirt. "I'm sorry I can't help you, Nora. I truly am. And I do hope this Air-Force general thing turns out to be a false alarm. Don't get up. 'Bye now."

She rushed off, leaving Nora full of confused thoughts—thoughts she did not like. She certainly was not, as Penny had suggested, considering having an affair with Brandon Hoyt or with anyone else in order to help get that vice-presidency for Dave. Why, what Penny had done for Bart and had hinted that she herself could do for Dave was no less than a form of prostitution. It was unthinkable—for her, at least. What the Penny

Austins of this world could do so casually, the Nora Osbornes could not do under any circumstances.

She was too much in love with Dave even to dream of being involved with another man for any purpose. She—

The ringing of the telephone startled her out of her train of thought. Certain that Dave was calling, she rose hastily to answer. Of course he would call, she told herself, because he had let her sleep this morning and had left the house without having seen her at all.

So she snatched up the phone and exclaimed, "Dave, I'm so glad you called! I've been—"

The man's voice that cut in on her was not Dave's. Her caller said, "Sorry to disappoint you, Nora. This isn't Dave; it's Brandon Hoyt. Remember, I told you I'd call."

Nora knew it was ridiculous to be frightened. No possible harm could come to her over the telephone, she tried to assure herself. But she recalled Penny Austin's saying a man had only one thing in mind when he called a woman—to have her for a playmate. If that was Brandon Hoyt's purpose in calling her, she couldn't help but be frightened. Her shaky voice gave her away.

"Oh, Mr. Hoyt ... How are you?"

"I'm fine, thanks," he said. "But I thought it was to be Brandon and Nora. Or have you decided we shouldn't be that friendly so soon?"

Reminding herself that she could not afford to appear uncordial toward him, she said, "I'm sorry—Brandon I slipped up."

"That's better, Nora," he said, laughing. Then: "You know, I was thinking of you a while ago and wondered if you'd have lunch with me."

"Today?" she said, alarm knifing through her. And then, as though an automatic safety control were touched off: "I'm so sorry, but I do have a luncheon engagement—one that I really can't break."

"Oh, what a shame—for me. I was looking forward to seeing you today."

"I am sorry, Brandon."

"Well, another time, maybe?"

"Yes," she said. "Another time."

They said goodbye and then Nora, putting down the phone, realized her mistake. She had failed to close the door against another invitation from him. Instead, she had left herself wide open. And could she plead another engagement the next time he called? She could, of course, but only at the risk of alienating him. And she could not afford to lose his friendship. What shall I do? she worried. How can I cope with him the next time?

She was still searching for an answer when the phone rang again. This time it was Dave and her heart leaped at the sound of his voice. She felt safe now; safe in his love and in the security of their marriage.

"Hi, honey," Dave said. "How are you feeling?"

"A little hung," she said. "And you?"

"The same, but I'll survive."

"You're not still sore with me?"

"Could I be, really?"

"I hope not," she told him. Then, in a more serious tone: "Dave, Penny Austin stopped by and told me about an item in Mike Harmon's column. Have you seen it?"

"I've seen it."

"Is there any truth in it?"

"I'm afraid there is, Nora."

"Oh, Dave!" she said, her heart aching for him. "I wish you'd told me. You were worried about it last night, and I was—well, I was nasty to you. Dave—"

"Yes, Nora?"

"Penny says that Brandon Hoyt must be the person behind it."

"He is, all right."

"Oh, dam him. I'd like to tell him a thing or two."

"A lot of good that would do," Dave said dispiritedly. "It's just one of those things that can't be helped. Well, I've got work to do, honey. Take care of your hangover."

Nora wanted to ask if there wasn't something Dave could do, but he said goodbye and broke the connection. There was not, she well realized, anything he could do. It would be unthinkable for him to go to Brandon Hoyt and try to make Hoyt understand that he, Dave Osborne, was far more capable of filling the vice-presidency, because of his experience, than any retired Air Force general. It would be a serious breach of office politics, to begin with. And such an approach would never change Brandon Hoyt's mind, for he was far from the type to permit himself to be influenced by a junior executive. Such a man would never be swayed by anyone, except perhaps—No, dam it, Nora told herself, I won't even consider such a thing.

When Dave came home that evening they made a point of not discussing the threat to their future. It was as though each felt that if they took no notice of General Lyle Wyman he might quietly go away, as a nightmare fades from memory by midmorning.

Saturday afternoon Carole Sundersen called Nora and invited the Osbornes to an informal little get-together that evening. If Nora and Dave could make it, fine. Carole and Herb Sundersen—he was chief engineer of Worden-Forbes—would love to have them. But in the event that they had something else planned, that would be all right, too. Nora said that Dave and she had nothing planned and they would be delighted to come.

It was, after all, a duty thing. Herb Sundersen was neither a company officer nor a member of the board, but as chief engineer he was a top executive and therefore a man Dave should cultivate. Despite the very real threat of General Wyman, Nora refused to give up all hope. She had to force herself to believe that Dave still had a good chance to have that vice-presidency.

The party turned out exactly as Carole had said the gathering would be, small and informal. There were less than two dozen guests and some of them, having other engagements, merely dropped in for a drink or two. Most were Worden-Forbes people.

Brandon and Julia Hoyt were present, as were Bart and Penny Austin. Penny's tall, lanky husband, a quiet type with dark-framed glasses and a preoccupied air, seemed an odd mate for the vivacious, oversexed Penny. At least he seemed so to Nora, now that she knew what sort of a person Penny Austin really was.

There was a buffet supper but, as usual, the food was held to be of secondary importance to the drinks. In spite of the continuously refilled cocktail glasses and highball tumblers, it was a sedate affair—at the start, at least—compared to the Hoyt's recent party. Conversation followed the conventional pattern, with the men discussing business, the administration in Washington, the international situation, juvenile delinquency, golf and sex. The women discussing clothes, children, recipes, servants, scandals, golf and sex. No flagrant flirtations took place; no couples sneaked away from the main group. Yes, this little party was, Nora told herself, quite different from the brawl at the Brandon Hoyts' home.

So the evening went until midnight when couples began saying goodnight and making their departure and Julia Hoyt suggested that Herb Sundersen show some of his home movies. By that time the only remaining guests were Dave and Nora

Osborne, Brandon and Julia Hoyt, Jim Matthews and a blonde young enough to be his daughter, and Bart and Penny Austin.

Nora could think of nothing more boring than being inflicted with someone's home movies. She gave Dave one of those wifely looks that said, "Let's go home—now." But when Dave and Nora got up and started to say that they must leave, big, blond Herb Sundersen grinned and told them not to be in such a rush.

"Don't worry—you may be in for a surprise," laughed Herb. "My kind of home movies carry a built-in, secret ingredient that makes them different from the usual run. You'll see."

The others joined in, urging Dave and Nora to stay.

And Julia Hoyt winked tipsily at Dave, saying, "You won't be sorry. Herb's movies are way, way out."

So Dave and Nora stayed, and Herb's so-called home movies proved to be way, way out indeed. He showed them in the darkened basement rumpus room and Nora was grateful for the darkness. She would not have liked the others to see the shock and then the embarrassed enjoyment that must have shown on her face. She would not have liked seeing the expressions of the other guests, either, at such a time. For Herb Sundersen's home movies were unalloyed, raw sex.

The film was in color with a background-music soundtrack, and the title, *Love Down on the Farm,* gave Nora a hint of what was to come. She was seated in a lounge chair and Dave was perched on the arm. Like the others, Dave and she had each brought a fresh drink to the rumpus room. Dave looked down at Nora, and in the glare from the screen she saw him grin. He, too, now knew what they were about to see and, like herself, he felt a bit shamefaced about it.

The first scene was of the house and barn on a typical small farm. A closer shot showed two men loading a pickup truck with sacks of grain. The one man was in late middle age, a homely sort, a true rustic type. The other was young, handsome. From their actions, apparently the older man was the owner of the farm and the younger one his hired hand.

The truck loaded, the farmhand disappeared into the barn. The farmer looked toward the house and a strikingly attractive blonde came from it and walked toward him. She was a most unlikely farm woman, for she had an unmistakable boudoir look even though she wore a simple house dress and an apron.

Obviously she wore nothing beneath the dress. Her over-sized breasts bounced freely and her heavy thighs were outlined with each seductive, hip-swaying step she took. She kissed the farmer and he embraced and fondled her. Clearly they were hus-band and wife. As he got into the truck and drove off she waved goodbye, smiling fondly. But once the truck was out of sight, she turned and hurriedly entered the barn. She began climbing the ladder to the hay loft, the camera remaining on her shapely legs as she climbed.

Comments came from the audience. Jim Matthews burst out, "So that's what farm life is like! Brother!"

Bert Austin said, "Boy, what a pair of gams!"

And when the girl on the screen reached the hay loft and found the young farmhand waiting there, Penny Austin exclaimed, "An honest-to-gosh roll in the hay!"

At that, Julia Hoyt asked, "Dave, Nora, now aren't you glad you stayed?"

Nora was at first amazed and then somehow disappointed in Julia, who had always seemed to her so proper, so much the lady.

The action on the screen had moved swiftly until this point. Now the film took on a more leisurely pace, showing the detailed, intimate love-play between the performers. They kissed and caressed and gradually the woman became the aggressor. She ripped off the man's shirt and flung it down, baring his heavy chest and torso. She ran her hands sensuously over his well-muscled body, her face registering pure lust. She was either doing a superb job of acting or true sexual passion consumed her. Suddenly, and with frantic haste, she bared her lover's body further and lavished caresses and long, lingering kisses upon it. After this amorous display continued for some minutes, she stood up and began to undress herself. Hastily she tore off the ridiculous apron, the absurd housedress, and kicked off her shoes.

And Jim Matthews burst out, "Man, get a load of those knockers!"

The young woman had a magnificent body. Her breasts were large, bell-shaped, her waist small, her hips more than adequate, her legs long and perfectly formed. She posed wantonly for her lover, fondled her own body; then he, by now stark naked, seized her roughly. Their bodies joined, the two fell together into the soft bed of hay. They writhed against each other for a time, then at last entered the ultimate embrace.

There was a fadeout at this point and the next scene showed the two, looking sexually sated, dressing and descending from the loft. Outside the barn, they parted. The man mounted a tractor to which a cultivator was attached and drove out into the fields. The woman returned to the house.

The final scene showed the husband returning in his empty truck. As he stopped and descended from the truck, his wife came from the house and ran to him. She kissed him hungrily, took his arm, tried to lead him to the house. He shook his head, gesturing to show that he had chores to do. She persisted, thrusting herself against him and squirming suggestively. Her face again registered lust. The farmer finally, reluctantly, gave in and they went to the house. The film ended with the closing of the door and the audience was left to imagine what took place inside.

The screen went blank, and Herb Sundersen shut off his projector.

"Is that all?" Julia Hoyt asked, sounding disappointed. "Haven't you more, Herb?"

"Well, I've one more new film," Herb said. "It's called 'Loves of a Salesman.' But there'll be a brief intermission while I change reels."

Dave rose from the arm of Nora's chair, saying, "To take another like that, I'll need a refill. How about you, honey?"

Nora hadn't touched her drink, and said so.

Dave went upstairs to the kitchen, and Jim Matthews and Brandon Hoyt, with his wife's glass as well as his own, followed. Herb turned on a lamp so that he could see to thread the new film into the projector. With the room lighted, Nora avoided looking at those who remained in the rumpus room. She gave her entire attention to her drink, too self-conscious to meet the gaze of the others. She could not talk and laugh about the film as they were doing and she wondered if she were something of a prude. Yet, she had to admit, she had enjoyed the movie. The images of those two naked people, the man as handsome as the woman was beautiful, remained vividly imprinted on her mental vision. Sexually aroused, she wanted only to experience, this very moment, the same actions that she had watched on the screen. She wished she were home with Dave.

Penny Austin crossed the room to her and asked, "How'd you like it, Nora?"

Forcing herself to look up, Nora said, "It was different, at least."

"Shocked you, I'll bet."

"Well, a little. I wasn't prepared for that sort of home movies."

Penny laughed, moved away. To Herb Sundersen she said, "I'm going for another drinkie, darling. Don't you dare start the next show until I get back."

"Don't be too long," he said, grinning at her.

Herb did start the second film before Penny got back from upstairs and before Dave returned. This film, fully as erotic as the first, had run several minutes before Dave resumed his perch on the arm of Nora's chair. A moment later Penny returned to the rumpus room, asking if she had missed anything. Suspicion nagged at Nora. She could not help but wonder why Dave and Penny had remained upstairs after Jim Matthews and Brandon Hoyt had come down again. She had a bleak vision of their embracing, kissing. She knew that Dave had long been attracted to the redheaded girl and she knew also what Penny's morals were like. But then Dave slipped his arm about her shoulders and in the semidarkness cupped her left breast with his hand. That small gesture, along with the torrid sexual activity on the screen, made her forget her suspicion that Dave might have been engaged in a little sexual byplay with Penny while upstairs.

But when the film was over and the lamps lighted, she saw evidence that her suspicions hadn't been groundless.

Hurt and angry, she said, "You should at least have thought to wipe her lipstick off your face."

Looking startled, Dave took out his handkerchief and sheepishly wiped at his face. He was unable to get rid of all the lipstick smear.

Nora got to her feet. "I've had more than enough of this," she said, speaking in a whisper so that only Dave could hear. She was angry but still she didn't want to create a scene. "Take me home, please."

The other guests were also talking of leaving and everyone went upstairs. There was the usual lingering at the door while goodnights were said. Jim Matthews insisted upon talking about the films with Herb Sundersen. Penny Austin stood talking with Julia Hoyt and the redhead noticeably avoided the gaze of Nora who was staring daggers at her. She would be wary of Penny's friendship from now on, Nora promised herself. When Bert Austin cornered Dave, trying to talk him into playing golf tomorrow, Nora found herself alone. Then Brandon Hoyt joined her.

In a whisper intended only for her, Hoyt said, "Monday, twelve-thirty, at the Lakeview Inn?"

She stared at him coldly, angry with him because she was angry with Dave. Could he actually think those films had made her ripe for an extramarital adventure? "I should think not," she said, and turned her back on him.

"I'll expect you," he said and turned away to join his wife.

Finally Dave and she got their goodnights said, told Herb and Carole that they'd had a marvelous time, and went out to their car. Dave had had too much to drink and he ran onto the lawn when pulling out from behind Jim Matthews' Thunderbird.

"Be careful, for heaven's sake," Nora said sharply. "Or maybe, seeing the condition you're in, I'd better drive."

"Are you saying I'm drunk?" he retorted, bristling.

"You're certainly not sober," she said, "which has been proved by the way you're acting. And have been acting."

He did not pretend ignorance of what she meant. "Listen: about Penny—"

"Yes, about Penny," she cut in, well aware that she was being pettish and unfair. After all, she had engaged in the same sort of thing at the Hoyts' party with Brandon Hoyt. But she couldn't help herself. "What about you and Penny?" she went on. "How far did you two go, anyway?"

"How far do you think we went?" Dave said disgustedly. "Do you think I laid her, right there in the lighted kitchen with other people walking in and out?"

"Those other people came downstairs before Herb started his second film."

"All right. So we were alone for a couple of minutes."

"So what happened?"

"Nothing that matters, damn it."

"It matters to me," Nora retorted. "And I want to know."

He swore under his breath and the car gave a sudden lurch as he swung back from too far to the left side of the road. He should not be driving, Nora thought—but she was afraid to suggest again that she should take the wheel. That, she knew, would really make him lose his temper. Luckily they had only a few blocks to go.

After a moment of sulky silence Dave said, "If you've got to know, she made a play for me. She gave me a buss on the cheek. You know what Penny's like; hell, everybody knows her."

"She gave you a buss on the cheek, did she? And what, may I ask, did you give her in return?"

"I kissed her back but I didn't mean a thing. I'd had a couple of drinks too many. And that damn film of Herb's didn't do me any good."

He ran through a stop sign, realized it afterward, and swore again.

After that, Nora decided to hold her tongue before they did have an accident. She managed to keep quiet until they reached home and Dave had run the Buick into the garage.

Entering the house, she asked, "Did you arrange an assignation with her?"

He stared at her. "I did not."

"Maybe you'd better."

He looked at her, scowling. "Now what do you mean by that?"

"I mean that you might get her out of your system if you once had her."

"Damn it; I don't want Penny Austin—and you know it," he said, striding into the kitchen. "I've got troubles enough without getting involved with any hot-pants dame like her." He opened the refrigerator, took out a tray of ice cubes. "For that matter, I've got enough on my mind without having you climbing all over me about something as meaningless as a kiss sneaked at a party. I'm losing out on the chance of a lifetime. I can see us having to give up this house and all that goes with it and that's plenty to worry about. So lay off me." He got a bottle of scotch from the cupboard. "Do you want a drink, too?"

"No, I don't want a drink, too," Nora said flatly. "And I don't think you need one, either. You can't drown your failure, remember."

"So now I'm a failure."

"That isn't what I said."

"It's what you mean, though," he said, going on with fixing his drink. "I'm not getting that vice-presidency because I'm not pushy enough. If I were more aggressive, I'd be getting it instead of that fly-boy friend of Brandon Hoyt's."

"If you think that, maybe it's true."

"All right, so it's true," he said and took a long pull at his drink. "Then I suppose I'm just not man enough to land a vice-presidency."

"To hold it, you mean," Nora said and wondered why she couldn't stop harassing him. "You already have it. You just aren't able to hold onto it."

"Thanks for pointing out my lack of ability."

"Nobody has said that you lack ability," Nora replied. "But what's the use of arguing about it—about anything? I'm going to bed."

"Go ahead," Dave told her. "Goodnight."

As she undressed, Nora realized that what had happened between Dave and Penny was not the only reason for her bitchy mood. She was upset by everything. The worry of Dave's not getting the vice-presidency. The fear of their having to give up this lovely house and a gracious way of life. And the secret shame she felt for having watched—yes, and for having enjoyed—Herb Sundersen's movies.

Abed in the darkened room, she was too keyed up to sleep. She felt torn apart, shattered, by this sudden contention between Dave and her. For one thing, she was haunted by the frightening prospect of losing their hard- won status of living in Wilshire Heights, of slipping from their place among the upper echelon of Worden-Forbes personnel, which only now was beginning to accept them. But on the other hand, she did not like the sort of people she and Dave were becoming. They had raised their standard of living, which was fine. Yet at the same time they had lowered their moral standards, which was not fine. These people, she thought. These people with their ultra-virtuous façade, but with no sense of decency or morality. Apartment keys and hundred-dollar bills up for grabs ... Erotic movies ... Sneaked kisses and cheap thrills ... Men winning promotion through their wives sleeping around ... Assignations arranged. And Brandon Hoyt, trying to arrange one with her. "Monday, twelve- thirty, the Lakeview Inn. I'll expect you," he had whispered. Okay, then. Let him be there and expect her. He was due for a big disappointment.

A sleeping pill, she thought. Or a tranquilizer.

She certainly needed something to put her to sleep.

But Dave came upstairs before she could get from bed and go to the bathroom for a pill. She lay still, hoping he would think she was asleep. He undressed in the dark, then came to her bed without having put on pajamas. Anger returned, stronger than before.

"I don't want you in here," she said flatly. "I won't have you in here tonight."

"Listen, honey." His voice was thick from the whiskey he had drunk and perhaps with soaring passion, too. "Damn it, I told you that stuff with Penny meant nothing. Forget it, can't you?"

"I just wish I could forget it."

"You're being utterly childish," he said, sitting on the edge of her bed and pulling the sheet down from her. "And you're no child, believe me."

"Sure, I know," she retorted. "I'm a woman. And after those filthy movies and that alley-cat of a Penny Austin you need a woman. Any woman. Well, just get over your itch some other way—damn it!"

She tried to pull the sheet back over her but he would not let her.

"I'm having you," he said angrily. "You're letting me have you. After all, you're my wife and—"

"Dave, I'm warning you!"

He ignored that, as she somehow knew he would. For the first time in their marriage, he was refusing to respect her wishes when she did not feel receptive toward his sexual demands. Also, for the first time in their marriage, he was making no effort to change her mood through the gentleness, the breathlessly intimate kisses, and the increasingly sensuous caresses that always before had brought them together to the ecstatic peak of passionate love.

Now his hands closed on her nightgown and ripped it off her, then reached hungrily for her breasts. She cried out and struck at him with her fists. She hit him several times with all her might but he seemed not to notice. She put her hands against his chest and tried to keep him from coming down upon her. This savage was not the gentle Dave she knew. This was a brutal stranger intent upon raping her. Her anger became wild fury and she fought him fiercely. But she couldn't stop him. He was too strong, far too strong. He spreadeagled her, dropped his weight upon her, invaded her so roughly that she cried out with pain. She lay helpless beneath him, telling herself over and over that she hated him.

Finally she sobbed, "All right. Use me. Use me—and pretend I'm Penny Austin!"

And to herself she said, I'll never forgive him … Never!

CHAPTER SIX

S UNDAY, THEIR day to visit Louise at Camp Wee-ni- toka, was
gray and wet. Waking to the rainy morning, Nora's spirits
remained at low ebb. She got reluctantly from bed and went to
shower her abused body. She dressed in a skirt, blouse and low
heels, suitable clothes for the trip and was ready nearly two hours
before Dave awoke. She knew that he wanted to get an early start
but, filled with disgust for what had happened last night, she did
not awaken him. She was still determined never to forgive him
for his mistreatment of her.

She ate a little breakfast, then got the Sunday newspaper in
from the doorstep and went through it with nothing she read
really registering. She wandered about the house and at last
heard Dave stirring upstairs. He was a long time in coming
down, lingering in his shower, over shaving and dressing. Hating
to face her, she knew. When he finally came to the kitchen where
she was fixing breakfast for him, he looked badly hungover and
extremely sheepish.

"Nothing to eat for me," he said. "My stomach's heaving. Just
give me coffee."

In silence she poured a cup of coffee for him and then began
putting away the breakfast things she didn't need.

Dave sat at the table and sipped the hot black coffee. He kept
glancing at her, trying to measure the extent of her displeasure.
She felt that he was pretending to feel worse than he actually did
feel, to play upon her sympathy in the hope that in pitying him

she would get over her anger. She simply hardened her heart, reminding herself of the brutal way in which he had forced her to submit to him last night. Raped by my own husband, she reflected bitterly—the kind of people we've become. She turned her back to hide threatened tears.

"Nora, listen," Dave began hesitantly. 'I—I'm sorry about last night. You've got to overlook it. I'd had too many drinks and—"

"I don't want to talk about it," she cut in. 'I don't want to talk with you about anything. I don't even want to be with you today, and I wouldn't go except that I want to see Louise. You can make it less unpleasant by keeping your excuses to yourself."

"All right," he said sulkily. "Whatever you say. Are you ready to leave?"

But the angry tattoo of her spiked heels was his only answer as she hurried to get purse, raincoat, and the things she was taking to her daughter.

The camp was only a seventy-mile drive from their house but because of the rain the trip took them nearly two hours, two endless hours of bitter silence. Dave attempted two or three times to break through her chill remoteness and, failing to get a response, he built up a wall of his own. His was a sulky silence and when sulking he always reminded Nora of a small boy denied some hoped-for treat. Today, however, he did not seem an engaging child, as he had sometimes when he was peeved, but rather a horrid monster of a small boy. Anyhow, she decided, he was in too foul a humor for her to try to salve his hurt. Let him sulk, she thought; the hell with him.

The visit with their daughter turned out to be far from rewarding. Seven-year-old Louise, too, was in a mood and Nora tried to blame Louise's dourness on the bleak day. Actually, as lovely as Camp Wee-ni-toka was with the fine grounds and attractive buildings and cabins, the place appeared gloomy in such weather. But Nora had to face the fact that the other girls, most of whom were gathered in the crafts building, seemed happy enough. Only Louise seemed depressed.

They found her sitting alone at a table with a book open before her, staring vacantly into space. So deep was she in her gloomy reverie that she did not notice her parents until they reached the corner where she sat in her loneliness.

"Hello, darling," Nora said, trying desperately to sound cheerful. "How's mother's girl?"

"I'm all right, I guess," Louise said, her wide gray eyes focusing on them. "You're late. I thought you weren't coming."

She spoke in a heavy, dispirited way, while all around them the other girls chattered and laughed gaily. They sat at the table with her, and Dave, discarding his sulkiness, tried to cheer her by talking in a forcedly amusing fashion. He was usually good with the child, able to make her happy when with her, but today she did not react. She remained grave, merely smiling politely. Nora thought: Something's bothering her; she's no happier than we are.

Nora could see little of herself in her daughter who had Dave's gray eyes and light brown hair. She was tall for her age and very thin. That, too, was inherited from Dave. Her temperament was also like that of her father, Nora suddenly realized—divining the reason for Louise's unhappiness. She knew that the child was slow to make friends, holding herself aloof. Like Dave, she was unable to mix with and impress herself upon others.

Unable to draw Louise out of her moodiness, Nora tried to get her to tell what caused her discontent with this charming camp. Nora was positive that she knew but she wanted Louise to admit it, to talk about it.

"I just don't like it here," the child said. "I don't like the other kids. I want to go home."

"But, darling, this is such a pleasant place. There's so much fun and things for you to do up here, and there's so little for you to do at home." She looked about the huge room, at the forty or more other girls. Not another child was alone. They were all in pairs or small groups. "The girls seem friendly, honey. Are you sure you've tried to be friendly with them?"

"Well. . . Louise stared at her shoes, her lips pouting.

"You see? It's you who isn't friendly."

"That's not so. They just won't bother with me."

"They would, if you bothered with them. You've got to mingle with them, join them in their games and in what they do. You've got to be—well, more pushy."

"Yeah, pushy," Dave muttered glowering. "You've got to be—pushy." He sounded bitter. "You must be aggressive."

Louise gazed up at him uncertainly. 'What's aggressive?"

"Ask your mother," Dave said. "She can tell you better than I can."

So it went, and the entire day was a horrible bust. Like all their days of late, Nora thought bleakly. She tried to make Louise understand that only by offering friendship could a person receive friendship. She talked for a long time and at last assured herself that she was getting her message across. At any rate, Louise promised to try to be friendly and she did not say again that she wanted to go home. After spending the afternoon with her, Dave and Nora talked to her counselor, Miss Le- land, who seemed understanding and sympathetic. Miss Leland said that she was aware Louise did not easily make friends, so she was making a special effort to get the child to associate more with the other girls of her age group. She promised to single out one or two girls to make friendly overtures to Louise and perhaps that would help her get over her shyness. They were not to worry about their daughter, Miss Leland told them.

But as they drove home through the rain, Nora did worry. And Dave burst out, "We should have brought her along. Damn it, the kid isn't happy there."

Nora broke her wall of silence long enough to take a stand against that. "We certainly should not have done any such thing," she said firmly. "Even if she is a little unhappy at the moment, the camp's good for her. She'll learn, somehow, that she must make an effort to win the attention of others."

"Sure," Dave said, turning sulky again. "She's got to learn to be pushy—aggressive. We can't have her growing up to be a Mr. Milquetoast, like her old man."

Nora chose not to reply.

They stopped for dinner at a roadside restaurant and arrived home shortly after eight o'clock. Though it was still early, neither one suggested going out or having someone in for the evening. Dave fixed a drink and sat down to watch television. Nora settled down with a best seller she had read halfway through, but as her thoughts wandered, the printed words became meaningless. Louises's discontent was one thing more for her to worry about. Maybe Dave was right; maybe they should have brought her home. It seemed that she didn't know what was the right thing to do any more. She was all fouled up. And so was everything else.

At nine o'clock she went upstairs and prepared for bed. While in the bathroom, she swallowed a sleeping pill. She debated a moment, took a second pill and went into the guest room where she opened the bed, then locked the door. There, she told herself, that will show him. She was not going to be raped tonight.

For a while, she thought the pills were not going to work. Her mind was racing, worrying about so many things, that she doubted if anything could slow it down. And abruptly she felt herself relax and grow drowsy.

She slept soundly, and overslept. It was nearly nine o'clock when she groggily unlocked the door and trudged into the bedroom—the bedroom that she and Dave had shared—to look at the clock on the night table between the twin beds. The master's bedroom for now, she thought bitterly. Well, the lord and master could have it all to himself for quite a while.

Dave was gone, of course. His empty bed was so badly rumpled that she knew he had had a bad night. She washed and dressed and the morning was as bright and cheerful as yesterday had been dark and dreary. Not that the state of the weather could change her feelings.

The phone rang. Mrs. Jensen was calling to explain why she had not come to work today.

"My daughter is sick," she said, "and I've got to take care of her and her three little ones. I'm sorry to let you down like this, Mrs. Osborne, but this is an emergency."

Nora told her that was all right, and not to worry. Putting down the phone, she thought that Mrs. Jensen's absence today was just as well. Nora would have a chance to get used to doing her own cooking and cleaning again, as she would have to do when she moved away from Wilshire Heights. She would not be able to afford help after Dave no longer had the vice-president's duties and salary.

She went downstairs to the kitchen where she sipped a glass of orange juice while the coffee perked. Even after two cups of coffee, she felt fuzzy-headed from the sleeping pills and decided that a walk about the garden might be good. Wandering about, she noticed that something had been nibbling at the rose bushes and she made a mental note to spray them later. She could do some weeding, too. Weeds were coming up through the cocoa bean hulls that their one-day-a-week gardener used for mulch. She spent an hour in the sun, hoping its warmth would lift her spirits. But it did not help and she felt like crying when she returned to the house. She did not want to move from here. She could not—just could not—give up the place.

The phone rang again, and this time Brandon Hoyt's now familiar voice said, "Good morning, Nora. How are you? Have you recovered from the effects of the Sundersens' party?"

"Yes, I have," she said, her voice sounding stiff and unnatural. "I'm fine."

"Good. And you can make it for twelve-thirty?"

She tensed. Her hand ached from gripping the telephone so tightly. "No, I can't make it. I'm sorry, but I just can't."

"Try," he said, his voice soft as a caress and somehow hypnotic. "Try, Nora."

"Well, all right," she said, her voice still sounding strange to her own ears. "But I'm afraid I'll end up disappointing you."

"I hope you won't," he told her. "Goodbye for now, Nora."

He broke the connection, and Nora quickly put down the phone as though it were an extension of his person and could do her harm. She stood in a trance, gripped by the unsettling thought that no real harm could come of her meeting him for lunch. Some good might come of it. She might be able to convince him that Dave should have that vice-presidency.

She glanced at the wall clock. Eleven-ten. She hadn't much time to dress and drive up to the Lakeview Inn at Crystal Lake. Still in a trancelike state but hurrying, she went upstairs. She entered the bathroom and started the water running into the tub. She would have to look her very best. She would have to make a good impression upon him.

Then, removing her clothes, she thought with something akin to despair: Heaven help me, I'm going to meet a man. And Penny Austin's phrase came to her: man who—who wants me for a playmate.

CHAPTER SEVEN

CRYSTAL LAKE was in the mountains, a thirty-five mile drive, and Lakeview Inn, a resort hotel, stood on a bluff at the lake's eastern end. Nora arrived late. The time by the clock on the station wagon's instrument board was twelve forty-five when she pulled into the Inn's parking area. She had driven slowly, even though she realized that she would be late. And now she sat for a moment in the car, not sure that she wanted to keep her date with Brandon Hoyt.

She knew what he wanted of her and he might have already made arrangements. A room for the afternoon here at the Inn. Cocktails and lunch, and then the room … No, she wouldn't do it. She simply couldn't go that far, even if he promised to back Dave for the vice-presidency.

So convinced, she got from the station wagon and climbed the three flights of stone steps leading to the hotel atop the bluff. She had been here a number of times for Sunday dinners with Dave. The place was pleasant with a magnificent view of the lake, the cottages dotting the shores and the forested slopes. But today, lost in troubled thought, Nora had no eye for the view.

She entered the lobby and thought that the desk clerk, who smiled and nodded, must sense that she was there for an assignation. That was foolish, of course. How could he imagine that? He did not know her.

She crossed the lobby and entered the dining room where most of the tables were occupied and told the hostess that she was joining a friend. A quick glance about the room showed her that Brandon was not there.

"I'll try the cocktail lounge, thank you," she told the hostess.

Brandon Hoyt was one of a half-dozen people sitting at the bar. He got from his stool at sight of her, smiling with pleasure.

"I'd about given you up," he said. "But the waiting has turned out to be worthwhile. You look wonderful, Nora."

She murmured, a little self-consciously, "Thank you, Brandon," and managed to smile for him. She knew that she looked less than wonderful. She was not beautiful and hardly glamorous but at least she did look her best. She was wearing for the first time her new gold cotton dress with a flared skirt, and it became her. Dave had not even seen it yet. "I'm sorry I'm late," she went on. "I had a bit of trouble making up my mind to come."

"Why, for pete's sake?"

"Well, this is all so new to me."

"I see," he said. "Well, maybe I can make it easy for you. A drink will help. Would you like to have it at the bar or in the dining room? I'm already one up on you, by the way."

She said she would prefer her drink in the dining room and then, when they were seated and the waitress came, she asked for a frozen daiquiri. Brandon had started with a martini at the bar and now ordered another.

Once she began sipping the daiquiri she felt relaxed and even managed to tell herself that it was going to be all right, that she could handle him. She would merely say no about the room upstairs.

"Feeling better now?" he asked, smiling directly at her.

For an older man, she thought that he was strikingly handsome. When he smiled, he had all the charm in the world. And certainly he was no ogre.

"Much better," she told him. "Of course, I'm scared to death that someone we know will see us."

"The chances of that are small," he said. "None of our crowd comes here. That's why I chose it. But look around if you want to, and reassure yourself."

"There's only one person here who knows me," Hoyt said, after Nora could see no one even remotely familiar. "That's Jim Matthews' ex-wife and she won't mention seeing me. She and I are old friends, so we're safe. By the way, I've arranged to be away from the office all afternoon."

Nora felt a quick thrust of alarm, but again she told herself that she could say no when the moment of decision arrived.

After they had finished their drinks, Hoyt summoned their waitress. "We'll have refills, please," he told her. "But we'll order lunch first."

She brought their drinks a moment later and shortly arrived with their food, a chef's salad for Nora and Hoyt's cold-cut platter. By then Nora was wondering how she could bring up the subject of the vice-presidency. She wished Hoyt would give her an opening.

He said, "How about you? Must you hurry back to town?"

"Well ... Not too soon."

"Good. I'd hoped you'd have time to go out on the lake. I've a friend who has a small boat I can use."

That seemed harmless enough, Nora decided. Apparently he had no intention of suggesting that they go to a room here at the Inn. He would not move that fast, she thought, reassured. He will wait until the second time to make a pass, but—surprise—there would be no second time.

As they had their coffee, Nora still sought a way to mention the vice-presidency, convinced now that Hoyt would not bring it up. At last, she decided to plunge in.

She said, "Brandon, there's something I want to discuss—seriously."

"Oh?"

"You'll probably think me out of order."

He shook his head. "Never you, Nora."

That gave her courage and she continued. She told him how much the vice-presidency meant to both Dave and her. She tried to make him see that Dave's experience made him the man best qualified for the office. He listened, an expression of sympathetic concern on his face.

"I agree that Dave can handle the job fairly well," he said. "But he doesn't impress me as having the all- around ability to be an executive officer of a firm as big as Worden-Forbes."

"He lacks only aggressiveness, Brandon."

"An absolutely essential quality in a key executive."

"He'd have more self-confidence—and therefore be more aggressive—if he got the job."

"You may be right, but I still have my doubts."

"Your friend, General Wyman, hasn't had Dave's experience."

"His contacts would more than offset that."

"Then your mind is made up?"

He did not reply at once but studied her in a speculative fashion. Finally he said, "Not so completely that it couldn't be changed. The general is a good friend, but I'm not exactly in love with him. We'll talk about it some more when we're out on the lake." He gave her one of his most charming smiles. "I'll give you the chance to change my mind. Fair enough?"

"Fair enough," Nora said, smiling back at him.

He stopped in the cocktail lounge, leaving her in the lobby and soon he reappeared with a Thermos bottle of martinis he had asked the barman to mix for him.

"We'll need refreshments out on the water," he said.

They descended the steps to the parking area and there he explained that the boat was at a cottage on the other side of the lake. He suggested that they go in their separate cars, he leading the way. His car was a blue Cadillac and she followed it in her station wagon, across the high bridge spanning the end of the lake. They drove along the north shore road, passing attractive cottages, and at last they turned in the driveway of an elaborate summer home built of stone, redwood and glass, and parked their cars alongside it. There was no other car about and no one seemed to be at home. The boat was tied up at a small pier.

"Well change into swim suits and really get some sun," Hoyt said. "Maybe swim a little."

"But I haven't a suit along."

"I'll get you one inside. Come along."

She held back, gripped by uneasiness. "Brandon, is this your cottage?"

He shook his head. "It belongs to a lawyer named Bob Newman. He's a bachelor who usually has a bevy of girls up here for weekends. So he keeps extra swim suits on hand for emergencies. We'll change and leave on the boat right away." He sensed her indecision and added pointedly, "You want the chance to convince me that I should back Dave for that job, don't you?"

Now she knew. He made it clear that his plans for her were made and that he would see them through unless she was willing to spoil everything for Dave and for herself, as well. She had played into his hands by mentioning the vice-presidency. She could still back out, of course, but—

He said, "Coming, Nora?"

"Yes. Yes, I'm coming."

With that she admitted to herself that she would go as far as he wanted her to go—even the whole way. She could not do otherwise with so much at stake. With Dave's whole future, her own future, in the balance.

"Yes," she said again in a choked-up voice. "I'm coming.

CHAPTER EIGHT

THE SWIM suit was two skimpy pieces of green material, a bikini.

In the bedroom where she had come to change, Nora felt rebellious for a moment. She would not go through with it. It was all so—so sordid. And shoddy. His wanting her to wear such a thing, his thinking he could have her. During that moment, she thought seriously of walking out on him. But it passed, for she remembered what he could do for her—for Dave. Slowly, feeling foolish and ashamed, she undressed and put on the two tiny pieces of cloth that were supposed to be a swim suit.

He called to her, asking if she were about ready.

She went out to the living room, feeling more naked than she ever had felt in all her life. He was in brief swim trunks, his exposed body deeply tanned and hard-muscled. He handed her a plastic swim cap, saying that she would need it if they decided to go into the water. He also held his thermos of martinis, a pack of cigarettes, a lighter, and a rolled beach towel.

"Nora, you're as lovely as I knew you would be," he said, his gaze moving slowly and intimately over her body.

"And I'm also as embarrassed as anyone could possibly be," she said. "I've never worn one of these things before."

"It becomes you."

"In an overexposed sort of way, perhaps."

"You've no reason to be self-conscious, believe me," he said. "Shall we be on our way?"

They went outside and down to the twenty-foot boat with its green canvas canopy amidships and twin outboard motors at the stern. He cast off the lines fore and aft, then started the motors. She seated herself beneath the canopy as he took the wheel and eased the boat out into the lake.

Other boats were out on the water, most of them sailing about the lake's east end. They headed west and soon passed through a narrow channel between the shore and an island. In the distance only two other boats were in sight on this part of the lake. Few cottages stood along the shore here and soon Nora saw none at all. After perhaps another mile they went through another narrow channel also formed by an island close to the shore. Beyond this second channel, the lake narrowed from about a mile across to about a hundred yards and this water they had all to themselves. The wooded slopes were steep here, rising directly from the water. There was no space for cottages in this wild and primitive spot.

Hoyt put in at a small island, dense with trees and brush. He cut the outboards, jumped ashore with a line, pulled the boat in, then tied the line to a tree trunk. The journey had taken only a few minutes but to Nora this quiet spot seemed as remote as another world.

Coming back aboard, Hoyt asked, "Like it?"

"It's lovely—but so lonely."

"The loneliness is what I like about it," he said, unscrewing the top of the thermos bottle. "Once in a while I like to go off alone."

"Alone?" Nora said.

He grinned. "Alone—with someone like you."

"And you often come here with someone like me?"

He shook his head. "Not often." He took two of the cups from the nest in the bottle's cap, poured martinis into them. Handing her one drink, he said, "Not often, and not for a long time."

She did not believe that. He was too much at home at the Inn, at the cottage, in this boat. His manner with her was too easy, too casual. He did this often and no doubt had done it recently. With whom, she wondered.

"To us," he said, raising his drink to her. "To us in our island paradise."

She drank with him, wondering what the martini on top of the two daiquiris would do to her. She took another sip, looking at him over the rim of the cup. He was an extremely handsome male, she had to admit. But could she give herself to him? She had always firmly believed that it would be impossible for her to give herself to any man but Dave. Now she did not know. She might panic at the last moment. Certainly she would not enjoy it. The martini along with the daiquiris was doing things to her. She felt lightheaded; her vision was a bit fuzzy.

"How about a swim?" Hoyt asked.

'Why not?" she said, glad of the opportunity to put off the moment of decision a while longer.

She donned the plastic cap, went aft with him, then lowered herself over the side. The water here was only up to her hips but a little distance off shore it was quite deep. They swam side by side for perhaps fifty yards, then Nora knowing her limitations as a swimmer, turned back. He came after her, taking her in his arms when they were midway to the boat. They went under together, then broke surface and treaded water. His arms remained about her, holding her body to his. He kissed her lightly and she laughed and slipped her arms about his neck. She returned the kiss. They went under again and their mouths were still locked together when they surfaced. They parted, gasping and laughing.

After they had gotten their breath back, Hoyt reached for her again. This time he ran his hands exploringly over her body and strangely she did not mind. It was almost as though he were fondling someone else, while Nora stood off to one side as an interested spectator.

Suddenly he said, his voice taut, "Let's go ashore."

They swam to shallow water and waded to the small beach. She removed the plastic cap and ran her fingers through her hair. He went aboard the boat for the martinis, cigarettes and beach towel, then led her through the brush and trees to a tiny clearing. He spread the beach towel and they seated themselves upon it. Filling the two plastic cups again, he handed her one.

"I really shouldn't," she protested. "I have a low tolerance for liquor."

"Just this one," he insisted.

She sipped just that one; then, with an almost total sense of unreality about herself and what was happening to her, she stretched out on the towel. He lay beside her, smiling faintly, his hand on her bare midriff. She felt herself shudder at the contact, but she told herself that the touch of his fingers was not so bad. Not wanting to look at him, she closed her eyes.

His hand caressed her for a time, then his fingers began working at the knot holding the strip of green cloth about her bosom. Soon the knot came untied, and he brushed aside the cloth, baring her breasts. He fondled them, caressing and kissing them repeatedly, while she kept her eyes closed, silently telling herself that this was happening to someone else. Aided by the drinks, she was almost able to convince herself of that.

After a time, he removed the lower part of the foolish bikini and bared all of her to his eyes, hands and lips. He began to stroke her thighs, and she, feeling suddenly tormented, began to squirm uncontrollably. She knew now. She was discovering that it was possible to enjoy the caresses of a man for whom she felt no real affection at all. This was pure lust, sex without any relationship to love, but it was no less enjoyable. She was fully aroused now.

"Brandon," she gasped, parting her thighs. "Please!"

He laughed softly, took his hands off her. She cried out with a shock, the pleasant shock, of his penetration. She wrapped her arms tightly about him and as of its own volition her body shared the rhythmic motion of his. He did not hurry. Indeed, it was a prolonged union. But it seemed all too short for her. She reached ecstatic fulfillment much too soon, and then, a moment later, he was experiencing the same tremendous explosive sensation. She held him even more tightly, wanting to enjoy with him every convulsive spasm.

Afterward, when his body was gone from hers, Nora lay there limply in an emotional calm, feeling physically spent and mentally inert. When she began to think, she marveled at herself. She had actually enjoyed it, which proved that she had not really known herself until this moment.

For a brief interval she was nagged by guilt. Then that, too, passed when she told herself that she had given her body to this man beside her for the best purpose in the world for any woman—to help her husband, to keep their home intact, and to assure their own and their daughter's future.

She recalled having read somewhere that after infidelity women were less bothered by their conscience than men. She now believed that to be true and was grateful for her own sake as well as that of all other women. She could return home to Dave and put this out of her mind. What had happened that afternoon was done and could not be undone, and she was sure that some good was bound to come of it.

If any part of the affair would continue to bother her, that would be the fact that she had enjoyed it so much. That troubled her even now. Uneasily, she wondered if she was by nature a— well, another Penny Austin.

The man who had been her lover, her extremely accomplished lover, raised himself on an elbow so that he could look down into her face.

"Another drink?" he asked. "A cigarette?"

"No, thanks. Nothing."

"Are you all right?"

"Very much all right."

"No regrets?"

"Not a one."

"Did I please you?"

"Yes. Oh, yes!"

He laughed softly, said, "We'll get along, you and I."

She looked up into his eyes. "Does that mean what I hope it does? That you'll back Dave for the vice-presidency?"

"As I told you," he replied, "I'm not exactly in love with General Lyle Wyman. Want to go back to the cottage?"

She said she did, because that seemed to be what he wanted. She rose to her knees and put on the no-longer ridiculous bikini. He gathered the things they had brought with them, and they returned to the boat. On the way across the lake she was both glad and sorry it was over. Glad because it should not have happened. And sorry because, like all stolen fruit, it had been so enjoyable.

When they tied up at the pier before the cottage, Nora noticed a small boat motionless in the middle of the lake. As she gazed toward it, there was a dazzling reflection of sunlight from some bright object held by one of the people in the craft. She wondered if someone were spying upon Brandon and her through binoculars and the lenses had caused the reflection. But that could hardly be, she assured herself, since no one had known she was coming here, and certainly Brandon would not have told anyone. Anyway, the boat now got underway and headed for the opposite shore. She promptly forgot it as Brandon patted her on the backside and told her to come along to the cottage.

Once inside, she went directly to the bedroom and removed the bikini. She had left the door open—privacy between them seemed unwarranted now—and Hoyt came in as she was hooking her bra after donning her panties.

"You're dressing?" he asked, sounding surprised.

She looked at him uncertainly. "Aren't you?"

"Well, I'd thought we could have each other again here," he said. "After all, it's still early—only three-thirty." He grinned at her. "Don't you want to do it again?"

She hadn't thought of it, but she said, "I want whatever you want. I want to please you, Brandon."

"Then come to bed with me."

Excitement instantly took hold of her. She slipped off the bra and removed her panties. They lay in each other's arms, facing each other, in no hurry this time. They kissed lingeringly.

After a time, Nora asked, "Tell me, why did you want me when you're married to such a beautiful woman?"

"Why, indeed?" he mused. "Well, I'm like a lot of men when they grow older. I have a yen for younger women. Even though Julia is a good wife, has given me a son and made my home life comfortable, it's not quite enough. You see, when I was a young man all my sexual experiences were with older—middle-aged—women. I was almost thirty before I bedded a woman my own age. I missed out on youth, so I crave it now."

"Why was that?" Nora asked, genuinely interested.

"I'd have to tell you the story of my life," he said, laughing. "And that would bore you."

"No, not at all. Tell me."

He moved away, sat up, reached for cigarettes. He lit two and handed one to her.

Then: "I was young during the depression. That doesn't mean much to you. Only people my age or older remember the really hard times. There could be no college for me and there was no decent job either. My father was an unemployed machinist. We were on relief. Rudy Vallee was singing about prosperity being just around the corner, but he didn't say which corner.

"I did any kind of work I could find. Odd jobs mostly and for what wouldn't even be tip money these days. I spent most of my time at the Y.M.C.A., at poolhalls, at the library. In winter, I was always glad when it snowed. The deeper, the better, because I'd take a shovel and go out looking for sidewalks to clean off—for a few cents. One night—a Saturday night, I remember—there was a heavy snowfall, but I didn't get many shoveling jobs. Too many men and kids were out for the work. I'd earned only thirty-five cents when I happened by the house of a teacher I'd had in high school.

"This Miss Anders was about forty-five, a stout and rather homely woman. She was shoveling her own walk, as most people did. I stopped, asked if she remembered me. She said she did. Flattered me to hell by saying she remembered me as the best-looking boy she'd ever had in any of her classes. For that, I helped her clean her walk. When we were finished, she asked if I'd like a cup of coffee and some cookies.

"I took her up on that—I was always a little hungry. She lived alone in a big old house that she'd inherited from her parents. Her home was pleasant, nicely furnished. The picture I got was that here was a well-off old maid. She had the house free and clear, I was sure. I knew her salary was about two thousand a year, which was big money in those days. While I sat in her warm kitchen, I began to get an idea—especially when she kept questioning me if I had a regular girl or went out at all with girls. I remembered reading at the library a biography of Benjamin Franklin. In it was some advice the old boy had given young men, advice about women. His idea was that older women could be very romantic—and very appreciative. From her interest in my nonexistent love-life, I thought that Miss Anders had an itch—possibly one she hadn't even admitted to herself. I decided to find out if she had. I thought—hoped—I might satisfy the itch if there was one and she might, in return, be appreciative to the tone of a few bucks."

As Hoyt paused to take a puff on his cigarette, Nora said, "And she turned out to have an itch?"

He nodded. "It was ten o'clock, which must have seemed late to her. But she invited me into the living room to listen to the radio. When the program was over she asked if I had to go home or if I could stay longer. I decided to force matters, so I looked her straight in the eye and told her there was nothing to keep me from staying all night if I wanted.

"She got the message—complete. And we didn't listen to any more radio. We were both virgins, but … Well, we made out fine. The next morning the temperature was down to zero outside and we stayed in bed. We got up only to eat and to throw coal into the furnace. By evening I was worn to a frazzle but she begged me to stay. She'd give me ten dollars, she said. I stayed and in the morning when she got up to go to church I kept on sleeping. When she got home we spent the rest of the day as we'd spent Saturday.

"It ended up a regular thing, with my coming around three or four nights a week. And once a week she'd give me ten dollars. I really had it made. I gave some of the money at home, used the rest for clothes I badly needed. Then I heard about a job open at a third-rate movie house. I went around to see the man who owned the theater. He turned out to be a lush and the job turned out to be that of combination janitor and ticket taker. It paid seventeen a week. I took the job, even though I would have to work nights and give up my soft snap with Miss Anders."

"How did she take your quitting her?" Nora asked.

"Oh, I sold her to a pal of mine."

"Sold her?" Nora was aghast.

Hoyt chuckled. "For seven bucks. He was as hard up as I was and so I thought of fixing it up for him with the schoolmarm—for a price. He said he could dig up seven dollars, so I bought a bottle of cheap wine and took him around to see her. She was all broken up, didn't like the idea at all. But I opened the wine and in a little while she was happy again. It was a going-away party for me, a welcome party for him, and a change-of-pace party for her."

Nora thought about it for a little while, smiling amusedly. "Tell me," she said finally, "did you and your pal both have her that night?"

"Uh-huh."

"What a Casanova you were."

"Were?"

"Are," she corrected herself. Then: "Was there another older woman after your schoolmarm?"

"Another—and more," he said. "The movie house where I worked was really run by the owner's wife, since he was a drunk. She was a good-looking woman of about forty. And a smart one. She booked the films, checked out the cash every night, kept the books, made out the payroll, kept me and the other employees on our toes. Her husband spent most of his time in a nearby bar, but he always showed up—dead drunk more often than not—just before closing time. Sometimes he was so stoned that I would have to help her get him to their apartment. Even help her undress him.

"I got the same idea about her that I'd had about the school-teacher, figuring that a lush wasn't much good in the sex department. One night I made my pitch, knowing I would lose my job if I was wrong about her. We'd dumped him on the bed and she was pulling off his clothes, bending over him. I laid my hand on her derrière. She jumped about a foot, then swung around and stared at me. I just looked at her. Like Miss Anders, she got the message. After getting her husband settled for the night, she turned out the fight and we went into the hall. I started toward the living room, but she told me—sounding angry—to come with her.

"She led me into the other bedroom, took off her clothes, lay on the bed. 'All right, Hoyt,' she said. 'You asked for it. Now see if you know what to do with it.'

"After that I got twenty-five dollars instead of seventeen in my pay envelope each week. But that didn't last. After a couple of months the husband suddenly went on the wagon and I got fired."

"How sad," Nora said, laughing. "Did you find another middle-aged woman to pay your way after that?"

"That was when I wised up," Hoyt said. "By now I knew that old Ben Franklin's advice was sound and I figured that if older women were such soft touches, I might as well make working them my profession. Stud service, I guess you could call it. The idea I got then was to go where there were such women with real money. The answer was Florida—Palm Beach. So I hitch-hiked south. It paid off, even though my first job was that of bus boy in a restaurant. In time I became friendly with three well-to-do women, one a divorcee and the other two widows. One really set me up, gave me a start in fife. Every couple of months she would give me a certificate for a hundred shares of stock in a manufacturing firm in Pittsburgh. The stock was worth only a little more than a dollar a share at the time, but ten years later, I sold it at thirty-two. And I had seventeen hundred shares."

Hoyt smiled wryly. "Older women were my meat, back then, but now I need young stuff."

He took Nora's cigarette, dropped it and his own in an ashtray on the bedside table, then reached for her.

"We're wasting time, talking," he said, rolling her onto her back and forcing her thighs apart.

CHAPTER NINE

THIS TIME, after they had finished, Hoyt immediately left her and went to the room where he had left his clothes. He returned fully dressed while she had only gotten into her slip. He lit a cigarette and gazed at her dispassionately and she sensed that he was impatient to get away from her. For her part, Nora felt drained and dispirited. Their love-making had been one time too many, she thought. They should have parted after returning from the island. Then the memory would have remained warm and pleasant.

Quickly she finished dressing, touched up her lips, ran her comb through her hair, then said, "All right, I'm ready to go."

They left the cottage, Hoyt making sure the door was locked behind him. Walking to their cars, they seemed as remote from each other as mere acquaintances, with nothing ever having been shared between them. To Nora came the unhappy feeling that she was but one of a long parade of women in his extramarital life. The thought depressed her.

Reaching his car and opening the door, he said, "Well, it was fun. I'll call you again soon."

She could not tell from his tone whether or not he meant that. At the moment she hoped he did not. How she would feel about it later, she could not guess.

"You'll keep your promise?" she asked. "You'll back Dave for the vice-presidency?"

"Of course," he said and got in behind the wheel "Don't worry about that."

He started the Cadillac's motor, put the car into motion. She went to her station wagon as he turned about in the driveway. He waved as he drove past, then he was gone.

She sat for a moment, unsure of him. Still, he had said he would keep his promise. He had told her not to worry. His abrupt departure meant nothing except that he had had enough of her—as she had of him—for the time being. Manlike, he would want her again and in wanting her again he would keep his promise. She would see to that. The next time he wanted to arrange an assignation, she would simply insist upon some assurance that he was dropping General Wyman and backing Dave. She would not give in to him again until she had that assurance.

She started the motor, turned the station wagon and drove away from the cottage. She saw nothing of the blue Cadillac when she reached the road. He was in a hurry to get back to town. She, too, should be hurrying for it was four-fifteen by the clock on the dash. She must get home and start making dinner before Dave got there; otherwise, he would question her about where she'd been.

But she did not hurry. Her mind was too filled with uneasy thoughts for her to drive at a high speed. She found that her conscience was going to bother her, after all, and she felt ashamed, guilty. And, too, she worried: What if I've played the role of whore for nothing? She had played it so well that certainly she should not be cheated out of her payment. The things she had done. She had wallowed in sex with Brandon that second time. She still had the feel of him in her nervous system. She had his male odor in her nostrils, his male taste in her mouth. She did not like herself very much at that moment.

By the time she was midway to town her spirits lifted some-what because of the remembrance that Penny Austin had won Bert his promotion by having an affair with Mark Hammond. Since Mark Hammond had kept his word to Penny, was there not a good chance that Brandon Hoyt would keep his word to her?

He's got to, she thought. He must!

At ten minutes past five she ran the station wagon into the garage. Dave would be home in another twenty minutes and she would have to make herself busy in the kitchen since Mrs. Jensen was not there to prepare dinner. Nora would have to appear busy— and innocent—so that Dave would not ask how her day had been and what she had been doing. Entering the house, she wished there were time for a bath. She had the foolish notion that Dave would be able to see that she was ... well, soiled. A leisurely bath would be the most wonderful thing in the world right now. She could wash away the taint of her infidelity, symbolically at least.

The phone began to ring as she entered the kitchen. She hur-ried to answer: "Hello?"

"Nora," came her husband's voice, "I won't be home until late. Same men from the Richmond plant are here and Bart Austin and I are elected to take them to dinner. It'll probably be pretty late."

She remembered last night and her sleeping in the guest room but knew that she could no longer punish him. After what she had done today, she could never again be peeved at any annoying thing Dave might do.

"It's all right," she said, no trace of a chill in her voice. "Mrs. Jensen isn't here, and I've not even begun to make dinner."

"You're not still sore?" he asked, sounding surprised.

"Of course not."

"No guest room tonight?"

"No, darling."

"Good," he said. "Well. I hope I won't be too late. I'll try to ditch these Richmond characters early. 'Bye now."

She put down the phone with a vast sense of relief. She had dreaded to face him so soon and now she had a reprieve; time enough, at least, to get herself in hand before he got home.

Upstairs she ran water into the tub, adding soap for a bubble bath and she remained soaking for a long half-hour, literally scrubbing herself pink. After toweling herself briskly, she put on lounging pajamas, combed her hair and carefully made up her face so that she would look attractive to Dave. She would love him tonight. Her mind was made up to that, tired though she was. Tired? She was half-dead. She could not understand why Brandon had exhausted her so much more than Dave usually did. Had she given more of herself?

She went downstairs and made coffee and a cheese- and-ham-on-rye sandwich. After that skimpy dinner she went to the living room and sat down with the novel she had been reading for the past week, but read only a few pages when her eyes grew heavy. To keep awake, she put the book aside and turned on the television. She watched two programs, then lay on the sofa.

She would not sleep she told herself; she would just rest for a while. But she did sleep, and did not wake up until Dave got home and shook her by the shoulder.

"What time is it?" she asked drowsily.

"Nearly one, honey."

"One!"

"Things ended up with a lousy poker game," Dave said. "I lost thirty-two dollars, besides wasting the whole evening. Better come to bed, Nora."

She got up from the sofa, trying to stifle a yawn that would not be stifled. "Oh, dam; I did so want to be wide awake for you, Dave," she said.

She went upstairs, changed into a nightgown, opened her bed and got into it. Dave came up a moment later, after turning out the lights and locking up.

She said, "I was going to do it tonight, but now I don't think I can."

"Tomorrow night, honey."

"Yes. Kiss me now, before I doze off."

He bent over her, kissed her.

She was happy then, happy in spite of what had happened. Or maybe because of it. For now, she told herself, Dave was going to be named to that vice-presidency and everything would be all right.

They overslept in the morning and there was a frantic rush when they woke up and discovered how late it was. He had a nine o'clock appointment. He gulped the orange juice she had fixed for him but skipped the rest of the breakfast. He kissed her and left.

Despite not having him at all last evening and only briefly this morning, Nora felt surprisingly happy. She fixed breakfast for herself and ate more than she should have for her figure's sake. After eating, she put a stack of show-tune records on the hi-fi and then, with music to brighten her mood even more, she went upstairs to dress, make the beds, tidy up the bedroom and bathroom.

She spent a pleasant day, one uninterrupted either by the telephone or callers. She dusted and mopped the whole house, worked in the garden; then drove to the shopping center to buy steaks for dinner. She wrote a little letter to Louise, reminding the child to be a friendly person. She drove back to the shopping center to mail the letter, so that it would still go out today. Returning home, she bathed and dressed for Dave's arrival, still two hours off, wearing an outfit she herself did not care for but one she knew that Dave especially liked—a low- necked green blouse and a straight beige skirt.

She had made a mistake in buying the outfit really, for the blouse was too snug for her ample breasts and the skirt too tight for her very well rounded hips. Surveying herself in the full-length mirror on the bathroom door, she saw that the outfit revealed as much as it covered. Her breasts were separately outlined in two sizable mounds, while the shape of her buttocks was brazenly molded. She decided that she looked like a movie actress playing the part of a cheap floozie. But that was what Dave liked about this combination and she wanted to please him. Moreover, she wanted to feel that she was seducing him.

All day, even while busying herself, she had had sex on her mind. Though she had never been one to dwell unduly upon sexual thoughts when not engaged in the act itself, today she had had fantasies running through her thoughts in a constant procession. She had tried not to think of yesterday at the lake, but her imagination simply refused to co-operate. Because of yesterday, she was ... well, in heat. She wanted desperately to make love, and she wondered, wryly amused, how she could possibly wait for bedtime, which seemed so far off.

The steaks were sizzling in the broiler and Nora was making a tossed salad when Dave arrived. His face brightened at the sight of her in the too-tight outfit.

"Well, well," he said, grinning. "Aren't you the sexy one?"

He came and kissed her, kissed her soundly.

"I've plans for tonight," she told him. "Martinis before dinner, whiskey sours afterward. No television. We sit in the garden until dark, getting slightly—just slightly looped. And then we go to bed."

"I'm afraid your plans are like those of the proverbial mice and men," Dave said. "John Fletcher is coming over this evening."

"Oh, no!"

"Oh, yes," Dave said glumly. "He said if we had no commitments for the evening he would stop by. I could not say no. After all, he's the one friend I've got among the top brass. I'm sorry, honey."

"It's all right," she said. "John never stays longer than eleven—and tonight I'll refuse to get sleepy."

She was a little disappointed, though. It would be a dull evening as was always the case when John Fletcher stopped by.

He would arrive promptly at eight, accept his first and only drink of the evening, discuss business from the comptroller's view point and then hint that he would enjoy a game of chess with Dave. They would go to Dave's study, and that would be it, for her, until John took his leave promptly at eleven. But he was a lonely man, a widower, and she could not really be annoyed with him for coming tonight.

The evening turned out as she had expected. Shortly before nine o'clock, Dave and their guest went to the study to start their chess game. She had been restless all evening and was more so now. She could not sit still to read or watch television. She could, she told herself, keep still for only one thing right now. And that would not happen until after eleven o'clock.

She got the idea of driving to the shopping center, both to be on the move and to pass some time. The stores closed at nine, except for the drugstore and she could certainly find an excuse to go there.

She looked in on the men at their chess game. "I've got to run over to the shopping center for some hair spray," she said. "I'll be back in half an hour or so."

Dave looked up, nodded and smiled as though he understood why she wanted to go.

The drugstore at the shopping center was next to the Pastime Bowling Lanes. As she got from her station wagon near it, a group of teen-aged youths standing in front of the bowling alley fell silent and turned their attention to her. One let go with a wolf whistle and another called, "Hello, Mrs. Osborne."

She glanced at them, wondering which one knew her and had called out but she could recognize none of them. However, she felt obligated to reply with a friendly hello. Walking toward the drugstore, she knew they still watched her. Kids, she thought—kids with grown-up ideas. She felt a little devilish and for their benefit she walked with an exaggerated movement of her hips. Again came the appreciative wolf whistle and she wore an amused smile when she entered the drugstore.

She drank a Coke at the fountain, then bought a can of hair spray that she didn't really need. She paused at the magazine rack, smiled at the pictures of bosomy females on the covers of the girlie publications. When she left the store, only one of the teen-agers remained in front of the bowling alley. She did not bother to undulate her hips for him.

Seated behind the wheel, she inserted the ignition key, turned it and stepped on the gas pedal. Nothing happened. After repeated attempts the car showed not a spark of life.

"Won't it start, Mrs. Osborne?"

She looked at the young man, a husky six-footer in a yellow knit T-shirt and dark slacks who was walking toward her station wagon. She found him vaguely familiar and frowned, puzzled, trying to identify him.

"The darned thing is completely dead," she said. Then, "I'm sorry, but I don't recall ever meeting you."

"We've never met, Mrs. Osborne," he said, his smile a flash of white teeth against deeply tanned skin. "But I've seen you around, often. Somebody told me who you are. I'm Phil Hoyt."

"Oh, yes."

She had seen him around and, of course, she had known that the Hoyts had a son. He seemed to resemble neither his father nor his mother so far as she could see. But he had a clean-cut, wholesome look. He was about seventeen, she guessed.

"Well, I'll have to call a garage," she said. "Do you know one that would make a service call at this time of night?"

"Why don't you let me drive you home in my car?" Phil Hoyt said, "and call a garage in the morning?"

"Well," she hesitated. "Maybe I should."

"Since the car won't start, you can leave your keys in it," he went on helpfully, "and the service man can fix it up, then deliver it to your home."

"A good idea, Phil, if you don't mind driving me home. I live over in Wilshire Heights."

"I don't mind," he smiled, opening the door for her. "Anyway, I'd like to show you my new car. It's a Corvette. Just got it last week."

She walked with him to his sports car, admired it enthusiastically, fitted herself into one of its bucket seats. He got behind the wheel, started the motor and switched on the headlights. They drove away from the brightly lighted shopping center but then turned off in the opposite direction from that which led to Wilshire Heights. She told him sharply that he was on the wrong road, but without answering her he pressed on the gas pedal. Puzzled and angered Nora watched the speed indicator climb from fifty to sixty, to seventy five.

"Listen, Phil, just what are you up to?" she demanded, frightened by him now.

"I want to talk to you, Mrs. Osborne."

"Talk to me? About what, for heaven's sake?"

"You should know, he said. "About your being up at Crystal Lake yesterday—with my old man."

CHAPTER TEN

STUNNED, NOHA could only stare at him. She would not have been more jolted if he had struck her suddenly and without cause. Long before she recovered from her shock, he swung the sports car off the highway onto a narrow side road running through a stretch of dense woods. After driving about a mile, he turned off onto a dirt road and the glare of the headlights showed orchards at one side and waist-high com on the other. Along the shoulders of this back road Phil Hoyt's headlights showed parked cars in which sat couples in prolonged embraces. Some of the cars were empty, their occupants gone into the deep shadows of the orchard or the corn field. A lover's lane, Nora thought dully.

She and Phil came to an old country schoolhouse, now long abandoned. Several cars were parked about the building, the radio of one tuned to soft music. Phil brought his Corvette to a stop at the deserted side of the schoolyard, as far as he could from the other cars. He switched off motor and lights and turned to Nora.

"Yesterday I was at Hutch's, a joint up the road from the Lakeview Inn," he said. "I saw my old man come down from the Inn with you, and watched you two drive to the other side of the lake." He grinned maliciously, white teeth gleaming. "My guess was that you were going to a cottage over there. So I hired an outboard at Hutch's also a pair of binoculars, then cruise out on the lake, looking for you love-birds. I saw you come back in a boat and go into a cottage."

Nora heard herself say, hoarsely, "I saw a boat, and a flash of reflected sunlight. I thought someone was watching … Did you do something to my car tonight?"

"Uh-huh," he said, grinning. "I took off the distributor cap."

"What do you want? My promise not to see your father again?"

"Not that, chick."

"What, then?"

"Don't be a square," he said, and cupped her right breast with his left hand. "I want some of what my old man had."

Nora felt suddenly sickened. "Phil, don't be ridiculous. I'm a married woman much older than you and—"

"So I've never had a married woman much older than myself. And that's what I want."

"You're only a boy."

"I'm as big as a man," he said, his hand squeezing her breast now. "Bigger than a lot of men."

She pushed his hand away. "I won't do it. It would be even worse than—than what happened between your father and me. Take me back and fix my car, please."

"You don't dig me, doll. The score is, you've got to put out for me. If you don't, I'll squeal. I'll tell my old lady about you and him, and she'll raise all kinds of hell."

"You wouldn't do such a thing," Nora said, uneasily and uncertainly. "Not to your father. Besides, you'd be hurting your mother as well as your father and me."

"So let everybody be hurt," he said. "I'll take you back, fix up your heap, then go home and tell tales."

She told herself he was bluffing. He had to be. It was not possible that even so precocious a boy would deliberately make trouble for his parents. "I won't do it," she said. "I just won't do such a thing. Now take me back to the shopping center."

He grinned nastily, seized her, pulled her against him. He pressed his mouth to hers, forced his tongue between her teeth. He slipped his hand under her skirt, grasped the soft flesh inside her thigh. She got her hands against his chest and shoved with all her might, thrusting him backward, away from her. The instant she was free, Nora opened the door and got quickly from the car. She thought frantically of flight but knew that was futile. Where could she run?

"Phil, please," she begged. "Please take me back!"

Still grinning, he got from the car. "Sure, chick," he said, reaching for her. "Just as soon as we've had our party."

She tried to elude him but he was quicker than she. He seized her by the left wrist, forced her arm up behind her. Then came a sudden, tearing pain in her shoulder and she had to clench her teeth to keep from screaming. Fearing that she would cry out, he clamped his right hand over her mouth. She was utterly helpless now. The slightest move on either her or his part caused her knife-sharp pain.

"Just do as I want, doll," he said, "and you won't get hurt." He applied pressure on her arm and the pain was so intense she feared she would faint. "Walk with me," he ordered. "Come on—move!"

She had no choice but to obey. He walked her toward a dark clump of trees, through it to a small clearing. He stopped there, his one hand still with its viselike grip on her left wrist and the other clamped over her mouth.

"You yell just once and I'll slug you," he said with low-voiced viciousness. "I'll slug you good. You catch?"

She jerked her head in a frightened, affirmative nod and he took his hand from her mouth.

"That's better," he said, when a moment passed without her attempting an outcry. "Why fight it, doll. Just relax and enjoy it."

He tried to force her to the ground but she said shakily, "Wait—Don't muss my clothes."

"You want to take them off?"

She nodded jerkily. She couldn't go home to Dave with any telltale signs of what had happened to her. He released her wrist at last but remained close, so as to grab her again if need be, while she removed her skirt and blouse. She laid them carefully on the ground, then he seized her and dragged her down. He tore off her panties, flung them aside, then roughly spreadeagled her. He came atop her, penetrated her with a hard thrust that caused her to gasp with pain.

She responded in no way at all, merely submitted to his frenzied use of her body. She was numbed physically, emotionally frozen. Her only reaction was shame and disgust. Fortunately it was quickly over. For all his size he was still a mere boy and did not know how to handle himself sexually. With no more than a dozen rapid thrusts, he came to completion. She waited, sick at heart, as he went through his series of climatic spasms and then, grown limp, removed himself from her. In a moment he got to his feet and zippered himself up.

Grinning, he said, "How was that, chick? The most, eh?"

"It was quick, at least," she said bitterly.

She picked herself up and hastily put on her clothes. She remained numb, frozen, from then on, only vaguely aware of their driving back to the shopping center, getting from his car into her station wagon. He raised the station wagon's hood, and after a minute or two told her to try the ignition. The motor started instantly. He slammed down the hood and she switched on the lights and drove away without another glance at him.

It was nearly eleven o'clock when she reached home. Dave and John Fletcher were at the front door, looking for her and worrying.

She stopped in the driveway, midway to the garage, and called to them in what she hoped was a natural-sounding voice. "I couldn't get the car started, dam it. I'd still be stuck at the shopping center if a kid hadn't come from the bowling alley and finally got it started for me."

"We were about to come looking for you," Dave said. "You'd better run out to the dealer's in the morning and have the car checked."

Later, after John Fletcher had gone and they were alone, she felt a little easier. Nothing about her showed, to Dave's eyes at least, what had happened. Dave and she had a drink and then went to bed. Locked in his arms, she tried to forget Phil Hoyt's fumbling use of her body. She tried, but did not quite succeed.

That morning, Thursday, Nora drifted into a low mood after Dave had left for the office. She had not been able to forget, even while making love with Dave, how Phil Hoyt had blackmailed her into submitting to him. And in remembering that, she was also reminded of her affair with Phil's father. She felt ashamed and guilty on both counts and she went about her household chores half-heartedly. Then increasingly upset, she called Worden-Forbes and asked for Mr. Hoyt. Hoyt's secretary asked who was calling.

"Mrs. David Osborne," Nora said reluctantly, yet knowing that any secretary of Brandon Hoyt's would be discreet.

Hoyt's voice, when he answered after a long moment, was brisk and noncommittal. "Hello, Mrs. Osborne. What can I do for you?"

"Have you a few minutes to talk, Mr. Hoyt?" she said, choosing her words carefully on the chance that the secretary was listening in. "I'm on the Hospital Fund drive and your name is on my list to contact. If you're busy at the moment, perhaps you would call back at your convenience."

"I'm afraid I'll have to call you back, Mrs. Osborne."

"Very well. You won't forget?"

"No, I won't forget," he said. "Goodbye."

He called back in twenty minutes, his tone now curt and unfriendly.

"You can talk now, Nora," he said "I'm at a phone booth. But, please never under any circumstances call me at the office. After all, I can't afford—"

Annoyed by his curtness, she cut in, "I didn't call because of a whim, believe me. Something very serious has happened. Your son saw us up at the lake."

Hoyt swore under his breath. "Has he been in touch with you?"

"He has, indeed," she said, and told him about last night.

She had expected him to be upset, and was shocked to hear him laugh.

"I'll be damned," he said. "Imagine the kid pulling such a stunt. I had him figured as too much of a mamma's boy for anything like that but I guess he's a chip off the old block after all."

"My God! You're not condoning what he did, for heaven's sake?"

"Well, there hasn't been any harm done, has there?"

"No harm done? How do you think I feel?"

"You didn't enjoy it?"

"Brandon, I don't understand you," Nora said, distraught. "A seventeen-year-old boy doing something like that. And there certainly was harm done, no matter what you think. Do you imagine I like being abused like that?"

"Abused?" He laughed. "That's a new word for it."

"I'm upset, whether you are or not. Why, he could try to make a steady thing of this—threatening to tell his mother if I don't give in. Can't you see that?"

"Oh, yes," Hoyt said casually. "He just might know a good thing when he has it. Well, if you really feel abused as you call it, and won't want it to happen again—"

"I don't, believe me!"

"All right. I'll have a talk with him. Don't worry—it'll be all right. Now I've got to get back to the office … By the way, Nora, I'll try to arrange to take an afternoon off next week. I don't know what day it will be. I'll have to call you."

"I don't think you should bother."

"I thought we made a bargain on Monday."

"The only bargain I remember is that you promised to back Dave for that vice-presidency."

"But I understood that my promise on that gave me certain privileges."

"Well, perhaps. But first I want to be sure you intend to keep your word. I don't feel quite able to trust you, Brandon."

He laughed. "You've got to trust me, baby. Anyway, we're so good together that I should think you'd want a rematch. We were good together, weren't we?"

"Well … yes."

"Anyway, I'll call you," he said. " 'Bye now."

He broke the connection and Nora stood holding the dead phone, her increasing uncertainty about him forming a cloud of worry in her mind. She could not trust him and she decided that her only hope lay in his wanting her again. Maybe if he wanted her badly enough, he would keep his word but that would mean a continued affair with him. And this morning, at any rate, she wanted anything in the world but that. She wanted to forget her one willing act of infidelity, and to become a faithful wife again. She wanted—

The door chimes sounded.

She put down the phone and, in her troubled frame of mind, started toward the front of the house. Penny Austin stood smiling in the open doorway—the last person she wanted to see this morning.

CHAPTER ELEVEN

Penny was wearing a sleeveless white blouse, brown shorts and green sandals, and she looked her usual delectable self. She smiled brightly. "Hi. Mind having a neighbor drop in this morning?" And she came in before Nora could answer.

Remembering the Sundersens' party and Dave with Penny's lipstick on his face, Nora felt a quick surge of anger. But then her reason took over and told her that she could no longer hold a few stolen kisses against Penny. Not after what she herself had done with Brandon Hoyt. The truth was, Nora told herself bleakly, that she and Penny were now sisters in infidelity. She was certainly in no position to cast stones at this lovely redhead.

"Coffee?" she asked.

"Uh-huh," Penny replied. "If you're not too busy. If you are, just kick me out."

"I'm not too busy, really," Nora said, pleasantly surprised to find that her rancor toward Penny had vanished.

But when they were seated at the kitchen table with coffee and cigarettes, Penny dealt her a low blow.

"What I really came for," the redhead said, grinning, "was to welcome you to the society of junior executives' wives who have given their all for dear old Worden- Forbes."

Nora stared at her, stricken. "What—what do you mean?"

"A little bird told me, darling. About your rendezvous with Brandon Hoyt at Crystal Lake."

Nora's heart sank; she was too jolted to speak.

Laughing, Penny went on, "Don't take it so hard, Nora. That sort of thing can't be kept a secret in a town the size of this. It's bound to be found out, sooner or later."

"Who told you, Penny?"

"Jim Matthews' ex, Karen Leighton."

Nora remembered Hoyt's saying that the woman was in the dining room of the Inn but she would not mention having seen them. He had been so very wrong. Or perhaps he had known and had not cared.

"But I don't know her," Nora said. "And she doesn't know me."

"She's seen you around and heard your name," Penny said. "But don't worry about it. Just because she told me doesn't mean she'll blab to anyone else. Karen knows the rules and plays the game. She told me because she knows I'm friendly with you. She thought I knew you were having an affair with Brandon. Dave won't hear of it. Husbands are never—but never—told." Penny took a swallow of coffee. Then: "By the way, how is he as a lover?"

"I—I don't want to talk about it."

"Oh, stop being such a prude, darling. It's too late for that. Besides, you haven't done what two out of three women we know don't do. So you went to bed with a man not your husband. So what?"

"I'm not exactly proud of it."

"Well, no. But you did it for a purpose and because of that you needn't feel guilty about it." Penny stared at her. "Are you such a prude that you didn't enjoy it?"

"I guess I did enjoy it, heaven help me."

"Sure you did—unless you're one of those unfortunate sexually frigid females. Did he promise to back Dave for that vice-presidency?"

"He promised but I don't quite trust him."

"I wouldn't trust him, either," Penny said. "I was luckier than you because Mark Hammond keeps his word. You'll have to keep working on Brandon, keep him panting for you."

"Even panting for me, he may not keep his promise."

"You should take out some insurance."

"Insurance?"

Penny nodded. "Get someone else to support Dave," she said. "Someone you can trust. Dave's got John Fletcher in his corner but John is a timid soul and won't be much help in a fight with Brandon Hoyt. Mark Hammond can be counted out. He's not here in town and I don't know if he'll arrive in time for you to work on him.

"At least three of the other board members can also be ruled out. Henry Forbes, our dear prexy, keeps a mistress in Baltimore and he doesn't cheat on her. Earl Holden is no chaser. Harlan Ames is an outsider, not connected with the company except as a board member and he does not live in Lanford. There's Vince Crane, though. He's an outsider but he does live here. He may be hard to meet socially, since he's not one of our crowd. Your best bet is Jim Matthews."

Nora stared at her incredulously. "You're not actually suggesting that I become involved with ¡him?"

"Why not?" Penny said. "You can't trust Brandon Hoyt but you could Jim—if he likes you. After all, darling, you're fighting for Dave's future. You've started to, anyway, and it would be foolish to stop at this stage of the game. Anyway, Jim Matthews isn't so bad. I admit he's a sort of roughneck but he's nice, in his heavy-handed way. And if he promises to back Dave, he'll do it. He'd give Brandon a fight, if Brandon continues to push his Air Force general. With John Fletcher, Jim Matthews and maybe Vince Crane on your side, Dave would be in—believe me."

Nora shook her head. "I couldn't do it. I can't see myself doing it again—and with another man. And I can't see how you can be like that, Penny."

"It's easy. I like that good stuff. The more, the better." Penny drank the last of her coffee. Then, eyeing Nora quizzically: "Honest, now wasn't it good? Didn't you have fun?"

"I don't like cheating on Dave, Penny."

"You were helping Dave."

"Well ... Yes."

"Keep that in mind. Quit worrying your pretty little head about being unfaithful. Anyway, you're still giving Dave his share, aren't you? You're not rationing him just because you gave in to Brandon, are you?"

"No, I'm not rationing Dave," Nora said. "But everything seems in such a mess." Suddenly she needed to confide everything in Penny who now seemed very much her friend. She told about her encounter with Phil Hoyt. "You see how fouled up everything is?"

"That kid," Penny said, laughing. "Imagine him pulling a stunt like that. How was it with him?"

"Not good."

"He needs more experience, a few years to season."

"Well, he can get his experience from someone else besides me. I've told Brandon about it, and he promised to talk to the boy."

"That was smart. Don't spread it around for free. If you must put out at this stage of the game, let it pay off. You give some thought to working on Jim Matthews and maybe Vince Crane too. That is, if you really don't trust Brandon."

Nora did not reply. But she couldn't see herself passing from man to man, from bed to bed, even to secure the vice-presidency for Dave. She was not like that. She was not entirely like Penny Austin.

❧   ❧   ❧

In his office at Worden-Forbes, Dave Osborne was giving some serious thought of his own as to ways and means of securing the vice-presidency for himself. He had an idea this morning, one that might give him a weapon to use against Brandon Hoyt. He considered it from various angles for a time, then had his secretary get Harvey Ward on the phone. Harvey Ward was in Purchasing, Brandon Hoyt's department. He and Dave were friends from high school days.

Into the phone Dave said, "Harv, it's been a long time since we've had a get-together. How about lunch today?"

"If you're buying, Dave-boy," Ward said. "The old budget is out of balance, and I'm not a credit-card man these days."

"I'm buying. Where do you want to eat?"

"You name it."

"Lorin's?"

"Fine, since it's on you. They make a swell deep-dish martini there and I haven't been in the place in months."

"Lorin's it is. What time do you go to lunch, Harv?"

"At twelve—always," Ward said. "Along with the rest of the working stiffs, since I'm one of them now. Or have you forgotten?" A trace of bitterness edged his voice.

"I haven't forgotten," Dave said. "See you at twelve, then." He hung up.

Dave lit a cigarette, sat lost in thought. What had happened to Harvey Ward was tough. He was now the lowliest of junior executives, hardly more than a clerk, actually. But until a year ago he'd been assistant to Brandon Hoyt and his future had looked bright. He had been given the job two years before when Hoyt's former assistant resigned to go with a trucking firm. Then, after the two years, Hoyt had brought in his nephew, a graduate of the

Harvard School of Business Administration, and had made him his assistant—putting Harvey back into his former job. Harvey had been given a raw deal but that, Dave told himself, was part of this game. A guy without pull had no security, and wasn't he the one to know that?

He had always hoped to find a way to help Harv and had planned, when and if the vice-presidency became his, to see that his friend was taken care of in some way. Now, because of the idea that he had latched onto, he was sure that Harv and he could help each other.

Ward came up to Dave's office a couple minutes after twelve o'clock. He was a thin, sandy-haired man whose heavy horn-rimmed glasses gave him an owlish look. Understandably, he was still bitter about losing out as Hoyt's assistant and habitually showed it.

Looking about Dave's imposing office, he said, "So this is how the upper one per cent have it. Think your title to that desk is clear, Dave?"

"Not too clear," Dave said, rising and coming forward. "You've heard the rumor about Brandon Hoyt wanting that Air Force general in this office, haven't you?"

"I've heard it. You letting him get away with it?"

"Not if I can help it. Let's go, eh?"

They drove to midtown in Dave's Buick. On the way, Dave inquired about Ward's wife, Lucy, and their two small sons. They were about as usual, Ward said glumly. Tim had a broken arm, and Dick an allergy. Lucy was unhappy because of his misfired career and the lack of money in the Ward household.

"Lucy still thinks I just failed to make good," he said. "And you know that wasn't the case, Dave."

"I know it," Dave said.

In the pleasant restaurant they were shown to a table immediately, had martinis and each ordered a medium- rare sirloin steak, baked potato, tossed salad, and coffee. When the waitress disappeared toward the kitchen, Ward picked up his drink.

"Here's to your tripping up Brandon Hoyt and that Air Force general, Dave."

After they had drunk to that, Dave said, "Harv, that's just what I want to talk to you about. I need help to trip up that pair."

Ward looked surprised. "Boy, if you think I can help you with that, you're just not well."

"I think you can help me—and help yourself at the same time. When and if I'm named to that vice-presidency, Harv, I'm going to take care of you."

"I've been hoping you would, Dave. It's about the only hope I've got left. But how can I help you, for Pete's sake?"

"Think back, Harv. Remember telling me, right after you got kicked out as Hoyt's assistant, that you had something on him and that you would use it except that you were scared it would backfire on you?"

"Oh, that?"

"What do you have on Hoyt, Harv?"

"He cut some corners while I was his assistant. Broke some company rules. One in particular."

"Which one? Give, man."

"Well, he was taking kickbacks from suppliers."

"I'll be damned. You're sure?"

"I'm sure. I was working with him, wasn't I? As head of Purchasing, he could work such a racket and get away with it. He had a thing going for him, believe me."

"And probably still does."

"He wouldn't give up a profitable sideline, that's for sure."

"Could you prove it on him, Harv?"

"I could. If I wanted to risk losing my job."

"How, Harv? What proof have you got?"

Ward looked uneasy. "Dave, I don't like this. I don't like it even a little bit. I can't gamble with my job, lousy as it is. I've my family to consider."

"You could be doing the right thing by your family. Just give me what proof you have and I'll have a talk with him. I'll cover for you and once I've got the vice-presidency, I'll bring you over into Public Relations. As soon as I can swing it, I'll make you my assistant. It could mean twice the salary you're now getting. Now give. What have you got?"

"A photostat," Ward said reluctantly. "A copy of a letter Hoyt wrote to the V. P. for sales of the Carmody Copper Corporation. In the letter, Hoyt said that he would procure a big Worden-Forbes order for Carmody, on condition that he received two hundred shares of Carmody common stock as a bonus for getting the order."

Excitement gripped Dave. "His signature was on the letter when you had the photostat made?"

"Sure."

"How'd you get hold of the letter?"

"I overheard him dictating it. After his secretary had typed it and he'd signed it, she placed it with the day's outgoing mail. This happened after I found out that I was to be washed up as his assistant. I thought I might use the letter as a club—but I lost my nerve. Anyway, I snitched it from the pile of outgoing letters on his secretary's desk. I took it home with me, the next day had the 'stat made, then put the original back in its envelope and mailed it. Nobody caught on."

"Harv, you've got to let me have the photostat."

"Dave, I'm scared to. Hoyt is nobody's fool. He'll know how you came by it. He could make the thing backfire on you—and on me. We could both end up out in the cold, cold world."

"We'll end up sitting pretty, believe me. We'll always be able to hold the photostat over him. He'll get down on his knees and beg me not to show it to anybody. Just the thought of H. M. Forbes seeing it would scare him witless."

Harvey Ward was a hard man to convince and Dave worked on him all the while they ate lunch. It was not until they were driving back to the plant that Ward gave in, and then he went along with the idea only conditionally.

"I'll have to talk it over with Lucy first," he said. "If she's willing for me to run the risk, I'll give you the damn thing. I won't take the chance on my own, then have her raising hell and tell me I'm a bigger chump than she thinks I am right now."

"You'll talk to her tonight?"

"Yes, tonight," Ward said.

Dave had to be satisfied with that. But he was tempted during the afternoon to call Lucy Ward and explain that his scheme would work. Before he had made up his mind to take that step, however he had a call from an acquaintance named Bill Marsten. The call made him forget Ward's photostat for the time being for Marsten, who had approached him before, had a job opening for him.

Marsten was head of Triton Electronics, a small but rapidly growing firm in a new and booming industry. He said, "Dave, I've been hoping since the last time I saw you that you'd get in touch with me."

"I've been pretty busy, Bill."

"Too busy to let me buy you a drink later today?"

"No, not that busy," Dave said, realizing that here was a chance to cushion his fall if he failed to win the vice-presidency. "Where shall I meet you, Bill?"

"How about the cocktail lounge at the St. Regis—about five-fifteen?"

"Right. See you then."

Dave put down the phone, asked Miss Marvin over the intercom to place a call to his home. He would have to tell Nora that he would be late again. He smiled fondly, remembering how she had told him he was not aggressive enough. She would have to change her tune, once she knew what he was up to with Harvey Ward.

When he talked to Nora, he said, "I'll be an hour late this evening, honey. I've an appointment to have a drink with Bill Marsten. You remember my talking about Bill some months ago?"

"The man who wants you to come work for him?" Nora didn't sound pleased. "Is he after you again?"

"Uh-huh."

"I'm not sure I like that, Dave."

"Well, the way things stand at the moment there's no harm in hearing what he has to offer."

"Don't commit yourself to anything, Dave—please."

"I won't. But it'll be reassuring to keep Bill's offer as a hole card—just in case."

"You're not going to need a hole card, darling. You're going to get that vice-presidency."

"Your woman's intuition tells you so, eh?"

"Well, yes."

"Do I detect a bit of uncertainty, though?"

"No, you don't. I refuse to believe anything but that you're going to get that job."

"All right, honey," he said, laughing, and put down the phone. Nora didn't want him to leave Worden- Forbes. She was counting on him to find a way to stay in this handsome office. Well, he was positive that he had found a way—if Harvey Ward would just play along with him.

He cleared his desk at a quarter to five and told Miss Marvin that he was leaving early. Walking along the corridor to the executive washroom, he noticed that someone was standing just inside the door, holding it slightly ajar, and talking loudly to someone farther back inside the room. He recognized Jim Matthews' booming voice and when he heard his name mentioned, Dave stopped several feet from the door, evesdropping on Matthews' end of the conversation.

Now he heard Matthews say, "Sure, it's true, Herb. I got it from my ex-wife. The cute little bitch keeps me posted—she should, the alimony she's getting. Anyhow, Karen says—"

Herb Sundersen, apparently, was the other man in the washroom.

"—that Dave has loaned that well-stacked wife of his to Brandon Hoyt. She saw them up at the Lakeview Inn together on Monday. You know what Dave's pitch is, don't you? He wants Hoyt to back him instead of General Wyman for that vice president's spot."

Dave felt as though he had been slugged. His brain reeling, he turned and walked back along the corridor, left the building and walked blindly to his car. For minutes, he sat slumped behind the wheel, telling himself that what he had heard was not true, could not be true. Matthews' ex-wife had simply been spreading lying gossip. But Dave could not convince himself.

Nora had openly told him that he was not man enough to win the vice-presidency on his own. She had heard about Penny Austin's winning Bart his promotion by having an affair with Mark Hammond. Nora had probably heard of other Worden-Forbes wives helping their husbands' careers by putting out. Hoyt must have made a play for her, either at the party he and his wife had given or at the Sundersens', and she had taken him up on it.

Nora—unfaithful!

My God, he thought—He wanted to bawl like a kid.

CHAPTER TWELVE

DAVE REMAINED in a state of shock and Bill Marsten, burdened though he was with the worries of a fast-growing company, asked immediately if Dave were not feeling well.

He could only reply that he was feeling a bit under the weather. "A lot of pressure on me these days, Bill."

"Better have a checkup. It could be more than pressure."

"You're right, of course."

They both sat in a booth in the St. Regis Hotel cocktail lounge and over scotches-and-soda, Marsten told Dave that he would still like to have him at Triton Electronics. The firm's present public relations head, an ex-newspaperman, lacked the proper touch for such work. He was talking of resigning.

"We're paying him seventy-five hundred a year, but we'd go nine thousand for you, Dave."

"I'm making more than that at Worden-Forbes, Bill."

"I know you are. But I also saw the item in the *Herald* about General Wyman angling for a vice-presidency. And I've had a tip that it's the same vice-presidency you're hoping to land. My informant tells me that the General has the inside track."

Dave could have said that he expected to take the inside track away from General Wyman but he was in no mood to do any bargaining. Hurt and despondent over this thing with Nora, he did not feel like talking at all. He simply wanted to be alone.

"How long do I have to give you an answer?"

"When will you know whether or not you'll get the vice-presidency?"

"After the director's meeting, a week from Monday."

"All right, Dave. I'll keep the offer open until then. You call me the following Tuesday. Okay?"

"Okay."

They finished their drinks and Marsten, sensing that Dave did not want to prolong the meeting, said that he had another engagement. They left the hotel together.

As they shook hands, Marsten said, "I don't like to see you miss out on that top spot, Dave. But I want you badly at Triton. Call me—and meanwhile take care of yourself. You really are looking down at the mouth." And Marsten went off.

Dave, having no desire to go home and face Nora, returned to the cocktail lounge and took a stool at the bar. He felt completely empty inside, as though the world had crashed about his shoulders. Nora, he thought bleakly, Nora how could you do this awful tiling? How could you smash everything we had together?

He downed his drink, ordered another. He had a third and then a fourth in quick succession and the barman began to eye him with misgivings. So he went to another bar and after that a third. He drank more in less time than he ever had done before but it did not keep him from thinking of Nora. Of Nora and of that son of a bitch, Brandon Hoyt. Dave left the bar, drove out to the country club and sat a a table, the drink before him forgotten, and tried to analyze the situation, and choose the proper course of action. He had reached the point, he concluded, where he should make a change. He should break away from Worden-Forbes and people like Brandon Hoyt. Never again would he place Nora in a position where she would feel compelled to give herself to a lecherous board member in order to help her husband in his career. With Triton Electronics there would be none of that sort of thing. All he need do, he told himself, was to go to the phone and call Bill Marsten and merely say that he would take the nine-thousand-a-year job. But it would be a big cut in income, which would hurt.

"Hello, darling," a woman said. "You all alone tonight?"

He looked up and saw Penny Austin. Two Penny Austins, actually, for he had drunk so much that he was afflicted with temporary double vision. He blinked several times and she became one—which, he decided, of Penny Austin, was quite enough.

"I'm alone," he said with alcoholic dignity, "by preference."

"But you're not including me out, too, are you, Dave?"

"You and the whole lousy world."

She was unfazed by that. Seating herself, she studied him for a moment. "So you know. And you don't like it."

He stared at her. "Does the whole town know, for chrisesake?"

"Not really. But who was the so-and-so that told you?"

"Nobody told me," he said bitterly. "Nobody tells the husband. I had to eavesdrop on a couple of jerks who were getting a big bang out of it. You alone again?"

"Uh-huh. My ever-lovin' is once more out of town. So if you want to cry on mama's shoulder, well, I've got all night."

"Tramp," he said thickly. "You're all tramps."

"You can't get under my skin, Dave. I've got a real thick hide." Again she studied him and abruptly seemed to make up her mind about something. "Let's go somewhere—and be alone."

Buzzed by his drinks though he was, Dave knew exactly what she meant. She was his for the taking. But right now he didn't want her or any women. Not even Nora. He was disgusted with women, sick of sex.

"I'll drive my car home," Penny said, rising. "You come by and pick me up. Have a cup of coffee instead of that drink. It'll be better for you. Okay?"

He thought of Nora and Brandon Hoyt and the pain was no less than before he'd started drinking. Liquor was no help. Maybe what Penny offered would be.

"I'll think about it while I'm drinking the coffee."

"You do that," she said and turned away.

He watched her leave the lounge, his eyes on her shapely rear. Most of the men in the room stared after her. But he was the one who could have her. He motioned to the waitress, told her to bring him coffee. His mind was not yet made up. But he would do as he had promised–think about it while drinking his coffee.

He was still undecided when he left the lounge and walked to his car. Even driving away from the clubhouse, he did not know if he would pick her up. He had never wanted to cheat on Nora. He had cheated on her only twice in all these years, once before their marriage, for therapy; and once afterward, but through no planning of his own.

The memory of those two sexual adventures came back vividly now as he drove slowly toward Wilshire Heights, toward either his own home or Penny's.

The first time he had cheated on Nora had been two days before their marriage. They had been engaged for two months and before their formal engagement they had had intercourse more or less regularly for nearly a year. Nora had given in to him from the time she admitted to herself that she was in love with him. She had been a virgin until then but no prude. They had understood that they were made for each other, that they would eventually marry. After announcing their engagement, Nora had decided they should wait for "the next time" until their wedding night. It had been as though, by denying themselves, she would now come to their marriage bed at least a halfway virgin. Whatever that was, he reflected sourly.

So he had gone along with her whim, of course. But he had become accustomed to having her and it was increasingly difficult for him to wait. He had begged her to give in—"Just this once," he had urged her on several occasions. He had tried sulking and even getting sore. But Nora had been firm in her resolution of no sex until they were man and wife. She had remained adamant and nothing had broken her down.

He had been aware that he could have borne the situation if he had not been seeing her every evening. But being with her had only increased his difficulty and he had actually suffered. He had been jumpy, on edge, irritable. The Wednesday evening before their wedding, which was set for Saturday, he had pleaded with her for hours to give in. However, she had refused, saying, "And mind you, none of that do-it-yourself stuff, either."

The next day had really been bad. He had been too nervous to sit at his desk, to get any work done. He had felt as though he would crack up if he did not find relief. Then he had remembered the name of a call girl, Helen Barsovitz, with whom a pal of his was friendly. During his lunch hour, he had decided to look her up in the phone book. And there she was listed.

He had said, "Helen you don't know me, but a mutual friend told me about you—Terry Andrews."

"Oh, Terry.—Well, any friend of Terry's is a friend of mine."

"Could I see you this afternoon, Helen?"

"I'm sorry, but I only make evening dates."

"Please, you've got to," he had said desperately. Knowing her rate was twenty dollars, he had plunged on. "I'll give you fifty dollars."

"My, my! You are in a dither, aren't you?"

"Fifty. Please?"

"Well, since you're so set on it. But you'll have to wait an hour before you come up." She laughed softly. "Can you wait that long?"

"Yes, I can wait that long."

He had called her from a phone booth and he was drenched with nervous sweat and shaking violently as he stepped out.

Helen lived in a small, modern apartment building, and when she let him in, Dave was doubly surprised. She was nothing like his idea of a call girl. She was "nice" instead of sexy, a small brunette in a plain green dress. And there were two small children in the tastefully furnished living room with her.

"Come in," she said, smiling. "I'm not alone, as you see. I had trouble getting in touch with my sitter but she's on her way now."

One child was a girl of five, the other a boy of three. They were quiet, well-mannered children sitting politely on the sofa, each with a toy. After asking his name, their mother introduced them. The door chimes sounded and the sitter entered, a stout, pleasant woman of about sixty with whom the children went eagerly. As the three went out, the sitter turned in the doorway, looked from Dave to Helen, and broadly winked.

Helen laughed as the door closed after them. "Kate knows, of course, But it's all right with her—she's an old pro. Would you like a drink?"

"Please," Dave said.

He needed a drink. He was inexperienced in dealing with call girls. He had had a couple of other girls before Nora, but they had been as young and no more expert at love making than himself. This woman seemed as knowledgeable as the most wayward of Eve's daughters and suddenly he felt embarrassed and callow with her. He was fearful that he would not be able to prove himself a man.

But she understood men and seemed to understand him especially. She had a drink with him and talked to get his mind off himself.

"You're probably wondering about me," she said. "This isn't a side of me many men get to see. I never have dates at home because my children come first, really."

She told him that she was married but that her marriage had been a mistake. Her husband, one of those unhappy men who never seem to grow up, had been a yeoman in the Navy. He kept re-enlisting, though she begged him to give it up and take a job and be with her and their children. He was now at sea in the Pacific.

"He comes home less and less often. And you can imagine what sort of life the children and myself would have if I tried to five on what money I get from him."

"They're nice children."

"And I'm determined to have them grow up to be nice adults, too," she said. "They will have at least some advantages." She paused, smiling, "Now I'm curious about you. Why should a young handsome joe like you have to buy it?"

"I'm getting married Saturday."

"Oh? And you want one last fling?"

"Not that. My girl—my fiancée—decided we should stop having each other until our wedding night. It's been two months now."

"Well, that is a new reason." She rose, took his empty glass. She slipped her arms about his neck when he got to his feet, pressed her body to his. "I've got all afternoon. The sitter and the kids won't be back until five. That should be long enough to get you over the jitters." She kissed him. "I'm going to make this afternoon one you'll remember, even when you're on your honeymoon, Dave. You can do anything to me you want, and I'll do anything you want me to do. Come along to bed."

He went with her to her bedroom, his taut nerves already beginning to ease.

And on his honeymoon with Nora, he had remembered—guiltily but with no regret at all—that wonderful, stolen, therapeutic afternoon.

The second time he had been unfaithful was during the third year of his and Nora's marriage. He had not sought a woman that time. She had come to him while he slept.

Worden-Forbes had been about to open its Richmond plant and he had been down there with a dozen of the firm's executives planning the ceremony for the dedication of the new factory. His job was to line up some local VIPs for the affair. He was sharing a hotel suite with Herb Sundersen—two bedrooms and a sitting room. The second night Herb suggested that they pick up a couple of women and take them up to the suite.

Dave wanted no part of it, but Herb, pretty well looped, did bring a woman up with him. Dave had a drink with them, then went to his bedroom. He closed but did not lock the connecting door, and was awakened an hour later by someone getting into bed with him. It was Herb's pickup, and she was nude.

Dave turned on the lamp on the bedside table, stared at her angrily. "Get the hell out of here. I don't want any part of you. Go on—scram!"

She was a big, voluptuous blonde. "Aw, honey, have a heart," she coaxed, rubbing her soft, naked body against him. "That jerk in the other room passed out on me after getting me all steamed up. I've got to have a man. Please—pretty please."

She took his hand, rubbed it over her rounded buttocks, then around to her mounded belly. Desire inflamed him. He could not help himself. He turned off the lamp, threw off his pajamas, seized her and lost himself in her warm, scented flesh. He performed well with her and he had her twice during the night and once in the morning. He felt guilty about it for a long time, even though he had been trapped into it and could not help himself.

So he had cheated on Nora only twice, and neither time because he had wanted to cheat on her.

Now, as he found himself pulling up before the Austin's house, there was Penny coming along the walk. He had come to her without really being aware of it, without actually desiring her. He knew why, of course. He needed to forget his wife's infidelity. Liquor had not brought him forgetfulness; perhaps Penny Austin could.

He reached across the seat and opened the door. "Get in, you redheaded tramp," he said, hating both her and himself.

CHAPTER THIRTEEN

THEY drove across town and entered the Expressway at the Northgate cloverleaf. Dave pushed the Buick up to sixty and for the next twenty-odd miles not a word passed between them. Near the Harrisburg-East Shore entrance to the Pennsylvania Turnpike, he swung off the Expressway to find a motel. They checked in at the first decent- appearing one they saw, a defiant mood causing him to sign the registration card as Mr. and Mrs. David Osborne instead of using a fictitious name.

Once they were in their room, he said, "We should have brought some liquor along."

Penny shook her head. "You've had enough and I don't need any."

He gazed at her without tenderness, with neither pleasure or desire. She was a damn attractive piece and he wondered on many occasions what it would be like to hold her in his arms. Now, hating her because she was a woman and all women were cheats, he felt more like roughing her up, hurting her, than making love to her.

She watched him with a half-amused, half-challenging expression. When he moved toward her, she quickly eluded his reaching hands.

"Let me get my dress off," she said. "I don't want to look as though I went through a war when we leave here."

He waited, watching as she removed her beige sheath, and put it carefully over the back of a chair. She turned toward him, smiling wantonly. She wore no slip, only panties and a bra which barely contained her abundant breasts.

"All right, you. You've wanted it for a long time, so now take it."

"Who said I ever wanted you, you redheaded bitch?"

"Nobody needed to say it. I've seen you looking at this chassis, big boy—plenty of times."

"And so you had to throw it at me, first chance you got."

"You've still got a choice—take it or leave it."

His fingers locked around her left wrist and his other hand clutched her hair in a twisting grip. She tried to get away but he pulled her against him and kissed her roughly. For a moment she submitted, then snapped her teeth hard on his lower lip. He swore with pain and released her.

She laughed at him. "So you're going to take it, are you?"

"Try and stop me."

"I just might. I don't like the mood you're in."

He caught her again, grabbing her about the waist. He felt her bare flesh beneath his hands and was instantly aware of surging passion. She put her hands against his chest, tried to keep him from pulling her to him. Failing in that, she struck him with her fist. He cursed her, slapped her in the face. She reeled backward, off balance and slumped against the foot of the bed. He got his fingers inside her bra and ripped it from her. She came at him fiercely, her fingers hooked, talon-like, her teeth bared, and tried to claw his face. He seized her right arm, spun her about and closed his arms tightly about her from behind. His hands cupping her breasts, he held her close while she strained frantically to break loose. Her breathing was labored and between gasps she spat obscenities at him.

Then she snarled bitterly, "You bastard, you're hurting me because you want to hurt your wife. You're taking it out on me for what she's done."

"What do you expect—tender caresses?"

"I can take anything you can dish out!"

She slammed her head back against his face. Again there was pain for him and he lost his hold on her. She twisted around, tried to knee him in the groin but he caught her upraised knee and toppled her backward onto the bed. He ripped off her panties, and now she wore only white plastic earrings, a matching bracelet, and white pumps. She lay still but her narrowed gray-green eyes watched him closely. The realization came to him that she was just waiting for a chance to kick him.

"Stay like that," he ordered her, "Move a muscle and I'll slug hell out of you."

"Bastard!" she said. "Oh, you filthy bastard, you!"

When he moved back to undress, she kicked off her shoes but made no attempt to get from the bed.

Then she taunted him as he stood naked before her: "What's so special about you that Nora shouldn't have another man if she wants one? Tell me. I certainly can't see for myself!"

He did not reply but moved warily toward her. She lay supine and motionless until he came down upon her, then fought him fiercely, raking his chest with her nails and closing her teeth on his left shoulder. He seized her wrists, forced her arms above her head, and pressed her face to one side with his own. She squirmed beneath him, trying to keep him from his goal. But in a moment he had her helpless and she gasped and went limp.

He took her with a passion fired by his anger and hatred and he brought her quickly to a shuddering peak. He continued his violent assault on her for his own pleasure now, even though she pleaded with him to let her go—crying that she had had enough. But after a few minutes she subsided again. Her body lost its limp submissiveness and once more began to respond. She moaned as with pleasurable agony and wrapped her now freed arms about him. He carried her along with him through soaring passion until, together, at last they reached the crest of sensation. Then came the aftermath of plunging downward into a passionless void. He rolled off her and lay spent beside her.

Minutes passed with neither of them moving or speaking. Then Penny turned toward him and tried to put her arms about him.

"Dave," she whispered. "Dave, it was wonderful!"

He pushed her seeking arms aside and got out of the bed. He dressed quickly and then, standing with his back turned, he lit a cigarette.

"Get up and get dressed," he said. "I want to get out of here."

"All right, darling."

For Penny, she sounded strangely subdued.

They drove the twenty miles back to town in as many minutes, neither one speaking the entire way. Another ten minutes brought them to Wilshire Heights. When they pulled up before her house, he immediately reached across her and opened the door. She turned to him pleadingly.

"Dave, please don't push me out as though I'm a cheap whore. I don't give myself to every man and I do have feelings—just as you do."

He stared at her coldly. 'What do you want now, for God's sake? A promise of undying love?"

"I could do with a promise—a promise that you won't be too rough on Nora. Just remember that she didn't go with Hoyt merely because she wanted another man. She went with him only because she thought she could help to get that vice-presidency for you. Promise me that, Dave. You must have worked off your anger on me. So promise—please!"

"Next you'll be saying you went with me just to get me to make such a promise."

"Maybe I did, in part, because I'm fond of Nora. And maybe I did partly for you, because you needed somebody tonight. You felt alone in the world and—"

"And your being a tramp had nothing to do with it, eh?"

"Maybe my being a tramp did have something to do with it, too. Oh, I'll be honest and admit that I wanted you. But do you promise?"

"Yes, damn it, I promise."

She leaned close, kissed him on the cheek, then got from the car. She closed the door, and looked in at him.

"If you love her, and I know you do, all this foolishness need not be the end of the world, Dave."

"All right, all right."

"Goodnight," she said, and started along the walk.

"Penny."

She faced about. "Yes, Dave?"

"I'm sorry about calling you that name."

"I know you are," she said, and stood watching as he drove away.

At one twenty-seven Dave arrived home. He entered the house reluctantly, knowing that he would quarrel with Nora—and knowing too that he would have to accept the status quo. What was done was done. There was no undoing her infidelity, which, after all, had been committed because she hoped to help him win the job he wanted. Or had she gone with Hoyt for only that reason? Possibly she had really wanted to stray—and had welcomed an excuse. Perhaps she had had a yen for Brandon Hoyt. Exasperated, he swore to himself. A man could not know what really motivated another person's actions—not even those of his own wife.

Dave found Nora in bed but awake and waiting for him. She was lying on her side, propped up on an elbow with a book open beside her. She closed the book, sat up, gazing at him accusingly. Her black hair was prettily tousled. She was wearing a pale yellow nightgown and she was so lovely. He looked away, for looking at her hurt too much. Another man had possessed her and Dave had the absurb feeling that she was now somehow different from the woman he loved.

"Well, you and Bill Marsten did make an evening of it," she said. "He really must have worked on you."

Removing his coat, he said tonelessly, "I spent about twenty minutes with Bill." He went to the closet, placed his coat on a hangar. "I spent the rest of the night going from bar to bar, trying to get stoned."

"Oh? And just why did you feel the need to get stoned?"

He looked directly at her. "I heard about you and Brandon Hoyt."

Nora remained very still, seeming not even to breathe. Her face drained of color, became chalky. After a long moment she lowered her gaze from his and stared at her hands that were clasped on her lap. Then she looked up again, her face stricken.

"You know why I did it, don't you?"

"I know why you think you did it. You convinced yourself you were doing it for me."

"You needed help."

"And you gave yourself to that bastard to get me that help. Do you actually think he'll keep his word—if he gave you his word on anything?"

"I'm hoping he'll keep it, Dave."

"You're hoping, for chrisesake." He removed his shirt, threw it and his tie onto the chaise lounge. "For your information, I have a way to handle Brandon Hoyt—and it'll be my way and no tyours that gets me that job."

"All right, Dave. If you can swing it on your own, I'll be glad. I want you to feel that you've done it on your own. But I was worried. I was scared to death that we would have to give up this house—the plans we've made for Louise and for the future. I didn't want Hoyt. God knows I didn't want to do such a thing. I hated doing it, believe me. I hated every minute of it and—"

"The hell you say," he cut in savagely. "Sex is sex, and you can't tell me you turned frigid just because you went to bed with another man beside me. Damn it, Nora, I never wanted us to be like this. It's a lousy situation for a man to be in."

He removed his T-shirt and Nora, gazing at him, said bitterly, "But your never wanting us to be like this didn't stop you, did it?"

"Just what do you mean by that?"

"Look at yourself. And don't tell me you got those marks pub-crawling. Only a woman leaves marks like those."

He looked down at himself and saw the four long red scratches on his chest from Penny's clawing fingernails. And on his left shoulder was a clearly defined set of teeth marks where Penny had bitten him.

"So I wanted to get even," he said, some part of him wanting to protect Penny. "And I picked up a twenty- dollar whore."

Tears welled in Nora's eyes. "All right. So you had to get even and you picked up a twenty-dollar whore. Just where does all this leave us? What has it to do with us?"

"All I know is that I'll get that damned vice-presidency for us. And I'll get it my way. I've got enough on Brandon Hoyt to make him drop his Air Force pal like a hot rock and back me instead. And that, my cheating little bitch, is more than all your fornication would do in a lifetime."

He turned and strode toward the door.

Frightened, Nora called, "Dave, where are you going?"

"Downstairs to get swacked," he said flatly. "To drink myself blotto and try to forget that you let that bastard lay you."

Nora began to sob painfully. To keep him from hearing, she buried her face in the pillow. She wept with the hurt of knowing that Dave had been with another woman and with fear of what was happening to their marriage.

Sobbing into her pillow until she was exhausted, at last she fell into a troubled, fitful sleep.

In the morning, during the brief interval between getting dressed and Dave's leaving for the plant, Nora saw the pattern of what their marriage was now to be. Dave was civil, even polite, but nothing more. He did not speak one unnecessary word. Their marriage was to be kept a going thing and for appearances' sake they would seem still a devoted couple. But actually they would continue to be as estranged and remote from each other as they were at this moment. Her affair with Brandon Hoyt would not be mentioned again—but it would not be forgotten.

Dave ate his breakfast, said goodbye, and was gone. He left her gripped by a chill feeling of impending disaster.

Clearing the table, Nora found his cigarette lighter beside his coffee cup—the little gold lighter engraved with his initials that she had given him when he had moved into the carpeted office where he now worked. She had wanted to give him something expensive to show how deserving she thought him. That he had forgotten the lighter this morning seemed somehow symbolic of all that was wrong between them. She gave way to the tears that had been so close to the surface since she awoke.

By mid-morning she could no longer bear being alone. She needed someone to talk to, a woman friend, and she had no confidante except Penny Austin, She picked up the phone.

"Penny, it's Nora. Are you busy?"

"I'm never busy, darling. But what's wrong? You sound so strange."

"It's Dave, Penny—he's found out."

"Oh, no."

'I need a shoulder to cry on. Do you mind if I come over?"

"Oh, I wish you would, Nora. I always seem to be running over to your place to see you."

"I'll be there in ten minutes," Nora told her.

Penny came from the house when Nora pulled into the Austin's driveway. She looked, as usual, fresh and happy, untouched by trouble. Envying her, Nora wondered why everything misfired for her while nothing ever seemed to go wrong with Penny's life.

They went around to the flagstone terrace where Penny had coffee ready.

"How bad was it?" the redheaded girl asked as she poured the coffee. "Did Dave give you a rough time?"

"Well, he didn't threaten me with a divorce," Nora said bleakly, "but he was rough when he came home late and half-stoned, slapped me in the face with his accusation. He was mad and said pretty rough things. But the worst part of it was that he'd been with a woman. And that just tore me all to hell."

Penny stared at her. "He told you he'd been with a woman?"

"No. She left marks on him."

"Marks?"

"Whoever she is, she's a scratcher and a biter."

Penny took a swallow of coffee, lit a cigarette, frowned in silence for a time. "You poor kid. What makes it so tough is that you're both such moral people—so puritanical. Both Dave and you magnify the importance of this playing around out of all proportion. But you've got to keep these relatively small missteps from smashing your marriage, Nora. You've just got to."

"We have a pretty badly smashed marriage now, Penny."

"I wish I knew what to tell you to do."

"To make matters worse, my affair with Brandon was probably pointless. Dave said he has his own way to force Brandon to drop General Wyman and back him instead."

"Oh, God—*men!*" Penny snorted. "They're all little-boy show-offs. Dave was just bragging to make himself feel better."

"You really think so, Penny?"

"Honey, I know men," Penny said. "To hear my Bart talk now, you'd think he climbed to his good job all by his own efforts but he's conveniently forgotten that little Penny was really responsible. I can't see Dave or anybody else forcing Brandon Hoyt into anything."

At ten-thirty that morning Dave had caught up with his most pressing work. He had Miss Marvin get Harvey Ward on the phone.

"Harv, did you talk it over with Lucy?"

"Yeah, I talked to her about it."

Dave waited, holding his breath. How weird, he thought, that my entire future depends upon a drab little housewife like Lucy Ward.

Harvey Ward went on, "She's all for the idea. I always thought that dame was more than a little wacky, and now I know it."

Dave began to breathe again. "Good for Lucy. I'll have to send her some flowers or something to show my appreciation of a very astute young woman."

"Just don't send candy," Ward said. "She's putting on enough weight. When do you want the—the thing, Dave?"

"Can I buy you lunch again today?"

"You can buy me lunch any day, pal."

"See you at twelve. You can give me die thing then."

"Right, Dave."

Dave put down the phone, leaned back in his chair, and frowning, lit a cigarette. He did not feel as good about his plan now, he told himself, as he should. The prospect of cutting the high-and-mighty Brandon Hoyt down to size should be pleasant to contemplate. Getting the man's support for the vice-presidency should seem sweet revenge for Hoyt's plan to put that Air Force friend into the office. But Dave could not feel smug about it. And he knew why: Because Brandon Hoyt had cuckolded him and even while the man was crawling, he would secretly be laughing at Dave.

Still, the photostat of that letter was a weapon powerful enough to force Hoyt to back him. His support, together with that of John Fletcher, should win Dave the vice-presidency hands down.

He asked Miss 'Marvin to call Dawson's, the florist where he had an account, and have some flowers delivered to Mrs. Harvey Ward.

The small gesture would tell Lucy that he was not unappreciative—that he would not forget.

Then, reflectively, he wondered why a man could not further his career without women being involved in the process. That was, he decided, a sad commentary on the state of modern big business.

CHAPTER FOURTEEN

THE weekend was no better than Nora had expected. Dave and she went to the club Saturday evening and made a public pretense that all was well between them. But they were uncomfortable in each other's presence. Their attempts at conversation were awkward, almost embarrassing. Dave drank too much and when they left for home, she had to do the driving.

They spent Sunday visiting Louise at Camp Wee-ni- toka. The child again said she wanted to go home but this time Nora felt sure she did not mean it. Louise was in a happier mood. Under questioning, she reluctantly admitted that some of the girls now seemed more friendly. As they walked about the grounds, one little girl stopped to chat with them; she was a child whose angelic expression was belied by the pixyish gleam in her blue eyes. This was Gretchen and Nora guessed that she was the one selected to break down Louise's reserve. And Gretchen was doing a good job, for in her presence Louise talked and laughed in normal little-girl fashion.

After they had talked to Gretchen, Louise suggested a walk in the woods. They agreed, and Dave said, with a heavy attempt at humor, that he hoped they wouldn't get lost.

"Nobody gets lost, Daddy," Louise told him. "That's silly. In all the time I've been here, nobody's ever been lost."

They walked a long way through the dense woodland, Louise saying that they were heading in a westerly direction. She proudly pointed out that she could tell this from the position of the afternoon sun and from their shadows being behind them. After perhaps an hour they came to a weed grown dirt road. The land beyond this road was out of bounds for the young people of Camp Wee-ni-toka, Louise informed her parents. The counselor Miss Leland, never took the girls of her group one step across the road that marked the camp boundary.

"But you could take me just a little farther," Louise said. "Will you, Daddy—Mommy?"

Dave said, "Well, just a little farther, honey."

So they went a little farther and found the Secret Cave, as the child immediately named the deep hollow beneath a rock ledge in the side of a bluff. In a sizeable area before the bluff only grass and bushes grew. Louise wondered at the lack of trees, and when she insisted upon an explanation, Nora made up a story.

"Once upon a time," Nora said, "long before the white man came to this country, a family of Indians—a father Indian, a mother Indian and a little girl Indian—lived where Camp Wee-ni-toka now stands. One day their wigwam was destroyed by some bad Indians. So the little family set out through the forest to find another place to build a new wigwam. Well, they walked and walked but the forest got thicker and thicker. They just couldn't find a place to live. But then—"

"—then they found this place," Louise broke in. "And lived in the Secret Cave."

"No, not quite," Nora told her. "The way the story goes, Father Indian and Mother Indian became very tired and oh-so very discouraged. They lost all hope of finding a new place to five. But Little Girl Indian said, 'Maybe if we pray to the Great Spirit'—which is what they called God—'He will help us.'"

"And the Great Spirit found this place for them?"

"Well, yes," Nora said. "But not right away, for the Great Spirit helped only those Indians who also helped themselves.

The Indian family asked Him to help them find a place to build their new home. Suddenly the sky grew black, black as night in the middle of the day, and there was wind and thunder and lightning. There was going to be rain, too. The Indian family had no shelter. They started running, looking for a place to protect them from the storm. Just before the rain came they found this Secret Cave, even though in those days trees grew right up to the mouth.

"And here, inside the cave, they huddled with their possessions. And a good thing, too, for the strong wind blew down all the trees in front of the cave. Then—"

"So that's why there are no trees here!" Louise exclaimed.

"Yes, that's why," Nora said, laughing. "But I told you that the Great Spirit helped only those Indians who helped themselves. When the storm passed, the three Indians realized what a nice place this would be for a home if they cleared away all those fallen trees. So they began working. They worked for days and days, clearing away the fallen trees. Then they had a nice yard in front of their cave and Little Girl Indian played there. Birds came to be her friends, and some rabbits, and even a little deer. But the strange part was that the trees never grew here again."

"Oh, that's a wonderful story!" Louise said, her face aglow. "Even though you made it up!"

Nora laughed, and so did Dave.

And just for a little while the three were happy again.

It did not last, of course. After they had taken Louise back to camp and were driving to Lanford, Dave and Nora were as much estranged as they had been before seeing their daughter. They stopped for dinner at a restaurant on the way home but Nora only picked at * her food. When they reached home at eight o'clock, Dave suggested they go to the club again. She pleaded a headache and told him to go alone if he wished. Then she felt hurt when he did go alone. Unhappy and depressed, she went to bed at ten o'clock, taking a sleeping pill.

Monday was a blue day, but in the afternoon Penny Austin phoned and asked if Nora would like to drive to Baltimore and go shopping. Nora said she would very much like to go. She hoped the trip would take her mind off her despondency about her marriage, at least for a few hours. She left a note for Dave, telling where she and Penny were going and that she might be a little late in getting home.

Dave found the note on his study desk when he got home at five-thirty. He read it with annoyance. Despite their estrangement, he wanted Nora there when he got home because the house seemed empty without her. Furthermore, he did not like her being away with Penny Austin. He wondered what Penny was trying to do. Sooner or later Penny would be sure to let her tongue slip and Nora would learn that Penny was the woman he had been with the other night. Damn Penny, anyway!

Well, no wonder he was in such a foul mood. He had had a bad day, starting from the moment he had learned that General Lyle Wyman, USF Retired, was in town, a guest of the Brandon Hoyts. Then during the afternoon Hoyt had taken the general through the plant and the offices, including Dave's. When the pair walked in unannounced—for Miss Marvin had been away from her desk—Dave had been possessed by a wild, compulsive urge to slug Hoyt. He had to use all his will power to smile pleasantly and acknowledge the introduction to the general. The thought had kept running through his mind: This is the man who had your wife ... This is the man who had your wife. He had found himself hating Hoyt as he had never before hated anybody.

As for Wyman, Dave had been impressed to a degree—as he would have been by any top flight military man. Wyman was tall and slender, with iron-gray hair and bronzed skin. Even in civvies he held himself stiff and straight. He was austere in manner, clipped of speech. With each utterance he had seemed to imitate a more famous general's pronouncement: "I shall return!"

But impressed or not by the visitor's military personality and bearing, Dave would have challenged the general's ability, given the opportunity, to handle this office. And as the two had left Dave to continue their sightseeing tour, he thought sourly: Get back to the golf course, pal, where all retired generals belong.

The visit had left him in a depressed mood. He had had in his pocket the photostat that would certainly end Hoyt's sponsorship of Wyman. He had had it since noon, Friday, when Harvey Ward rather reluctantly had handed the copy to him.

That afternoon he had planned to have Miss Marvin call Hoyt's secretary and make an appointment for him. Then he would confront the man with the photostatic evidence of his taking kickbacks and his serious breach of that important company rule. But back at his office after lunch, he had been reluctant to put the call through. He had let the afternoon get away from him and today, Monday, he had still hesitated to seek an appointment. He had begun to wonder if he lacked the nerve to carry through his plan, or if he had scruples against blackmail.

So now, he told himself: Tomorrow ... I'll see him first thing in the morning ...

But next morning, Tuesday, he waited too long, and not until nearly noon did he ask Miss Marvin to call Hoyt's secretary. A moment later she told him over the intercom that the appointment was set for next Monday afternoon at four o'clock.

"That's the best I could do, Mr. Osborne. Mr. Hoyt was in his office for only an hour this morning. And he won't be in again the rest of the week. He's going out of town."

Jolted, Dave silently cursed the subconscious motive that had kept him from contacting Hoyt earlier. The directors' meeting was scheduled for ten o'clock and an appointment with the man at four would be too late. More, it would disastrous.

"Listen, Hilda," he told Miss Marvin. "Get me his secretary. I want to talk to her. And by the way, what's her name?"

"Kulaski, Mr. Osborne."

"Well, let me talk to her."

A moment later she told him that she had Miss Kulaski on the phone.

He said, "Miss Kulaski, it's very important that I talk to Mr. Hoyt before the board meeting on Monday. Important to him as well as to me. See if you can't work me in early in the morning, won't you?"

"I'm sorry, Mr. Osborne, but Mr. Hoyt's schedule is filled for Monday morning. I could squeeze you in at nine, if you don't need more than, say, ten minutes."

"I won't need more than two minutes, Miss Kulaski."

"Very well. I'll put you down for nine."

Dave thanked her and set down the phone. He felt shaken, unnerved. This was cutting it pretty close. Still, it might work out better this way. He would give Hoyt the jolt just before the meeting and the man would be reeling under it when he went to the board room. Yes, that might be better.

General Wyman's visit to Lanford and to Worden- Forbes was given adequate press coverage, even though the publicity was not arranged by Dave's department but by Brandon Hoyt. Both the Monday evening *Bulletion* and the Tuesday morning *Herald* carried interviews and pictures of Wyman. The general had denied to reporters that his visit to Worden-Forbes meant that he was considering joining the corporation as an executive. He was quoted as saying he had no plans for the future other than to live on the nearby farm that he had bought several years ago. His farm was close to the Idlewild Golf Club, and he hoped to get in a great deal of golf.

Nora read the publicity given the general and she felt sick at heart. She was completely convinced now that Brandon Hoyt would not keep his promise to her. He had never intended to keep it when he made it, she told herself. He had simply used her, made a fool of her. She came very close to giving way to tears over the way she had been misused and for the wrong being done to Dave.

Again she turned to Penny Austin, needing to cry on someone's shoulder. And Penny, inviting her to lunch at the Red Mill on Harverford Road, was understanding and sympathetic.

"Well, you never did really expect Brandon to keep his word," Penny said as they sipped daiquiris. "But that doesn't make it any easier to accept, I know. How is Dave taking it?"

"Hard. Or I imagine he is, at least. He doesn't talk about it. He doesn't talk anything over with me these days." Nora's voice was unsteady, and she had to blink away tears. "We're just two strangers sharing the same house, Penny. He doesn't say one word more to me than is absolutely necessary. And I wouldn't dare bring up this thing."

"One thing sure, he was just talking through his hat when he said he could force Brandon to back him. As I was sure he was."

"I suppose so."

"I wish I knew what to tell you to do."

"I wish you did, too," Nora said bleakly.

The waitress returned and they ordered lunch. Nora asked for a salad of fruit and cottage cheese but Penny, who never seemed to worry about her figure, said she would have the veal scallopine with noodles. They talked little; Nora was lost in a gloomy reverie and Penny was in one of her rare thoughtful moods. But later, after ordering dessert—for Nora a lime sherbet and Penny a hot- fudge sundae—they resumed their discussion.

"Maybe Dave does have a way to force Brandon to back him," Penny said, "then, being Dave, he just hasn't the nerve to make use of it."

"But what do you think Dave's scheme could be, Penny?"

Penny shrugged. "I haven't a single, solitary idea. I wish I had. You couldn't sound him out, could you?"

Nora shook her head. "I wouldn't dare. You just don't know how it is between us. If I even mentioned Brandon Hoyt, there would be a battle. It preys on Dave's mind that Brandon was my—my lover."

"Then there's only one thing to do."

"What, Penny? What could we do?"

"Not we, just I. I could see Mark Hammond."

"Oh, Penny—would you?"

"For you, yes," Penny said. "You and Dave are like a couple of lost, frightened children. Somebody's got to help you, and I'd never forgive myself if I didn't try. Anyway, Mark Hammond will arrive in town a day or two before the directors' meeting and he always calls me, even if he doesn't want a date. Poor Mark's dating days are about over now because he's getting on in years. But when he calls, I'll ask him to meet me. And I'll plead your—and Dave's—case."

"Penny, you're a doll—a real pal."

"I'm just an old softie," Penny said, smiling wryly. "Next, I'll be taking in stray cats and dogs. But don't get your hopes too high. I can go only so far with Mark; he's not indebted to me, or at least he doesn't feel that he is. I'll tell him what the situation is between Dave and Brandon and try to make him see Dave is experienced where that Air Force character is not. That's as far as I can go without stepping out of bounds. But if Mark should feel that Dave will make a better vice-president than General Wyman, he'll squash Brandon like a bug. One thing always comes first with old Mark, and that's Worden-Forbes."

"Penny, I think you'll save Dave and me," Nora said, frantically clutching at this last straw of hope. "If you do, I'll love you forever."

Penny laughed. "Please, darling, I'm not like that. I've never been double-gaited in my life."

"Oh, I didn't mean—"

"I know you didn't," the redheaded girl said. "I was just having my little joke."

Penny pleaded another engagement when they left the restaurant but she did not hurry away when they reached their separate cars on the Red Mill parking lot. She got behind the wheel of her convertible and waited until Nora drove off in her station wagon. Then she got from her car and went to the telephone booth at the side of the old stone building. She called Worden- Forbes and asked for Mr. David Osborne, Public Relations.

"One moment, please ..."

Another feminine voice said, "Mr. Osborne's secretary. Who is calling?"

Secretaries, Penny thought and made a face. They guarded their bosses more staunchly than wives did their husbands.

"Mrs. Bart Austin."

"One moment, Mrs. Austin. I'll see if Mr. Osborne is in his office."

"You know damned well he's in his office, dearie," Penny said. "You just put him on now, you hear?"

Miss Marvin did not answer, but in a moment Dave said guardedly, "Hello, Mrs. Austin."

"This is Penny, Dave. Let's not play games. If you can't trust your secretary not to listen in, you'd better get one you can trust. Dave, I've got to see you."

Sounding annoyed, he said, "I'm pretty busy, Penny."

"Well, just don't be too busy. I've come from having lunch and an interesting discussion with Nora. Now I've got to see you."

"Well ... All right."

"Make it five o'clock, at that place east of town—the Florida Room. Okay, Dave?"

"Okay," he said grudgingly.

Leaving the booth and returning to her car, Penny decided that she did not quite understand herself. She sat there for a moment, wondering why she was going to all this bother. It was not at all like her to help others. She was essentially selfish, and believed that charity began and ended at home. Never in her life had she gone out of her way to help anyone. But here she was, in a dither to help the Osbornes.

Though seldom self-analytical, she did try to puzzle out this act of unselfishness on her part. She was fond of Nora. She had never been as friendly with another woman. Penny was no woman's woman, that was for sure, and she never had been. But Nora liked her and she liked Nora. Why that should be, Penny had no idea, for they had little in common, actually. Nora was pretty much of a prude, and she—well, she was just the opposite.

Still, she liked Nora and held a sort of protective feeling toward her. That was a part of it. Dave was another part, she supposed. It was odd how she felt about Dave Osborne. Usually when she had had a man other than her husband, she forgot the relationship immediately after leaving his arms. But she had not forgotten that night at the motel with Dave. She had told him then that being with him had been wonderful, and she had meant it. He had given her the most excitingly pleasurable hour she had ever experienced. He might not be much of a business go-getter but as a lover he was something special. True, he had taken her in anger and maybe that had made it more exciting.

However he had taken her, she had enjoyed him more than any man she had ever had and, she wryly admitted to herself, that statement covered a wide territory. But she was not able to forget Dave. So that fact, too, must be behind her wanting to help the Osbornes.

Whatever her motives, she didn't want to see their lives completely smashed. They were fouled up enough already, poor kids.

Penny drove into town, left the convertible on a parking lot and spent the early part of the afternoon in the stores. She made but one purchase, a two-strand set of orchid beads with matching earrings. She paid twenty- two dollars plus tax, an outlandish price for something she would wear only a few times. But she had felt an urge to buy something and she saw really nothing she needed or cared to have. She had reached the point at which shopping was no longer a thrilling and novel past-time, as it had been in the old hungry days when Bart and she had lived on a tight budget.

At four-thirty she walked to the parking lot, got in her convertible and drove west through town. She felt a rising excitement because of the prospect of seeing Dave again and wondered if she wanted a rematch with him. Would she have another date with him, realizing—as she now did—that Nora was her one woman friend? She did not know the answer to that.

The Florida Room, on Route 30, was a squat, white, windowless building with a pair of phony royal palms out front to supplement the subtropical decor inside. She parked the convertible among the half dozen cars already there and went into the cocktail lounge. Taking a stool at the bar, she ordered a daiquiri and almost immediately a Latin type right out of *The Untouchables* tried to move in on her.

"Blow, Joe," she said, freezing all over him. "Blow, or I yell to the management."

He gave her a scowl that would have done a hoodlum proud, but moved back to his stool farther along the bar.

She lit a cigarette, took a sip of her drink, and then, promptly at five, Dave arrived. He, too, was wearing a scowl.

Taking the stool to her right, he said, low-voiced, "Damn it, Penny, what are you trying to do, mess things up for me more than they already are?"

"Now, why would I do such a thing, darling?"

The barman came and Dave asked for a scotch on the rocks.

Then he turned back to her. "Seeing Nora all the time, you're sure to give it away—about us, I mean."

"She already knows you were with a woman that night, remember."

"She doesn't know the woman was you."

"Would that bother her more?"

"You know it would. She thinks of you as a friend. Nora's pretty naïve about some things."

"So are you, darling," Penny said. "Let's have a little privacy for this conference, shall we?"

They took their drinks to a booth. Dave got out cigarettes, gave her one and took one for himself. He lit both with his lighter. He was still scowling and watching her warily.

"Knock off the grudge, for Pete's sake," she told him. "I didn't ask you here to make a pass at you. I want to talk."

"About what?"

"About you," Penny said. She drained her glass. "Buy me another, lover."

Dave downed his own drink before signaling the waitress. When their second round came, Penny said, "I'm going to say something I had not intended to say, Dave, but I think I'd better lay it on the line for you right now, so here goes: You're being completely unfair. Sure Nora did something that hurt you, but she did it for you—for the future of you both. She didn't stray because of any natural inclination on her part. She—"

"Cut it out, Penny. I've heard that record too many times."

She ignored that. "It's even-steven between you. You squared accounts when you had me. So why the grudge against her?"

Dave did not reply.

"All right, clam up. But you're being damned rotten unfair to her."

"If you've said it all, let's break this up."

"I haven't got around to saying what I came to say," she told him. "You told Nora that you have a way to force Brandon Hoyt to drop his Air Force pal and to back you. Were you just bragging?"

"No, I wasn't just bragging."

"So? What have you got on him?"

"Penny, it's none of your business."

"I'm going to help you, Dave—in spite of your nasty mood."
"How?"

"Did you ever hear that Mark Hammond, chairman of the board, is an old and good friend of mine?"

"I'm not exactly deaf to gossip."

"Well, goody for you. Anyway, I'm going to see Mark before the board meeting—to go to bat for you. But I've got to have some specific information, some facts, to get you beyond first base. Right now, all I've got is the argument that I'm fond of the Osbornes and think you deserve the vice-presidency, and that's not much to sell Mark. So if you do have something that will smear Brandon Hoyt in Mark's eyes, that will make this operation a lot easier for me, and for you, too, will you give, or must I go to Mark empty-handed?"

Dave's face was dark with anger. "Dammit, Penny, just keep out of my affairs. I'm fed up with women who try to excuse their sleeping around because they're "helping someone,' for God's sake. Do it for Bart if he puts up with it, but don't do it for me. I can't take that phony stuff."

He swallowed the rest of his drink, slammed the glass down on the formica table top and got up from the booth. He stood bitterly gazing down at her. "I'll tell you what I told Nora. I'm getting that vice-presidency and getting it strictly on my own. Not through any of her two-timing "help'—or any of yours. And that's it."

"Dave, don't go," Peggy begged. "Please don't go."

But he strode away and out the door.

Penny sat there in the midst of her shattered good intentions, telling herself that she was a fool and that she should have known better. You simply could not reason with anyone like Dave Osborne. He would try to bull it through alone and naturally he would mess things up for himself and Nora. Penny was quite sure that he did have something on Brandon Hoyt and she was equally sure that he lacked the nerve to make use of it. She would not pity him when that Air Force general got the vice-presidency but she would feel sorry for Nora. She sighed, finished her drink, then picked up her purse and left the booth.

About to turn away, she noticed that Dave had left his cigarettes and lighter on the table. She picked them up and put them in her purse, having no idea when she would have a chance to give them to him. This was probably the last time she would ever be alone with him. The thought saddened her.

For in one way, at least, Dave Osborne was very much a man.

CHAPTER FIFTEEN

To Nora's despair, the breach between Dave and her widened during the next few days. Dave did not come home until late Tuesday night and when he did arrive he was well stoned. He offered neither explanation nor apology for his late arrival or his condition. He merely stared in silent accusation at Nora as he stalked stiffly through the living room on his way upstairs.

In the morning he looked deathly ill with a hangover and again had nothing to say to her. He was no longer being polite or even civil.

As she was about to go to the garage, she found the courage to say, "Dave, please—is this because you think I've done something wrong again? If you do, it's all in your imagination. You've got to believe that!"

"Quit nagging at me," he said angrily. "I'll be damned if I'm going to be nagged at."

And with that, he drove off to the office.

Wednesday evening he came home early but was still in an ugly temper. He ate little at dinner and then spent the evening drinking alone. She had been rebuffed that morning and did not try to get to him that evening. Discouraged, she concluded that any attempt to break down the wall between them was useless.

Thursday morning was no better and Thursday night he did not come home until nearly one o'clock. He had been drinking again and he looked tormented. Nora was badly frightened and dreaded to think how this nightmare would end. Friday morning, after he had left the house, she wept for him, for them both. She was convinced now that her affair with Brandon Hoyt was only a part of the reason for Dave's behavior. The other part, she felt sure, was his gnawing fear that he would not get the vice-presidency. He was being torn apart and to Nora it seemed that he was slowly destroying them both.

In desperation, she put through a call to Brandon Hoyt. As usual, she got his secretary and had to give her name.

"I'm sorry, Mrs. Osborne," the secretary said, "but Mr. Hoyt is out of town and won't be in his office until Monday morning." And then, slyly: "Didn't Mr. Osborne tell you?"

"Perhaps he did," Nora said, "and it slipped my mind, Thank you, anyway."

She put down the phone, her desperation now a frantic thing. She had hoped to beg Brandon, humbly and abjectly, to give Dave his support, offering in return to do anything he wanted. But she was denied even the chance to so demean herself.

There was still Penny, of course, and her promise to talk to Mark Hammond on Dave's behalf. But Penny had not phoned or stopped around and she did not answer when Nora phoned her. Penny, too, must be away ... She picked up the phone again, dialed the Austin's number. Her hands were trembling violently. If Penny had forgotten to see Mark Hammond, all was lost.

This time, however, Penny answered.

"I'm so glad I caught you in," Nora said. "I've been trying and trying to get you."

"I only got home an hour ago," Penny said. "I ran up to New York for a couple of days with Bart to a convention. He's back in Dayton again and won't be home until the middle of next week. . . How are things with you, Nora?"

"Bad, Penny. Worse than ever."

"Dave's still being the heavily wronged husband?"

Nora said that Dave and she were becoming more and more estranged. "He's drinking heavily all the time. He's hardly ever at home and he won't talk to me at all now. At first I thought he suspected me of—of cheating again. But now I think he's broken up because lie's convinced he won't get the vice-presidency. I tried to call Brandon Hoyt but his secretary says he's out of town and won't be back until Monday morning."

"And this board meeting is Monday?"

"Yes."

"Well, it's a cinch that Dave won't have time to force Brandon into backing him—even if he does have something on that character."

"I've lost hope, Penny. Unless you ...

"I haven't forgotten," Penny said. "I'll keep my promise. Mark Hammond is in town at the Harrison and I spoke to him on the phone before I went to New York. I'm seeing him this evening at seven, for a talk. So I'll give it the old college try, Nora. I'll do my best."

"Thanks, Penny. You don't know how grateful I am."

"As I said before, don't get your hopes up too high. I can only tell Mark how deserving you and Dave are, and that really doesn't carry too much weight. If I knew what Dave had on Brandon, I could tell the old boy. If Dave's got something really serious, Mark might go after Brandon's scalp at the board meeting. But I don't suppose there's any way to make Dave tell what it is."

"No way that I know, Penny."

"Too bad. But I'll do my best, and you—well, you keep your fingers crossed."

"You'll call me right after you've seen Mr. Hammond?"

"As soon as I leave him," Penny promised. " 'Bye now."

Nora said goodbye and put down the phone. She was unsure of whether or not to hope. Penny seemed not at all certain she could influence Hammond. If Penny failed now, it could mean real disaster. Dave was showing a weakness she had never suspected and she feared that if he failed to win the vice-presidency, he would have lost the will to try again for promotion. He seemed to be going to pieces even now. And if that were actually the case, could he ever again get hold of himself? She could see him, her beloved Dave, wasting himself, chained forever to some mediocre job, like his friend, Harv Ward. Oh, no—not that, she thought in despair.

She could not know if Dave would be home early, but she made her preparations for dinner. She removed two steaks from the freezer, got together the ingredients for a tossed salad, cutting them to size in the olivewood salad bowl. That done, she went upstairs for her bath. She put on a sheer, pale blue dress, white pumps, and white plastic jewelry. She did her hair and her face with extra care, which took more makeup than usual. Like Dave, she was showing signs of the strain they were under and her color was not good. There were blue black smudges beneath her eyes.

Just before five-thirty, Dave's usual time to arrive home, she was so on edge that she felt the need of a drink. She placed ice cubes in a shaker, added the makings for a daiquiri. She shook the mixture briefly, poured it into a cocktail glass. Sipping the daiquiri, she went to the living room and stood at the picture window. Far down Elm Drive, a car appeared but it turned in at the Jenkens' driveway. Another car came in sight but that was not Dave's either. She knew by the time she had finished the daiquiri that this was another evening she would spend alone. Depressed and sorry for herself, Nora returned to the kitchen and made another daiquiri. She ate a few crackers with pineapple cheese spread while drinking the second cocktail and that was her dinner. Presently she made a third daiquiri. The drinks were making her lightheaded without lifting her spirits.

Penny called much sooner than Nora had expected. When the phone rang at twenty minutes past seven Nora's first thought was that Penny had been unable to get anywhere with Mark Hammond.

"Didn't it work out, Penny?" she asked.

"It's too early to tell," Penny said. "I spoke my piece and Mark's being nice about it. That's why I'm calling so soon. Are you alone, Nora?"

"Yes. Why?"

"Mark would like to talk with you. I think you should come and join us. You can tell him far better than I can just why Dave is the man for the job."

"I'll come, of course."

"Can you make it right away?" Penny said. "I have a date and can't stay here much longer."

"I'll leave now."

"Good," Penny said. "We're in the cocktail lounge at the Harrison. 'Bye now."

Nora put down the phone and hurried to her bedroom to check her makeup and run a comb through her hair. She gave herself a quick inspection in the full-length mirror, decided that her dress would do, snatched up her purse and rushed down to the garage. She reached midtown in fifteen minutes, then spent ten more finding a parking lot three blocks from the Harrison. The hurried walk to the hotel left her breathless and flushed as she entered the lobby.

Pausing just inside the cocktail lounge, she tried to let her eyes adjust to the semidarkness but Penny saw her and waved. As Nora approached the booth, Mark Hammond rose so that she could seat herself. Once she was settled and he sat beside her, Penny introduced them in her breezy manner.

"Nora, my good friend Mark. . . Mark, my good friend Nora."

Smiling, Nora looked directly at Mark Hammond for the first time.

He was a big man, a giant of a man, an outdoors type with a deeply weathered face. A rim of silver hair surrounded his massive bald head. He was in his sixties, but his smile was youthful and his bright blue eyes alert and knowing. Nora could see at once that he had been a handsome man, was still a handsome man, in a rugged, well-aged fashion and he radiated a sense of virility that had an immediate impact upon her. Here is a real man, she reflected.

"Nice of you to come, Nora," he said, offering his hand. "You're every bit as lovely as Penny said."

She gave him her hand and had it swallowed in the vastness of his. He held it a little longer than was necessary, smiling at her while his knowing blue eyes appraised her, as they had doubtlessly appraised a thousand women before her.

"What would you like to drink?" he asked, finally releasing her hand.

'I've already had my quota," she said. "But since this is an occasion—well, I'd like a daiquiri, please."

"Another for you, Penny?" he asked.

Penny shook her head. "I've got to rush. I'll finish this one, then leave you two to talk things over. I'm awfully sorry but I do have this other engagement."

Penny finished her drink soon after Nora was served her daiquiri, then picked up her cigarettes and lighter and dropped them into her purse. Nora noticed the gold fighter and thought how like Dave's it was. Only after the redhead had gone did the thought strike her that she had never seen Penny carry a fighter before; she had always used matches. Then the lighter must be Dave's—the one she had given him to celebrate his new job.

But when and how had Penny gotten the costly gadget? Nora could guess but she hated to believe the obvious answer. Why, Penny was her friend. She would not be having an affair with Dave. Surely, he could not have been with Penny that night—and perhaps since. Penny could not—would not—be on her way to meet him now. Repeatedly Nora kept telling herself that her fears were foolish; then she realized that Mark Hammond was talking to her and she had not caught one word he had said. She tried to rid her mind of these dark thoughts and listen to him.

"I doubt if your husband has anything on Brandon Hoyt," he was saying. "Brandon's too foxy to let anybody maneuver him into a tough spot. Besides, it seems to me that if your Dave has any valid evidence that Brandon has been cutting corners, he would have used it."

"Dave does have something, Mr. Hammond," Nora said. "I know he has. He doesn't say things he doesn't mean. He's not—well, a bluffer or a liar. If only you'd talk to him, I'm sure he'd tell you what it is."

"Oh, I don't think it will be necessary for me to see him."

"You mean—?" Nora said, feeling her heart give a wild, hopeful lurch.

"I mean," he said, smiling at her, "that I'm in a mood to let you convince me that Dave, and not some retired Air Force general, should fill that vice-presidency."

Nora went rigid, for his hand moved from atop the table to her thigh.

"Why don't we go upstairs to Worden-Forbes' suite?" Hammond went on. "This is a matter that needs privacy to discuss properly."

CHAPTER SIXTEEN

H IS oversized hand moved slowly back and forth over her thigh in a sensuous caress. Nora inwardly shuddered and wanted to cry out: Stop this, you nasty-minded old man, but the reasoning part of her mind warned her to keep silent. One wrong move and she would irreparably destroy not only Dave's future but hers and Louise's as well.

His fingers started to knead the soft, smooth flesh of her thigh. Her mind raced frantically this way and that like a mouse in a maze, seeking some way of escape. But she knew that this was a trap from which she herself had blocked every exit—unless she wanted to throw everything away. What did it matter? she thought bleakly. Dave was involved with Penny and she had lost him forever. But there was no need for her to lose everything else.

How could she be sure, though? She had gone through this sort of thing with Brandon Hoyt and his promise had turned out to be only a ghastly joke. How could she be sure that this man's word was any better than Hoyt's? Because Penny had said he kept his promises? Penny, she thought bitterly. Her dear, loyal friend, Penny.

"Penny—she set this up for you, didn't she?"

"For me?" Hammond said, looking surprised. "My impression was that she set it up for you."

"How can I be sure you'll keep your word?"

"My word is as good as my bond, my dear. Penny must have told you that I kept my promise to her."

"She did. But it was a long time ago that you helped her husband. You could have changed since then."

"I've changed in some ways," he said, smiling wryly. "But not in that way."

'You'll see that Dave gets the vice-presidency?"

"I will."

"You can swing it, even over Brandon Hoyt's objections?"

"I can shut him up before he even starts to talk," he said confidently. "I have the board in the palm of my hand."

Nora reached for what was left of her daiquiri. She drank it down and stared bleakly at the empty glass while his insistent hand still caressed her thigh. She told herself that he was not really touching her—not the real Nora. She could let him use her body, up there in the ninth-floor suite, but she would hold her inner self aloof from it. She would not let him reach her, no matter how much he caressed her. She would be merely an empty, unfeeling vehicle for his physical pleasure, and would reject the taint of his maleness even as he labored over her in panting quest of sensual satisfaction.

"All right," she said, and was surprised by the steadiness of her voice. "All right, I'll go."

"Good," he said, and now took his hand away. "If you'd rather not have people see us go up together, I'll go first. The suite number is—"

She thought of Dave and Penny, perhaps together this very moment. Dave lost in Penny's lush, lovely flesh—because he wanted to be.

She said, "If you're not ashamed for us to be seen together, why should I be?"

He gazed at her with surprise for a moment, then shrugged.

"All right," he said. "Let's be on our way."

He left the booth and she picked up her purse and followed. As they walked together across the lobby toward the elevators she felt dwarfed by his hugeness. He was slightly stooped, in the manner of many enormously tall men, but even so he must have stood six-feet-four. It seemed to her that the eyes of everyone in the lobby were on them, knowing where they were going and exactly for what purpose. She held her head high, thinking: Go on and stare. If you've never seen a whore, you're seeing one now. A sob welled up in her throat.

As they entered an elevator, Hammond said, "Ninth floor, son."

"Yes, sir, Mr. Hammond." The door slid closed, and they were whisked upward.

Stepping from the elevator, Nora thought, Welcome to the Ninth Floor Club, darling. The initiation is quite simple, merely a matter of taking off your panties and climbing into the hay.

She walked beside the huge old man along the corridor to the suite. He produced a key, unlocked and pushed the door open, moving aside to let her enter first. She hesitated, held back by a sudden revulsion until his hand closed on her arm and its vast strength moved her into the sitting room of the suite.

"A drink?" he asked, going to the bar in the corner. "I'm having one."

"Yes, thanks," she said tonelessly.

The more numb she became, the better.

He returned to her with two tall drinks, handed her one, then, his hand gripping her arm again, led her into one of the adjoining bedrooms. He shut the door and Nora felt herself a prisoner in a remote, ugly corner of the world where she would be soiled forever. In this large room, with the two double beds and chaise lounge, Nora guessed, the visitors must spend most of their time in a horizontal position.

She took a fast swallow of her drink, then placed the tumbler and her purse on the bureau, removed her plastic costume jewelry, her dress and slip. She turned to him in panties and bra. He stood sipping his drink, feasting his eyes on her partially nude body.

"As I said downstairs," he told her, "I've changed in some ways. Age has caught up with me, to my sorrow. Unfortunately, I seem to have more failures than successes with women nowadays. This may be another failure."

"If it is, you can't hold me to blame," Nora said. "You'll still keep your word?"

"I'll still keep my word," he said. "And you'll get an A for trying."

He finished his drink and set down his empty glass, then began removing his clothes. Hoping this would be another failure for him, desperately wishing so, Nora went to one of the beds and turned down the spread and upper sheet. She took a long time doing it, dreading to face him again. When she turned, he was completely disrobed. With a sinking heart, she saw with revulsion the sagging of his flesh. But, too, she saw—and was even more impressed than before—the great size of him. Despite herself, she wondered what it would be like to be possessed by a man so huge. With the thought came self-disgust, and she strove to reach that state of aloofness she had promised herself to attain. He came to her, this great, gaunt man, and ran his hands over her. She unhooked her bra, freed her breasts, and he captured them, fondling them roughly. She removed her panties, closing her mind to the things his hands did to her. He drew her down onto the bed with him, and she lay supine and he on his side. Mercifully, she was able to force herself into a remoteness from it all and so she remained essentially untouched by his caresses.

After a time, he said plaintively, "It's no good. You'll have to help me. You know how?"

Nora knew how. She knew from the times when she had wanted Dave and he had been slow to be aroused. She turned toward the big old man and with her hands and lips tried to do what he was unable to accomplish for himself. She did all the mad, erotic things but in a numbed, mechanical way, striving to earn the vice-presidency for Dave. Yet Hammond's impotence refused to yield. At first she merely succeeded in doing what she did not want to do—arouse herself. She went from total lack of feeling to soaring passion and then to torment in the face of his continued inability.

Unleashed desire drove her to a frenzy. And suddenly, miraculously, her desire was communicated to him. He seized her by the shoulders and turned her roughly onto her back.

"Oh, yes—yes!" she gasped.

He came onto her, and she had to throttle a scream that rose in her throat with the hard jolt of his manhood. After that she moaned with the joyous sensation of passion accommodated and finally shrieked with the agonizing ecstasy of fulfillment.

Afterward, when he had removed himself from her, she lay at rest in the surcease of passion. Disgust came and it was entirely for herself. She had joined in the coupling of bodies with all her being and so she was to blame for her own degradation. I'm wanton, she thought; I deserve all the ugly things that happen to me. She felt that she should weep for herself but she was far beyond tears.

The man beside her had fallen into a deep sleep and his loud, asthmatic breathing rasped against her nerves. She got from the bed and snatched up her clothing, dressing with haste to hide her body. She got her purse from the bureau and, without really looking at herself in the mirror, touched up her lips and combed her hair. She walked quickly into the sitting room and closed the door behind her. She had not looked again at the sleeping man. She had no thought of waking him, even for reassurance that he would keep his promise.

She left the suite and the hotel. Reaching the street, she paused to orient herself, not knowing in which direction lay the parking lot where she had left her car. Finally she got her bearings and started walking. She walked fast, not like a person in a hurry to reach a pleasant destination but like one fleeing a feared pursuer. She was trying to run away from herself.

Driving directly home and seeing the house dark, she knew that Dave had not yet arrived. She ran the station wagon into the garage, then sat for a time with her arms folded on the steering wheel and her head resting on her arms. She simply wanted to die and wondered if she would ever rid herself of this nightmare feeling of self-disgust.

The ringing of the telephone summoned her out of the car and up to the kitchen where she spoke a toneless hello into the extension.

"Mrs. Osborne?" a voice said. "Mrs. David Osborne?"

"Yes."

"Mrs. Osborne, this is John Hadley at Camp Wee-ni- toka."

"Oh, yes, Mr. Hadley," she said, remembering him as the camp director. Then, alarm knifing through her: "Is something wrong? Is Louise ill?"

"She isn't ill, Mrs. Osborne, but I thought it best to call you. Louise has run away from camp. She's been gone since four o'clock this afternoon. That's six hours now, and I am, to say the least, becoming upset. I've been trying to reach you for the past two hours and—"

"Aren't you searching for her?" Nora cut in, her fear for Louise making her voice sound frantic.

"We are searching, Mrs. Osborne. I've called in the state police and have also gotten more than thirty volunteers to help. But we're having a severe electrical storm here and that makes looking for her difficult. I'd suggest that you and Mr. Osborne come up here as soon as possible."

"Why? Why did she run away?"

"It seems she had a quarrel with one of the other girls," the man said. "Will you come, Mrs. Osborne? The child will be frightened as well as unhappy when we do find her and we feel strongly that her parents should be here to comfort her."

"We'll be there," Nora said. "We'll leave right away."

We, she thought cradling the receiver. If only she could reach Dave … She picked up the phone, dialed Penny's number and waited a long time but Penny did not answer. She would have to go alone. Oh, Dave—Dave! was her silent, anguished cry—the cry of a woman forsaken, who must face trouble with no one by her side.

She picked up her purse and car keys, returned to the garage and drove a dozen miles before the thought occurred to her that she could have left a note for Dave. But then, she told herself bleakly, he would not have found it. He would come home drunk and go to bed, never even noticing that she was not there.

CHAPTER SEVENTEEN

DAVE again spent the evening pub-crawling, trying to drown in liquor the constant, stinging awareness that his marriage was a shambles. He felt that nothing could ever repair the damage, not even his getting the vice-presidency. That Nora had given herself to Brandon Hoyt had cut him deeply and the hurt would be with him all his life. Her faithfulness, which he had never even thought to question, had always made him vastly proud, especially when he heard gossip about the extramarital flights of other men's wives.

But Nora's reason for having the affair with Hoyt had struck him an even harder blow. In effect, she had told him that she had little or no trust in his ability to give his family the security they deserved, so she had sought to help him by selling herself. Thereby she had destroyed his pride in himself as a man and even his self-confidence as a business executive.

She had ruined the fine thing their marriage had been but without accomplishing what she had set out to do. There had been no reason on earth for Nora to make a whore of herself, as she had so tragically done. By his own efforts alone, he would win the vice-presidency. The photostated letter was safe in his pocket. And on Monday morning at nine o'clock he would walk into Hoyt's office and give him an ultimatum:

"Either back me for the vice-presidency at the board meeting," Dave would say, "or I'll go to H. M. Forbes—or to Mark Hammond—with this."

Then he would show Hoyt the photostated copy of the man's own letter, offering to place an order if he could get a return.

So Dave would get the vice-presidency and his future with Worden-Forbes would be bright and assured. But that would not straighten out his marriage. Even if Nora threw herself into his arms and told him that he was an all-time wonder-boy, he would never be able to forget her lack of faith in his ability—nor her flagrantly degrading affair with Hoyt. Never could she salve the sickening hurt to his pride. Nothing could ever be the same between them.

Tonight he sat in a grubby midtown bar, the Barrel. He was on his fifth rye-on-the-rocks and the stuff was not doing a thing for him. If he could not soon find a way to forget the troubles of his marriage he felt that he would crack up. Hell, that would really be something—having a breakdown before getting a chance to face that Brandon Hoyt bastard.

Well, if whiskey would not give him forgetfulness, a woman might. That thought insinuated itself upon his mind and took a tenacious hold. He had not forgotten the night he had had Penny Austin. Maybe if he had her again ... Well, why not? If Nora saw fit to sleep around, there was no reason why he should not do the same. One thing was certain: with Penny he would feel whole again in the manhood department. At least, for a little while.

He left his fifth drink barely touched, rose from his stool and walked steadily enough out to his car.

Fifteen minutes later he pulled into the Austin's driveway. He knew that Bart was in Dayton again and he hoped that no one else would be with Penny. There well could be someone, of course, for Penny was a real tramp. She could be with anybody. He switched off motor and lights, got from the Buick. He crossed the lawn to the door and pressed the bell button.

The outside light came on, the door opened and Penny frowned at him. "Oh, it's you. Well, what do you want?"

"You need to be told?" he asked, pushing the door farther open and stepping inside. "I want you, of course."

"Get out of here, Dave," Penny said flatly. "Go home to your wife. I don't want you. I've decided I don't like you even a little bit. You're a sulky, overgrown child. I'd feel I was robbing the cradle ever to have you again."

"Knock it off," he said, shutting the door. "If you're peeved because of what I said at the Florida Room, I apologize. Now come on—be nice."

He reached for her but she quickly sidestepped.

"I told you to go home to Nora," she said angrily. "She's the one who wants you—not I."

"There's never a time when you don't want a man, damn you I"

"Oh, yes there is. That time is right now. Get the hell out of here!"

He shook his head. "Not until I've had you," he said and moved toward her. "And I'm going to have you, even if I've got to rape you."

She backed away, looking frightened now as well as angry. Once across the entrance hall, she whirled and ran into the living room. She grabbed up the telephone and began dialing. He came and wrenched it from her hand.

"Who do you think you're calling?" he demanded.

"Nora, of course. Give it to me, Dave."

"No, I won't give it to you."

He put the phone down and grabbed her about the waist when she tried to pick up the phone. She whirled, struck at him with her fists. He jerked her off balance, forced her to the floor. He held her flat on her back with his left arm across her chest and his right leg across her legs. She fought fiercely to get free but was no match for him. He slipped his right hand under her skirt and forced it between her thighs. With the touch of his hand on her bare flesh, Penny abruptly stopped struggling.

"All right, you louse," she said. "But not here. Not on the floor, damn you!"

He held her for a while longer, not trusting her abrupt surrender. But the fight had gone out of her and now, as he caressed her thighs, she parted them so that he could touch the warm, nylon-sheathed nest there. She was ready and willing now, even eager.

'Where?"

"On the couch down in the rumpus room," she breathed.

"All right, come along," he said. He got to his feet and helped her rise.

She stared at him angrily for a moment, then turned and walked from the living room. Following, he saw that she was hastily unbuttoning her blouse ...

Nora ran into the storm when still a dozen miles from Camp Wee-ni-toka. Traffic had been light and she had kept the car at an even, quiet seventy miles an hour. But now she was forced to cut her speed because the sluicing rain, which the windshield wipers could scarcely cope with, limited visibility. Lightning flashes slashed the darkness, each blinding chain followed by an ear-shattering thunderclap. Nora gripped the wheel until her fingers ached, frightened in spite of herself. She could not stop worrying about Louise, lost and panic-stricken in the fury of this storm ... then Nora had to turn her full attention to guiding the station wagon along the narrow, tortuous mountain road.

Actually, Nora's fear for her daughter went farther than the image of the child, lost and alone in the storm. Her thoughts were haunted by something much worse that could have happened to Louise. Almost every day the newspapers carried stories of children falling into the hands of sex maniacs. Heaven help me, Nora thought, knowing the blame was hers. For she, rather than Dave, had believed that sending Louise to this summer camp would help them in their quest for higher status in the company hierarchy. And she, rather than Dave, had insisted that Louise stay on at Wee-ni-toka when the child had wanted to come home. Yes, this was one thing she could not blame on Dave.

She finally reached the little town of Pine Grove and Camp Wee-ni-toka was only two miles farther. However, the place was reached by a side road, made even more difficult in this storm than the road behind her. In running off, Nora reflected, Louise must certainly have planned, in her seven-year-old way, to go home. And she must have set out along this road, intending to get to Pine Grove and probably hitching a ride there to Lan-ford. Louise had been told always that she should never accept a ride from a stranger but under these circumstances, of course, she would have forgotten that. In her unhappiness, her desperation to get home, she would have seen no harm in accepting a lift.

She may have been picked up along this road, Nora thought. She may not have gotten even as far as Pine Grove and have been taken into the woods, into the thick growth of trees, dark and forbidding, that pressed down on either side of the road. Nora shuddered.

Brilliant blue-green lightning streaks, followed by crashing thunder, heralded stronger wind-swept torrents of rain. But now Nora's headlights showed her the stone pillars marking the entrance to Camp Wee-ni-toka. Another quarter mile and she saw the lighted windows of the administration building before which a dozen cars were parked, among them three state police cruisers.

Nora parked, got out and ran through the rain to the stone steps leading to the veranda. The door was opened before she reached it by Mrs. Hadley, the director's wife.

A dozen people were gathered inside the large living room, and all showed the same tense anxiety shared by those commonly touched by a grave emergency. A state trooper sat talking into a portable two-way radio but his frown showed that he was not receiving good news. Another trooper and two men in civilian clothes stood at a buffet table, eating sandwiches and drinking coffee. Each still wore a glistening wet slicker, so Nora knew that they had been out searching and intended to go again. The others in the room were women, members of the camp's staff. Louise's counselor, Miss Leland, came hurrying toward Nora, a look of distress on her rather plain face.

"I'm so sorry, Mrs. Osborne," she said in a rush of words. "I feel that it was my fault—I really do. If I'd paid more attention to Louise, I might have kept her from running away. But she told me she was tired and wanted to go to her cabin and rest until dinner. I gave her permission, of course. Then, when she didn't come to dinner, I went to her cabin. And she was gone."

"There's been no word about her at all?" Nora asked.

"None at all," Mrs. Hadley said. Stout and middle- aged, she was obviously distressed. "We know definitely that Louise did not go to the village. My husband and I went there as soon as we discovered that she was missing. The troopers checked later and no one at Pine Grove saw her. She must have gone into the woods, Mrs. Osborne. The men are searching there now, as they have been since shortly after six o'clock. Five troopers and most of the men from the village are looking for her, and the forest rangers have also been asked to help. If Louise isn't found by midnight, more men will come in."

The trooper at the radio was saying, "Nothing at that abandoned farmhouse, eh, Charlie? Okay. Stay with it."

The trooper and the two men at the buffet table bolted the last of their sandwiches, buttoned their raincoats and went out into the storm.

Then Miss Leland was again profusely apologizing for not having kept a closer watch on Louise. There had been a quarrel between Louise and a girl named Harriet Morton. Miss Leland had learned of it only after Louise had disappeared. Evidently that was the reason for the child's running off.

"If only she had told me about the quarrel," Miss Leland said miserably.

Mrs. Hadley said, "Come sit down, Mrs. Osborne. We'll have coffee. It may be a long wait, though 1 hope and pray that it won't be."

Nora let herself be led to a sofa but no sooner had she seated herself than she got up again, crossing the room to the trooper at the radio. He was young, capable looking, and she intuitively felt that he would know if there was a possibility that someone had taken Louise away.

"I'm Louise's mother," she said, "I'm worried that someone with—well, with criminal tendencies may have picked my daughter up. Do you think that has happened?"

"We've no reason to think it has, Mrs. Osborne."

"I'm awfully worried—frightened, really."

"That's understandable," he told her. "It's only natural to fear the worst. But there has been absolutely nothing like that—even molestations—reported in this area recently. We're assuming that your daughter is lost in the woods and we've no reason to think otherwise. She was upset over that quarrel with the other girl. Probably she brooded about it, then just wandered off."

"But shouldn't you people act on the possibility that she might have been picked up by someone? Why don't you set up road blocks?"

"We weren't notified of the child's disappearance until seven forty-five, Mrs. Osborne. By that time she had been gone for at least two hours, and possibly four hours. If some person had picked her up and taken her from this area, he's now long gone. Road blocks wouldn't catch him. If he didn't take her out of the area, we'll find him—and her. But for now it's better to act on the assumption that she's simply lost in the forest." He smiled at her. "You try to think that. Okay?"

"All right, I'll try." Nora smiled wanly, unreassured.

She returned to the sofa and sat there sipping the coffee Mrs. Hadley had brought her. Then, too upset to sit still, she asked if she could use the telephone.

"I wasn't able to reach my husband before I left home," she said. "He was at a—a business meeting. I'd like to try to get him now."

"Yes, of course," Mrs. Hadley said. "You can use the phone in my husband's office."

When the phone began to ring, Penny was lying in Dave's arms on the couch in her rumpus room. Dave and she had made vigorous, uninhibited love and then, exhausted, lay beside each other, silent and unmoving, until the emotional dullness of lovemaking's aftermath had dissipated itself. Still without words, they had turned to face each other and entwined their bodies in their approach to new passion. That they disliked each other intensely mattered not at all. For them mutual dislike and even anger served merely to heighten the enjoyment of the sexual act.

So, when the phone first rang, they were attempting to fan the embers of desire back into flame. Penny at first decided to ignore it, then, thinking that Bart might be calling, she broke away from Dave and moved through the darkness to the extension at the opposite side of the room. Picking up the phone, she was startled to hear Nora's voice:

"Penny, I'm calling from Louise's camp," Nora said. "Louise has run away. She's been gone since four o'clock this afternoon. The police are searching for her but there's a bad storm and—well, they haven't found her. Dave should be here. If he's with you, Penny, tell him to come—please."

And with that, Nora broke the connection.

Penny put down the phone and stood by it, badly shaken. How in heaven's name did Nora know about Dave and her? She felt guilty and ashamed.

From across the darkened room, Dave's voice, thick with whiskey and passion, called to her. "Come back here, you," he shouted.

"Dave, get up," she said. "Get up and get dressed."

"The hell I will."

She crossed the room to where her clothes lay in an untidy heap on the floor. She picked up the blouse and put it on.

"That was Nora." Her voice was flat. "She called from Louise's camp. Louise ran away and they can't find her. Nora wants you up there. Now get up, you louse, and get dressed. I'll have some black coffee ready for you by that time—so you can be halfway sober."

She put on her skirt and padded barefooted upstairs to the kitchen. She was pouring hot water onto the powdered coffee when Dave entered. He looked as though the frightening news had somewhat sobered him. He also looked as though someone had clobbered him. She was angry with him—as she was with herself, too, she had to admit—but she could be sympathetic.

"Drink it while it's hot," she said. "You've got a long drive ahead of you and you'd better be sober. I'd drive you, but—well, I just can't face Nora."

"How did she find out about us?"

"I don't know. Not from me."

"It's a mess," he said self-pityingly. "Everything's such a god-damn mess."

"Quit feeling sorry for yourself," Penny told him. "Worry about Louise—and Nora. That poor kid running away and getting lost."

He did not reply to that; he did not speak again. He drank the coffee, set down the empty cup, then turned to leave. She went to the door with him, watched him half run to his car and then drive away. She closed the door and leaned heavily against it.

For the first time in her life, Penny felt a disgust for sex, for the murky, devious byways, the cheap lies and shoddy intrigues that formed the lifeline of sexual unfaithfulness. She had wanted to help Nora, not to hurt her. But even when trying to help her, she had probably hurt her in one or two ways: Tonight at the hotel cocktail lounge when she had pleaded a nonexistent engagement and had left Nora with Mark Hammond. Of course she had known the moment Mark had said he would like to see Nora that he would try to take her to bed. But also, of course, she had not known how Nora would react to old Mark's proposition. But now she did know, too late, that Nora would forever regret giving in to Mark, if she had really done so. Yet, if she had not given in, she would have spoiled Dave's last chance for the vice-presidency. So, reasoned Penny, she had hurt Nora, not helped her. And she had hurt her even more by having this silly but highly enjoyable affair with Dave.

The thought occurred to Penny that Dave and Nora were people essentially doomed to a tragic life. Basically decent people, they had been pushed into a world that destroys their kind. It would be better, Penny conjectured, if Dave did not get that vice-presidency; if he and Nora were forced to return to the dull, conventionally moralistic world that they were really a part of. It was a world that held lasting values for them—moral values actually as necessary to their lives as the oxygen in the air they breathed.

As for herself, Penny decided that she did not want sex in any form whatsoever for a long, long time. Her self-disgust was no small thing.

CHAPTER EIGHTEEN

Nora stood facing the big window, staring out into the rain-slashed blackness until her eyes ached. When, she wondered, would she have word of Louise?

Despite Nora's urgent pleas to join the other searching groups, the trooper at the walky-talky radio had ordered her to remain here. He had pointed out that the men had enough to do without looking after a distracted mother, unfamiliar with this rugged, wooded terrain. She would get lost, too.

"So you take it easy. We'll bring your little girl back in fine shape, Okay?"

Okay, Nora thought, nodding miserably. Sure. Great.

So she had waited, her heart jumping at every scratchy sound from the walky-talky receiver and no one had anything really to report. This area, that place, had been searched. Results: Negative. And Nora's knuckles were raw from striking the dusty window sill. Why, why did they not set up road blocks? Damn it, they should realize that every day little girls like Louise were horribly mutilated and killed by these sex maniacs. Right now the child might be lying out there, her clothes torn, her little body bloodily ravished, dead, the victim of one of these monsters. Nora's vision suddenly blinded her with tears.

Here she was, alone, in this place …

When she saw the car's headlights searching up the road-way, she knew that Dave was coming to the camp. Then, as the headlights came closer, she felt a surge of jealous resentment rise in her, like a viciously clawing wild animal. Her mind was filled with a tape recording that constantly repeated: Penny and Dave … Penny and Dave …

Yet, when a tense-faced Dave opened the door and appeared with an extra raincoat over his arm and a flashlight in his hand, the sight of him made her heart ache. His face was so white and drawn that he looked as frightened as she felt. She hurried to him, clung to him.

"Oh, Dave, I've been so worried—so frightened."

"They haven't found—?"

"No," Nora said. "Not a trace." Then, hysteria threatening: "Dave, I'm so afraid someone has picked her up and—"

"Don't think it," he said. "We mustn't think such a thing."

She began to cry, at last giving way to painful sobbing and nothing Dave could say helped. Mrs. Hadley came quietly in and told him to take Nora to the office where they would be alone. She led them there, then left them.

Dave held Nora in his arms, letting her cry until, after a time, her sobbing quieted. She took the handkerchief from his breast pocket, wiped her eyes and blew her nose. Dave murmured what he hoped were comforting sounds, but she jerked away from him.

"We're being punished," she cried hysterically. 'We've done terrible things and now we're being punished. We've turned ourselves into awful people, just for the sake of—of belonging. I did wrong in forcing Louise to stay at this camp when she hated it. Children always sense what is wrong for them and Louise sensed that this camp was not right for her. She hasn't been happy since we moved to Wilshire Heights. And anyway, she left her friends in our old neighborhood and she misses them terribly. Dave, listen: we're trying to be what were not cut out to be. If something bad has happened to Louise I'll hate you and myself the rest of my life!"

Dave nodded, his face grave. "I understand how you feel, Nora," he said. "We have made a mess of our lives these past few months. I've got to go out there and find our daughter. Will you be all right alone?"

"I'll be all right alone," Nora said bitterly. "Haven't I been alone for a long while?"

He left, and in the main room he donned his raincoat. He ignored the advice of the trooper at the radio, which was not to go into the woods unless he was familiar with this wild country. Into the stormy night he went, crossing the wide clearing where the camp stood, then plunged in among the dense trees and undergrowth.

Afterward, he had no idea how far he tramped through the thick wet woodland in his frantic search for his daughter. He merely knew that he kept on the move the remainder of the night, wandering one way and another. Twice he encountered other searchers, small groups of weary men, and to them he identified himself as Louise's father but learned that no one had found any trace of the child. He continued to go it alone and was surprised to find how quickly he tired. Then he realized that his heavy drinking and his love-making with Penny had sapped his endurance. But he had no thought of giving up.

He stopped every few minutes to call his daughter's name, waited hopefully for an answer and then, failing to hear one, pressed on. The beam of his flashlight lanced into dark gullies, among clusters of rock, into a deep ravine. And despite legs that were leaden with weariness and laboring lungs, he persisted in his search through this night of storm.

He came finally to the weed-grown road which Nora and Louise and he had crossed on their trek last Sunday. He recalled how happy the three of them had been for a little while as Nora told her little story of the Indian family finding the place which Louise had named the Secret Cave.

Abruptly, Dave felt his heart leap with sudden hope.

Louise would not have forgotten that place, which had touched off her imagination as well as Nora's. A child's mind magnifies such small incidents, he told himself, and retains them forever as cherished memories. In running away, Louise would have realized the impossibility of her reaching home. But she would have had some refuge in mind. That might have been the Secret Cave, which, in Nora's fantasy, had been the refuge of the Indian family in a fierce storm like this one.

Suddenly Dave knew that his daughter was there. She would be huddled under the rocky ledge, sheltered from the storm and safe in every other way. Sheltered and safe, but undoubtedly as frightened at being alone in the stormy darkness as any seven-year-old would be.

Dave drove himself on, across the road and into the dense woodland just as the rain stopped and the sky began to turn gray with approaching dawn. He did not come to the place he sought, however, because he had not crossed the road at the same point where Louise and Nora and he had crossed last Sunday. Again he wandered one way and another, pausing often to call his daughter's name. He began to think that he would not be able to find the Secret Cave, that he would have to stop and turn back for other searchers to help him. He did stop but tried calling out once more. And this time he thought he heard a faint answering call.

He shouted more loudly: "Louise! Louise, baby!"

And, yes, there was again a faint answer.

Running in the direction from which the answering call seemed to come, he tripped over a root. His forward momentum carried him through a tangle of brush and then he plummeted down a steep slope. He sprawled at the base of the slope, dazed and in pain. His head hurt and there was a knife-sharp ache in his left side. When he picked himself up after several minutes, he felt an even greater pain in his left ankle. He was barely able to endure the sharp stabbing hurt when he put his weight on his left foot. Halting to rest, he called out once more.

This time he knew that it was Louise who answered. "Daddy—Daddy!" she called.

Minutes later he made his painful way out of the trees to the small clearing by the bluff in which the Secret Cave was located. Louise stood in the hollow at the base of the bluff, her hair disheveled and her blue denim camp uniform wet and bedraggled. But she was alive and unharmed and Dave sobbed with vast relief.

She came running to him, crying happily, "I knew you'd come, Daddy! Where's Mother? Didn't she come with you?"

Dave caught her up in his arms, too choked with feeling to answer at once. He could only mutter, "Thank God! Oh, thank God!"

Though Louise was in better physical shape than he was, Dave insisted upon carrying her but after a short distance he was forced to stop and put her down. He leaned against a tree trunk and gently felt his sore ankle, which he found badly swollen. The throbbing pain was agonizing even when he was not placing his weight upon that foot. Too, since carrying Louise, the sharp ache in his left side was more severe.

"I fell and hurt myself, honey," he said. "You think you can walk the rest of the way?"

"Oh, sure," Louise said. "I'm fine. Or I will be if you take me home. Will you take me home, Daddy?"

"You bet your boots I'll take you home."

Louise giggled. "I'm not wearing boots, you silly." Then, anxiously: "Are you mad at me because I ran away?"

"No, I'm not mad, baby. But you shouldn't have done it."

"Well, a girl called me names. She said I was—"

"You forget it," Dave told her. "It's over now, and you're going home. But first, we'll have to find our way back to the camp."

"Find our way?" Louise said, her eyes grown round. Are we lost?"

Dave laughed despite his pain. "No, not really," he said.

He took her by the hand and, limping badly, walked with her through the dense woods. He began to think he would not be able to return to the camp. The pain in his ankle was becoming unbearable.

They had traveled perhaps a half-mile when they heard a voice calling the child's name.

"Listen, Daddy," she said, surprised. "Somebody's calling me. Isn't that strange?"

"It's strange, all right," he said, smiling. "You call back, eh?"

As Louise called, "Hello, hello, who are you?" Dave sank to the ground and sat with his back to a tree trunk. His ankle was swollen to twice normal size and throbbed with pain even now.

A trooper and four civilian searchers emerged from the surrounding trees and brush. They moved slowly, weary from spending the night tramping through the forest. But they managed to grin at sight of Louise and to show surprise at seeing her father with her.

"So it took a greenhorn to find her, eh, Mr. Osborne?" the trooper said. Then, to Louise: "Hiya, honey. How are you feeling?"

"I'm fine," Louise said. "But my daddy's hurt. I guess it's lucky you came along. He needs help to get back to the camp."

Dave did need help. He required a stretcher to bear him back to Camp Wee-ni-toka, the attention of a doctor summoned from Pine Grove, and a state police car to take him to the hospital at Lanford. There he found that his head and his side were not seriously injured, but the X-ray showed a fractured bone in his ankle. The ankle went into a cast, and Dave into a hospital bed.

For her mother, Louise's return alive and unharmed seemed a miracle, and the ordeal of that stormy night brought Nora to make a momentous decision. After stopping at the hospital with Dave's pajamas, robe and toilet kit she started home with Louise. And at that time she made up her mind about the future of the Osborne family.

She needed still more time to think things out and she concentrated on her plan the remainder of the day. That night she lay awake for hours, pondering how she would tell Dave tomorrow.

Nora drove Louise to Sunday school in the morning, then returned home and called a sitter, a college girl she trusted, to stay with the child while she went on to the hospital. Picking Louise up at eleven o'clock, she told her about the sitter. Louise fussed a little, saying that she, too, wanted to visit her father.

"I've something to talk over with Daddy," Nora told her. "Something important."

"Something too important for me to hear?"

"That's right, darling," Nora said, laughing.

She was surprised that she was able to laugh, for she felt so-so grim. But maybe her ability to laugh again was proof, she reflected, that her decision was the right one. She merely had to make Dave see how important her course of action would be to all of them.

The sitter came at one-thirty, and Nora left in the station wagon a few minutes later. After parking at the hospital, she sat in the car for a moment, mentally rehearsing what she would say to Dave.

She must make two points clear to him. One, she could no longer put up with their estrangement. He would have to forgive and forget her affair with Brandon Hoyt, and she would forgive and forget his with Penny Austin. Being a party to a halfway marriage was an impossible role for her to take. The second point was that she no longer wanted to be a part of the group in which they now moved. If dropping out meant that Dave would have to resign from Worden-Forbes, then that was all right with her. If he would not give in, she would have no recourse but to consider a divorce.

That was what she had decided, and she intended to give Dave that ultimatum. If she was wrong in believing that he still loved her and wanted to keep their marriage intact, she would take Louise and leave him. She would not go on being what she had become. The price they were paying for belonging was far, far too high.

Tears came but she blinked them away and left the station wagon, walked purposefully into the hospital and took the elevator to the fifth floor. But while going along the corridor to Dave's room, she found that her nerve was failing her. She began to doubt that she could go through with her plan. The trouble was, she was too deeply in love with Dave.

He was out of bed and learning to use a pair of crutches.

He gave her an uncertain smile. "How am I doing?"

"You're doing fine, Dave."

"I'll be on these things quite a while," he said. He moved awkwardly to the bed. He seated himself on its edge, then asked, "How is Louise?"

"She's all right. She went to Sunday school this morning.

"And how are you feeling?"

"Not happy."

"Neither am I," he said. "Sit down. I want to talk."

"So do I want to talk," she replied. "And I'd better stay on my feet to say my piece."

He gazed at her bleakly. "Well, go ahead. Get it off your chest."

She shook her head. "You first," she said realizing that her nerve was just about wholly gone.

He fumbled in the pockets of his robe, brought out a cigarette. He didn't speak until he'd lit it and then he searched for words.

"I don't know how to say it, Nora, without seeming to be placing the blame on you. But it's this way: I became involved with Penny because I was sick with jealousy. And because my pride was hurt. I never really wanted her. I don't even like her. I guess I was acting like a kid trying to get even."

'So you got even."

"And I hurt you," he said bitterly. "One of the two people I love. But, damn it, you shouldn't have given yourself to Brandon Hoyt—even if you thought it would get me the vice-presidency. It was a lousy thing to happen to a man in love."

"And now you're no longer in love with me?"

"I didn't say that. I am in love with you—I always will be. But I don't like what you've become—or what I've become."

"You're echoing my words, Dave. You know that, don't you?"

He nodded. "I know. But I made up my own mind about things. Nora, I want out. I'm not going on with Worden-Forbes, even as a vice-president. And I don't care to be a part of the crowd we're associating with. I want to make a clean break."

Now you're echoing what I've been wishing, Nora thought. Aloud, she said, "You mean you want to resign from the company?"

"Yes."

"And have to start all over?"

"I can go to work right away for Triton Electronics. Bill Marsten will pay me nine thousand a year. Of course, that's not nearly what I'm getting at Worden- Forbes and we'd have to move out of Wilshire Heights. But I won't do it unless you agree. If you won't agree, I'll go after that vice-presidency. Oh, I know you doubt that I can get it, with Hoyt backing that Air Force general. But I was telling the truth when I said that I had something on him."

He explained about the photostat of the letter he had gotten from Harvey Ward, then continued. "I won't be able to see Hoyt tomorrow because of my ankle. But I can just as easily lay it on the line for him over the phone."

Nora sank weakly into the bedside chair feeling utterly jolted. So Dave's talk had not been mere boyish bragging, after all. He actually did have a way to force Brandon Hoyt to back him. What a fool she had been to think that he was incapable of getting and holding this top job. How stupid she had been to hurt him by her traipsing from bed to bed, honestly thinking that she could help him by acting like a cheap little whore. She had let herself be used and degraded by three different men and all to no purpose. If Dave should ever find out about Mark Hammond, God help her!

"The strange thing is," Dave went on, "I could have settled this with Hoyt days ago. I kept putting off getting in touch with him. I didn't know why I kept stalling until this thing happened to Louise. That opened my eyes to what a mess both of us have made of our marriage. I hate Brandon Hoyt for having had you in bed, Nora, but when I face it, I know I wouldn't get any real, honest satisfaction by forcing him to back us. That suddenly struck me as a lousy way to get a promotion. Damn it, I guess I'm just not cut out to be a good blackmailer. Hell, I don't even want that silly vice-presidency now. But if you're set on holding onto the house in Wilshire Heights and being part of the crowd—well, I'll call him. And clobber him with that photostat."

Nora's voice was husky and her eyes brimming as she turned to him. "Anything you want to do, darling, is just what I want, too."

"Better give me a signed memo on that," Dave grinned. "Some day you might forget what you've just said."

"I won't Dave. Cross my heart, honest and truly. Know why? Because what you've decided is exactly the same thing that I had made up my mind to since the first day you were in the hospital. I'd planned to tell you that I don't want you to keep on at Worden-Forbes. That crowd is just no good for us, Dave, and the price we've been paying for all this plushy kind of life is too high. Nothing is worth all the heartache it costs."

They gazed at each other wonderingly for a brief moment and in the flash of time each had the same thought. Nora got from her chair at the same instant that Dave adjusted his crutches and got from the bed. He hobbled to her and, balanced on his crutches, put his hands to her waist. Nora's arms were about his neck, and their lips met, gently at first then opening with the long-missed fire of their love and passion.

After they had kissed, Nora whispered, "Darling, how long will they keep you here away from me?"

"Until tomorrow morning," Dave said. "Can you wait?"

"Hardly. Can you?"

"Hell, no," he grinned.

"Well, neither can I," Nora smiled softly, that smouldering glow coming into her eyes. "But isn't there anything that we can do about it?"

A slender young brown-haired nurse silently entered the room at that moment. Her eyes twinkled as she answered Nora's question. "Not one blessed thing can you do," she said. "And isn't it a crying shame!"

THE END